FALLEN WARRIORS

MARK ANDERSON SMITH

First published in Great Britain by Mark Anderson Smith, 2017
This paperback edition published in 2017 by Mark Anderson Smith

A catalogue record for this book is available
from the British Library.

ISBN: 978-0-9929883-8-8

http://www.dragonlake.co.uk
books@dragonlake.co.uk

SIGN UP FOR NEWS AND OFFERS

Season Two of Fallen Warriors is being planned. If you would like to sign up to the author's mailing list and receive news about the book's progress, the chance to get previews of short stories and occasional notifications about blog posts then please sign up at http://www.dragonlake.co.uk

Everyone who signs up to the mailing list will get the author's short story—Dragon Lake—for free.

You will find a glossary at the end of the book. If you are unfamiliar with terms used in the novel you will hopefully find this helpful.

For Carol

'I form the light and create darkness,
I bring prosperity and create disaster;
I, the Lord, do all these things.'
Isaiah 45 v7

CHAPTER ONE
The Vision

Zafar drummed his fingers on the steering wheel as he waited for the lights to change. The orange light lit up, then the red and he thumped the wheel, looking to his left towards the railway tracks. Not a single car had moved in either direction through two light changes. How was it such a small city could be gridlocked almost every single day? Maybe he should switch to taking the train from Leeds, though that meant either parking in the city centre at exorbitant rates or taking a bus.

Looking back up the hill he wondered what the delay was this time: someone broken down and unable to move their car off the road; drivers exchanging addresses after an accident; or was it simply that there were too many cars on the road?

They had been inching forward until about ten minutes before when for some reason the cars in both directions had ceased moving. Normally traffic into York in the evening moved faster than those leaving, the situation reversed in the morning with all the surrounding villages emptying into the city each day.

The lights changed to green and Zafar groaned, beginning to drum his fingers again. He kept his foot away from the accelerator pedal knowing that he would end up revving the engine.

It was never usually this bad. Slow, especially at this T junction where the cross bar of the T headed up a small artificial hill and the stem continued up over the railway tracks. He always had to wait here, the cars inches apart, always wary of the driver in front rolling back.

He glanced to his right and saw a smartly dressed man nodding his head. Listening to music perhaps. Or mad. Now there was a thought, sitting next to a mad man who was nodding his head to… what? Possibly a conversation, with the demons in his head. Maybe he imagined himself on a roller coaster being shaken about, or was he just imagining music. What do mad people think about when they are stuck in traffic he asked himself. Do they think that everyone around them is mad… He allowed this thought to sit unchallenged until he became aware the man was looking back at him and was frowning.

Zafar forced a smile, then turned back to look at the lights. Now showing red.

His eye was caught by movement on a cycle path that cut under the road then curved up to join it. Three kids on bikes, dark clothes and hoods up over their heads. They wove in and out of the cars and then were gone. Zafar turned to look, but couldn't see them, only rows of cars in three directions. No-one moving, no-one tooting their horns or revving their engines. Sheep, sitting patiently waiting for the… slaughter.

The image of the dark figures weaving in and out of the traffic played over in his mind. How easy it would be to point a gun and shoot. It wouldn't take many shots either, he thought as he looked round again. A few shots and the junction would be paralysed for hours…

If you were to target a few other key junctions at the same time…

Zafar saw how it would play out, the attacks co-ordinated to seal off York, turning the traffic into one huge barrier that would allow them to take the city. A few kids at each junction is all it would take. Kids with guns. With grenades. Firing into the open windows of cars, running round and dropping a grenade into one window then running before the explosion.

What would the drivers do? What could they do? Get out of their cars, no, anyone who did that would be shot. Yet, if they stayed still, they were easy targets. There was no escape, if one driver tried to move his car, he would find himself unable to do so, even if he mounted the narrow pavement, the road narrowed at the lights and there was just not enough room.

Some would phone for help, dial 999, but what good would that do? The police could not get here quickly and even if they did, how would they stop the killing?

Zafar had tried different routes out of the city in his attempts to reduce his commute, but almost every road into and out of York was the same at this time. Far too much traffic concentrated in such a small city.

As his thoughts raced, Zafar could still visualise one young gunman walking between the cars towards him, stopping next to each window and firing directly into it. Until he reached Zafar and stood there, black trousers, black jumper and balaclava over his head. The man rapped the muzzle of the gun on his window and then aimed...

'Allah Akbar,' Zafar blinked and saw he was again looking directly at the mad man in the car next to him. The man was staring back at him, a look of fear in his eyes. Zafar studied him for a moment, the man eventually becoming uncomfortable and looking away before Zafar heard someone behind him sounding their horn. Finally the cars were moving.

As he followed the train of cars slowly through the junction and away from the city he felt acutely aware of everything he was doing and around him. It was like his senses had been dialled up to ten and he hadn't even realised he was only hovering around a four. His pulse was racing and his breathing shallow, like he had actually been in a fight.

What was it he had seen? It had not just been his imagination, it had been real, a vision even, of the future.

CHAPTER TWO
Fallen

Emma placed one bare foot in front of her, feeling the coolness of old stone soaking up exhaustion—the perfect cure for an evening's dancing. She focused her eyes on Monk Bar while shifting her balance forward, conscious of her toes hugging the angled apex of the parapet.

'You're beginning to scare me,' Rachel said. 'You realise how high you are now?'

'I'm trying not to look.' Emma took another small step. 'You need to live a little, Rachel. Take a few risks.' Just like earlier with Paul—now that was scary. This was simply a distraction, something to help forget that kiss.

Concentrate, Emma told herself, enjoy the moment. She allowed herself a smile at her personal mission statement.

'Only one risk I can see, a rooftop three metres down. You keep going and it's six metres to the road.'

Ignoring her, Emma glanced to her left to see the towers of York Minster lit up against the sky. As always—the sight took her breath away as she imagined how the Minster must have looked centuries before, the massive structure dominating the flat landscape for miles around York.

A breath of air—nothing more—and Emma paused. It's okay, she told herself, just a few more metres and you're at Monk Bar. She had a sudden urge to kiss the ancient sandstone tower when she reached it. 'Do you think it's like Blarney Castle? If I kiss the stone will I receive a gift?'

'Are you high?'

'Always!' Though high was the wrong word, Emma thought. Exhilarated! Now that's how I feel, except... 'Did Jennifer see us?'

'Is that what this is all about? I don't know what goes on in your head

4

sometimes, Emma. How does tip-toeing round the walls of York help you deal with the fact you got off with Jennifer's boyfriend?'

'It wasn't like that.' Except it was and regardless how hard she tried to distract herself now, Emma knew she had crossed a line.

'Sure, try telling Jennifer that tomorrow.'

'Did she see us?' Emma insisted.

'What does that matter? You still need to tell her. Honestly, what were you thinking?'

She hadn't thought, had just acted on instinct as she always did, as she had all evening—focusing on Paul, teasing him, resting her hand on his shoulder when talking with him even though Jennifer was there.

'He kissed me back.' Emma noticed Rachel stop but continued her own slow advance, looking forward to Monk Bar.

'She is never going to forgive you,' Rachel sighed and then swore. 'The stairs are blocked off! We're going to have to walk back to Sainsbury's. Come on, Emma! It's 1am and I've got a shift tomorrow.'

'I'm almost at Monk Bar.'

'You can't even get the whole way on the wall…'

'Parapet,' Emma interrupted.

'Whatever! You're not going to jump that gap.'

'Are you filming me, Rachel?' Asked Emma.

'You want this to be your YouTube moment? If I'm not going to pick up the pieces, why would I encourage you? Will you just get down from there?'

'Two more minutes and I'm done, it's just a longer step really,' Emma said, only half looking beyond the half metre gap in the parapet to where her foot would land. Her focus was still on the ancient stone tower that was now almost close enough to touch. She held her breath and allowed herself to fall forwards, lifting up her foot to step over and continue until… Yes! She stopped, touching the smooth stone.

'Hooray,' Rachel said in a flat voice. 'Now can we go and call a taxi?'

Having reached her goal, Emma wished she could climb higher, perhaps stand on one of the Minster's towers and look over the city. Drink in the beauty of the lights spread out underneath her, highlighting ancient stone walls. She turned, facing away from the city and spread her arms as wide as wings, feeling the chill air with her fingertips, and closed her eyes, imagining what it would be like to soar over the city.

'Emma,' Rachel said softly. 'You're freaking me out. It's really high here.'

Letting her breath out slowly, Emma opened her eyes. 'I'm sorry.' She turned, but something felt wrong. Her right foot caught on the parapet and in trying to correct her balance she twisted and felt herself tip too far backwards.

'Emma!'

Rachel was there, her hand stretched out towards her but Emma couldn't reach quickly enough. Oh please no! This wasn't happening. Emma tried to grab at the wall but she was falling backwards, was too far away. She heard Rachel scream, saw fear in her eyes but it was too late and Emma tried to turn, to lift and protect her head but she was already below the arch and there wasn't enough time.

Reaching up as she fell backwards, her shoulders were pulled forward. Emma felt something snap as she landed and then could not stop her head whiplashing backwards to crack on the unyielding tarmac. Stunned, she was only aware of a sense of regret and then unconsciousness mercifully took her as her heart stopped beating.

~~~

'Emma!' Rachel looked down at her friend's still body, Emma's scream still echoing in her head. The way Emma had landed… Rachel turned away, thinking she was going to throw up.

No! She can't be. Rachel forced herself to take out her phone and tried to punch in 999. Her hand shaking so hard she pressed the wrong numbers. She cleared them and this time managed to dial.

'What service please?' An impatient voice answered.

'Ambulance.' Rachel looked back over the parapet. Was that blood around Emma's head?

'What's the emergency?'

'My friend's fallen… from Monk Bar… in York… her head… she needs an ambulance… now!' Why couldn't she stop shaking?

'Are you with your friend?'

'Of course I'm not with her! How could I be with her? The stairs are blocked off, wait… Hey!' Rachel shouted at the man who had appeared from under the archway and was now kneeling beside Emma. 'Does she have a pulse?'

As he looked up at her, Rachel groaned. His dirty blonde hair and ragged beard covered most of his face. She now noticed his dark overcoat making him look like one of the hundreds of street beggars that haunted York's tourists all year round.

As she watched though, he placed two fingers on Emma's neck. She found herself counting but after twenty seconds he shook his head.

Her chest tightened and Rachel blinked back tears. This was not the time to lose control. 'Do you know CPR?' She called, but he did not respond, just continued to kneel beside Emma. Rachel remembered the phone in her hand. 'Are you still there?'

'I've dispatched an ambulance, they'll be with you in five minutes.'

It could still be okay, Rachel knew. They were only two minutes drive from York's A&E. She tried to remember where the ambulances were based. Not far... Oh no, what is he doing? 'Stop that!' She shouted. She needed to get down there and protect Emma. Rachel started running back along the wall.

~~~

She was beautiful with flame-red hair that framed an oval face; high cheekbones with a scattering of freckles; pouted lips still open as if about to speak, only... Her green eyes showed no sign of life. They stared upwards, unfocused, still.

Calvin carefully knelt beside her, not wanting any more hurt to come to her. Only a minute before he had been looking for a quiet corner where he could crawl into his sleeping bag and hide from the police or drunks who might have a go at the homeless.

Who are you? He wondered. How did this happen?

'Does she have a pulse?' Calvin heard from above. He looked up and saw a face looking down from above the Bar wall.

Gently, he placed two fingers on the girl's neck. He realised his fingers were trembling. Pressing down, he could feel no beat. For a second an image of a different face replaced the one before him, rain drumming down as he had leaned over and checked for a pulse. Calvin shook his head to clear the image. It was happening again—someone was going to be taken away and there was nothing he could do. For the first time in over a year, Calvin felt a tear roll down his cheek. He reached up and wiped it away, studying his wet fingers.

His father would have called on Jesus, shouted and commanded the girl to rise. A memory came to him—hiding at the back of the room, scared he would be called on to join his father as he healed, knowing he did not believe. Yet that night he had seen something amazing: a man at the edge of death, wracked by coughing. First he grew still and then he sat up—his face showing release from the sickness that had, only minutes before, almost ended his life. Years later Calvin had recalled this event, faced with an even more desperate situation and there had been no healing. And now...

'Is this some kind of sick joke?' He muttered and immediately felt a sense of shame—that night had been no-one's fault but his own.

Calvin brushed a strand of the girl's hair from her face. Despite his shame a stronger emotion was building inside him. Calvin looked up. 'Are you listening, Jesus? Are you watching this from your throne up there?' He took a deep, shuddering breath. 'My father saved that man in your name. Why then? Why not when I... when he needed you? Can you save this one or was it all a far cleverer deception than I realised?'

It was nothing. A gentle gust of wind—barely enough to register on his skin. Calvin looked around but there was no-one on the road.

'I want to believe,' he whispered. 'Please, Jesus, help me.'

The feeling started in his head, a warmth that quickly flowed into his chest and then down his legs and along his arms. His fingers which had been trembling, grew still even while he felt them tingling. Before doubts had a chance to voice in his head, Calvin put the palms of his hands on the girl's head and face. 'In the name of Jesus, be healed.'

Calvin stayed still, waiting for something, unsure what to expect. Nothing was happening.

'Please Jesus, I don't know how to do this. Help me!'

He desperately thought back to his childhood, to times he had watched his father—wanting the gift his father possessed, wanting to believe.

'But father, how?' He had asked. Only to be told, 'you have to listen. Let Jesus tell you how.' What help was that? Yet, there was a dead girl before him and despite all reason, Calvin wanted to believe she could be brought back. Closing his eyes to shut out all distraction, Calvin asked again: 'Jesus, what do I have to do?'

Long seconds went by and Calvin became aware again of the distant noise of traffic. 'Jesus, I don't know how else to ask this, heal her, wake her, raise her from the dead!' An image in his mind, a memory from a previous life. It had not made sense then and although it made no sense now, Calvin knew he had to act quickly—the warmth he had felt was now like a pressure in his skull, a hand bearing down on him. Calvin prostrated himself over the girl, placing his hands on the road, covering her with his body; sheltering her head and chest. 'Be healed,' he shouted.

Tears now running freely, he rose and then covered her again. 'Please Jesus! Heal her, restore her,' he cried. Then a third time he rose before prostrating himself over her again and whispered: 'Wake up. Please, you can do this. Wake up.'

Lying there, supporting his weight with his hands so not to crush her, Calvin listened for any sign she was responding. Someone grabbed at his coat and pulled him backwards.

'Get off of her!'

He had been concentrating so hard, he had not heard anyone run up behind him. Calvin landed on his back, managed to avoid banging his head and then felt a kick to his side. He rolled sideways and managed to get to his feet but the girl—it was a girl attacking him—kept coming towards him, trying to punch and hit him now that he was upright, yelling at him to get away.

'What were you doing to her? How could you hurt her like that!'

Fending off her punches, Calvin saw blue flashing lights and an ambulance fast approaching on Lord Mayor's Walk. There was no way to explain. Unable to even say goodbye to the girl he had tried to save, Calvin turned and headed at a run under the Bar arch.

~~~

Rachel watched the man run into the city, wondering where the strength had come from to pull him away from Emma and fight him off. How could he assault her like that? Before she could check Emma, she heard the ambulance pull to a stop and the siren switch off. Rachel moved to check for a pulse but stopped, her chest tightening as she saw thick, straw coloured liquid oozing from Emma's ear.

Hands reached down and took firm hold of Emma's head then Rachel felt someone lifting her up.

'…I'm Jim, that's Carol, we're going to help your friend. Now just stand back there.'

Rachel felt herself being walked away from Emma. 'I couldn't stop him, stop her… I was too late,' she heard herself say.

'That's okay love,' Jim said as he kneeled beside Carol. 'What's your friend's name?'

'Emma, Emma Hunter. I'm Rachel, I'm a nurse.'

'Okay Rachel, you know the drill then, we're going to look after Emma.'

'There's a lot of blood,' Rachel heard Carol say.

'I know. Steady while I check her airway, okay, that's clear. She's breathing and,' he paused. 'And I've got a good radial pulse.'

'We're going to have to stop this bleed.'

Jim cursed. 'Spinal fluid in her ears.'

'Skull fracture?'

'Looks like it. Okay, I'm going to get the collar and then I'll cannulate and get a drip running.'

Carol looked up at Rachel as Jim ran back to the ambulance. 'She's doing okay but we need to stop the bleed and get her into Resus. Do you want to come with us?'

Rachel heard the words but they made no sense. Carol was kneeling in a wide pool of Emma's blood, holding Emma's head still. The blood was everywhere, how could Emma still have a pulse? And the way she landed, a skull fracture... Rachel had seen the results of head trauma in A&E before.

There was no coming back from that. She felt her legs give way and stumbled to the ground, weeping for her friend.

CHAPTER THREE
Run & Hide

Out of breath, Calvin slowed from his run but kept walking. He couldn't go back, did not want to risk it now. His sleeping bag was gone. The only possession he had other than the clothes he was wearing. It wasn't important except that now he was cold and had no way to keep warm unless there was space in the Drop In.

Walking would keep him warm until he got there. He could walk for hours and had frequently done so. Some nights you had to walk to stay alive. He had had friends on the street who had chosen to stay put and had never moved again.

He was cold but alive. He had lost his sleeping bag but somehow he would get another one. What had happened back there?

In his mind, Calvin saw his father place his hands on a friend who was ill. As he had watched, his friends pale cheeks had flushed with colour and then he had coughed and sat up.

How old had he been then? Five? Six? Calvin looked down at his own hands. His father's hands had healed many people but those same hands had taken a cane and beaten him as a child. He could not remember what he had done to deserve that punishment. He had never asked why.

The beatings stopped when he was seven. After that, he never saw anyone healed.

It had never occurred to him since then that this was something he could do.

Why now? Why had he prayed for her? In none of his memories of his father's healings had he ever brought someone back from the dead. Calvin did not even know if he had tried though surely he had prayed for people when Calvin was not there.

He had never wanted to be like his father. Did not want to hurt anyone like he had been hurt. Yet, in the end, he had turned out worse. A car drove past and Calvin felt himself stiffen. It didn't matter that he had done nothing to hurt the girl. No-one would believe him. Maybe he still deserved to be punished.

He kept walking though. Why do I bother? Why go to the Drop In? What is it going to take to make me give up? He had no answer. Maybe this was the real punishment, to keep going and face the loneliness and the beatings and the rejection.

A crushing sense of despair seemed to grab at his chest. Calvin felt tears well up in his eyes and he angrily tried to blink them away. God, how long are you going to keep punishing me?

There was no answer. Had he expected one? Roughly pulling his coat sleeve across his face, Calvin walked on. He was almost there. Just had to keep it together for a bit longer.

~~~

'Her blood pressure seems normal. No sign of any bleed. Pulse still strong. I'm not going to risk intubating.'

'Looks like your friend's been very lucky.' Carol shouted back to Rachel as she drove.

Rachel held Emma's hand, trying to keep out of the way as Jim ran his tests. She was breathing. Everything sounded normal but there was no way... The straw coloured liquid had congealed in Emma's ear. A clear sign of major spinal or head trauma. There had been at least a pint of blood pooled round her head. Then that man, the way he had shaken his head when she asked about Emma's pulse.

How could she be okay?

The ambulance swerved round and Rachel put her other hand against the cot to steady herself. Looking forward she could see York Hospital.

A couple more swerves and they braked sharply. Rachel opened the door and got out of the way. Carol ran round to help Jim and together they manoeuvred the cot out, set the trolley base down and wheeled her into A&E.

'We'll take her straight to Resus.' Jim told her. 'Take a seat, I'll be back in a minute.'

She stared at the rows of seats in A&E reception. Two men sitting together, one with blood running down the side of his head. A woman holding her child who kept coughing. A different woman who sat away from the others, her face guarded. Rachel could not face sitting and waiting.

She walked over to reception.

'I just came in with my friend.' Rachel told the woman on reception. 'What paperwork do I need to fill in?'

'The woman taken through to Resus?' Seeing Rachel nod, the woman—her name tag read Janice—selected forms and attached them to a clipboard. 'You need a pen?'

'Yes.' Rachel felt herself sway and held out her hand to the wall to steady herself.

'Are you okay?' Janice asked.

'I just need to sit down.' Taking the clipboard and ignoring Janice's look of concern, Rachel went over to the nearest seat.

She held the clipboard up to her chest and stared down the corridor.

~~~

'Not usual getting you in here, Calvin.' It was Phil, one of the many volunteers who staffed the Drop In at nights.

The temperature had seemed to plummet as he had approached the Drop In and Calvin found he couldn't speak, his teeth chattering together.

Phil frowned at him then reached behind himself for a blanket. 'Have you lost your sleeping bag?'

Nodding, Calvin accepted the blanket and wrapped it round himself. It was heavy but he had got too cold and it did not stop his shivering.

'Fancy something hot to eat or drink? Sally Army are here tonight.'

Yes, anything to heat him up. The shame he normally felt from accepting charity at the Drop In was on hold.

Phil took him through to the hall which was packed with familiar faces. Some nodded in recognition. Many couldn't have noticed him if they wanted. There were several tables set up and most were empty. The others there had obviously arrived earlier and eaten. Now most were lying down in sleeping bags or with blankets trying to sleep. Phil walked him to a table and waited while Calvin sat down. 'I'll get some soup. Tea or coffee?'

'Tea, white.' As Phil walked away Calvin tried to think whether he'd thanked Phil? He couldn't remember.

Just being inside was starting to help. Calvin felt himself shiver uncontrollably as his body tried to warm up. He counted the people inside while he waited. Nineteen including himself. There were more homeless on the streets in York than that but some of them would have bolt holes kitted out to enable them to get through the worst weather. He would have to find one himself. He didn't want to go through another winter like the last one, freezing cold night after night, barely warming up during the day.

Phil brought soup and tea, both piping hot and both delicious. Thick vegetable soup with fresh crusty bread. The tea strong and sweet after he had put three sugars in.

Calvin pulled the bowl and mug close to get the benefit from the warmth, breathed in the steam. He dipped the bread in the soup as he could eat the soaked bread faster than the hot soup. By the time he had finished the meal he had stopped shivering. He carried the bowl and mug back to the little kitchen.

A lady with the Salvation Army was washing bowls, her jacket hung over a chair.

'Are you going to stay here tonight?' She asked after thanking him.

Calvin nodded.

'There're more blankets at the front desk.' She smiled and then turned back to the sink.

Phil was back at the front desk, reading a novel with one of the Drop In blankets around his shoulders.

'Any chance of another blanket?' Calvin asked him.

Phil looked up. 'Sure.' He grabbed another blanket and gave it to Calvin, then reached down for another. 'Pillow?'

Calvin took the blankets and left before Phil started a conversation. He didn't want to talk about losing his sleeping bag. Didn't want to think about finding the girl and failing her. He found a space on the floor and cocooned himself in the blankets, using his arms as pillows and taking all the protection he could get from cold.

He closed his eyes and saw the girl's unseeing eyes stare back at him, her red hair fanned out, hiding the blood underneath. He squeezed his eyes tight to drive out the image but it haunted him until he fell into a disturbed sleep.

~~~

Dripping with sweat, Danny rolled off of Natalie and onto his back. He turned and kissed her before getting up. Behind him, he heard Natalie reach down for the duvet and pull it up. Her flat was small with just a combined kitchen and living area and one bedroom but the rooms were large and modern. A small hallway connected the rooms, the bathroom and the entrance door and Danny padded in his bare feet across the wood effect laminate that had been used throughout the flat.

There was a separate shower cubicle in addition to the bath, in an extremely efficient use of space that still impressed him three months on. He turned on the spray and waited for the water to warm before stepping inside.

Getting soft in your old age, Danny.

Less of the old now, he allowed himself to retort. He was old though, old for a serving officer. When he turned forty eight in January it had hit home that he could retire in two years. Retire…

He turned, letting the spray dance over him before he washed.

They had made love in the shower once, but neither had wanted to try again.

Clean, he grabbed a towel and rubbed himself dry then stood for a minute, conscious his breathing was still rapid. His reflection studied him from the mirror as he focused on regaining his breath. Every year the physicals got a little harder, the recovery took a little longer. Not enough to cause concern, he was still in good shape. Had to be or the stress would eat him up.

The whole war on terror in the North seemed to have landed on his desk: two dozen cases he was being asked to run simultaneously and even though he was liaising with detectives in Manchester, Bradford and Newcastle, the cases they each were tasked with managed to cross over in enough ways that none could afford to ignore what was happening elsewhere.

A detective's nightmare: too much information and no quick way to sort the dross from the genuine. He shook his head wondering how they had managed to intervene successfully in any case so far.

What are we fighting to protect, he asked his reflection in the steamy mirror. It wasn't a question he wanted to answer.

With a last look round the bathroom wondering if he could persuade Cynthia to let him remodel theirs, he left the towel and padded back to the bedroom and began to dress. Natalie watched him side on, her form curled up underneath the duvet.

He checked himself in her mirror. No shirt tails hanging out, tie on straight. 'I'm just going to head out,' he told her. Natalie nodded. He could never read her expression and knew better than to ask what she was thinking.

Danny took the stairs.

Walking out towards his car, his phone buzzed. Pulling it out, he answered brusquely: 'D.I. Martin.'

'Sorry to disturb you, Sir but we've an unusual case at the hospital. Girl claims her friend fell thirty feet from Monk Bar and smashed her head, but an A&E surgeon is claiming it's a hoax and is demanding we send someone over.'

'Can't you send a uniform?'

'Incident on the A64. Two fatalities. Also, situation may require someone more senior. I understand the surgeon is one of their top people.'

'Okay. I'll be there in ten...' He hesitated. 'Make that fifteen minutes.'

He ended the connection and looked up at the flat. It would be helpful to have Natalie along.

He started to jog back up unaware of a blue transit van that had been parked before he arrived. There had been no movement visible from behind the tinted rear windows of the van as a camera had zoomed in on his face and took shot after shot.

CHAPTER FOUR
Nightmare

'Is this her?'

Rachel looked up at the question and saw a surgeon in green scrubs walking up to her, an angry expression on his face. The Paramedic, Jim, was keeping pace and appearing to be trying to hold him back, though the doctor kept brushing him away.

'What kind of a sick joke were you trying to pull?'

Rachel stood, still holding the clipboard against her chest. 'What's wrong with Emma?' She managed to gasp out. She realised she was starting to cry.

'Nothing! Not one thing! Is this some sort of stunt? You trying to prove something?'

'I don't understand. She fell. She hit her head.'

'You don't fall thirty feet, crack your head open and then have no injury. Pretty clever hoax—the blood on the hair and fluid in her ears. All looked genuine until we couldn't find a single thing wrong with her.'

'She's okay?' Rachel felt for the back of the chair and lowered herself down to the seat. 'How could she be okay?'

The surgeon shook his head in disgust. 'It's bad enough that people make hoax calls but to set up something to look like an accident... You're both nurses aren't you? I've worked with your friend before. Seen you around as well. Consider yourself suspended from duty. You can explain yourself to the police when they get here.' He turned to Jim. 'Keep an eye on her and make sure she doesn't run off.'

The surgeon turned before she could respond and headed back down the corridor. Rachel glanced round and saw everyone looking at her. Jim was still there, standing slightly away from her.

'It wasn't a hoax.' She felt her eyes well up again and brushed the tears away before they could fall. 'It wasn't.'

Jim looked away. 'I believe you, but I was there in Resus. She doesn't have a single cut on her. We gave her an MRI and there is sign of trauma but it's old. A scar too, but fully healed. Years old. It just... doesn't make any sense.'

'Can I see her?'

'Yes. I'll take you through.'

~~~

Emma had been cleaned up, the brace the Paramedics had put around her neck had been taken off and she simply looked to be sleeping. The only sign something had happened was that she was lying on a hospital bed, her hair still matted from the blood.

'Can I sit with her?' Rachel asked.

'Sure.' Jim started to back away but then hesitated. 'Would you like some tea?'

Fighting back tears, Rachel nodded.

~~~

Someone shook her on the shoulder and Rachel woke with a start. She sat up and saw a nurse she didn't recognise.

'The police would like to ask you some questions.'

There was a man and woman standing outside Resus, dark overcoats but no uniforms.

'Okay.'

The Nurse waved them in.

'I'm Detective Inspector Daniel Martin, this is Detective Natalie Henderson. Can I ask your name?'

'Rachel Phillips.'

'Do you have ID on you?' Asked Henderson.

The question was said in a neutral tone but immediately Rachel felt threatened. 'In my purse.'

'May I?'

Reluctantly, Rachel found her driver's licence and handed it over to Henderson who took down her details.

Martin then asked her to tell them what had happened. Once she finished, they both shared a glance. She couldn't read what they were thinking.

'We have CCTV covering the area so we should be able to confirm your story. The man you say attacked her... Did you see his face at all?'

'Yes. He was blond, long hair, beard, but ragged... He looked as if he was

18

homeless.'

'Would you be able to help us produce a photofit?'

'Of course.'

'Okay, thank you.' Martin glanced at Henderson again before asking: 'Can you give us your contact numbers so we can reach you?'

Rachel recited her mobile and home number. Henderson took these down. They asked the Nurse to call them when Emma was awake and left.

She checked her watch. It was 4am.

~~~

A beautiful day. She looked up past trees full of blossom and the city skyline to the soft blue sky and took a deep breath. It was good to be alive. Everyone seemed to be smiling, business men in their suits, tourists walking hand in hand, mothers pushing their children in buggies.

Everyone smiling, except one angry man. So tall he seemed to be a giant, striding towards her from outside the city walls. She couldn't see his face but she knew he was angry, a hatred so deep within him that the sky seemed to turn cold and she froze with fear. She tried to take a step back but found her feet would not move. She managed to look round to her right and to her horror saw two others heading towards her. Like the first man, dressed in black, their faces hidden.

She looked round to her left and saw three more. They were holding guns. Huge, ugly things. Again, turning, she saw they all carried guns, and metal tubes that would spit out explosions, would spray death.

She tried to run. Her feet stayed still.

She looked round and realised that no-one else had noticed. The business men were still smiling and laughing. The mothers were unconcerned for their children. She tried to shout, to warn them, but her voice did not seem to be working. She waved her arms, tried to signal a warning and found herself sitting in her bed, heart beating too fast, her breathing rapid and shallow.

'You foolish old woman,' Mary scolded herself, still frightened from the dream. 'Nightmares at your age,' she muttered, trying to calm down her breathing.

She sat until she could not feel her heart thumping inside her and she could breathe normally. Then she stayed where she was, the memory of the dream seeming to hold her in place even though she tried to put it out of her mind.

'This is ridiculous!' Mary turned and switched on the lamp beside her bed. The clock that sat next to it showed it was almost quarter to one. 'I've not even been asleep two hours!'

It wasn't going away. Mary pulled at the sheets and eased herself out of bed. 'Some hot milk, that will do the trick.'

Before she stood, Mary paused and glanced upwards. 'Lord God, I'm sure you've better things to be doing but please, let me get back to sleep.'

As she went downstairs and began heating some milk, she ignored a voice deep inside that whispered: not tonight.

CHAPTER FIVE
Awakening

At 7am Emma opened her eyes. She wasn't at home. Looking around she saw she was in a hospital. Rachel was leaning on the side of the bed. She seemed asleep.

Sitting up, Emma shook Rachel's arm. She tried to push Emma's hand away but Emma tightened her grip.

'Stop that...' Rachel looked up and then sat bolt upright. 'You're awake!'

'Yeah, and in a hospital. What happened last night?'

'You don't remember?'

'Uh, no. Must have been some party though.' Emma yawned. 'Good sleep though. How long have I been out?'

Rachel stood up and took a step back from the bed. 'How do you feel?'

Emma shrugged. 'Fine. Why am I here?'

'What's the last thing you remember?'

Yawning again, Emma stretched. 'We went out last night. Dancing... Oh! I made out with Paul!'

'That's what you remember? Paul?'

'That was stupid. Jennifer's going to kill me.'

'What's the last thing you remember?'

Emma looked away, frowning as she thought back. 'We were at the club. Did someone spike my drink?'

'No! No-one spiked your drink. You don't remember walking home? Climbing on the wall?'

Emma shook her head.

'Do you have any headaches, any pain?'

'No, should I have?'

'You fell off of Monk Bar. Cracked your head open. I watched you die!'
Rachel had tears running down her face.

'No. No, that's not possible. I feel fine.' Emma put her hand up to her head and noticed her hair felt strange, like paint had dried on it. She felt around and then put up her other hand. Under her hair, the skin felt strange, a jagged line that she had never noticed before, covering an indentation in her skull that ran for a couple of inches. 'I have a scar. Have I been in a coma?'

'It was just last night. I tried to stop you but you wouldn't listen. It was like you were high or something. I couldn't catch you... it was too fast and then you hit your head and there was so much blood but the paramedics said you were okay even though that guy had attacked you. It doesn't make any sense.'

'Somebody attacked me? Was that how I fell?'

'No, it was after, when you were lying there. At first I thought he was going to give you CPR but he...' Rachel looked away.

'What? What did he do?'

'He, he climbed on top of you. I thought he was going to rape you!'

'Rape me! Why didn't you stop him?'

'I did, but I had to run back to find somewhere to jump down from the wall and I chased him off.'

Emma closed her eyes and tried to slow down the thoughts that were racing through her mind. I fell. I hit my head. I don't have a wound but do have a scar. I was attacked by some guy. 'This all happened last night?'

'Yes. The police will want to speak with you. They think, the surgeon...' Rachel seemed to stumble forwards and Emma found herself throwing back the sheets and rushing to support her friend.

'It's okay, sit down.' She helped Rachel sit.

'What are you doing out of bed!'

Emma turned to see a doctor standing in the doorway. The face was familiar but she couldn't place the name. 'She looked like she was going to faint.'

'Never you mind that, get back into that bed now! Rushing about after a serious accident, you should know better!'

'Connie?'

'Yes. Haven't completely addled your brain then. You lie back while I check on your friend. I'll get to you in a minute.'

Emma watched as Connie checked Rachel's pulse and then blood pressure. After asking Rachel some standard questions, Connie gave her diagnosis: 'Exhaustion. Possibly also still in shock.' Connie gave Emma a hard look. 'Something very odd about all this.'

Connie then turned to Emma and gave her a full work-up. Extracting three vials of blood and examining her head and neck very carefully.

'You have a scar. An old head injury?'

'No. Never.'

'Well, you didn't get it last night, that's for sure. I would say more than a year old. Do you remember what happened?'

'Nothing.'

Connie ran through a series of questions.

'Your memory is fine, up until yesterday evening. No sign of any cognitive disturbance. I could almost let you go home now but will keep you in another night. You had a lot of blood in your hair when they brought you in and even though your MRI was clear you also had spinal fluid leaking out your ears. Has she told you?'

'Told me what?'

'You're suspended until there's been an inquiry. Our good friend Mr Cole has made a formal complaint against you accusing you of perpetrating a hoax. Quite a serious allegation. We had to take samples of your blood and the fluid in your ears last night and send them away for analysis. Was it?'

'What?'

'A hoax? Better to come clean now and maybe we can put some positive spin on it all.'

'Look, I know what people think of me, say about me, but I would never do that. I wouldn't even know how!'

Connie studied Emma for a minute and then shrugged. 'Maybe we'll never know what happened. The police are going to want to question you though. I need to call them and let them know you're awake.'

'Whatever.'

'Try and get some rest. And you...' Connie said looking at Rachel. I'm going to call you a taxi. Your friend is in good hands. You need to get some sleep.'

After Connie had left the room, Emma turned to Rachel. 'Why do they think this is a hoax? What did she mean I've been suspended?'

Rachel stood, holding onto the bed to steady herself. 'I don't want to talk about it. I'm going home.'

'You can't just leave me.'

Rachel paused in the doorway. 'It's both of us you stupid cow! They've gone and suspended both of us! All because you had to go messing around on the wall. Look, I'm glad you're okay but I haven't slept all night and I can't deal with this anymore. I'm sorry.'

The door closed behind Rachel leaving Emma on her own.

~~~

'That's all there is?'

Will met Archer's suspicious gaze and held it. 'Minus my normal commission. We agreed thirty percent, didn't we?'

'Thirty percent for you, not for me...' Archer picked up one of the boxes of mobile phones and seemed to weigh it, still keeping his attention on Will.

'We need to talk about that...' Will started, but Archer raised a hand in a clear signal.

'There's nothing to talk about. When you work for me, you work for me. You want to set up your own jobs, go right ahead. But when you're working on my information, when I tell you, it's on my terms. How many boxes in total?'

'Two hundred and fifty. I've kept seventy five.'

'Normally you take the cash. What's up?'

'A friend of mine was looking for some gear to sell. He offered a good price.'

'And I don't?'

'He's a friend.'

Archer grunted. 'Two fifty... That's only one pallet. There was supposed to be two.'

'There was only one pallet.'

'That wasn't the information I had.'

'Your information was wrong.' Will knew it was a mistake as he said it.

Archer's gaze narrowed. 'My information is never wrong.'

There was no point in answering him. Will knew that there were lots of reasons why the second pallet might have been moved, but even giving one would just make him look guilty. He'd challenged Archer and would just have to live with the consequences.

'Well?' Archer demanded.

'Well what?'

'Aren't you going to answer me?'

'There was one pallet in the lockup.' Will kept his gaze on Archer, but noticed his "assistant" started to slowly walk round the small storeroom.

'What happened to the other one?'

'How am I supposed to know?' Will tried to inject some frustration into his tone. Archer's information was not always correct. Sometimes shipments were moved early. Sometimes there were security guards when none were supposed to be on duty. Sometimes the quantities were less or even more than expected. He'd always been up front about times when quantities were more which had led Archer to trust him.

'You're short on the delivery.' Archer tossed the box back onto the pallet.

Will shook his head. He wasn't under contract to deliver a set amount and Archer knew it.

'I've promised two hundred and fifty units. I need to deliver two fifty. If you'd brought back two pallets you could have kept your thirty percent and I'd still have had spare units.'

Will grimaced. He had made a deal to supply seventy five units to a friend. But Archer was his main source of generating leads. Researching the kind of jobs Archer passed to him took a wide network of contacts which would take Will years, if not decades, to develop.

The problem wasn't that Will couldn't honour that deal... By stiffing Archer on the second pallet he had over three hundred units. He could backtrack for Archer and still provide a whole pallet to his friend. The problem was whether word would ever get round that those extra units were now in circulation. If so, would Archer suspect Will had cheated him?

'This was my chance to make something extra on the job.'

'If you'd brought back two pallets you would have made extra.'

Shaking his head in frustration, Will thought quickly. The decision to hang onto the second pallet had been an impromptu one, built up by annoyance at the low cut he took from each job. But he had few contacts himself to shift the units. Was it better to concede the seventy five units and try and rebuild the relationship with Archer?

'I'll tell my friend he'll have to wait. The other units are in my van.'

~~~

He had left the house just to get out, driven around for an hour and then returned, but now sat in his car, reluctant to get out and go into his house.

A tear formed in his right eye and he allowed himself a minute to remember their first days here after they were married. The days before the cancer.

Why God? Why?

Locking the car behind him, Zafar walked up to the house and let himself in. Normally, he would put on a CD or the radio almost immediately to fill the house with some sign of life but he knew today he needed to be quiet, to think.

While he boiled a kettle on a gas hob, Zafar put some green tea in one of the tea pots they had received as a wedding gift and took out a mug. Shireen always used the delicate cups that matched this pot but while he liked this pot which never dripped, left to himself... He paused at that thought and allowed it to run through his head over and over.

The whistle on the kettle blew interrupting his thoughts and Zafar took a deep breath and wiped away his tears before filling the tea pot with the hot water, steam billowing up in the cold air. He shivered, only now realising it was cold in the house.

He could not think if he was cold. Turning, he knelt down to look at the controls of the electric radiator attached to the wall.

Satisfied it would begin to heat up, Zafar took off his suit jacket and went to get a jumper. Checking the tea when he came back he decided it was ready to pour.

Sipping the fragrant liquid, he allowed himself a smile. Definitely better in a mug.

The fragrance from the tea filled his senses, the warmth of it heated his hands and mouth and belly, and Zafar found himself reliving his vision.

He didn't consider himself a violent man, tried as far as possible to live in peace with those around him, but lately there had been an anger building at the treatment of his brothers and sisters around the world. Whatever anger he felt could not compare to those who were oppressed on a daily basis and so, when he heard of yet another suicide bombing, he tried to imagine what would drive someone to blow themselves up. Perhaps he was built differently as he was unable to find any sympathy for those who carried the bombs and certainly not for those who undoubtedly gave the orders. Would The Prophet ever have been so careless with the lives under his command?

As a child, he had fought with his cousins and with anyone who wanted to fight. Wrestling mostly. Harmless usually. Sometimes with fists, though once Jani, his youngest cousin, had deeply embarrassed him by showing him how effective fists could be when one was not afraid to use them. That had been a valuable lesson and when he had picked himself up, he had kept attacking until it was Jani who fell.

Jani was at university now, studying in Manchester. Jani's two elder brothers, Faruq and Jaleel were settled in jobs and with families. Strange to think back to when they all lived as neighbours on the same street in York, fighting and playing.

But this, was it from Allah or just the ravings of his mind. He had a sense he had been given something incredibly profound. There was such a simplicity about it, a few young men capturing a city through their bravery and audacity. It was something that Mohammed would have done. Something that was even now being done throughout the Middle East, establishing a Caliphate for the first time in hundreds of years.

Yet, what would even be the point of carrying it out? They would need thousands of people to keep a city once they had captured it. Even with guns against them, Zafar did not think a whole city would submit.

And if not to capture a city, what would be the aim of such a co-ordinated attack?

It was madness. If Shireen was still alive, he would have told her and she would have scolded him. His heart almost broke at the thought. With her gone was there anyone he could talk to, go to for advice? He had not talked to his father in months, had never been that close to him. His Mullah…? No, he would not trust him with anything of importance.

Faruq and Jaleel would not understand, would not listen to him, their younger cousin. And, smiling at the irony, he himself would not go to Jani for advice.

And with great sadness, he had to admit, he no longer had anyone he would call a friend. He had shut himself away from everyone that he and Shireen had called friends and eventually, they had given up trying to reach him.

He missed her. So much. Laying his head on the table, Zafar allowed the tears to come freely and great sobs to shake his body.

CHAPTER SIX
Questions

'Let's run through this one more time, how many drinks did you have at the club?'

Emma sighed and looked up at the ceiling. Detective Henderson had appeared at just after 11am and had now been asking her questions for half an hour.

'I said already, I don't remember leaving the club. I must have had three cocktails. Two shots of Tequila on top of that but that's all I remember.'

'What is the last thing you remember?'

Kissing Paul. There was no way she was going to put that on record though. 'Dancing. I don't know what time.'

'Where did you get your drinks from?'

'The bar.'

'Any possibility someone spiked them?'

Emma shook her head. 'I got two rounds. Rachel got two and...' Paul. Paul got a round, but no, he wouldn't...

'And...'

'A friend, but he wouldn't have.'

'What is his name?'

'It's not possible.' When did Paul buy his round? Was it before or after they kissed? Emma felt suddenly sick.

'His name?'

'Paul, I don't... I don't know his last name. He's Jennifer's boyfriend. But he wouldn't, couldn't...'

'Most rapes are carried out by people known to the victim. If Paul or someone else spiked your drink it would explain the memory loss.'

'So would a blow to my head.'

'Except there is no evidence of that.'

'What do you call this?' Emma pulled her matted hair away from her head.

'Well, we'll be checking the CCTV footage—both at Monk Bar and at the club. Maybe we'll get an image of the man your friend says attacked you.'

'You have CCTV of what happened?'

'We should do. My D.I. ordered it sent over this morning.'

'I want to see it.'

Henderson sighed. 'Let us review the footage first. Can you remember anything from walking on the wall?'

'No.'

'Was all this simply a practical joke?'

'No.'

Henderson closed her notebook. 'Okay, Ms Hunter. We'll be in touch.'

The detective walked out and Emma slumped back on the bed. At some point during the interview she had started to get angry. She wasn't sure if it was with the detective who obviously distrusted her, or with Rachel for walking out on her, or was it just anger at the fact she couldn't remember a single thing after leaving the club? 'Are you up there, God?' She directed at the ceiling. 'Enjoying yourself are you?' Turning over and curling up she put her hand to the back of her head to feel the scar that had somehow formed overnight. 'What is going on,' she whispered to herself.

~~~

'Nurse. Nurse!' Emma glared at the young girl who had ignored her, walking straight on to the nurses' station. What's her problem, she thought to herself. Sighing, Emma sat up. It was almost 3pm. She'd spent the last hour watching the nurses and doctors doing their rounds. Had submitted to another series of checks but despite her efforts to start a conversation with the people she thought of as her colleagues, they had remained impersonal, distant.

If she was at home, off shift, spending the day in bed would have been the normal way of working off a hangover. For some reason she felt no ill effects from drinking. Her head was clear, she was alert, she was bored and she was… Disgusting!

She put a hand up to the back of her head. Her hair was a solidified mass. She'd tried to ignore an increasing desire to have a shower, knowing she wouldn't be allowed, but how long were they going to make her wait? The gown they had put her in was irritating her skin. Even if she could get a sponge and some water… Well, if they wouldn't come to her, she would just have to go to them.

Easing her legs off the bed, Emma paused before standing up. Putting her hand back up, she found the scar that was troubling her. It had definitely not been there before. A scar like that took weeks to form. Would have required some major trauma to produce it. She'd seen that sort of trauma before. Emma shivered.

Standing, she noticed no sign of dizziness. She felt healthy, strong. Checking her gown was covering her at the back, she barefooted it over to the nurses' station. Connie was there, the only nurse she knew on that shift.

'When can I get a shower?'

Connie looked up. 'You shouldn't be walking around.'

'I'm fine.'

'How many times have you heard a patient say that just before they collapse?'

Shaking her head, Emma shrugged. 'Never.'

'Happens here a couple of times a week. Should get out more.'

'A shower?'

Connie sighed. 'Not today.'

She'd had to try… 'Okay. Where are my clothes?'

'They had to cut them off. They were in a right state from what I heard.'

'That was my favourite dress!'

Connie gave her a look that seemed to ask: really?

'Can I at least get my phone?'

'We don't have it.'

'You're joking! Wasn't my purse brought in?'

'I'll try and find out.'

'And what is it with these nurses? Not a single one will speak to me.'

'I'll have a word with them. Now get back into bed.'

Clutching at the back of the gown, Emma headed back to her bed. The man in the bed next to hers watched her walk over. He looked like he was going to speak so Emma glowered at him. He wisely remained silent.

~~~

She had finally managed to get one of the junior nurses to speak to her and asked for some magazines. The TV was too far away and she had never been terribly interested. The junior brought a few magazines over but even though she would have happily browsed them waiting for a hair or dentist appointment, the photos seemed flat and lifeless. The stories were irrelevant.

Emma glanced at the clock. Three minutes to eight. Visiting hour had livened the place up, for everyone else. Rachel hadn't showed and without her phone, Emma couldn't check to see if she was coming over.

The other patients all had family or friends round them. Laughing, chatting. Some of the visitors seemed more interested in the TV than the people they were there to see, but at least they'd turned up.

She could have called her Mum. Never occurred to her during the day. Why would she? Hi Mum, I had a fall. I think. I don't remember it. I'm fine, apart from a scar I didn't have the day before. And they cut my clothes off me so I'm stuck here unless I can steal some scrubs.

No. She couldn't imagine trying to have that conversation. Not when she hadn't spoken to her Mum in six months.

Too late to call anyone else. Unless for a chat. But who would she chat to? Rachel was her best friend and she'd been royally upset with her that morning. They couldn't really suspend them both for an accident, could they?

Lying back, Emma tried to recall what had happened the previous night. They had been dancing and drinking all evening. She could remember images from the evening but everything was in the club. She tried to picture leaving but there was just a blank. She closed her eyes and relaxed hoping that would help. Within a few minutes she was asleep.

~~~

The blonde man approached her. He had sad eyes. Kind but sad. They looked into her eyes and she felt herself wanting to cry at the depth of his sorrow.

He reached out a hand and brushed hair from her face. He laid a hand on her cheek and she felt his warmth.

Leaning closer, he whispered words so quietly that she could not hear them. His voice was soft, his tone gentle.

She wanted to take his hand, hold it and feel his skin warm hers. She tried to reach out to him but he was moving backwards, no wait, she was the one moving. He reached out his hand for her to take it but her arms would not respond. She was falling, spinning and the ground was rushing up to meet her. She tried to scream but there was no time…

Emma sat bolt upright. She looked around and in the gloom confirmed she was still in the ward. A nightmare, that was all, just a really bad dream.

She realised she had been sweating. Great! All she needed. Getting out of bed she went to relieve herself. Returning, she gingerly sat back on the damp sheets.

Had that been how it happened? Falling like that? She didn't know whether she wanted to really find out. Had it been the guy Rachel spoke of? Had he tried to stop her falling? What had she said? Thought he wanted to rape me? Was I trying to get away from him and that's how I fell?

Rachel would tell her. In the morning. Emma lay her head down and closed her eyes. A second later she opened them again. She wasn't quite ready to go back to sleep. She lay like that until the ward came to life again, the nurses bustling around checking the patients and she finally felt safe enough to sleep.

CHAPTER SEVEN
Release

'You have got to be joking! I can't wear that!'

'Fine, go home in your gown. Just make sure to wash it and bring it back.'

Emma looked in disbelief from Connie to the clothes she had brought her. Women's tan slacks; a cream blouse; and cream cardigan. 'Whose clothes are those?'

'Yours. Unless you don't want them and I'll give them back to the laundry.'

Emma shuddered. She was being unreasonable she knew, but the thought of wearing the second hand clothes filled her with disgust for some reason.

'Whose were they?'

'How should I know. You know how it works. People donate clothes all the time.'

'Yeah, from people who died.'

'Okay, that's enough. Keep your voice down.' Connie glanced round to the other patients. 'You wear them home and you can burn them for all I care. You were the one asking for your clothes.'

'My clothes, not these…' Emma picked up the cardigan. 'They're just… wrong. The colour…'

'Whatever. I need to run through the same checks as yesterday.' Connie attached the strap to check Emma's blood pressure. 'Any headache?'

'No.'

'None at all?' Connie was frowning.

'Nothing.'

'Okay… Right, blood pressure a bit low. Is that normal?'

'Yes. I've never had high blood pressure.'

Holding a pen torch up, Connie shone it in Emma's eyes and asked her to look left, right, up and down.

'Any tingling or loss of sensation anywhere?'

'No.'

Connie ran through several additional questions and poked and prodded her until Emma actually pushed her hand away. 'Enough already!'

'Patient appears impatient, grumpy and inconsiderate. Perfectly normal in fact.'

'I can go home then?'

'Please do! Though you may want to shower first. We've got some toiletries in a box at the desk, I'll bring some over.'

Emma nodded her thanks. As Connie returned to the nurses' station, Emma saw Rachel walk up, Emma's Dolce & Gabbana bag in her hand.

'Tell me that you've brought me some clothes!'

'Pleased to see you too.' Rachel tossed the bag on the bed. 'They letting you out then?'

'Just need a shower. Thanks!' Emma grabbed the bag and padded over to the bathroom.

It took a while to get her hair clean, trying to ignore the dark splattering on the shower floor. Finally she felt clean enough to get out but knew she would have to wash again when she got home.

Rachel called a taxi and they sat in silence during the short trip to their flat and then up the stairs.

Rachel put the kettle on as soon as they got inside. 'Take it you've had breakfast.'

Emma dumped her bag outside her room and took off her jacket, shouting through to Rachel: 'Had some toast. Do we have any milk? I'm really craving some Cheerios.'

'I bought some yesterday.' Rachel shouted back.

Their flat was not big. Two single bedrooms with just enough room for wardrobes and tables; a small shower room; and a kitchen diner with a sofa and TV crammed in at the end. It was functional and they could just afford it on the painfully low nurse's salaries they were both on.

Emma walked into the kitchen and headed straight for the pantry cupboard. Found the Cheerios and then pulled out a bowl and spoon and made her way to the table.

Rachel was standing facing the kettle which was beginning to boil.

'Pass the milk would you?' Emma asked, pouring out the Cheerios.

Rachel offered her the milk bottle without turning round. Emma grabbed it and poured before handing it back to Rachel.

'You said a guy attacked me. I think I dreamt about him last night,' Emma said, her mouth half full of Cheerios.

Rachel turned to look at her but didn't say anything.

'Did he push me? Is that how I fell?'

'No-one pushed you.' Rachel's shoulders slumped and she stopped stirring the tea bags in the pot. 'You still don't remember?'

'Nothing. Unless what I dreamed actually happened. The guy definitely didn't push me?'

Rachel carried over the tea pot, two mugs and the milk. She sat, poured the milk in the mugs and then the tea. I'm only going to tell you once, okay? Just once and then I don't ever want to talk about it again. I hardly slept yesterday. Kept closing my eyes and seeing you...' Rachel looked up and Emma saw her eyes had welled up.

'I don't want you interrupting me every five seconds with some stupid question either. I'll tell you what happened. Everything I can remember. Then I don't want anything to do with it. You understand?'

Emma nodded and listened in silence as Rachel told her how she'd been when they left the club. The confession about Paul. Walking on the parapet of the wall and then how she'd slipped... Slipped and Rachel tried to catch her but she was too far away. It hadn't been the man in her dream after all, it had been Rachel. But she had fallen.

Then it became difficult for Emma to concentrate and Rachel had become detached, her voice flattening out as she continued. Emma had fallen badly. Rachel had called an ambulance but the way she'd hit the ground... Rachel tried to describe it but the words would not come out. Her monologue stalled until finally she looked directly at Emma. 'I thought you were dead. I was speaking to the operator but I thought there was no point. Then that homeless bum turned up and at first I thought he was checking for your pulse but now I wonder if he was just looking for a purse. Then he got on top of you and I thought he was going to... I don't know... Rape you? Right there. In the middle of the street. I had to run back half a mile before I could jump down. Broke a heel and had to run back barefoot. I chased him off. I don't think he did anything to you but... I couldn't see. I'm sorry.'

Emma couldn't take it all in. She wanted to ask something but then Rachel started up again.

'Then the ambulance turned up and you weren't dead, like you'd just landed in someone's take-out curry. And they couldn't find anything wrong with you and it makes no sense because I saw the blood and I saw the stuff in your ears but you're here and unless Zombies prefer Cheerios to human flesh you seem very alive.'

Emma let the spoon go loose in her bowl and reached up slowly to the back of her head. 'I have a scar.'

'I don't want to know.'

'I didn't have a scar before.'

'Seriously!' Rachel held up her hand. 'I do not want to know. I've told you all I know. I'm seriously angry with you right now and I think it's better if we don't talk about it anymore.'

'Don't talk about it? What are you saying? You think I died? Is that it? That I'm some sort of ghost?'

'You got me suspended, okay! One stupid night on the town and I might lose my job because you just had to go messing about.'

'You're angry because they suspended us?'

'No. I'm angry because they suspended me! There is no "us" in this. They think we set this up together but I sure wasn't in on the game. Tell me...' Rachel's tone softened. 'This isn't just some ultra-elaborate prank you're pulling is it? Am I being Punk'd for some new reality TV show because if I am... I'm not sure I can forgive you.'

'I don't know what happened. Honestly. I wouldn't do that to you.'

'You'd cheat on Jennifer with her boyfriend but wouldn't pull the mother of all practical jokes?'

Emma put her hands up over her eyes and pressed until she could see stars. 'Jennifer...'

'She is going to kill you when she finds out. Ironic really.'

'I am in so much trouble.'

'Is this a bad time to ask if you ever did sign up for the Union?'

Emma looked blankly at her.

'Thought not. Might be worth calling them tomorrow. You never know. They might be able to help.'

'I don't really...' Emma stopped out of embarrassment. 'I don't really know what it means. Suspended.'

'You kidding me, girl?'

Emma shook her head.

'Suspended. We could be out of a job unless we can sue them or get the Union to put pressure on them or something. How can you not know that?'

CHAPTER EIGHT
Expelled

'Do you ever take a break, Boss?' Natalie sat down opposite Danny, setting down her mug on the canteen table.

Danny looked up and watched as she pulled out her notebook and pen. 'I'm sure I had a Saturday off last year.'

The touch of her foot on his inner leg made him start. Even though he knew there was no-one else in the room, Danny wanted to look round and check they were alone. 'Not in the office,' he said.

'Doesn't look like the office to me...' She gave him a mischievous smile as she looked round the room. 'Want to come round tonight?'

'You know I try and get home early on a Sunday.'

'So come round this afternoon... You're not supposed to be working today anyway.'

A foot running up and down his leg should have been inconsequential, but Danny was finding it hard to concentrate. 'Toxicology report on Emma Hunter?' He asked, opening the first of several files he had taken to review.

Her foot ran up his leg one last time and withdrew.

'I ordered it yesterday.' Natalie opened her notebook and flicked through, her gaze withdrawing from him.

'We need to get the CCTV footage.'

'I went to Monk Bar yesterday. There are three Council cameras that will probably have captured some of the incident and an additional one belonging to Monkbar Hotel that may be useful. I put in a requisition for all the feeds.'

Danny nodded approvingly. It could take officers eight years just to make Detective Constable but Natalie had achieved the rank within three and her attitude to the job showed she had every chance of being promoted up to Inspector rank or higher. 'What possibilities should we be investigating?'

Natalie shrugged. 'The surgeon making the complaint was right to do so. Hunter showed no sign of having any injury from a fall from the Bar. Not even grazing or bruising.'

'The blood…'

'She's a nurse. It wouldn't have been that difficult for her and her friend to extract some of her own blood and plant it on the scene.'

'Not so easy to take out spinal fluid though.'

'No. They're going to do DNA tests on the fluids. We'll know soon enough.'

'It would take some level of acting though…' Danny put his hands behind his head and studied the ceiling. 'Her friend, Rachel… Not easy to fake that shock or distress.'

'What's the alternative? She slipped, fell and landed without a scratch? Rachel pushed her… Attempted murder is kind of hard to prove when the victim is perfectly healthy. Suicide is no easier. It has to have been faked. We get the CCTV and we can prove it.'

Danny put the file to the side and picked up the next one. 'Burglary at T. C. Bennett's Off-Licence…'

~~~

'I don't see what the problem is, Mary. Tony's trying to reach out to these people. What's wrong with that?' Arthur Thompson looked to his wife, Edith, for support.

'It's the first two commandments!' Mary realised her voice was becoming shrill and checked to see no-one was looking. 'Have no other gods before me. Do not bow down before other gods.'

Edith Thompson shook her head. 'Tony's not bowing down to other gods. He's been quite clear what he does when he goes to these meetings.'

'They're praying together… How can a Christian pray with a Muslim or a Buddhist or a Hindu?'

Arthur leaned forward on his walking stick. 'I am uncomfortable with that, truth be told. Meeting with people is one thing, but worshipping together… No. That I don't understand.'

'Tony's a good man. You should really speak to him directly,' Edith said.

'I have, but he insists he won't stop attending these meetings.'

'Well, I don't see what we can do.' Edith said, shaking her head.

'We can vote to remove him.' There! She'd finally said it. Mary looked defiantly at Edith and Arthur who she could see would need a lot more persuading.

'We can't do that...' Arthur protested.

'We voted him in as Minister, we can vote him out again.' Mary insisted. She stole a glance round and saw Maggie Blythe was walking towards the exit. 'Will you pray about it? Excuse me, I must speak with Maggie.'

Mary hurried away, not seeing the looks Arthur and Edith gave each other.

~~~

'Zafar!' Tariq all but yelled out his name and quickly gathered him in a hug.

Zafar, embarrassed, gave Tariq a couple of pats and was relieved when Tariq finally stood back and only offered a huge grin.

'You actually came... Thank you so much for honouring me with your visit. You must come in!' Tariq stood aside and ushered Zafar into his house.

The house was astonishingly bare. Zafar took in the plain white walls of the hallway, a glimpse of a functional kitchen and then a simple lounge with an old sofa and low table, with perhaps a dozen wooden chairs around the walls. The lounge at least had a television implying that Tariq had not become a total hermit.

'How long has it been,' asked Tariq, gesturing for Zafar to sit on the sofa. He himself took one of the wooden chairs.

Zafar shook his head. 'Not since high school.'

'Six, maybe seven years then.'

Zafar nodded, thinking back.

'First, brother... I heard about your wife. I am so sorry.'

Zafar looked away. 'It was as God willed.'

'No,' said Tariq causing Zafar to look directly at him. 'I do not believe all things are in God's will.'

It was almost blasphemy to say such a thing and yet it instantly reminded him of times in the Mosque as kids when Tariq had challenged the teaching they had received. Zafar felt himself starting to relax.

'Ah Zafar,' Tariq continued. 'I do not want to remind you of sadness. I am delighted you have come.' He jumped up. 'And I am a terrible host. You will eat with me, please!'

Zafar laughed. 'Do you have food in this house?'

'Of course not, we will eat wallpaper!'

Zafar looked around. 'It looks like you may need to buy some more.'

'Ah yes, I was peckish last night.' They both grinned.

'Come with me, I was going to buy some supplies this morning. And you look like you could do with some fresh air.' Tariq examined him closely. 'Are you ill, Zafar?'

Zafar found he could not meet Tariq's gaze. 'No. I... I haven't been sleeping well.'

'Maybe a walk and some good food will help. Well, food anyway...'

Zafar smiled and shook his head. It was good to see his old friend again.

~~~

They left Tariq's house and walked along the short street to a longer one which cut through the rows of terraced houses.

'So Zafar,' Tariq eventually said. 'Are you working just now?'

'Yes. Since leaving school. For the last three years I've been at an accountants in York.'

Tariq nodded his approval. 'A very respectable job.'

Zafar glanced at his friend and waited good humouredly for the inevitable follow up question.

'Do you not find it somewhat tedious?'

'Well, it is funny you should ask that. No. I quite enjoy working with numbers.' Zafar left it at that. He knew that any attempt to explain what he enjoyed and found satisfaction with in accountancy usually fell flat.

Tariq simply looked approvingly at him. 'You always were one of the brighter ones at school.'

Zafar could not detect any sarcasm, and decided to accept the compliment.

'And how about you, Tariq? What is it that you do?'

Tariq smiled but did not answer straight away. They walked for maybe twenty paces before Tariq motioned for them to stop and he then turned to look Zafar face on. 'I make things happen, Zafar.'

Zafar held Tariq's steady gaze, feeling a growing sense of excitement. He wanted to ask Tariq what he meant: what things? How do you make them happen? Do I know of any of them? He held back, worried he'd sound like he was babbling. He thought back to the drive home on Friday and the vision—if it was a vision—that he'd had. He was wary of sharing that. It was one thing to have a thought, quite another to share it.

Tariq gave another smile, though Zafar noticed a look of uncertainty, or puzzlement even, for a brief moment.

'The shop is just around this corner.' Tariq gestured ahead. 'Let's get some food and we can make a meal.'

The custom was that a visitor was an honoured guest, to be waited on, to be served. A guest never helped make a meal! But then he and Tariq had lived out of each other's houses, dodging slaps and driving their parents up the wall. Tariq had been as close as a brother for as long as he could remember and there were no rules between brothers.

He just watched as Tariq bustled around the small store, chatting freely with the owner and then, when Tariq introduced him, he offered a respectful greeting. He noticed Tariq nodding his approval.

After he had paid and they had left, Tariq chatted freely as they walked back.

'It is good to get outside. I try not to store too much in the house and so force myself to get out a couple of times each day, if only to buy food.'

'Surely you don't spend the rest of your time in the house,' Zafar asked, disbelieving.

'Of course not! But there are days when I am not working, and days when I work from home and I need to get out, see the sun and feel the wind.'

Zafar looked up at the cloudy sky and raised his hand to still air. They both laughed.

~~~

A productive morning, Mary thought to herself. She had managed to speak with four families in the church, making it clear to each of them that she wanted them to join with her in voting out the Reverend Anthony Wright.

She'd not been sure about him when the church had originally voted to call him as their minister. Too young. Too full of himself. And her suspicions had been confirmed when, within a few short months of taking the position, he'd announced his intention to take part in Inter-faith meetings in the city.

Didn't he know what the Holy God did to Israel when time after time the nation had turned to false gods? Well, he did know because she'd told him. Challenged "Tony"—as he liked to be called—time after time…

Mary closed her eyes and took a deep breath to calm herself. There was no point in getting worked up about it now. She'd prayed and sought God and the only answer she'd received was the assurance that what he was doing was wrong. There was only one way to deal with a false prophet and that was to expel them from the church.

She picked up her Church Directory and scanned the names. Still a lot of people to speak with, but she had time.

When the doorbell rang, she sat in puzzlement for a minute. She wasn't expecting anyone and didn't normally receive callers unless they had phoned in advance. Hopefully it was not someone begging for a charity or trying to sell her something. As she got up, Mary set her face. They would soon know not to waste time calling at her door.

'Miss Birch.'

Mary stared at a solemn faced Anthony Wright who she saw was flanked by Philip Blythe and Cynthia Martin. 'Reverend Wright. Philip, Cynthia...' she acknowledged.

Normally, "Tony" would ask her to use his first name when she addressed him formally, but this afternoon he just asked her if they could come in.

'Would you like some tea?' Mary asked after showing them into her sitting room. She watched as they glanced uncomfortably at each other.

'No thank you. Mary, please sit down.'

Mary forced a smile at Reverend Wright and turned to Cynthia as she sat down. 'It's so good to have you visit, Cynthia. How is Daniel?'

'Mary!'

The Reverend's tone was abrupt and Mary turned back to him in annoyance. This was her house he was in...

'Several members of the church have informed me that you have been trying to organise a vote to have me removed as minister.'

Mary glanced at Cynthia and Philip. She had not yet spoken with them, but had been sure they would support her. Both shared her view of God's word. She raised herself up.

'You left me no choice. You insist on worshiping false gods. You can't expect the church to accept your teaching when you keep going to those... Inter-faith meetings,' she struggled to say the words, the anger rising up within her.

'Mary, you know full well that I don't meet with these leaders to worship with them. I do pray—to Jesus—as a witness to them whenever I meet. I listen as they pray, but don't think for a minute that I would say amen to what is being said. Have you not read the book of Acts? Paul in Athens pointing to the altar of the unknown god and using that as an opportunity to witness to the worshipers there... If we never meet with people who worship foreign gods, how can we ever hope to win them to Christ?'

Mary looked at Cynthia for support, then at Philip, but they both seemed happy to let Mary and the Reverend sort this out.

'We're told to come out of the world, to have nothing to do with those who sin,' she replied.

The Reverend shook his head. 'No, no, no, Mary. We're told to go out into the world, to make disciples. That is our commission. Not told to bury our heads in the sand and only meet with fellow believers. It is not the healthy who need a doctor, but the sick—those are Jesus words. However, you are right, we are told to have nothing to do with believers who turn their backs on God's word and embrace sin.'

'Well, there you go then!' Mary looked round triumphantly. 'That is what I was doing, warning the church about you.'

'No. You were sowing division in the church. Gossiping about me when you should have followed God's word—as I am doing here. Discipline is not something to be taken lightly, Mary and what you have done may have done irreparable damage to the church.'

'How are you following God's word?'

'Jesus gave clear instructions on how to discipline believers. Go to them in private and try and win them over. I accept you came to me in private initially, but Mary, you never tried to win me over. You simply argued with me and refused to listen as you still seem to be doing tonight.'

'How dare you come into my house and…'

'Secondly,' the Reverend interrupted. 'Jesus said that if a person will not listen, you should take two fellow believers with you—as I have done today—and speak with the person.'

'Cynthia? Philip?' Mary turned to each of them.

Cynthia held out her hand to Mary who grasped it. 'Mary, I understand why you are uncomfortable at the thought of meeting with leaders of other religions. Please understand, this is not about worshiping with them, it is trying to witness to them.'

Mary let go of Cynthia's hand.

Philip leaned over. 'Please listen to Tony.'

'What are you saying? You think I've sinned?'

'Mary, you cannot go behind my back trying to turn people against me. Gossiping and sowing division within a church are serious issues.'

'I was not gossiping!'

'You told Arthur and Edith that I was worshiping false gods. That is gossip, Mary.'

'I don't have to listen to this!' Mary stood and pointed to the door. 'Get out!'

'Mary…'

'I said get out!'

The Reverend stood reluctantly. 'You leave me no choice, Mary. You have refused to accept the discipline of the church. In the presence of witnesses I am excluding you from the church for the next month. You will not attend any meetings or contact any members excepting myself, Cynthia or Philip. If you wish to repent we will be glad to talk to you.'

'You can't do that…' Mary felt her strength fail as she saw Cynthia stand, an expression of sadness on her face. 'The church is my life. Cynthia, please...'

Cynthia just shook her head.

The three of them slowly filed out of the room, Mary following them to the door. Once outside, the Reverend turned to her.

'Have you ever talked with a Muslim, Mary?' The Reverend asked. 'A Buddhist? Do you have Atheist friends? If you are not willing to spend time with people who do not share your faith, how can you ever win anyone to Christ? Look at Christ's example. Even on the cross he was willing to forgive a thief and a probable murderer. If he can do that, can't you find it in your heart to reach out?'

CHAPTER NINE
Challenged

After they had gone, Mary couldn't stop shaking. She walked up and down, asking God to help her, but as usual, there was only silence.

How could Cynthia betray her like that? She had known her since she married Daniel thirty years ago. Had known Daniel his whole life, had been his God-Mother.

Mary eventually walked to the kitchen, hoping a cup of tea might calm her nerves, but her hand shook so badly as she tried to fill the kettle that she decided to wait. Back in her sitting room she sat in her favourite armchair and studied where they had each sat. She had abstained from voting for Anthony Wright when the church had met to appoint their new minister. Too young. Not even married. How could he have enough experience to lead a church?

But many others had voted for him, enough that there had been no question about inviting him.

Arthur and Ethel had also abstained. She didn't need the church directory, they were old friends. Taking several deep breaths to try and calm herself, she managed to still the shaking enough that she could dial their number.

'York 899.' She heard Ethel answer, still quoting only the last three digits even though the number had changed to six, decades ago.

'Ethel! It's awful. The Reverend was here…'

'Mary? Is that you?'

'Yes, I'm sorry, I'm just so upset…'

'Let me get Arthur…'

'No, wait…' But Ethel had already laid the phone down and she could hear muted discussion.

'Mary?' Arthur's voice.

'Yes. I'm sorry to disturb you. I just had to speak with someone.'

'I don't think that's a good idea, Mary. Has Tony been to see you?'

'Yes, that's why I'm calling.'

'I spoke with him after you spoke to us. He was very concerned, Mary and I have to agree with him.'

'You… You spoke to him?'

'Of course. He's our minister. He reminded me of God's warning in the book of Numbers. The many times the people complained against the appointed rulers of God and each time God sided with his chosen leaders.'

'That's not the same…' Mary thought desperately. 'What about the kings? God removed them from office.'

'God did. Even David refrained from attacking Saul, even though God had promised him the kingdom.'

'But you didn't even vote for him, how can you defend him, what he is doing?'

Arthur sighed deeply. 'I made my peace with Tony soon after he arrived in York. As I said to you earlier, I am uncomfortable with the Inter-faith meetings, but I accept what he says. I don't believe he is leading us to worship false gods.'

Mary stared ahead, the room seeming to close in on her.

'Could I at least speak to Ethel?' She asked.

Another sigh. Clearing his throat, Arthur replied: 'Ethel and I are in agreement that you need to make your peace with Tony. We encourage you to humble yourself, to seek God and to be willing to listen to Tony.'

Mary let the phone drop and laid it back on the receiver. She tried calling two more of her closest friends at the church. Each of them gave her similar advice.

For a long time she was unable to get up. Thoughts tumbled round her head, a battle raging in her mind. A question she did not want to face kept asking, was she wrong?

~~~

Tariq took on a different persona once they reached his house. The friendly and joking manner did not disappear, not entirely, but he took charge, instructing Zafar to wash his hands and then guiding him through some of the preparations for the meal.

This was simple enough, lots of carrots, thinly sliced along their length. Rice stewed in a mix of oil and water. Lamb, spices and herbs added to the mix and the whole stew left to cook in a wok on Tariq's basic stove.

This was far removed from a traditional experience of visiting a friend. Instead of being served, he was doing the serving, but even conscious of this, Zafar did not mind. They were working together and Zafar was getting to know his friend once again, Tariq chatting as they readied the meal, telling him about places he had visited since he left school, the adventures he had experienced. Zafar was surprised that his friend was so well travelled. He had visited South America twice, once to Peru where he had journeyed to see the ruins of Machu Pichu. He had spent time in China, with the Tajiks in Xinjiang and had also backpacked throughout the former Soviet states of Central Asia.

His stories of corrupt border police, wild plateaus and travel disasters were so wild, Zafar did not initially know whether to believe him, but this was his friend, so he gave him the benefit of the doubt and laughed and shook his head at Tariq's stories.

'We are done,' Tariq said, drying his hands on a towel. He tossed the towel to Zafar and Zafar also washed and dried his hands.

'The Osh will take an hour more to cook, we can leave it simmering.' Tariq paused and his expression turned solemn. 'Now perhaps you should tell me why you came here today.'

Zafar wanted to laugh off the question, but he had called Tariq for a reason. 'Maybe we should sit down,' he suggested.

Tariq led the way back into his sitting room and sat cross legged on the carpet. Zafar sat opposite him, studying the carpet, the walls, anything but look at Tariq who seemed to be waiting patiently.

Eventually Zafar cleared his throat, looking up at Tariq. 'I don't know where to begin.'

'Most people start at the beginning,' Tariq smiled. 'But if it's easier to start at the end or somewhere in the middle…'

'What I'm going to say, it's… People go to jail for less.'

Tariq nodded in understanding. 'What you say will not leave this room.'

Eventually Zafar found the words to begin and shared the whole experience he'd had on his journey home from York. Tariq nodded throughout, but kept quiet, not interrupting. When he finally finished, Tariq gave him an encouraging smile, but remained silent, as if he was waiting for more.

'Aren't you going to say anything?' Zafar asked after a while.

'What do you want me to say?'

'Something. Anything!'

'Thank you for sharing this story with me.'

'That's it?'

Tariq leaned forward slightly and brushed a section of carpet.

Zafar let a sigh of exasperation escape. 'What should I do about this?'

'Nothing. You should go home and forget about it.'

'How can I forget it! The last two nights I've been unable to sleep!'

Tariq said nothing and eventually Zafar continued: 'I've been lying awake at night thinking about this. When I go to sleep, I wake up from dreaming of it. Only two days and I'm exhausted. My body aches as if I've been pummelled. My food has no taste and I have no desire to eat. How can a vision have such an effect on me?'

'I have no idea. Perhaps you are ill, you should see a doctor.'

'Don't make fun of me!'

'I am serious,' Tariq said. 'Why should you feel so ill?'

'I worry that God has given me this vision, and he will punish me for doing nothing.'

Tariq studied him. 'So what are you going to do about this vision?'

Zafar looked at the floor. 'To be honest, I have no idea. It terrifies me.'

Tariq nodded. 'Understandable. Well, when you have decided, let me know.'

Zafar looked up sharply. 'That's all you have to say?'

Tariq considered him again. 'It is not enough to "think" God has spoken to you. That will not sustain you. A mission like this will test your resolve in every way. You have to believe it wholeheartedly.'

'You believe this is a mission?'

'It is not for me to say,' Tariq responded. 'I'm simply commenting on what you've told me… Do you want to have victory against the infidel?' Tariq continued after a pause. 'Do you believe that this mission will aid us in our struggle, or will at the very least give the infidel reason to fear us?'

Zafar realised he had not considered the implications of his vision as deeply as he'd thought.

Tariq continued: 'Or perhaps you do not believe the words of the prophet when he told us to fight against the infidels until they are made our servants.'

'I believe the prophet.'

Tariq raised his eyebrows.

'I do! It is just, from this… There would be no going back.'

'We are at war already. Just because you have lived in luxury all your life, you have been able to ignore this fact. But no, you should go home now. You obviously have forgotten you are a Muslim and a stranger in this land.'

'I have not forgotten who I am!'

'Zafar, there is no shame in not being able to fight. Perhaps all God wanted you to do was pass this message on to me so I can act on it.'

'You believe this is from Allah?'

'What does it matter? You do not want anything to do with this.'

'Tell me!'

'Yes.'

Zafar let out a moan. 'Allah, give me strength.'

He felt Tariq taking hold of his shoulder and looked up at him.

'Zafar, my brother,' Tariq said. 'You need to think very carefully now about what you say and what you do. It is not for me to tell you this is from God. You need to know it in your own heart. And even if you know it, you need to know you are willing to be obedient.'

'But how can I? I am not a soldier.'

'What God asks us to do, he gives us strength to carry out. How did you feel when you first had this vision?'

Zafar thought back to sitting in his car, watching his vision of a gunman walking towards him, raising a gun. 'Exhilarated, terrified... Like I knew I was about to die and could feel everything all at once.'

'No-one knows how they will react the first time they go into battle. The strongest man will turn into a coward while the weakest will turn into a leader. Fear is a natural instinct and without it none of us would ever survive past childhood, but at some point we have to decide to control our fear or it will control us.'

'I'm not a...' Zafar began, but Tariq had already left the room. Zafar realised he was shaking. I'm not a coward, he told himself as he struggled to calm his body.

After a few minutes Tariq returned carrying a huge plate of Osh which he placed on the carpet between them. Two spoons were balanced on top of the food. He left again and returned with a small bowl with a jug sitting in it and a towel draped across an arm.

Turning to Tariq, Zafar placed his hands over the bowl and allowed Tariq to pour water over them while he gently washed them. Then he dried his hands before offering the same service to Tariq. It had been years since anyone had performed the ritual of cleansing for him before eating and Zafar felt himself deeply moved by the gesture. As Tariq sat himself opposite, he lifted his hands and said a short blessing. Zafar lent forward to pick up a spoon and realised his hand was no longer shaking.

They ate in silence. Tariq seemingly content to enjoy the meal, Zafar lost in his thoughts.

Tariq laid his spoon down while there was still a third of the plate uneaten. Zafar looked at the amount of food remaining, then up at Tariq.

Tariq raised his eyebrows in expectation and Zafar found himself chuckling. 'I cannot, brother.' He sighed, laid his own spoon down and patted his belly. 'A meal fit for kings.'

'Are you sure?' Tariq asked.

Zafar nodded and Tariq then cleared away the plate returning a few minutes later with a teapot and the traditional small round tea cups. He took his time over the ritual, eventually handing Zafar an aromatic cup of steaming tea.

'From China,' Tariq said as he poured his own cup. 'I find the aroma to be relaxing.'

They sipped the scalding liquid. Zafar looked across at Tariq. 'I'm not a coward.'

'I know, but you are untested.'

Zafar felt himself grow tense. 'Have you been tested?' He asked.

Tariq did not answer straight away. He appeared to ponder Zafar's question while considering him. Eventually he simply said, 'Yes. I have.'

Zafar wanted to ask how, why, where… Eventually he asked: 'Don't you trust me?'

'With my life, brother.'

'What are you holding back?'

Tariq breathed deeply and let it out slowly, all the while examining Zafar. 'To trust is not the same as to blabber. Your whole life you have tried to fit into a culture that is alien to you, now for the first time you are considering turning back to Allah, but it is difficult to shake off what has become normal to you.' Tariq hesitated. 'But you're right, I am holding something back. Wait here.'

Tariq stood and left the room, Zafar looking round wondering where he was going.

A couple of minutes Tariq returned holding a DVD case. It was plain with no cover. As he loaded it into the player built into the TV, Tariq said: 'I had not planned to show you this, but maybe I should.'

'What is it?'

'A documentary I have been working on with some friends.'

'You have made a film?' Zafar tried to imagine his friend as a film maker and couldn't do it.

'I've been helping with the project.' He turned to Zafar. 'It is not an easy documentary to watch… Maybe I shouldn't…'

Zafar saw tears in his eyes.

'I'm sorry,' Tariq said. 'This was a mistake.'

'What was? Why have you changed your mind?'

'I can't.' Tariq shook his head.

'What is on the DVD?' Zafar demanded. He surprised himself at his assertiveness.

'Forgive me, Zafar. Sometimes I am too proud, I forget...' Tariq met Zafar's gaze. 'It is a documentary of attacks on our people in this country. Films taken by the attackers... Follow up interviews with the victims.'

Zafar recalled increasing news reports of assaults and vandalism against Muslim businesses and Mosques. They never showed footage of the attacks though.

'How did you obtain this, the films?'

'We have had brothers set up fake online profiles, infiltrate sites and online groups where the attackers plan and share what they've done.'

'But wouldn't the police arrest these people?'

'These sorts of sites are on the dark web. The police don't even know most of them exist.'

'Then how did you find them?'

Tariq sighed. 'We staged an attack. Some students doing media studies helped us and we posted the film on a FaceBook group. It opened a door for us and once we got access to one site, we began to get invited onto others. I've been working on this for over three years.'

'Will you show it to the police?'

'What would be the point?'

'You know who these people are, you've got access to their websites...'

Tariq shook his head. 'The police know about all these attacks. They investigate, but even when they know who the attackers are they do nothing.'

'Then release it to the media, show the world what is happening.'

'Zafar, the people in the films, the people who would do this... They are your neighbours, your colleagues. The people you sit next to on the train, the people standing in front of you at the supermarket. They are the people flying their Union Flags and singing God save the Queen.' He shook his head. 'I attend Friday prayers and the Mullah's preach peace and the next day meet with the infidels to pray, ignoring the prophet's warnings. We are living in the house of war, Zafar. We should expect the infidels to behave like this. There will never be peace here until all accept Allah.'

Zafar considered why he had chosen to visit his friend. The first time he had sought out one of his Muslim brothers in five months. Five months of mourning. And he had come here to seek advice about his own vision of death. This could not be a coincidence.

'Play the DVD,' Zafar commanded.

Tariq again hesitated. 'Are you sure?'

'Yes. Play it.'

Tariq pressed play on the TV and the DVD started.

It was indeed a documentary and Zafar watched in horror as film after film showed attacks on his brothers and sisters followed by interviews with the victims, at least, those who had survived. As he watched, he wasn't aware that his expression subtly changed and his fists began to clench.

~~~

Danny closed the front door and slid the chain into place, took off his overcoat and hung it on the hook closest to the door. 'I'm home,' he shouted through to Cynthia. There was no reply.

Taking his briefcase upstairs to his study, Danny hung his jacket on a coat hanger and left it in the study. Walking downstairs, he ran his hand down the large flower patterns Cynthia had wanted for wallpaper. The colours had faded over the last ten years.

Cynthia was in the dining room, a bible open in front of her on the table.

'I'm here,' he said, giving her a brief kiss on the cheek.

She gave him a distracted smile. 'Dinner's in the oven.'

'Thanks.' Danny turned to the door.

'We need to talk.'

He slowly turned back. Cynthia was looking pensive. Worried even. A knot formed in his stomach. 'What is it?'

'Maybe you should sit down.'

Danny pulled out a chair opposite Cynthia.

'It's about Mary.'

The knot began to loosen. 'Mary?'

'How many Mary's do you know? Your God-Mother…'

Danny shook his head. 'I know which Mary, what about her?'

'Tony asked me and Philip to go with him to see her today. She's been trying to have Tony removed as minister.'

He couldn't help laughing. 'Mary? Seriously?'

Cynthia's expression remained unchanged and he sat back, now studying her. 'What happened?'

'Tony's excluded her from the church. She's been told to repent. She's not allowed to speak to anyone.'

'He can't do that, can he?'

'I think… I think he can.'

'But… Mary?'

'I know.'

'I've never heard of…' Danny trailed off. 'This is a church, right? You don't just chuck people out.'

'She wasn't willing to repent...'

'Repent? Mary... What does she have to repent of?'

Cynthia looked like she was about to cry. 'Tony showed me some passages. It's serious, Danny.'

'What is?'

'Gossip. Spreading division in the church. It goes against everything Jesus said about being united.'

'The Christian message is about love, forgiveness.'

'Not just that. Jesus said some scary things. He tells us to rebuke someone who sins against us.'

'And then forgive him.'

Cynthia shook her head. 'No. Jesus said we should forgive if he repents.'

'So, we're not supposed to forgive people now?'

'We're supposed to repent of our sin, Danny. Listen to this...' Cynthia turned some pages in her bible and began reading. 'You must not associate with anyone who claims to be a brother or sister but is sexually immoral or greedy, an idolater or slanderer...' She looked up at him. 'It says with such a person do not even eat, expel the wicked person from among you.'

He couldn't speak, just stared at her, the words reverberating round and round his thoughts.

'Then there's this from Matthew... if they refuse to listen even to the church, treat them as you would a pagan or a tax collector.' Cynthia finished and looked up at him.

Danny realised she was waiting for a response, but he'd missed most of what she'd said. 'Why was Mary trying to have Tony removed?'

Cynthia told him.

'Let me get this straight. Tony is meeting with leaders from other faith groups, something Mary is perfectly entitled to be concerned about— possible, what's the word, idolatry? But she's the one who is thrown out of the church?'

'You meet with faith leaders.'

'I'm a police officer, it's part of the job. Tony's a Christian minister.'

'Are you saying he shouldn't meet with them?'

Danny bit back his initial response. 'No. I'm not saying that. I just... You went with him, to see Mary?'

'Yes. We tried to talk with her, but she wouldn't listen. Then she threw us out of her house. It was horrible, Danny.'

He watched as a tear rolled down her cheek. There had been a time when he would have rushed to hold her. Would have moved Heaven and

Earth to stop her crying. He stood. 'I'll make time to go and see her. Tony as well. Try and sort it out.'

'Thank you.'

He nodded. Stood for a minute, but then went to heat up his dinner.

CHAPTER TEN
Sticky Wicket

'D.I. Martin, you're in early, Sir. Again.'

'That's the only problem with days off, Don. Twice as much work the next day.' Danny waved his ID at the door sensor and pushed open the security door.

What was he doing coming in for 7am? Danny asked himself as he made his way to his office. Don had been duty officer twice last week and had seen him in early each time. He was coming in earlier and earlier but did not seem to be making any headway on the ongoing cases.

Four high profile cases currently in North Yorkshire and nineteen other active investigations that his team were working on. He chose not to keep track of the dead cases, ones that had not been closed but as there were no current leads they could do no more work on them.

The office was dark as he swiped his ID and opened the door. At least one of them switched off the lights on their way out last night, he thought.

Switching on the lights revealed a familiar mess of files stacked on the seven desks, the walls covered in a blizzard of post it notes, photos and red marker pen. Twenty three active cases each fighting for space. He'd had wet behind the ears detectives try and introduce different methods to tame the chaos, but the reality of managing live investigations had always tamed them before too long. As he scanned the cases that were in progress on the walls, Danny's eyes fixed on the one dirty rectangle that had no paper pinned over it, no post it notes or photos. Their next number one priority.

Taking off his coat and jacket, he allowed himself a minute's reflection on the system. You could never tell when they would be landed with the next big case. The FBI in America had a saying that it was all about the first

24 hours. Whatever you found out in that first day was likely to determine whether the case could be resolved or not. Of course, it was overly simplistic but they had a point. It was vital to gather as much information early on as they could and to do that required organisation. When a new case came in, it went straight up on the empty section allowing them to begin cross referencing all new information immediately and follow up on it. Then Danny would decide which of the other active cases was about to be dropped off the wall because who knew when another blank section would be needed.

Shaking his head, he checked the coffeemaker. Yesterday's wet grounds were still sitting in the filter paper. He emptied them out, put in new paper and filled it up with fresh coffee. He filled up the pot from the water dispenser in the office and switched the machine on. This was why he was coming in so early. So many active cases they would not all fit on the wall. It had become a nightmare to manage and most weeks Danny felt he was losing the battle.

~~~

'Take a seat, Danny.'

Chief Inspector Kevin Rudd gestured to one of the chairs in front of his desk.

Danny studied Rudd for signs of what the meeting was about. Rudd, as usual was reading through briefing papers and signing forms. He had a stack several inches high on both sides of the desk. The piles always seemed to balance each other out, no matter when he met with Rudd it was as if the paperwork was never ending. Much like his own.

Rudd signed one form with a flourish and set it and a stack of papers to his right. He went to take a different briefing pack from the left hand pile, hesitated and then withdrew his hand and placed it and his other hand flat on the desk.

'We have a vacancy for a CTSA.' Rudd announced.

Danny made an internal curse.

'Roger Harbrook is being promoted and we need someone to step up to take his place. I'm going to recommend you.'

Danny didn't respond immediately other than a restrained nod in acknowledgment. He'd always found it best to avoid speaking as long as possible in situations like this. A move to Counter Terrorism Security Advisor was a promotion, especially over the last decade as more and more funding was diverted to combating terrorism, but it was a move away from the role he'd joined the police for, the role he'd always felt he was born for. Effectively his own career had reached it's peak, but when you're doing the job you always wanted to do, why would you want to move on from it? Because Rudd saw potential in him and to give Rudd credit, he wasn't afraid of recommending his team for better roles, even if it meant possibly losing them. Rudd was more generous than other Chief Inspectors he'd known, but if he was to refuse this "opportunity," what would the consequences be?

'What would the role involve, Sir?' Danny asked. He knew the answer of course. Everyone did. But the question did deflect the need to directly respond to the offer.

Rudd sat back, his hands still palm down on the table. 'Why don't you tell me what the role involves Danny.'

So much for deflection. Danny looked away, thought back to a leaflet he'd read. 'CTSA's identify potential sites that could be targeted by terrorists. They prepare plans to prevent attacks or minimise the potential impact of an attack. They work with businesses and councils.'

Rudd moved his hands to the arms of his chair. Began drumming his fingers on an armrest.

Danny swallowed. 'How much time would the role involve?'

'This would be a full time role.'

'I've invested a lot of time building up relationships here. Working with local businesses, Neighbourhood Watch schemes, Community Councils... I think I have a lot still to contribute in York.'

'For all those reasons I am recommending you. You have got excellent contacts in the community and you'll be able to draw on those in this role. Also, the fact you are good at building relationships shows you are more than capable of managing the networks you will need to build as a CTSA. You are a good detective and the skills you have will be valuable to the National Counter Terrorism Security Office.'

'But my case load...'

'Can be taken over by your team. Again, the fact you have built such a solid team around you shows you will be perfect as a CTSA.'

'Except I won't have a team, will I?'

'No. That's correct. This is much more about managing a wider network. Although the people you will be working with: landlords, company directors, managers etc. won't report directly to you, you will be responsible for them. Indeed, this role basically places you with a much greater responsibility than you currently have.'

'With all due respect, Sir, that is a different type of management.'

'And one I believe you have demonstrated the skills for.' Rudd picked up a sheet of paper that had been on his desk. 'There's an Argus Project meeting in York tomorrow. It's been planned for months and Harbrook was going to attend. I want you to go in his place. It will give you an insight into the role and they will benefit from having someone with your experience working with them.'

'That gives my team no notice, Sir.'

'Even police officers get the flu, Danny. They'll cope.'

'Can I at least have some time to think about it?'

Handing Danny the paper, Rudd leaned forward. 'This isn't a request, Danny. Be at the York Royal for 9am tomorrow.'

CHAPTER ELEVEN
Discarded Sandwich

The voice seemed to be coming from a distance away. She tried to ignore it, she was close to finding him, though who was it she was trying to find?

'Emma!'

He'd been there, she was sure of it. Just a few more minutes and she'd find him...

'Emma! Wake up.'

There was a loud rattle and someone had turned on a searchlight in her face. 'Go away,' she managed to mumble, turning away from the light and pulling her covers over her head.

The covers were pulled away and Emma felt a weight sit beside her. The dream was almost gone and she resisted opening her eyes in the hope she could recover it.

'I need you to wake up.'

'What is your problem!' Emma screwed up her eyes and managed to open one of them and turn back to see Rachel sitting looking at her.

'I'm going to see the Union Rep. You should come with me.'

'What time is it?'

'Eight o'clock.'

'It's too early.'

Rachel gave an exaggerated sigh. 'You were supposed to be on shift this morning. 6am start.'

'That was before I fell off the wall.'

'And fell on your obviously too fat...'

Emma tried to slap her, but Rachel dodged and stood.

'We're suspended, remember?'

'I don't care.'

'You don't...' Rachel crossed her arms. 'If we lose our jobs... I can't afford to blow all my savings on rent until you start to care. I know you're not loaded. How are you going to pay next month's rent?'

Emma forced herself up. 'I've never not paid.'

'It's been close though, hasn't it. Have you saved anything?'

Her last paycheck took her out of overdraft with enough left over to go out on Friday night. 'I don't want to think about it just now.'

'You have to think about it. This doesn't just affect you, I live here as well.'

'Can you lend me the money,' Emma couldn't believe she'd just asked that and from the look on Rachel's face, she couldn't either.

Rachel shook her head and took a step backward towards the door. 'Lend you...? No, you need to get up now and come and speak to the Union. This isn't going away, Emma.' She looked at her watch. 'I'm leaving in half an hour. You can get some breakfast on the way.'

Emma watched Rachel leave and close her door then threw a pillow at her light switch, lay back down and pulled her covers over her head.

She didn't hear Rachel check on her half an hour later or the doors slam as Rachel left the flat.

~~~

She woke suddenly. Opening her eyes, Emma listened but couldn't hear any alarm. Rachel... Emma had a vague memory of Rachel talking to her, something about the Union. It wasn't important. What was important was her dream. The same blonde haired man she'd dreamt of in the hospital. It wasn't normal to dream the same thing twice, was it? She got up and headed through to the small shower room, her thoughts buzzing about her head.

The dream had faded already, but she still thought she remembered his face, would recognize him if she saw him. Emma decided she must have been conscious when he checked her pulse, when he... She shook off that thought. What had he been doing? He'd been close enough for her to see him, to have filed away a memory even as she was losing consciousness. She put her hand to the back of her head. Water from the shower made the scar slippery to her touch. Scars don't form in a day, the voice in her head told her loud and clear. Then how did I get this one, she thought back.

Did he know, this nameless man she had dreamt? Had he poured out the blood that had matted her hair when she woke up? She squeezed out shampoo, lathered her hair and rinsed it off then repeated the process scrunching the shampoo through her hair again. Would she ever feel clean?

Eventually she turned off the shower, wrapped a towel round her and stood in front of the steamed up mirror, her vague outline visible through the fog. She tried to see his face, to remember what it looked like, but only the faintest memory remained. Did he know what had happened? Had he seen her fall, this man Rachel thought was homeless? The centre of York was only ten minutes walk away and there were always beggars on every street, no matter how often the Council tried to get rid of them. Beggars were homeless, weren't they?

~~~

He prayed as he walked. Not out loud of course, that would be too terrifying to do, the looks he got now were bad enough. But sometimes he felt like it wasn't enough, to talk silently to God. Like his words did not have meaning unless he gave them flight. All trapped up in his head, sometimes he couldn't pray any more, the words seemed too many.

So, when it got too much, Michael stopped praying, and just walked. Walked until the words calmed down and ordered themselves in his mind and he was able to talk to God again. He had thought about whispering. Speaking softly to God so no-one else would hear. That would not have worked though. His mother had told him off for mumbling as a child, shouted at him when he whispered. It would be worse on the streets.

He didn't know if God was disappointed with him. If his fear of bringing even more insults down on himself was justified or not. Surely God understood. Michael hoped He did. Hoped his prayers would be heard. Hoped they would be acted on. Just as he hoped that some people would read the message on the boards he strapped to himself three times a week.

Sandwich boards people called them. Michael didn't feel much like a sandwich. They were heavy for starters. He had never eaten a sandwich that was an effort to carry round. The boards had to be heavy, otherwise the wind took and played with them. He had experimented with different grades of plywood but 12mm seemed to be the best thickness. Painted a smooth white with thick black letters that stood out even fifty metres away.

The words were usually the same, but sometimes Michael sensed God telling him to change them and so he carefully painted over the old letters and used stencils and a spray can to create the new. Often he had had to scrape and sand off layers of old paint and begin again to make sure the finish on the boards was right.

The words on his front board were smaller today than normal. You would need good eyesight to read them from fifty metres. 'Jesus wept for Lazarus. Jesus died for you,' was carefully painted on the front. The back posed a question that he had struggled with. Was it too inflammatory? Would it encourage people to talk to Jesus or drive them away? In the end he painted on the words: 'What will you do for him?' and asked God to use them.

~~~

Normally she wouldn't even look at them, let alone consider speaking to them. Emma had passed three beggars on her walk into the centre and for the first time in her life had studied them as she walked by.

Some of them were filthy, like they thought they would be more likely to earn sympathy if they looked unwashed. It just made her want to walk on, face straight ahead.

Others were more presentable, though none looked well dressed. Was there a perfect state between dirty and clean; ragged and respectable that made it more likely people were going to put money in your cup, Emma wondered.

And people did put money in. Now she was paying attention to them, she began to notice coins being dropped, the odd person even standing talking with one of them. Was it just tourists who were so generous, York's residents being so jaded they had stopped caring?

Rumour had it that a beggar had been seen climbing into a Mercedes after a hard day's work conning money from the gullible. Was it just a cruel rumour, Emma now wondered for the first time, or could someone actually make real money begging on the streets?

Few of the beggars seemed happy. Old, young, men and women—most had vacant expressions. Forced smiles if at all but as Emma looked she could see a... she didn't want to use the term... a deadness in their eyes. She shivered despite the warm sun.

She had not been counting but must have seen at least a dozen beggars as she walked down Parliament Street and then round and up Spurrier Gate. None of them were her man. She needed a photo to show them, to ask if they knew him, where she could find him. She didn't think she could just walk up to any of them and explain: I'm looking for a blond, homeless guy. Emma realised she was finally starting to feel hungry and began looking for a sandwich shop.

~~~

He was asking God to speak to the people walking past him when the first businessman jostled him. Michael felt himself being propelled forward, and stumbled. Not to fall, he kept walking, but he turned to see what had happened and saw a young man in a suit, his arms outstretched and waving up and down. He had a large grin on his face and he was walking side on to Michael, keeping pace with him.

There was another shove at his back and someone else laughed, 'What is this then? Community service?'

'Nah, he's got a phone number for a gay chat up line on the front!'

Michael didn't know where to turn. He kept walking, hoping they would get bored and leave. Most times they did.

There were at least four of them. Each walking in front of him now. He wasn't sure if anyone was still behind him. The one who was waving his arms was walking backwards now, facing Michael. He still had that grin. Michael tried not to look at him, at any of them. He tried to ask God for help but it was as if his mind had frozen.

'Jesus wept!' The young man waited until the others looked his way. 'I forgot my wallet! I'll have to go back.' He stopped abruptly and Michael had to quickly change direction to avoid hitting him. He had to ease through the group of men as they all stopped, conscious of how close they all were, of trying not to hit them with the boards. He was only just by them when the young man spoke again. 'No, wait, you owe me from last night's poker game, Jonesy! Are you good for it?'

'Sure.' Came the reply, far louder than it needed to be.

Michael could not stop his eyes looking around, wondering what they were going to do next. He tried not to flinch but couldn't help it when a knock came again. The grinning man was back, pushing roughly past him, even though the pavement was not crowded.

He felt his mouth open, but couldn't think of anything to say. Turn the other cheek... That was the verse, the killer verse that crippled him. Not that he would have been able to do anything anyway, but if he had been able to do something, to stop the pushing and the insults, he would have sinned. Please God, let some good come out of this. He managed to form as a conscious thought.

'Got the time, mister?'

Michael caught the young man's eye and saw the mockery there. He shook his head and looked past him, looking for a way out. He didn't see a woman standing in a shop doorway, shaking her head as the group of them walked by.

'Reckon you do have the time, plenty of time to be out doing this.'

Michael couldn't understand how he could walk backwards like that. Wasn't he worried he would fall over?

The young man gave one last malicious grin and turned, stepping off the pavement corner. Straight into the path of a bus coming through the junction.

Michael could only watch in horror as the bus hit the young man, taking him out of sight before the bus driver had time to react and stop the bus. It was not going especially fast, but to Michael it seemed to be speeding past. The anxiety and fear he had been feeling dulled, overshadowed by shock.

'God, no!' He whispered. Then asked: 'Why?'

He felt people pushing past him, realised dimly it was the young man's friends. One of them looked at Michael and swore at him. Michael vaguely realised he couldn't hear him. There was a ringing in his ears. He took a step back and realised someone was pushing him forward. He turned his head and saw a pretty, red haired woman who was opening and closing her mouth. He was finding it difficult to focus on her.

He gradually realised the woman was not pushing him, she was holding him up. Realising this, he tried to stand straight but only succeeded in starting to fall forwards. The woman moved round, grabbing the front board and steadied him.

'Thank you.' He managed to say. Hearing his own words, he became aware of other sounds, car horns tooting, shouting, and the woman saying: 'Are you all right?'

Michael gently shook his head, feeling every move and becoming aware of just how unsteady he was. 'I need to get out of this,' he told her.

'Okay, how can I help?'

'Just hold the boards steady.' Michael crouched down and let the boards sit on the pavement. Then, very carefully, he eased himself down and then out from between them. He felt the woman take his arm and lead him to the window of a shop.

'Sit here. I'll bring your sandwich boards over.'

He put an arm behind himself and eased himself down until he was sitting on the pavement, his legs pulled up in front of him. He leaned his head forward feeling as if he was going to black out. His heart was racing, the blood seemed to be pumping too fast through his brain, he felt a buzz and tried to slow his breathing down.

She was back, leaning his boards carefully against the shop window. She crouched down by him and put a hand on his shoulder.

'You're in shock. Give yourself time.'

He turned to look at her and saw over her shoulder the men who had been jostling him pushing past a gathered crowd. His eyes widened.

He didn't see her look of concern or really register that she turned to see what he was looking at.

She stood, turning fully to face the men. She put one arm out, hand flat towards them. 'Back off!' She said clearly to them.

They stopped, all three of them. Michael could see the anger in their expressions.

'Get out of the way.'

'I saw you assault this man, you will back off or I'm calling the police.'

'We've already called them. This is nothing to do with you. Get out of our way, we're going to make sure he pays for what he did to Freddy.'

'And who's going to make you pay for what you did to him? The four of you picking on one man, shoving him, insulting him? You enjoy bullying people who are weaker than you?'

Michael felt shame at that, wanted to stand and show that he wasn't weaker than them but his head was spinning and he really thought if he stood he would collapse.

Another of the three spoke: 'He killed Freddy. He's not getting away with that!'

'This man did nothing to your Freddy but I saw your Freddy hit him. I saw your Freddy insult him. No-one pushed your Freddy. No-one made him step in front of that bus. You care about your friend so much why aren't you with him now?'

'She's nothing, push her out of the way.' The third man said quietly but not quietly enough that Michael couldn't hear him as well. Michael reached out to try and warn her but before he could do anything the man in the centre had stepped forward, only to stop, clutching his face and screaming.

He watched the young woman step deftly to her right and saw she had a spray can held out straight in front of her.

'Either of you two morons want some of this?' She asked. 'You are not laying a finger on me or him. You say your friend is dead? Go and bury him before I bury you!'

'What did you do to him?' One of the men asked, a horrified expression on his face.

Michael saw red drip through the man's hands onto the pavement.

The sound of an ambulance siren tore through the silence and Michael saw blue strobing lights pass by them and head round the corner. A second siren with a different tone soon followed. The men had not moved other than to support the man in the centre who was doubled up.

'You wanted the police.' The woman shouted. 'There they are. Go and tell them everything! Tell them how this man was so weak you just had to attack him and then this little girl stood in your way and you had to attack her as well! GO!'

Finally they began to shuffle the man in the centre around and lead him towards the corner where the ambulance had stopped.

Once sure they were not coming back, the woman sat down beside Michael.

'I'm not weak.' Michael told her.

She looked at him, her face pale. 'You might as well be if you let people like that push you around.'

'Jesus said if our enemy strikes us on one cheek we should let them strike the other.'

'That's just stupid.'

'I'm not stupid either.'

'Definition of stupidity: believing you have to let people bully you and then giving them a reason to.'

His breathing was coming under control and the buzz had stopped but he couldn't understand what she had said. 'I don't give them a reason.'

'You wander around with a sandwich board telling people you're a target. What did you think was going to happen?'

I thought they were going to attack me. I thought they would insult me and mock me and despise me. He didn't say any of this but for the first time he allowed himself to feel the truth of all his fears. Then he felt ashamed. You didn't say a word against them when they hit you. He silently prayed. You didn't stop them mocking you. Why shouldn't I suffer when you went through so much for me?

The woman was shaking her head at him. He wanted to make her understand but knew that one of the reasons God told him to use the sandwich board was because he was so terrible at speaking to people.

'God only tells me what to do. I just need to be obedient.'

'God tells you to walk around like this?'

'Yes.' Maybe she understood.

'You hear God talking to you?'

'Yes!'

'He tells you what to write on the boards?'

'He does!' She was listening to him! She was nodding her head. She smiled at him! He smiled back.

~~~

Emma felt a great sadness as she smiled at this poor little man. He was trying to smile back but he obviously wasn't used to it. Wisps of hair that he had combed over his bald patch were blowing about in a gentle breeze. His pale skin had not benefited at all from walking outside with his boards.

Was he insane? Hearing voices that he thought was God telling him what to do? He was so slight it was a wonder he could lift the heavy boards. She had struggled to carry them over. He looked underfed as if he had been starving himself. She wondered if he worked or if the voices in his head would not let him.

'Emma Hunter, isn't it?'

She looked up and saw Detective Henderson standing in front of them.

'Is that pepper spray?'

'Perfectly legal.' Emma tossed up the can to Henderson who caught it at arms length as if it was going to explode in her face.

'FarbGel?'

'Non toxic, no harmful chemicals. I'd rather have used pepper spray on him but for some reason you lot don't want us to be able to defend ourselves when we're attacked.'

'So that isn't blood on his face?'

'I only sprayed this gel. What happened to him after I scared him off was nothing to do with me.'

'And the man knocked down by the bus?'

'They were assaulting this man. The idiot was walking backwards, not looking where he was going.'

'A man died. Watch what you say.'

Emma bit down the response that she wanted to give. 'This man was insulted, pushed and hit by that group of men. At no point did he respond in any way. Neither he nor I had anything to do with the man's decision to walk backwards across a road.'

'I'll need a full statement.'

'I'll give you one. I think this man needs treating for shock though. You might want to ask if he wants to press a formal complaint of harassment and assault against those men.'

The man was shaking his head.

'You should. They'll just think they can get away with it again.'

Emma went to stand up but felt the ground sway and had to put a hand out to steady herself. She forced herself to stand upright and touched the man on his shoulder so he looked up.

'I don't know your name.' She told him.

'Michael.'

'Pleased to meet you, Michael. I'm going to give the officer a statement. Don't go anywhere okay?'

He nodded and she beckoned Henderson to walk away with her.

Once they were out of earshot, she spoke quietly. 'He said he's been hearing voices. Telling him to walk around with the sandwich boards and to write things on them.'

Henderson looked over at Michael, a frown creasing her otherwise smooth forehead. 'What are you saying?'

'I think we should take him into the hospital, get him a psychiatric evaluation. Probably best if he doesn't know why he's there. Just tell him it's for the shock.'

'Do you think he might have started all this?' Henderson gestured towards the bus at the corner.

'No, I saw the whole thing. He was minding his own business, just shuffling along when the men started insulting and hitting him. But...' Emma sighed. 'I'm not a doctor, I know that, but I've taken courses and done regular shifts in Psychiatric wards. He should be admitted. It's possible he's never had anyone in his life who could recognize the symptoms.'

'No-one noticed him walking around the city with two sheets of plywood strapped to him?'

'Not everyone has friends to look out for them. You work in a hospital long enough and you see a whole bunch of people with no-one.'

~~~

'Where have you been?'

'Ease up, Rachel. It's been a long day.' Emma dropped onto the sofa, her jacket still on.

'What's that supposed to mean? What have you been doing?'

Her eyes still open, Emma found herself seeing the bus crash into that foolish young man. She shook her head to clear the image.

'If you don't want to talk, I guess that's okay. I'm trying to be sympathetic here but either you're still needing to rest or you're not. If not, then I really need your help.'

Rachel walked over to the sofa and stood, her arms folded. 'No? Nothing?'

Emma felt like she was falling, like in her dream, someone reaching out to her. A blonde man, or was it Rachel... In the background she was dimly aware Rachel was speaking.

After a few seconds, Rachel walked back to the breakfast counter.

'I spoke with the Union. You should have come with me, but... They think it will be better if we fight the case together. They can sign you up as a member. I brought a form for you to sign. Emma, I need you to do this for me. Will you sign the form?'

Emma managed to nod.

'Thank you. I'm going to go out and get something to eat.' Rachel waited a minute. 'Do you want to come?'

Emma didn't know how long it was before she realised Rachel had gone. Emma wasn't even sure what she had been thinking about. Trying hard not to think about anything. It had worked.

She stood feeling stiff and cold. She walked across to the thermostat and turned the heating up then went to bed. It seemed to take forever for the bed to warm up and when it finally did, the events of the day kept playing back in her mind. She was still awake a couple of hours later when Rachel came back. Heard her curse and then silence for a minute before her door opened.

'Emma!'

Emma didn't respond. Kept her eyes closed and lay still. She heard Rachel move round to the side of her bed.

'Are you awake?'

She would go away in a minute. Emma kept her breathing shallow and slow.

'You said you would sign the form.'

Form? What form? It didn't matter, she'd deal with it tomorrow. She heard Rachel move away and the door close. Eventually there were sounds outside her room and she felt safe enough to open her eyes. She stared at the wall until sleep finally took her.

CHAPTER TWELVE
Tick Tock

'...One last thing, Boss. Emma Hunter was involved with the fatality.'

Danny stopped making notes, his mind going blank for a second before remembering. 'The Monk Bar girl? From the hospital?'

'That's the one.'

'What was her involvement?'

'She claims she witnessed the incident then defended Michael Irving against the friends of the man who died.'

Danny leaned back in his chair looking up at the ceiling. 'That's quite a coincidence...'

'And I know how you feel about coincidences,' Natalie said.

'Was she involved in any way with the man's death?'

'There's no evidence she was and none of the witnesses places her anywhere near him at the time.'

'Still, to be at the scene only a few days after being involved in an alleged fraud... I don't like it. Was she violent towards these friends?'

'She used a defensive spray against them: FarbGel, have you heard of it?'

'No. I'll check it out.' Danny made a note of the name.

'She claims it's legal. I checked and there doesn't seem to be any restrictions on its use.'

'Still, there's a potential for an assault claim.'

'No-one wanted to press charges against her and when I pressed them on what happened they clammed up. I'll pull the CCTV but it's possible her story will check out.'

'If we get the CCTV... If you haven't got the initial request through tomorrow let me know and I'll escalate it.'

'Will do… You coming round later?'

Danny hesitated. 'When do you think you'll be finished.'

'Wrapping up now.'

'See you in an hour.'

~~~

A clock ticked in the corner. A steady beat yet, as she listened sometimes it seemed slightly louder. A tock more than a tick. Mary drew a deep breath and then, realising she was nodding off, opened her eyes hurriedly. She sat up in the chair. She couldn't doze now, not after spending the whole day waiting for God to speak. Her stomach growled and she placed her hand on her belly. For others it might be inconsequential, spending a day fasting and praying, but not for her. A day trying to hear, trying to find any sign that she wasn't completely, totally on her own.

'If I can't turn to you then who can I turn to,' she whispered.

He would speak, she just had to be patient. She had tried closing her eyes earlier on in the day, hoping God might send her a vision or even just a picture of comfort, but she was so tired from not sleeping properly the last few nights that she quickly felt herself dropping off and had to keep shaking herself awake.

'Lord, give me a sign,' she prayed again. 'Show me you haven't left me.'

As she waited there was only the ticking of the clock, a sound she had almost forgotten was always there. A steady beat in the background of her life.

Why didn't he say something? Not that God had ever spoken directly to her. No, that was for other people. But had she ever given a whole day like this, a whole day without food, waiting on God? Surely he could see how desperate she was. Surely this meant something to him.

Some half forgotten words entered her thinking and she tried to ignore them. Only a day…

Fasting had always been difficult for her. Going without food made her faint, made her temper more prone to explode at the slightest provocation. Missing a single meal, a breakfast or lunch was her usual sacrifice. Very occasionally she had skipped her evening meal, but never had she gone a whole day. God would know how much this meant to her. Would see how important it was.

Only a day… The words had begun to circle in her thoughts. The more she tried to block them out, the more forcefully they returned.

'I have humbled myself,' she told him. 'What more do you want from me? Why won't you speak to me?'

She closed her eyes once more, but opened them as she began to picture the words. Would she have to sit here all night waiting for God to speak? Maybe it would be a blessing. If she didn't sleep she wouldn't have that nightmare again. Two nights in a row, waking in a sweat... Did you have nightmares if you slept during the day? She didn't want to find out.

It wasn't normal to have the same nightmare more than once, was it? It had been so long since she'd last had a dream that scared her so much, probably not since she was a child, but even then, she couldn't remember having the same nightmare over again. Such a strange dream. The people unaware of the danger. The giant men towering over her, over the whole city. The weapons they carried, things she'd never seen and yet she knew they would kill and maim.

Both times she woke with the same sense of fear. It was so childish, to have nightmares at her age. She was so tired...

Her eyes closed. Dreams were supposed to be quickly forgotten. What had she read once, nature's way of sorting out the memories. God's way...

Her eyes snapped open again. She reached for her bible and flicked pages until, there! "I will pour out my Spirit on all people. Your sons and daughters will prophesy, your old men will dream dreams, your young men will see visions."

As she stopped reading the tock, tick, tock of the clock seemed to grow louder.

'Lord, is this dream from you?' She asked.

Silence.

'Please Lord... What does it mean? What am I supposed to do?'

There was no still, small voice. No angelic beings appeared to guide her. No command from Heaven. Just the relentless ticking of the clock.

CHAPTER THIRTEEN
Argus

There was a sign board set up in the lobby of the York Royal hotel. Doberman Owners Association had top billing in the Clifton suite. Below this, Danny read Argus Project, Heworth suite.

Walking up to the hotel reception, he nodded at the young man standing there. 'Where can I find the Heworth suite?'

'Through the double doors there. Turn left down the corridor and first on your right.'

Danny thanked him and made his way through the hotel. It was... Posh. No other word for it really. Carved wood decorations, thick patterned wallpaper and plush carpet. How much would it cost to stay here, he wondered. How much did renting the suite cost for that matter, he thought as he reached it.

The suite itself was more business like than the corridors but still had an air of expense—currently being paid for by the taxpayer. Two women and one man already in the room, seated round a large conference table. There were several flipcharts in a row at the far side of the suite.

'Hello, I'm Detective Inspector Daniel Martin.'

'Detective Inspector, thank you for joining us today,' said the woman closest to him. 'I'm Irene Carr, Home Office Counter Terrorism Liaison. We have Claire Avery from City of York Council and Jim Stark from BBC Radio York already here.'

'Roger Harbrook sends his apologies, he had a previous meeting arranged for today.'

'As did the Chief Inspector I understand.'

Danny blinked. 'I'm sure that's true.'

There was a frosty expression on Irene's face as she smiled in response. 'Well, you are welcome. Hang up your coat and help yourself to tea or coffee and a pastry. We are waiting on representatives from the city Shop Owners Association and retailers.'

Danny shook hands with Jim and Claire and loaded up with coffee and pastries. It was going to be a long day.

~~~

Rachel was sitting at the breakfast bar drinking coffee when Emma got up. 'Finally decided to show your face... What was wrong with you last night?'

Emma looked at the clock on the wall. Just before 9am. She ignored Rachel, walking past her to check the kettle had water before switching it on.

'Still not talking to me? Have I said something? Done something to upset you?'

Emma didn't reply, just listened to the sound of the water beginning to boil.

'Emma, what's going on? Emma!'

She turned at Rachel's shout, vaguely aware something wasn't right. Rachel looked upset. She knew she should care about that, but she didn't want to. Behind her the kettle reached a fever pitch before the circuit cut.

'Aren't you going to say anything?'

Emma couldn't remember why she was standing there. Why had she got out of bed? There didn't seem to be a good reason so she walked back to her room.

Behind her Rachel kept asking if she was alright, asking about a form. She sounded like the kettle had, an increasing level of noise that cut out when she closed her door. Sleep was what she needed. The noise outside her room didn't fully stop for a few minutes, but eventually there was quiet and Emma surrendered to the dark.

~~~

Mary started awake. She looked around in confusion for a minute then realised her hands were gripping the arm rests of her chair. She'd finally been unable to stay awake, had fallen asleep sitting up only to have that stupid dream wake her once more. The third time in a row.

When had she fallen asleep? She thought back, trying to place herself in the real world and shut out the nightmare she'd woken from. She had made herself a cup of tea at seven in the morning, deciding that she would drink that then get herself washed. She looked at the table beside her chair and saw she'd barely touched it. The clock showed it was almost nine. She must have slept almost two hours. It had seemed much longer.

Normally when she woke she spent some time praying and reading from the bible, but what would be the point? She'd spent the whole day and night praying and reading, asking and hoping that God would tell her what to do. Nothing. Not a word.

She leaned over and put her hands to her face. What was she supposed to do, keep fasting and praying until she collapsed with hunger? She felt so weak. How was she supposed to listen when she was tired and hungry?

Only a day...

Those words popped into her head again. She thought she'd managed to put them out of her mind. Had managed to for most of the night though at some point everything had seemed to blur in her head. Almost as if she'd been asleep while awake.

Only a day for a man to humble himself. That was where the words were from. How did the whole verse go? She couldn't remember. Eventually picked up her bible and flicked pages backwards and forwards. It was one of the prophets, she was sure of that, but which one? Isaiah, Jeremiah? She didn't think it would be Ezekiel though it could easily be one of the smaller books.

It took her several minutes scanning through Isaiah until she saw the chapter heading: True Fasting. Mary started reading. It didn't take long before she found the words that had been circling her thoughts for hours. "Is this the kind of fast I have chosen, only a day for people to humble themselves?" 'No, Lord,' she heard herself saying. 'But how can I keep going? I've no more strength. Do you really expect me to keep fasting? And if so, how long?'

She waited, the silence a loud buzzing in her ears.

Mary's eyes fell to the page and she read out loud: 'Is not this the kind of fasting I have chosen: to loose the chains of injustice... to set the oppressed free... share your food with the hungry... provide shelter... clothe the naked... Then you will call, and the Lord will answer; you will cry for help, and he will say: Here am I.'

Mary looked up, feeling a weight had been lifted. Why didn't she know this? Had she never read this passage before? She must have to have had the words echoing in her thoughts, but how could she have forgotten. Hadn't Jesus referred to this when he taught in the synagogue, or was that a similar passage from Isaiah? She would have to check, later.

'It was never just about food. I'm sorry, Lord,' she prayed. 'Does this mean I can eat?' She asked, realising she had started to smile. 'I should wash first, that's what you're supposed to do when fasting... Wash yourself and act as if you aren't. Only for a day… I thought…' She stood, feeling stronger than she had for hours. 'Yes, wash first, then eat.'

The good feeling faded as she washed. The memory of the Reverend's words came back with force: "If you are not willing to spend time with people who do not share your faith, how can you ever win anyone to Christ."

She wasn't an evangelist. Had never had the confidence to speak to strangers. It wasn't fair for him to expect her to suddenly start being someone she wasn't.

Except… She'd never believed life was fair…

No! She wouldn't let herself be bullied into doing something she didn't want to do.

'What I want to do I do not do, but what I hate I do…' The words came to her unbidden. No, she told herself. That's not relevant, not what Paul was saying.

She shook her head, tried to focus on what she was doing, searched for peace in the routine but it was no good, the feeling she'd had only a few minutes before was gone.

She made a simple breakfast and sat at her kitchen table to eat. She ate slowly, conscious that it wasn't healthy to rush eating after a fast. Maybe it didn't matter so much if it had only been a day, but she didn't want to take the chance.

To block out the noise in her head, she turned on the radio and the reassuring voices of the presenters filled the room.

'…less than half of all patients receive visitors. The study shows that while it is hard to prove a direct relationship between support of family and friends and a speedier healing process, anecdotal evidence from doctors and nurses suggest a strong correlation. The authors of the study…'

It didn't seem possible. Half of all patients never received a visitor while they were in hospital? Mary had been in hospital twice, fortunately only minor surgery each time. Each time though she'd had visitors from the church. Close friends and others she hardly spoke to. It had been helpful, surgery was scary. She herself had visited many people through the years as they'd waited or had recuperated. There were always people in wards who sat on their own, but she'd never given thought to them. Maybe their family and friends had already been, or would be along after she left. Or maybe not…

Standing to clear up the table she remembered faces. Women and sometimes men—though why they'd stopped segregating the sexes she didn't know—who'd been just as scared as she was. None of them wanted to show it. All put on a brave face before and all were equally exhausted after. Mary supposed it might be a bit like the army. Everyone in the same uniform, those shapeless, revealing gowns. Stripped of their dignity, poked and prodded and ordered about.

It had never occurred to her to be scared to talk to anyone there. Scared of silence. Scared of what might happen later. But not scared of her comrades in the trenches.

Mary went to get the phone book and a minute later stood listening as a hurried voice asked, 'York Hospital, how should I direct your call?'

'What time are the visiting hours?' She asked.

~~~

The other "representatives" arrived before 9am. Alice Stanford, head of the York Shop Owners Association followed by Douglas Thomson, a Regional Manager and a Chief of Operations, Janet Lendel. Danny was starting to feel distinctly under ranked.

After introductions were completed and everyone settled, Irene stood up. 'As you will know from your briefing packs, Project Argus is an initiative from the National Counter Terrorism Security Office. Our aim is to enable you to prevent, handle and recover from a terrorist attack.' She paused for breath.

'Our agenda for today begins with taking you through a simulation of a terrorist attack on York city this morning. We will break for lunch from twelve till one and then have three 45 minute sessions looking at prevention, dealing with an attack and recovery. We will have five minute breaks between each session and a fifteen minute break after the third session. Then a final hour to address any specific concerns you have for each of your organisations and businesses.'

Irene handed out a glossy folder to each of them. 'These packs contain our general guidance on prevention, management and recovery from terrorist incidents. You can refer to the guidance notes as we run through the simulation if you like, and you will be able to take these away with you.'

Danny pulled his pack towards himself and began flicking through the material. He noticed that Douglas Thomson pushed his pack to one side. Claire Avery opened her pack but did not look through it while the others followed his lead of skimming the material.

'You will each be taking the part of your organisation during the simulation. Suggesting how your organisation would act at each stage. I will be providing updates to you as the scenario changes and prompting you for your organisation's response. We'll take notes on the flipcharts. This is a role play and you should feel free to discuss options or thoughts you have as we go through the simulation. This is not a pass or fail situation.' Irene smiled at the group.

'We will begin now. The time is 09:10. Douglas, a phone call is made to your York store at The Pavement. A group calling itself Raj Istal claims to have planted a bomb in the store timed to go off at 11am.'

Danny couldn't help himself, he laughed. It came out more as a bark.

'Detective Inspector?'

'I was just...' He hesitated for a second then laughed again. 'I was expecting a more realistic scenario.'

Irene leaned over and placed both hands on the table, fingers splayed and turning white at the ends. 'We have limited time today. I can assure you that this is a realistic possibility, Detective Inspector.'

'When the IRA were planting bombs on the mainland, sure.'

'We can't predict what terrorists will do, Detective Inspector!'

'Sure you can, that's what we have you for. To dream up ways we can be attacked and find ways we can guard against it.'

'Well, that is what we've done.'

'We're not still living in the Seventies! The last time someone tried to plant a timed explosive on the mainland was over two decades ago. Since then we've had a wave of actual and attempted suicide bombings in the UK and witnessed this trend growing worldwide. The reason terrorist groups use suicide bombers is because you don't have all that messing around with timers that nine times out of ten fail to go off.'

'So what are you suggesting, Detective?' Asked Douglas.

'The government has spent millions warning us about chemical, biological and dirty bombs. If none of these are likely threats, fantastic! But I think we're missing the point. You have to think like a terrorist. What are his objectives, what does he want to achieve? Around the world they are still recruiting gullible young men and women to blow themselves up in crowded places. Why? To destabilize government and society. Terrorists don't care how many civilians they kill, they want civilians to be afraid, to bring about a form of anarchy that they can exploit.

'Think back to 2001. After 9/11 we had several attempts to seize aircraft or blow them up. Attacking air travel has always been high profile and now guarantees we will crack down with greater travel restrictions. The attacks on London in 2005 had the same purpose, to try and cause panic in our transport system, to make us afraid to go to public spaces.

'The purpose of terrorism is to cause fear—to terrorize. Yet, that isn't their ultimate objective, just a means to an end...' Danny tailed off, a cold feeling chasing down his back. His thoughts were racing now. It wasn't just about Iraq, Afghanistan or Syria was it.

Irene cleared her throat. 'Well, thank you for your insights, Detective Inspector. Can we continue with the scenario?'

Danny leaned back and studied Irene. 'My apologies, I hadn't realised how passionately I feel about this subject.'

'I'm sure we all do, that's why we're here. Now, Douglas, you have had a bomb threat to your store…'

'Excuse me, Irene,' Danny interrupted. 'I am going to ask for a change to this scenario. What if the bomb threat did not mention a specific store?'

Danny let the thought hang in the air for a minute and looked around at the group. Claire and Douglas both seemed to be considering the implications. Irene looked annoyed at another interruption while Jim and Alice looked bored. Janet simply looked confused.

'I don't get it,' said Janet. 'Why wouldn't they say where the bomb was?'

'To cause maximum panic, maximum chaos.'

'He's right,' said Claire. Douglas was nodding. 'We could not ignore the threat simply because it did not name a store. We would have to consider evacuating them all.'

'No.'

They all looked at Irene.

'You can't evacuate every store because of a vague bomb threat.'

'Well, surely we have to at least consider the possibility,' Douglas said leaning forward.

'No. That is what they want. That would be their objective.' Irene said looking at Danny.

Danny sat back and looked around the room. No-one looked bored anymore.

'We can't risk lives,' said Claire.

'Claire's right,' said Douglas. 'We have to protect our staff and our customers.'

Irene was shaking her head.

Danny leaned forward. 'It's happened before.' He looked at Irene but she would not acknowledge he was right. Am I wrong, he wondered.

'I've never heard of a mass evacuation before,' said Janet.

Danny barked a laugh and looked upwards as he put it together. 'Because they didn't evacuate.'

Everyone looked at Irene.

'Was there a bomb?' Asked Jim.

Irene gave an imperceptible shake of her head.

'You were lucky!'

Irene took a step back. 'Home Office stance on an unspecified threat is to place only those who need to know, on alert.'

'I've never heard that,' said Claire.

'Well that is something our listeners will want to know more about,' said Jim.

'No!' Irene seemed to realise she had over-reacted. 'Terrorists do give a warning to cause fear and also send a message that they are not the bad guys. It worked very well for the IRA back in the Seventies and Eighties. Giving a vague warning is different, it's a trap. Either there is no real threat, no actual bomb and the aim is to cause panic and to make the government look stupid. Or there is a bomb and the terrorists are able to cause far greater disruption than they would have just by blowing it up. If we don't tell the public and there is no bomb, we avoid the panic. If we don't tell them and there is...'

'You can't expect us to do nothing!' Interrupted Claire.

'She didn't say do nothing,' said Danny.

'We expect you to take any threat seriously, but also to avoid causing undue panic.' Irene looked at her watch and sighed. 'Very well, we have a new scenario. The time is 09:26. Detective Inspector, a phone call is made to Fulford Road police station. A group calling itself Raj Istal claims to have planted a bomb somewhere in York city centre timed to go off at 11am...'

CHAPTER FOURTEEN
Decision

Zafar reached the top of the grass mound and placed his hand on the stone of Clifford's Tower. Several other people had already spread out around the bank that surrounded the base of the tower and Zafar walked round until he found a space with a view towards the Ouse.

He occasionally came here to have his lunch, but today he had decided to fast and instead had come to think. The documentary Tariq had shown him had filled his thoughts since the weekend, almost drowning out his vision. He'd said very little after it had finished, eventually telling Tariq that he needed to go away and think.

Yet he was struggling to focus. The previous morning even his manager had asked him if he was alright…

For several years he had listened to reports of the struggle in the Middle East. From nothing, the Caliphate had grown in size, conquering the West's puppet army in Iraq and even defeating Syrian forces. But the call to arms had seemed distant, irrelevant. If the Caliphate was genuine, it would grow until the whole world was finally united and Zafar had not been able to see that happening in the near future.

Then the documentary had opened his eyes. If we were already at war, then this was no longer a distant call, but an immediate one and what if Allah had given him the answer? What if his vision was the means to wake up his brothers and sisters and save them from the oppression they were under?

Then it would be a treason to turn from the path before him.

Tariq had been right. This was no easy task. They would need an army of warriors and commitment to fight and keep on fighting until the whole country had been won. The lesson from the current struggle was that such a task would be long and arduous. Gains made by the Caliphate had been lost in recent years. But rumours suggested that despite their denials, British and American forces were working undercover to disrupt the Caliphate. The Prophet had warned against deceitful men, how could a battle be won against forces that never showed themselves?

Yet if Britain was distracted by the establishment of the Caliphate within their own borders, they would have no choice but to pull back. And if brothers in surrounding countries saw their success and were themselves inspired to fight… The whole world could be turned on its head. It was easy for the countries of the West to unite against Islam when they were distant from the battle, it would be impossible for them if they were each fighting their own war.

It was a heady thought that he could have been chosen to lead others in this final battle. Zafar bowed his head and thanked Allah for entrusting him with the vision and prayed for courage to follow through with it.

When he looked up, the sky seemed to have brightened and the air was fresher. He stood, made his way down to the street and, before he set off back to work, sent Tariq a text: I have decided, it is my turn to cook the Osh, when shall we meet?

CHAPTER FIFTEEN
Walking the Wall

She felt stiff and cold when she woke, as if she hadn't had enough sleep. She had dreamed again, the man trying to save her as she fell. Emma forced herself out of bed hoping a coffee would revive her and maybe help her forget. Rachel didn't seem to be in the flat, but Emma didn't feel like checking her room.

She made herself a hot drink and then turned to sit at the counter. She pushed some paperwork out of the way so she could set down her mug, then pulled it back when she saw the word Union. Had Rachel said something about this? Emma tried to remember, but other than a sense there was something important, she couldn't recall.

It was a membership form. Emma was sure Rachel had mentioned something about this. She looked it over. Lots of boxes to fill in. She sighed, could she be bothered?

I've been suspended, she thought to herself. I've got no savings and might be out of a job. Rachel had said something about asking the Union for help, she was sure of it... and in order for us to do that we need to be members. Figures... I wonder how much the membership fee costs? She imagined Rachel saying a lot less than having no job...

Rachel had left a pen on the counter. Typical... No excuses. Emma took a sip of her coffee and started filling in the form.

It didn't take as long as she thought it might. Half an hour later she checked the time: mid afternoon. She absentmindedly put her hand up to her head to scratch, but stopped when she felt the scar. Was it in the shape of a question mark? She traced the ridge then started to feel a sense of urgency. She dressed quickly and left the flat.

Half an hour later, Emma cursed herself for even considering going back up on the wall. The first section from Sainsbury's to where she now stood, frozen in place looking towards Monk Bar, had been fine. The sun was out, clouds were light and there was a soft breeze. It had seemed the most natural thing to head up the steep stone stairs and get away from the traffic.

The closer she had got to where it had all happened, the slower she found herself walking. She still couldn't remember any of it. Not walking on the parapet, not reaching the Bar, not even falling.

Yet she had dreamed of it again, seemed to start dreaming as soon as she fell asleep and woke up each time with his face growing more distant, his hand still trying to catch her. She had wanted to ask him who he was, but it was a dream and neither he nor she could speak, though she saw him moving his lips, obviously trying to say something.

She must have been conscious if she had seen his face, must have landed badly enough to stun her. She was tough and all the time she saw people admitted to hospital who only had minor injuries when they should have broken half the bones in their body. Stunned, concussed, that was why she couldn't remember anything except in her dreams, but that in itself was encouraging—the fact she could remember through the dreams meant her memory was coming back.

Not her courage though. She turned away from Monk Bar and crouched down with her back to the parapet. The stone was warm in the sun and she sat and contemplated her toes through her sandals. The varnish was chipped. She hadn't touched it up since before the... It didn't seem to matter anymore.

That wasn't good, was it? She would never have gone out without her nails having been carefully painted. Why didn't she care?

She put a hand to her head in sudden panic then relaxed having remembered she had brushed her hair before leaving the flat.

'I'm losing it,' she whispered to herself. 'Yep, first sign of madness—talking to yourself. Definitely losing it.'

~~~

Two hundred yards away and six metres down, Calvin Smith walked quickly under Monk Bar. If anyone had been watching him they would hardly have seen him looking towards the spot where he had tried to revive the girl. Ever since that night he had broken with his normal custom of choosing differing routes each day when he headed into the city. Now every morning and night he walked under Monk Bar.

He prayed for her as he walked, even though she was dead, even though it was too late, he prayed God would have mercy on her, that he would forgive her and accept her.

He didn't pray for himself anymore and wasn't sure God would even be willing to hear his prayer for another anyway, but even though he was damned, he had to try.

~~~

Clouds were beginning to turn pink in the West as Danny made his way out of the hotel. He had parked in the hotel car park but felt like he needed some air before going back to Fulford Road. Irene Carr had been distinctly frosty towards him the whole day, though several of the representatives had quietly expressed their appreciation for making the day more interesting.

Role playing, what a waste of his time!

He made his way across and up Station Road until he reached the monument and could climb up onto the wall. Traffic was gridlocked as always, with cars queuing in both directions as far as he could see towards York Minster. It was turning into a beautiful evening, the air still with large patches of blue beginning to fade in colour as the sun dipped lower towards the horizon.

He needed to think and there was something about the walls around York that allowed him to distance himself from the traffic that was only metres away. So, he was walking and thinking. Walking because it helped him to think, kept him away from distractions and also postponed having to talk to anyone else about the whole CTSA situation.

Maybe it would all go away. He'd been downright aggressive at points during the day. Had stepped in several times to stop Irene going off on some flight of fancy and made the whole group face up to the reality of what they were considering.

Not that he thought any of it all that likely. Sure, there were terrorists and sure, there was a threat but the whole fight against terror was meaningless to most people. A waste of money and effort.

Danny knew from bitter experience that the police could not protect people from crime and if they couldn't prevent crime how on earth could they protect people from terrorists?

People needed empowerment. They needed help to set them up to protect themselves. Help to rebuild their communities.

He stopped, looking at the people crossing the River Ouse. He could never say this out loud but secretly he knew it was true: we've let too many people with too many different beliefs into our country and now we wonder why our communities have no cohesion. You only had to look across at America and see that at least they had a common uniting factor. Their belief in their constitution. Belief in their flag. Belief in the land of hope, liberty and freedom. But what do we believe in here in our so called United Kingdom?

Christians, Muslims, Hindus, Buddhists, Atheists... None of them united by a common belief. Conservatives, Labour, Liberals... Three political parties that had embraced liberalism while alienating their traditional supporters.

He turned back, letting his thoughts play out, hoping he would find some resolution to the turmoil. He'd become a Detective because he believed that would make a difference. That he could make a difference. That if he stopped people committing crime then communities would be safer.

But if anything, things just got worse every year. The government kept cutting back resources and manpower but expected the police to improve their rates of detection and prevention. But how could the police prevent crime? It was maddening. You would need a police officer in every house, on every street and even then you couldn't absolutely guarantee no-one would ever commit a crime.

It was the same with terrorism. Except much, much worse. Danny had read the editorials and rotated the newspapers he read to get as broad a view of opinion as he could. Newspapers weren't the sole barometer of public opinion and sentiment, but they did still give insights he couldn't get anywhere else.

The statistics revealed the insanity of the Government's focus. 571 murders in England and Wales in the last year. The number of people killed through road traffic accidents had been 1,732 and throughout the UK not a single person died as a result of terrorism! Looking at those hard cold facts would he have the same focus if he had the power to change anything? Danny shook his head. Britain was broken. It used to be Britain united by faith. Now—if anything—Britain was only united in greed. Millions longed to emulate the rich and famous. Queued up to audition for talent shows in the hope they might be allowed to join the elite for fifteen minutes.

He'd read recently that ten percent of people in the UK owned ninety percent of the wealth. The poorest were slowly being strangled by austerity cuts that were justified by implying people were lazy. He knew crime was a problem, knew terrorism was the least threat the country faced and couldn't shake the feeling that the hidden danger was that Britain was headed for a revolution. The whole country in a slow motion car crash. Happening without anyone's knowledge but everyone about to hit the windscreen.

He was back at the steps near his car. Maybe he'd done enough to persuade the organisers he wasn't suitable material to join the Argus Project, wouldn't cut it as a CTSA. Britain had bigger problems than he was able to deal with but maybe he could at least continue doing what he was best at. As he climbed down the steps, Danny glanced up, then hesitated. He couldn't remember the last time he'd asked God for help, why would he do so now?

~~~

The drugs gave everything a dreamy quality. Michael held up his hand and moved his fingers, marvelling at the way they seemed to glide through the air. He no longer felt angry. Why had he been angry? Oh yes, because they wanted him to stay in the hospital.

Why had that bothered him? He couldn't remember, wasn't sure he wanted to try.

'How are you feeling, Michael?'

Who was this? Michael turned to look at her. She wasn't wearing a white coat or scrubs like the other doctors and nurses, just a smart dress. She had a friendly smile. He smiled back.

'Michael? How are you feeling?'

'I'm feeling good,' he told her. And he was. Though just then he started to feel a bit queasy. Like he'd felt once on a ferry on the way to France. He grasped the arms of the chair to steady himself. Closed his eyes.

'It can take some time for your body to get used to the drugs. We'll take the dose down slightly and see if that helps.'

He nodded, took some deep breaths and gradually the feeling the room was moving under his feet started to ease.

'Could I ask you some questions?'

'Of course.' Michael opened his eyes and saw the woman had pulled up a chair in front of him. She was still smiling. It felt so good to have someone smile at him.

'Thank you. You said that God speaks to you sometimes. What does he say?'

The good feeling lessened as Michael remembered God's command. That's why he'd been angry...

'I have to... I can't stay here.'

'It's okay, Michael.' The woman leaned forward. 'Try to relax.' She was still smiling.

He wanted to please her so he tried. It didn't take much effort and the bad feeling slipped away.

'Why can't you stay here, Michael?'

'I have to warn everyone.'

'What do you need to warn them about?'

'They're in danger, they need to repent.'

'What are they in danger of?'

'He's sending... I don't know. He hasn't told me.'

'That's okay, Michael. What has he told you?'

'To write the words. To show them to everyone. To warn them.'

'How long has he been telling you to warn people?'

When had it started? Michael thought back. It was hard to focus. 'I was... Fifteen.'

'How does he tell you?'

'God speaks to me.'

'You hear a voice?'

'Of course.'

CHAPTER SIXTEEN
Searching

York wasn't that big a city and yet Emma suspected it crammed more streets into it's tiny space than many larger cities. She had ended up retracing her steps back along the wall, unable to approach Monk Bar and had made herself walk into the centre of York, determined that she wouldn't be put off by the accident she'd witnessed. But now she found herself questioning what she was doing. Dozens of tiny snickets, lanes and courts led off from the main streets. Was the man she searched for waiting in one of them or was he wandering round himself, even following her so that no matter how long she searched for him she would never find him?

Not that she knew what he looked like, unless her dream was a memory. Had her imagination just constructed a photofit? Maybe he had been the smooth shaven man with the dog she had passed a few minutes ago. He had a dog though. Rachel had said nothing about a dog.

He could be sitting right there, the lanky, grey haired, grey bearded man that looked like he had escaped from Auschwitz. Emma didn't believe it though. Didn't want to believe it.

She pictured herself meeting him, able to ask: Hi! What happened to me? What were you trying to do to me?

She shook her head. What was she thinking? She had no idea what he was trying to do to her, except…

Except what? She couldn't finish the thought.

She stopped walking causing a woman who had been following to swear at her as she dodged round.

It was time to go home.

~~~

'You don't talk to me for two days, are out who knows where, I'm left on my own trying to persuade the Union to help us and you can't even sign one simple form! What is wrong with you?'

Emma closed the door to the flat. 'Nice to see you too.'

Rachel put her hands on her hips. 'This isn't a joke, Emma. Where have you been?'

'I really don't want to…'

'Talk about it?' Rachel interrupted. 'No, I got that. But you need to talk about it. We need to talk about it.' She stopped, took a deep breath, but Emma held up her hands.

'Can I at least get into the flat?'

Rachel shook her head. 'I don't know. Will you clam up like you've been doing?'

'Seriously, Rachel. Just let me in, okay!'

Rachel stood aside and Emma squeezed through.

'I signed your stupid form,' Emma said, seeing the paperwork was still on the counter.

'You signed it…' Rachel walked over and picked up the form. 'I didn't check, I mean I did check… this morning.'

'I found it when I got up. I can't remember you talking to me about it.'

'Really? You came in and were talking to me. You nodded when I asked you.'

'I don't remember.'

'How come? You seemed kind of spaced out. Then you wouldn't talk to me this morning. What's up, Emma?'

She saw an image of a blue bus, remembered the sound of a body being hit and thrown.

'You're doing it again…'

Emma focused on Rachel who was looking concerned. A wave of dizziness hit her and she reached back and found the sofa. Made her way round to sit. Rachel walked over to stand over her, then sat beside her.

Eventually Emma realised that Rachel had stopped asking questions. She glanced at Rachel and saw she looked even more concerned. 'I'm alright,' she said, looking away again.

'You could have fooled me. Should I be taking you back into A&E?'

'No!' Emma regretted the way she spoke immediately after. 'I'm just… Something happened. On Monday.'

'Okay…'

'I saw… There was an accident, these guys were hassling this poor guy and then one of them wasn't looking where he was going and he stepped in front of a bus. I saw the whole thing.'

'Oh my…'

Emma saw Rachel put her hands up to her mouth.

'Why didn't you tell me?' Rachel asked.

Emma shook her head. 'I thought I was handling it. I guess I wasn't.'

'Oh, Emma…' Rachel leaned over and hugged her. 'You need to talk to me, girl. You shouldn't try and deal with that sort of stuff on your own.'

'I know,' whispered Emma.

~~~

Joan Cairns took a sip from her mug and grimaced at the cold tea, half a mug left too… What a waste, she thought. Setting it down she pushed away her sudoku puzzle and picked up the ward clipboard. Standing and stretching, she wondered how long she had been mulling over the puzzle. It was a tough one but a good way to pass the time when she didn't have a book with her. She preferred not to watch the TV when she was on nights just in case she couldn't hear a patient.

First name on the list was Michael Irving. Admitted yesterday, involved in an incident in York and lucky to have had a nurse on hand who recommended an evaluation otherwise he might have ended up in jail. He had signs of schizophrenia which, though not initially dangerous, could have been interpreted that way by the police if things had gone differently.

His light was on as it had been the past two nights. Afraid of the dark? He seemed to sleep poorly at night and had been dozing on and off during the day. The sedatives he had been prescribed may have been causing that of course. Approaching his door she could hear him talking, quite agitated. She peered through the toughened glass window and saw Michael, sitting defensively on his bed with his knees up and arms wrapped round them, his back against the corner of the room.

Joan knocked gently and opened the door. Stepping carefully into the room she heard him: 'Emma, please don't, please be careful, Emma, don't go on the wall...'

He was babbling, thought Joan. A bit disturbing that he was focusing on the Nurse that had found him on the street but with psychiatric disorders that went with the territory.

'I'm going to get you a sedative, Michael. I'll be back in a minute.'

Joan could hear Michael continue to talk as she went to unlock the drugs cabinet, made a mental note as she was doing so to write up her observations for the psychiatrist. Entering the room again, she was focused on pouring water into a cup and didn't see him glance up in fear at the far corner of his room.

~~~

Tariq stood by his first floor window looking down at the dark street. He had not dared to hope that Zafar would contact him again, and initially his text had puzzled him: "...my turn to cook the Osh..." They had not agreed any code though Tariq knew he had cautioned Zafar against sharing his vision. Zafar had hardly spoken after they had watched the documentary—in truth—not a film Tariq planned to release to the general public. No, it's purpose had always been intended for more select viewing.

Zafar's visit had taken him completely by surprise. His old friend had appeared to have gone native, going to university, getting a normal job, marrying, settling down. Yes, he had heard about the loss of his wife, had wondered about contacting him then but... It just would not have been right.

Now, out of the blue, Zafar had come to see him and not only that, he also appeared to have been sent with a vision of such power Tariq could not discount it.

The timing could not be ignored. His own plans had reached a stage where he would have to decide soon when to act, but he had not considered such a breath-taking plan, was almost ashamed that his own plans had been so limited. He looked again at Zafar's text. "I have decided" was neutral. Decided to act or decided not to act. Either way was a decision. But would he be so keen to meet, offering to cook Osh if he had decided to do nothing? No, Tariq couldn't believe it, wanted to believe his friend had turned to the true path.

Ultimately though, even if Zafar had not committed to the cause, he had shared his vision. Tariq felt like a baton had been passed to him. To follow through with such a scheme would require all his resources, all his contacts. He would have to call in every favour, risk everything... Would it be worth it?

The repercussions would be swift and deadly. There was no guarantee whether it would spark a holy war or set their ultimate goal back by a generation. Yet if he did nothing, would they ever see the Ummah established here?

Very little of value was ever accomplished without violence. He had studied their history since he was a child and there was not a single Islamic nation that had not been claimed by war.

Tariq closed his eyes, trying to imagine what Zafar had seen. His interpretation of it was hazy, but he again caught the excitement of the moment. A mass attack... dozens, maybe even hundreds of foot soldiers waging war on an unprepared city. It could be the trigger to finally cause his brothers to wake from their apathy, the spark that caused a holy flame to burn the infidels to the ground.

He turned away from the window and lit a candle to light a small wooden table. Taking a single piece of paper he wrote down ten names in pencil. Tariq studied the list for a time then crossed out four.

He looked at the remaining names for a minute longer then nodded, satisfied they were the right men to lead others. He would need to buy a new phone to make the calls. He also sensed it was time to move, possibly was time to become a nomad and abandon all thoughts of being settled. Whether Zafar intended to act on his vision or not, Tariq knew he must. He had always been careful, but would have to ensure there could be no trail left behind. If the authorities caught wind of what was going to happen, they would crush anyone connected with it.

He held out the paper to the candle flame and waited until the whole sheet was on fire before dropping it on the room's stone fireplace. There would be no evidence left anywhere.

CHAPTER SEVENTEEN
Pressure Mounts

'Sir, I've a Mr Anthony Cole on line two for you.'

Danny laid his pen down and looked up from his paperwork to the blinking light on his phone. Anthony Cole... That was the surgeon who'd made the complaint against the Hunter girl at the weekend. He picked up the phone and accepted the call.

'Detective Inspector Daniel Martin.'

'Detective Inspector, This is Anthony Cole. Have you charged Emma Hunter and Rachel Philips yet?'

Did the man realise how insulting his tone was? Danny took a moment before replying.

'We are investigating the allegation.'

'What's to investigate, Detective Inspector? They have obviously faked this fall and wasted valuable NHS and police resources.'

'We've requested footage from the scene and a toxicology report. My team has not yet received these, but we will be chasing them up.'

'Please do. I've had the Union on at me this morning telling me they will be representing these women. I would like to have this situation resolved quickly.'

Danny's attention was briefly distracted by a meeting request from Rudd's PA popping up on his screen. 'I understand, Mr Cole. My team will be in touch.'

'Ensure they are.' He ended the call.

Danny looked across at Natalie. 'Am I right that we still haven't received the CCTV or toxicology report?'

'Not yet. I chased both this morning.'

'What's keeping them?' He put his hands behind his head. 'That was our esteemed Mr Cole asking if I'd charged those girls yet.'

'What's his urgency?'

'The Union is on his case. Guess he's worried that if we don't back him up he'll be forced to make an embarrassing apology.'

'The CPS will never prosecute without evidence.' Natalie put her head to one side. 'We've only interviewed Philips and Hunter so far. I could expand to the group they were with at the club, see if they confirm the story.'

'Do it. And find out why the CCTV and toxicology are taking so long.' He hesitated and then said: 'Rudd wants me in for a meeting at... 11:45.'

'That's precise. He's giving you a full fifteen minutes then?'

'Only five,' Danny smiled. 'You'll be called in at 11:50.'

~~~

'Come on in, Danny. Take a seat.' Rudd smiled at Danny as he sat down. 'I had a good report back from the Argus meeting. They say you made a valuable contribution.'

Danny waited for the "but" yet there was none. Rudd continued to smile and seemed to be waiting for him to respond. He took a deep breath.

'The scenario they were using was out of date and pointless. It would have been useful in the Eighties or early Nineties but we don't face that sort of threat anymore.'

'Go on.'

'I have to admit, I'm surprised they were positive about my input.'

'Irene Carr did note that you were blunt.'

'I would be happy to accept that.'

'She went on to say that the feedback she received from the other participants was extremely positive. There was a consensus that you brought a reality to the event that has been lacking and that she's never had such a high rate of feedback for any event. Some of the participants have even suggested bringing in colleagues and requested scenarios they would like to explore.'

Unaware he was doing it, Danny grimaced. How could he have been so wrong? He'd been rude. Had questioned and challenged Irene the whole day. She'd not offered him her hand when he said goodbye and he'd assumed she'd write up such a poor report that the whole CTSA idea would be crippled.

'Still not convinced this is the right move for you... Very well. MI5 have requested we accompany them as they carry out an operation in Leeds on Friday. Normally Harbrook would attend, but I've said you will go in his place.'

'Sir, I've already lost one day this week, the backlog isn't getting any smaller.'

'This is a valuable training exercise for you. An opportunity to see what we're facing and how the intelligence community are dealing with it, find out the sort of things CTSA's get involved in, find out what they do. You can ask all the awkward questions you want but I suspect you'll be intrigued, Danny. In this role you'll have greater involvement with MI5, interaction with police forces across the country. It is quite a progression.'

Danny forced a smile. 'I'm not sure I'm the right person for this role, Sir, but I thank you for the opportunity to find out more.'

'Good man. I'll have Harbrook send the details onto you.'

CHAPTER EIGHTEEN
A Secret

'What are we going to do with you, child?' Najwa's mother stood looking in the mirror while she adjusted her hijab as they got ready to leave the house.

Najwa didn't reply. It wasn't her fault her periods seemed unable to keep to a schedule, that sometimes only a couple of weeks would pass before the bleeding started again. If that meant she missed school another day, what did it matter? Her parents only ambition for her was that she marry well.

Her mother satisfied, she checked Najwa's hijab and then opened the door. Najwa carried a novel she'd borrowed from the school library. If she was going to have to wait at the clinic to be seen, she would rather not have to read one of the tatty magazines they left lying on the table.

It wasn't a long walk to the clinic. Najwa noted the gardens that were well tended and those that were overgrown with grass. A rusting car blocked a driveway, sitting high with bricks in place of wheels. Najwa couldn't remember how long it had been there.

She saw an old woman walking towards them and moved behind her mother to let her past, her face was familiar—a neighbour she had seen before.

The woman almost looked as if she was going to say something, but then they were past her. Najwa looked back to see the woman had stopped, a look of sadness on her face.

~~~

'Najwa? Are you feeling better? I could use some help making the tea.'

Najwa hid her book under her pillow and turned over in her bed. If her mother came into the room she would pretend to be sleeping.

The doctor had poked and prodded her and asked lots of questions. Had weighed her, checked her height and eventually said that many girls had irregular periods. That she was underweight for her age and height which may be the cause and that it would probably settle over the next year or so.

Her mother had asked if being underweight would explain why Najwa was always tired and the doctor said it was a possibility.

'Maybe it's just school, Mum.' Najwa had said. Her mother had nodded in agreement and had let her go to bed when they got home instead of sending her off to school.

Her teachers would not be pleased. She had already missed many days this year and with the exams due the following year, they kept going on about the need to study. It all seemed so pointless.

After a couple of minutes it was clear her mother wasn't going to check on her so Najwa retrieved the book. She had first seen a copy in RE class. Several of her friends—all Muslim—had been given permission to be excused from the class when they taught Christianity, but Najwa's parents hadn't objected so she'd gone along. She knew about the Injil, every Muslim did. Knew that the book had been corrupted first by the Jews and later by the Christians, yet she had immediately liked the title on the cover: Good News Bible. She wanted some good news and was intrigued to find out why it was called good news when it had been corrupted. So far she couldn't see anything to object to.

They had a copy in the Library and she'd borrowed it to find out more. She re-opened the book. The story was much more interesting than doing chores or studying for a boring exam.

~~~

Why am I doing this, Emma thought to herself as she climbed the stairs back to her flat. Two more days of walking York's streets and alleyways and still no sign of the man in her dream. She knew it was becoming an obsession, but she had to find him, find out why she kept dreaming about him.

Last night she had been lying down and he was sitting beside her. He had been talking, she was sure of it, a calm voice that made her feel at peace but she couldn't remember anything he had said.

She reached her landing and opened the door. Almost immediately Rachel was running through.

'The Union wants to meet with us, plan how we're going to challenge the suspension. Monday is the earliest they can do, but that's only been a week, Emma! I'm sure once the Union starts to put pressure on the hospital they'll fold. They've got nothing other than a wild allegation against us.'

Rachel said everything in a rush, barely pausing to take a breath. Emma could see she was so excited and knew she should be as well, but at Rachel's last words her hand went to the back of her head and she gently ran her fingers over the scar that was becoming so familiar to her.

'It's at 10am on Monday. I've got a doctor's appointment at nine so I'll be heading out early. They need both of us to be there, okay?'

'Sure,' Emma said.

Rachel cocked her head and gave Emma a searching look. 'You don't seem all that excited? I thought you would be happy.'

Emma forced herself to give Rachel a smile. 'I'm just tired. It's good news. Really good news.'

Rachel frowned, but didn't challenge her and Emma used the pause to squeeze past so she could close the door.

'We should celebrate,' Rachel said.

'We should,' Emma said over her shoulder as she walked through to the sitting room. 'Do we have any wine in the flat?'

'Don't you want to go out?'

'I've just been out.' Emma turned and saw Rachel was standing with her hands on her hips, that searching look back again.

'Don't you want to go out and celebrate?'

No, not really, Emma thought to herself. She shook her head. 'I'm just tired.'

'Well, okay, but we have to go out tomorrow. This is good news, right?'

'Really good news.' Emma managed another smile then walked into the kitchen. 'I'm starving, do we have any food in?'

CHAPTER NINETEEN
First Meeting

His heart thumping inside his chest, Zafar checked the number on the door. In the streetlights, the faded number was hard to see but it was the right house. When Tariq had told him they would meet at a different location it had confirmed the enormity of what they were going to discuss. He pushed open the gate and walked up the short path.

Standing and waiting after he had knocked, Zafar tried not to look around to see if anyone was watching. He felt like ants were crawling up his back. There was no sound from inside and no lights visible through heavily curtained windows. He was just about to knock again when there was a sound of a lock opening and the door was pulled back.

'Zafar,' Tariq smiled at him and gestured for him to come inside.

The hallway was unlit and narrow and Zafar had to squeeze past until Tariq could shut the door. He waited until Tariq had locked the door and stood still as darkness surrounded him.

'Saving electricity?' He tried joking, becoming aware that there was light coming from underneath a door off the hallway. Zafar heard a swishing sound and then had to blink as the light was turned on. He saw Tariq smiling, standing in front of a black curtain that now covered the door.

'I have invited some friends to join us,' Tariq said. 'I would like you to share your vision with them.'

'You trust them?' Zafar felt foolish asking the question.

'With my life.' Tariq excused himself and eased past Zafar to open the door Tariq had noticed earlier. He gestured to Zafar to follow him in.

Walking in, Zafar saw five pairs of eyes studying him. He nodded towards the five men who were sitting on traditional mattresses around the wall, none of them older than himself he noticed. Was that a good thing?

He closed the door and sat down next to Tariq and waited.

Tariq looked round at each of them, his expression solemn. 'No introductions. You are here because I asked you to come. I hope you will stay because you believe as I do that God has given us a mission to carry out.'

Zafar saw that the others were focused entirely on Tariq who continued. 'Last week I counted five separate attacks on our brothers and sisters in this country alone. You've all heard the stories. Seen the news getting steadily worse for months now. We hoped we could live in peace here but the truth is there is no peace outside Islam.'

The tallest stranger nodded his agreement, his fringe falling across his face before he pushed it back. 'The infidels still insult Allah by attacking his lands, their foreign troops desecrate our soil in Syria and Yemen,' he said. 'Still they threaten Iran. They blaspheme Allah at every turn, waving their fists at him. They do not listen when we tell them to leave our land, they steal our oil, kill our brothers and rape our sisters.'

An image from the documentary Tariq had shown him came unbidden to Zafar's mind—a young woman being beaten and kicked while her attackers filmed her.

Tariq acknowledged the interruption, indicating he wasn't yet finished. 'You remember September the Eleventh when the world trembled in fear. You remember July the Seventh when London came to a standstill. You may be surprised, but these dates are not important to me. I fear that they have done our cause more harm than good. But what is our cause? This is the question I believe Muslims everywhere have failed to ask. Because we have failed to ask it, we do not know or agree on an answer. We are divided and a divided people are weak. Because we are weak, our brothers and sisters are not safe on the streets, because we are weak, our lands are occupied by the infidels.'

Tariq paused to take a breath. 'Allah has given us this world. Our fathers understood this. There was a time when Muslims controlled much of the known world. We came so close to conquering Europe, to establishing the Ummah in China and Africa. The same situation has arisen time and again in our history. Our fathers who rode their caravans and traded throughout Asia were often robbed and killed. It took Prince Laskar to subdue the tribes of Central Asia and unite the people under Islam before our fathers could trade in peace.

'Hundreds of years later, our fathers took to the seas and took their trade to Malaysia, Indonesia and the great islands. But the islanders were pagans, worshiping spirits and ancestors. Our fathers could have ignored this, could have profited despite knowing these people were headed for Hell. But they chose instead to risk their own lives to share the message of The Prophet. The Prophet was given a mission, was commanded by the angel Gabriel to declare to the whole world that Allah alone is God and to take Allah's message of peace to all people everywhere. Yet our leaders are frightened of this message because they know that Allah has not just commanded us to speak of peace, we are commanded to bring peace.'

Tariq took a deep breath, keeping eye contact with them all. 'The reality is that to bring peace to this world, we have to subdue it, conquer it. Not just in Syria or Iraq. Not just in Afghanistan or Yemen or Libya, but everywhere. Here. In the UK. This is our duty, this is the mission that Allah is still calling us to complete. Will you join me in accepting this mission today?'

Zafar looked round at the other men. The tall one was nodding. Beside him, the youngest of the group looked deep in thought, the dark skin of his forehead creased. To Zafar's left, he caught the eye of the man sitting next to him and saw a flash of amusement before the man looked away, examining the others himself. Zafar had to lean forward slightly to see the fourth man. Bearded but with the lightest skin of them all. He could easily pass for a Westerner, even the style of his clothes seemed to set him slightly apart and yet Zafar suspected that he was as much a Muslim as himself. The fifth man was inscrutable, his expression betraying nothing.

'Are you proposing we declare war on the United Kingdom?' Asked the youngest of the group.

'The United Kingdom is at war with us,' Tariq responded. 'It is time we accepted that and responded in kind, but remember a war is won battle by battle.

Sitting next to Zafar, the man with the amused look shifted. 'I only count seven of us. What kind of battle or war are you planning?'

Tariq smiled as well. 'There is a plan I want to share with you but suffice to say for now that we will need many more men to join us. However…' His expression became grave. 'Mohammed would have carried on alone if no-one had joined him. If the Prophet would have done so, it befits us to follow his example.'

'I am sure that many of our brothers will join us, but as I asked, what battle are you planning?'

Tariq held his gaze. 'Again I must ask you, will you join me in accepting this mission? If not, then I must ask you to leave.'

Zafar felt his mouth dry. He had resolved though that this was his direction. 'I will join you,' he said vowing to himself that he would see this through to the end.

Zafar heard the tall one speak: 'I will join you.'

'As will I, though I have many questions.' This was the young man.

'You will have ample opportunity to ask and discuss but it is imperative that you are willing to submit yourself to your leader even if you disagree. To execute a war will require determination and sacrifice and the willingness to act when ordered to do so. Will you accept the orders given?'

'Yes, Tariq.'

'Yes, Tariq,' echoed the man on Zafar's left. The sing song way in which he said it made Zafar doubt his commitment but Tariq said nothing.

The Westerner looked round at them all. 'It will be my honour to join you.'

Finally the fifth man spoke to say he would join them. Zafar saw and heard no trace of excitement or fear as he did.

'Brothers, thank you. It was important that we agree together before discussing further. And now, I feel I should introduce you. I know and trust each of you otherwise you would not be here, but I suspect you have not met.' He put his hand out towards the Westerner. 'This is Darius, an engineer. Born in the UK though his parents are from Iran.'

'Refugees who have almost rejected Islam,' interjected Darius. 'I do not intend to follow their path.'

How close had he come himself to turning away from Islam... Zafar silently thanked Allah for entrusting him and calling him once more.

Tariq was now looking at the man sitting on Zafar's left. 'Rani was born in Iraq. His father brought him here after his mother was killed when the war began. His expertise is in electronics and software programming.'

'My friends call me Psycho,' Rani said, giving Zafar what was becoming a familiar amused look.

'I call you Rani,' Tariq told him.

'I said my friends.'

Zafar looked between Rani and Tariq and decided Psycho was beginning to seem appropriate. Tariq held Rani's amused look for a minute without signalling amusement or annoyance and then turned to Zafar's right.

'Raj has managed to disguise an interest in explosive compounds and a high IQ by posing as one of the clumsiest chemistry students Leeds has ever seen.'

'May Allah bless me for having to take on such a demeaning disguise!'

Zafar could not work out whether the young student was being sarcastic or serious.

'Philippe has received training from Al Qaeda and is an expert in weapons and combat.'

'It is a pleasure to meet you.' Zafar could hear a French accent as Philippe spoke.

'This is Mohammed,' Tariq said, gesturing at the expressionless one. 'He has trained in Somalia and has knowledge of explosives and combat.'

Mohammed acknowledged the others silently.

'Finally, I am delighted to introduce you to Zafar.' Tariq looked at Zafar and he felt his blood begin to race.

Raj leaned forward. 'What is your expertise?' He asked looking at Zafar.

'I'm an accountant.'

Tariq laughed. 'More than that! My brother here has been given a vision. I will let him tell you what he saw and, if he is willing, what he came here to tell me.'

Since he had made his decision and texted Tariq, Zafar had thought of little else, carrying on his work on automatic pilot while he built on the original vision. He had only expected to be speaking with Tariq but now he looked round at these men and felt a rush of adrenaline as he realised they were here to help him make his vision a reality.

'We live in a country that is enslaved to greed and apathy. Every day I drive into and out of York surrounded by people stuck on a treadmill, trapped in their metal boxes and oblivious to their slavery. Last week I saw some children playing on bikes, weaving in and out of the gridlocked traffic and had a...' Zafar hesitated, searching for a better word than vision. 'I believe Allah showed me a way to set this country free. Just as our brothers have conquered the infidels and established the Caliphate, so we can do the same here.

'The city of York is a perfect location to establish the Caliphate here. An easily defensible city right at the centre of the UK where we can establish a base and from there launch attacks to grow our territory, while inspiring our brothers and sisters throughout the UK and the world to join us and finally take this world for Allah.

'I saw an attack taking place during rush hour in the evening, when traffic is at it's heaviest, cars unable to move forwards or backwards. Multiple units of men targeting the key junctions into and out of the city, seizing cars, forcing people out and using those cars to blockade the city. Within a short time the city would be ours and the message would go out that there is no God greater than Allah!'

There was silence after he finished and Zafar looked round immediately noticing Rani's knowing grin. Refusing to let himself be unsettled by Rani's attitude he examined the others who all had thoughtful expressions.

Tariq broke the silence: 'Before Zafar came to me I was in despair at the daily attacks on our brothers and sisters in this country. Our Mosques are firebombed, our people are threatened and harassed. You all know I have been working on a documentary highlighting the injustice our people face. Yet you will remember conversations each of us have had where we have agreed that unless we act, the situation will never improve.

'For too long those who call themselves Muslims in the West have become fat and lazy. They have rejected Allah as they have been tainted with the immorality around them. I believe that Zafar has been shown a vision just as the prophet received from Gabriel.' Zafar felt his face flush at the comparison. 'I believe that Allah is calling us to now rise up and claim this land for him.'

Raj leaned forward. 'There is anger in the universities and I believe a willingness to fight, but in the Mosques they are preaching peace. How likely is it that many will join us?'

'It does not matter whether anyone joins us,' Philippe responded. 'Allah will enable us to overcome.'

'Yet Allah has not always done so in the past, no, let me finish,' Raj said, holding up a hand as Philippe fists clenched, his handsome face cold with anger. 'Allah has given victory in the past but I have studied our history and there are times when faithful Muslims have received no help.'

'Raj is right,' Tariq said in a calm voice that seemed to distract Philippe. 'The will of Allah is not for us to question but we should not be ignorant of the past either. You believe that the students will join us?'

Raj nodded. 'Yes. But even so, this country has 60 million people, even if every Muslim joined us, we are outnumbered thirty to one.'

'Only a tiny number of them are armed,' Rani said dismissively.

'The police have access to weapons.'

'Which they do not carry on normal duty.'

'That is another point,' Raj said forcibly. 'If we attack now and our brothers do not rise up to join us, we will have lost the element of surprise. Every terrorist attack in recent years has resulted in greater surveillance of our people, increased measures to prevent further attacks. What we are proposing…' He looked pointedly at Zafar. 'Is the beginning of the end game. If we cannot achieve it, then we make it harder for those who come after us.'

'I am worried our little brother is afraid,' Rani said.

Zafar looked at Tariq, wondering if he would intervene, but he was sitting calmly, observing the exchange between Rani and Raj.

'We want to win Britain for Islam, that is the end game, yes?'

'You talk about games little brother, perhaps you are not ready for such grown up talk,' drawled Rani.

'Game theory is part of the study of war. To put it very simply...' Raj said, returning Rani's disdainful look. 'If we conquer York for Islam but in doing so, sacrifice all other Muslims now living in the UK, what have we gained?'

'We will claim this land for Islam and once we have done so, it will always belong to Islam!'

'This land already belongs to Allah,' Mohammed interjected, his voice soft and measured. Raj and Rani both turned to him. 'We must not think we are claiming this land for Islam but remember we are taking it back.'

'This is semantics,' Philippe responded. 'What is important is that we act.'

'If we act without purpose we make it harder to achieve our goal,' Raj told him.

'Enough!' Zafar shouted. In the silence that followed he realised his voice may have carried next door. He looked round at the group and saw anger reflected back from Philippe and Raj. Rani still looked amused while Darius and Mohammed appeared unaffected by the discussion.

'We are going round in circles,' Zafar said, trying to speak in a calmer tone. 'The points you are making are all valid but if we cannot agree in this small group then how can we ever hope to work together, let alone inspire others to join us.'

'Who are you to lead us?' Mocked Philippe. 'An accountant!'

'If Allah could use a merchant then he can also use an accountant. Each of you sat here and swore you would join Tariq in accepting his mission. Yet less than five minutes later you squabble like children. I cannot answer all your questions. I cannot take away all your concerns. I can only tell you that Allah has given me a vision. I believe Allah intends us to seize the city of York and use that as a base to sweep throughout Britain. If I have to act on this vision myself I will but...' He looked at Tariq. 'I trust that Tariq had good reasons for inviting you here tonight and each of your skills will be needed.'

'May I speak?' Darius looked to Zafar for permission.

'Of course.'

'Do not judge us too harshly, my brother. The questions and points that have been raised are all valid and it is not childish to debate them. A true warrior knows the importance of tactics and strategy. A commander considers whether retreat will allow the war to be continued elsewhere when there is greater advantage.'

'Well said,' Tariq interjected. 'I called you here because each of you is a leader. It is not surprising or concerning to me that the first time you meet you test each other.'

Zafar felt a sense of shame at how he had spoken and the rebuke he sensed from Darius and Tariq. 'Darius, you are right,' he acknowledged, looking round the group. 'How would you respond to what has been said so far?'

'I am an engineer. As such my training is to think through problems and find solutions. You give ten engineers the same problem and each of them will find a different solution. How many engineers does it take to change a light bulb? As many as the ways a light bulb can be changed. Raj, you are quite right to consider history and game theory. If we look at our homelands in the Middle East and Africa, none of these places are truly governed as Mohammed instructed and even the Caliphate has its failings. The uprisings over the past few years are a sign that while Islam has spread, it has also been corrupted. There are a few who are rich but many who are poor. Is this what we want to see happen in Britain? No...' Darius held up a hand as Philippe made to speak.

'The question is rhetorical. And your point, Philippe, is also valid. Allah calls us to act, not to rest and wait. We now have an opportunity to extend the borders of Islam. Let us set ourselves focused on this task while also being mindful that few people have been truly able to bring peace.

'Rani, you have passion and a desire to fight. We all need your courage.

'Mohammed, you remind us of a great truth, this whole earth was created by Allah. Shaitan led the people of the earth in rebellion against Allah and it is our privilege to reclaim the earth for Allah.'

Zafar looked on in amazement as the group which had seemed ready to splinter only a few minutes ago were now all nodding in agreement. Could he ever learn to speak as Darius had? To unite people who otherwise despised and mocked each other?

'Our brother's vision...'

Zafar looked round sharply as he realised Darius was talking about him.

'...is our rallying point. A clear instruction from Allah to take the fight to the infidel. To strike a blow that will terrify him and give courage to our brothers around the country. Zafar, your plan, would you share the details with us?'

Zafar shifted and raised himself up. 'York is strategically vital. One of the few remaining walled cities left in Britain, it is small with key roads acting as arteries into the city. Each of these is a choke point. Block the roads at the right place and traffic will grind to a halt. Block the roads and capture the walls and the city will be easy to defend, difficult to attack.

'There are cycle lanes threading their way through York which we could use to travel unseen and to avoid the congestion we will be creating. We will need hundreds of foot soldiers operating in small teams to surround and capture the city. Once we have it under control these small teams can circulate on patrol acting as watchmen. Like all cities, there is an extensive CCTV network. We will capture this and can use their defensive system against them.'

Zafar stopped as a buzzing noise came from near Tariq. He watched as Tariq pulled out a phone and checked it.

'I am sorry, my friends,' Tariq said. 'We will have to discuss plans in detail at another time. I'm afraid we must disperse now. Be under no illusions, what we are planning will be thought of as terrorism by the infidels. We will need to maintain absolute secrecy. If one of us is identified and monitored by the police, we will all be at risk. I will go over protocols to use for contacting me. You will eventually be responsible for networks of small cells, the easier to remain hidden.' He paused. 'You will not be a martyr if caught,' Tariq said, his gaze intense. 'You will be a failure. Allah will only acknowledge our absolute victory when we have taken this country and hold it in his name. I believe that together we can inspire our generation of brothers to rise up around the country and overthrow the corrupt government of the infidels!'

CHAPTER TWENTY
Unsettled

Mary checked the clock—Two in the morning—then lay back and stared at the ceiling. The same nightmare every single night for almost a week. Maybe she needed to go see a doctor. No. Didn't trust them. They'd probably lock her up in one of those padded cells.

Was it connected to being thrown out of the church? Some way of enabling her to deal with what had happened? Except the nightmares had started before that, so...

Unless she kept having them because of that...

She shook her head slowly and groaned. She was so tired! She really should pray, ask God to enable her to sleep, but she had been praying and kept having the dreams, so what was the point?

She'd been putting off going to bed, listening to the radio long past the point where she'd lost interest. Eventually though she had to try and sleep, but without fail, every single night, she'd woken with the same sense of fear.

Maybe the doctor could prescribe her a sedative? Or the pharmacist? Yes, she could try that. Something over the counter might be all she would need.

Mary closed her eyes, willing herself to block out the images of people falling in the streets.

CHAPTER TWENTY-ONE
Training Day

Danny had been for training at the Leeds District Police Headquarters before. He had found the modern, white, square cut buildings and sheer size of the complex intimidating then. It was no better as he drove into the visitor's car park at 07:50 that morning. It was a symbol, not of a police force there to serve, but one of an occupying army.

When did we become a country that required this scale of operation, he wondered as he locked his car. Not a question he expected his superiors would appreciate.

He told the Desk Sergeant he was there to meet Oscar Barnes and signed in. He only had to wait a couple of minutes when a short, well rounded man approached and held out his hand.

'Oscar Barnes. Are you Daniel Martin?'

'I am.' Danny shook his hand and stood.

'Your ID please.'

Barnes compared the image on Danny's card with his face, then smiled as he saw Danny studying him. The man had a healthy, rugged tan and was almost bald, just stubble that was kept short. If it wasn't for the name—and accent—Danny wouldn't have been surprised to see him waiting on tables or behind a shop counter in Greece or Turkey.

'Not what you were expecting?' Barnes smiled.

'Just thinking you could blend into a good many places.'

'Leeds and Bradford especially. Come on, let's get moving.'

Barnes led Danny back out to the visitor's car park, to a battered white van with a plumbers logo on the side.

'Moonlighting?' Danny asked.

'Perfect cover. We use basic utilities all the time. No-one thinks twice about someone working inside a house, or an engineer at a telephone cabinet.' Barnes unlocked the van and pulled out overalls. 'Pull these on.'

'I was told this was a training day...'

'I train on the job.'

Once in the van, Barnes texted, talking as he did so. 'Just sending a message to my team, telling them we're on the way.'

'Where are we going?'

'Into Leeds. Got a possible terrorist safe house and we're going to investigate.'

'This is a live operation?' Danny felt a surge of adrenalin at the thought.

'They're all live operations.' Barnes drove off. 'You get the standard briefings right?'

'Sure.'

'And you've been recommended for a CTSA position?'

Danny hesitated before answering, glancing at Barnes who was dividing his time looking at the road and him. 'Yes.'

'Not sure about it?'

'No. I'm a detective. The only career I ever wanted.'

'Understandable you're not sure about switching. What we're going to look at today, that won't be your new day job, but you need to understand what we're doing to understand why your role is important.'

'Okay.'

'If you accept the role then you'll be given a different level of access and you'll see a substantial increase in the volume of briefing information. Some of it will be more detailed, some less.'

'Less?'

'You're about to find out how much we don't know.'

~~~

Barnes drove into Leeds, following directions from a Sat-Nav that took them into a residential area where he slowed. Ahead, Danny saw flashing lights and a cordoned off street with people standing about. Barnes stopped near the cordon. 'There are two tool boxes in the back,' he told Danny. 'Get them out while I speak with the police.'

He could smell the gas as soon as he stepped out the van. What is going on, he thought as he looked at the people, probably residents, all standing around. He saw Barnes walk up to a uniformed officer, hesitated, then decided he better do as told for now.

The boxes were bulky and heavy. Just what he'd expect a plumber to have to carry. Was Barnes really going to fix a gas leak as part of his cover?

'All set?' Barnes was back.

'We're really going in there?'

'Of course.'

'Is it safe?'

Barnes gave a strange smile. 'You didn't become a detective to be safe, did you?'

He picked up a toolbox and turned, walking towards the street. Well, Danny thought, if they wanted to give me a reason to turn down the role, this is perfect. He picked up the other box and followed.

Away from the cordon, Danny hurried to catch up. 'You do know what you're doing, right?'

'I'm a trained professional.'

Barnes stopped at a manhole cover and used a long tool to turn off the mains gas supply to the street.

'Isn't there a risk of explosion?'

'There's always a risk of explosion. You see it on the news sometimes. Operations that went wrong... A house blows up... A family killed...'

'Those are MI5 operations?'

'Usually the family isn't dead, we've put them in witness protection since they've endangered their lives by providing information to us. But sometimes it goes wrong...'

Danny couldn't think of a response. He recalled images from news reports, house roofs collapsed, blackened walls and smashed windows. The bodies he'd seen investigating house fires...

'Do they train you to be so gullible, or is it the inbreeding?'

Danny saw Barnes was now grinning at him. 'This is a wind up?'

'You know gas has no smell right?'

'Yeah.'

'So they add the smell so people know if their gas is leaking...'

'Right...'

'All we had to do was release that chemical and suddenly a whole street evacuates. No danger, no fuss—apart from people worried their homes are going to explode—and in the grand scheme of things, it doesn't hurt them to get a scare, might make them more careful about turning their gas off.'

Danny shook his head. 'Nicely done.'

'Thank you. Now the real danger comes when we enter the house. I wasn't joking about the risk of explosion...'

~~~

With the residents out of the way, Barnes picked the lock on the front door of a terraced house. He had Danny put on blue booties before they entered. Danny watched as Barnes pushed past a thick black curtain that hung behind the door then followed him inside. In the hallway Barnes handed him gloves and a hair cover. 'You're a detective, you know the drill.'

'What are we looking for?'

'Anything. Underneath the tools in the boxes are evidence kits. Take what you need and let's sweep the house. Meet back here in ten minutes. Don't move anything and watch for trip wires.'

'They use those?'

'The IRA used to. At some point these guys will as well. You take upstairs.'

Danny made his way down the hallway. The walls had been painted magnolia, but now were dirty and uncared for. He glanced inside a room as he passed, no furniture he could see. The stairs were bare wood, a thick band of paint running up the centre. No footprints visible, no carpets so far.

The house was long and narrow with a front room he had passed and he guessed a kitchen, maybe dining room at the back, the stairs in the middle of the house, switching back on themselves. He climbed slowly, conscious of the stairs creaking. There probably wasn't anyone still in the house, but... He stopped. Tripwires? He had forgotten to check.

Take a deep breath, Danny, he told himself. You haven't blown yourself up yet. It wasn't another wind up, was it? It didn't matter. There was a risk and so he would act accordingly. Scanning the stairs in front of him, he kept climbing.

The hallway was similar to downstairs. Bare floorboards, walls that had not been painted in years. There was a door to a room at the front of the house right at the top of the stairs. Looking down the hallway, Danny could see three other doors. Bedrooms and a bathroom? Four rooms in all to check.

He reached for the door handle. A clever terrorist would have rigged up a device that exploded when the handle was turned or the door opened. Barnes wouldn't have sent him up here if that was a real risk, would he?

Danny got down on his knees and looked under the door. The room was clear as far as he could see. It didn't mean it was safe though. Danny turned the handle and slowly opened the door. Nothing except a long, drawn out creak.

Stepping in, he quickly looked round. Empty. A large window to the front, again with heavy curtains that currently were drawn back. A fireplace was the only feature in the room. Danny ran his finger over the skirting. No dust. He got on his knees again and looked between the floorboards. They had been cleaned out. He could search every inch and maybe find some clue, but not in ten minutes. He went over to the fireplace. There were some ashes in the grate. He pulled an evidence bag out his pocket and tweezers. Tried to pick up a piece of ash but it crumbled away.

Leaving it, Danny went to check the other rooms. Hesitating each time he opened a door, but finding nothing once he was in the room. No furniture, no scraps of paper. The bathroom was as spotless as it could have been. The iron bath had no bath panel which could have hidden something behind it. There was no cupboard under or over the sink. Someone had gone to great lengths to cover their tracks. He made his way downstairs.

'Is this normal?' He asked Barnes who was waiting in the hallway.

He shook his head. 'No. This has been professionally cleaned. Anything upstairs?'

'Some ash in a fireplace.'

'Show me.'

Upstairs, Barnes crouched down and studied the ash. 'Paper. Carefully burnt. Surprised they didn't hoover it away like everything else.' He looked up at Danny. 'I had another house like this in Bradford last month. Cleaner than a hospital ward. Somebody doesn't want to leave any trail.'

'Yet we're here…'

'Yeah. It's complicated. I'll show you later. Right, we have three other houses to check before we can get rid of this smell.'

~~~

The chemical had been released by a gas canister buried in a flower bed next door to the safe house the previous night. After carrying out a perfunctory check of the neighbouring houses, Barnes walked Danny back out to the police cordon.

'We've found the source of the leak.' Barnes told the senior officer. 'It's at number 37. I need to call in a team to replace a section of pipe. The gas should disperse in an hour and you can let people back to their homes. We'll wait until the other team turns up.'

He headed back to the van and they stowed the tool boxes before getting back in themselves.

'What happens now?' Danny asked.

'My team arrive, set up a tent over the gas canister, dig up the soil and then have a cuppa for a couple of hours before tidying everything away.'

'All that just to cover your tracks?'

'Maybe there isn't just one safe house on the street. Maybe they have someone watching the property. A large part of my job is making sure they—whoever they happen to be—don't know I'm investigating them. You have to deal with some of that, right?'

'Sometimes. Though usually we're only investigating because a crime's already been committed. No need for secrecy at that point. It's all about speed, trying to capture any evidence before it's destroyed.'

'Our evidence walks and talks. The biggest problem we have is that terrorists are people. People who have contacts that we want to find, but also family and friends and colleagues and sometimes just random strangers they interact with. We start watching one terrorist suspect and in a month we can end up with two hundred people they've interacted with. Each of those has to be flagged as a potential suspect. Each has to have a basic file opened and if those people trigger any warning flags, a deeper investigation has to be carried out.'

Barnes rubbed his hand over his stubbled head. 'Have a guess how many people I'm currently investigating?'

'Thousands.'

'Fifteen thousand and change. That's just my case load.'

'Sounds like you need to recruit more MI5 officers, not CTSAs.'

'We do. We are. You're welcome to apply, but you'd probably take a pay cut. That's part of the problem—the budget only stretches so far. We're at war, Danny. It's just the government doesn't want to admit it.'

'Nobody can manage a fifteen thousand suspect caseload.'

'Most of them are innocents. The problem is that most terrorists don't want to advertise their guilt. The really good ones, like…' Barnes broke off and checked his mirror. 'They're here. Hang on, I'll be back in a minute.'

Barnes got out and Danny saw him speaking with another man in a van. Nothing Barnes had said so far was all that shocking to him. The briefings Danny had access to were bad enough and they all knew the government wasn't going to reveal everything. But was what he was seeing enough to make him accept the role? Was any of it really relevant to a CTSA?

~~~

Barnes drove Danny back to the police headquarters where they left the van and then in Barnes car to his office in the outskirts of Leeds. From the outside, the building looked like a business premises with a small warehouse. Inside, Danny quickly spotted what appeared to be a walk through metal detector at the entrance, steel doors and palm scanners.

Barnes took him upstairs and introduced him to two team members who were working phones and computers. A large map of Yorkshire took up most of one wall. Pinned ribbons fanned out from various locations to photos and notes. Danny looked for the street they had been on and found a pin as expected. Only one ribbon was attached and it went to a blurry photo that had a dozen ribbons stringing off it.

'Our mystery man.' Barnes said, bringing over a coffee to Danny.

'That's all you've got?' Danny said, pointing at the photo.

'We're not even sure it's him. He's one of the suspects we picked up when we started trailing another guy. None of these locations are definitely linked to him. Maybe there's more than one person, we don't know. He was captured in that photo and linked to a safe house in Bradford, the one I told you about. When we went in it was as clean as the one we were in today.'

Barnes took a drink of his coffee. 'The house had obviously been used, but the paper trail was worthless. He'd paid cash up front, no problems for the landlord. His references had never been checked and the name he'd given and the references all proved false.'

'So how'd you link him to the house we were at today?'

'I'm guessing. A similar pattern. This time the landlord did try and check out the references, not as quickly as they should have done, but at least they tried. They then tried to contact mystery man but weren't able to and at that point they called the police.'

'An honest landlord…'

'Just wish they'd been more timely, might have gotten the surveillance team in place sooner. This is what I'm facing, Danny. Thousands of leads, most of which are just time wasters. In amongst it are a few radicals who intend us harm. If we arrested every suspect we'd probably cause a civil war. Some suspects, we know they're trouble but we can't arrest them because we need them to lead us to the real bad guys. The problems is, we usually don't know who the real bad guys are until we can properly investigate and that takes time.'

'So how do we deal with it?'

'This is where you come in. The war on terror isn't going to be won by my team, it's going to be won by you—the Counter Terrorism Security Adviser. We need people who understand the dangers, understand the risks and who can win over communities, business leaders, religious leaders. We need people working with the community who can act as an ambassador, feed back their concerns to us, share our concerns with them and come up with a plan to deny these terrorists support. Now, let me show you some of the cases we're working on…'

~~~

'Maybe we should all emigrate.'

Barnes laughed. 'That would be one option. We could all move to Saudi Arabia, upset the balance of power there and maybe launch our own takeover bid. Imagine it—more oil than the North Sea and 365 days a year sunshine.'

'I'd probably miss the rain.'

'I wouldn't.' Barnes shook his head to emphasize the point. 'So Danny, has any of this helped you with your decision?'

Danny walked back to the map of Yorkshire to look again at the attempts to identify suspects. 'I think I'd be more comfortable working with you.'

'Well, that is an option you could pursue…' He sighed. 'There is something else we need to cover today.' Barnes retrieved a plain white envelope from his desk and handed it to Danny.

'What's this, my Gas Safe certificate?'

When Barnes didn't laugh or answer, just stood and watched him, Danny felt uneasy. He opened the envelope and slid out…

'What are these?' He didn't need Barnes to answer. A quick shuffle through the photos left his mind reeling. 'Have you been following me?'

'You were flagged as a possible candidate for highly classified documents, Danny. Of course we followed you. Ms Henderson isn't it.'

Danny didn't answer.

'We just have photos from the outside of the flat, though that was interesting enough. Do you socialize with all members of your team in the evening, Detective Inspector?'

'Why are you showing me this?' Danny finally managed to say, letting his anger mask his confusion and fear.

'Consider it a friendly warning.' Barnes held his hands up defensively. 'Now, no need to look at me like that. I could have passed those straight onto your Chief Inspector. Rudd isn't it?'

Restraining himself, Danny took a slow breath. 'Why didn't you?'

'Now, what would be the point of wrecking a good man's career?'

'Is this some kind of blackmail?'

'No. There's no value to us or anyone in you being forced into anything. No, this is one professional to another telling you that you've crossed a line and you need to deal with it. Sooner, understand?'

'Why?' Danny shook his head. 'Why bring me here, spend so much time, give me all this information? I don't understand.'

'You're a good cop, Danny. At least according to your C.I. From the little I've seen of you today I think you'll make a difference in whatever you end up doing. I'm not telling you you've failed a test. But you have to know that continuing an affair with a colleague is like tap dancing in a mine field, sooner or later you're going to take a wrong step. Nobody's perfect. I'd probably be more suspicious of you if we hadn't dug anything up. Now shall I order in some lunch?'

Danny could only stare at him.

'You'll get over it,' Barnes assured him. 'Now I fancy Chinese. Remember, the government's paying...'

CHAPTER TWENTY-TWO
A Consultant Accountant

Zafar shook their hands and embraced them as his team left, Tariq letting them out of the house one by one. His team… The second meeting had gone much better, with a coherent plan being formed and each of them taking responsibility for different aspects. There was so much to do…

Tariq came back into the room. 'You should wait another ten minutes before leaving. How did you feel the meeting went?'

'It went well. I just wonder, is the timeline achievable?'

'It is better to have a sense of urgency. The longer we wait, the worse the situation gets for our people. I'm sure you've realised by now, for you to lead this mission will require your absolute focus. You can't hold down an ordinary job and devote yourself to the cause.'

'So I hand in my notice.' Zafar took a deep breath as he thought about the change this would bring to his life. 'That is not a problem.'

'You need to be careful though, not to attract suspicion.'

'So I don't start wearing a Kaftan,' Zafar laughed.

Tariq remained serious. 'What we are proposing to do… If anyone suspects, they may inform the authorities and they will not stop until they have hunted us down.'

'I understand.'

'Good. You need a cover story. We have a company set up for this purpose, we use it to channel funds in and out of the country. They can offer you a contract—doing what you have been doing to all intents and purposes.'

'A consultant? A consultant accountant…' Zafar could not stop a smile, but sobered as Tariq's expression remained steady.

'Yes, a consultant position, well paid with the opportunity to travel and reason enough to justify leaving your current role.'

'I will have to give notice though. A month.'

'Do they owe you holidays?'

Zafar shook his head slowly as he thought how he had focused solely on his work after Shireen's death. He had even resisted taking the offered public holidays. 'I must be entitled to three full weeks.'

'Then you can start your new job in a week. In the meantime, I think we should start you recruiting at nearby universities. I can arrange some events in the evenings so as not to interfere with your work.'

Zafar felt his stomach clench at the thought of standing up in front of an audience. 'What will I say?'

'I can help you prepare something short. We will show my documentary and we should invite our brothers to join a civil defence group we are setting up. It should tie in well with the documentary and if word does get out, we can simply say we are running patrols round Muslim communities to protect our people from the acts of violence they are experiencing.'

'And it allows us to identify those who feel defence is not enough...' Zafar said, admiring the elegance of the idea. 'Very well, we should make a start so I can practise this weekend.'

CHAPTER TWENTY-THREE
Slug and Lettuce

Emma almost walked out when she saw Jennifer and Paul were in the pub. 'You didn't tell me you'd invited them,' she whispered to Rachel.

'What's the problem?'

'You know what the problem is.'

'Get over yourself. I'll have a large wine.'

Rachel left her. Emma watched as she walked over to Jennifer and Paul then hurriedly turned away as they looked over at her. Going to the bar she ordered herself a J2O, uncertain whether she should be drinking. This is a mistake, she thought while carrying their drinks over to the table.

Jennifer was pointedly looking away from her while Paul seemed to be fascinated with a beer mat. Rachel had sat next to Paul leaving Emma with no choice but to sit next to Jennifer.

'How was your day, Rachel?' Jennifer asked.

'Just killing time. Meeting with the Union on Monday and I'm fairly hopeful they'll put pressure on the hospital. How about you?'

'Too many patients and too few staff.'

Emma exchanged a glance with Rachel and was relieved when she didn't respond.

'And how about you Emma?' Jennifer asked.

Emma almost choked on her drink. 'What?'

'How are you? Have you recovered after your accident?'

'Well...'

'Rachel tells me you've been out and about almost every day.'

Emma looked at Rachel who shrugged.

'She did? I mean, yes. I've been doing a lot of walking.'

'So you're fully recovered?'

'I, uh, I guess so.'

'I'm so glad.' Jennifer gave her a sickly smile and then, without warning, slapped Emma hard across the face. 'I wouldn't want to hit a cripple now, would I.'

Emma gasped and put a hand up to her cheek.

'Paul told me what happened that night. We almost broke up because of you.'

Emma saw Paul shift uncomfortably, still studying his beermat.

'Have you anything to say?' Jennifer asked, her voice cold.

Emma looked again at Paul and back to Jennifer. 'I'm sorry.'

'I hope so.' Jennifer stood. 'Come on Paul.' She gathered up her phone and purse while Paul stood. 'I thought you were a friend,' Jennifer said to Emma. 'See you Rachel.'

Emma watched them walk out the pub. Paul hadn't said a word.

'Time was when you'd have slapped her back,' Rachel said, bringing Emma's attention back. 'You really are out of sorts.'

'Did you know Paul had told her?'

'News to me, though I have to say, you sooo deserved that. How does it feel to be the other woman?'

'We're going to have to stop hanging round with them.'

'Speak for yourself. I still get on fine with Jennifer. Nice to see she can hold her own too. Look, you messed up. Maybe she can forgive you. Not that I would, but hey!'

'Thanks a bunch.'

Rachel gave her a wry smile then went solemn. 'Seriously though, if you ever cheated with my boyfriend... I'd put you back in hospital.'

'Fair enough. I think I'm off men for the foreseeable future.'

'Good. Now are you going to have a real drink?'

Emma shook her head.

'Suit yourself.'

CHAPTER TWENTY-FOUR
Break Up

He'd asked her if he could come round that evening, told her to take an early night. As he walked from his car to her flat he couldn't help looking round to see if anyone was watching. No-one that he could see.

She had changed into a dress. Had glasses set out with wine. She kissed him when he walked into the flat and he knew then that he wanted her.

Danny took Natalie's arms and gently pushed her away. 'We need to talk.'

'I thought talking was something we didn't do…'

'Please.' He lifted the briefcase. 'I need to show you this.'

'A present?'

He guided her to the sofa and opened the briefcase. Took out the envelope and passed it to her.

Natalie laughed as she pulled out the photos. 'What are these!' Then her smile faded. 'Is this what I think it is?'

He nodded.

'So what?' She tossed the photos on the coffee table. 'Are you worried? This isn't going to hurt you.'

'You're right. At worst I'll be the butt of jokes for the next few years. Maybe they won't be so quick to promote me, but plenty of senior officers have had affairs.'

'Don't call it that.'

'They would understand, maybe not in public, but long term I would still progress.'

'So what's the problem? Worried about Cynthia?'

Danny ignored that jibe. 'It ruins your career.'

'How?'

Did she not see it? 'How do you think you've advanced so quickly?'

'Not because of you!'

'Do you really think anyone else is going to see it that way? You are promoted faster than all your colleagues, reach detective grade younger than anyone else currently. No-one's going to care how brilliant you are, or how hard you've worked. They're just going to see these pictures and the word will be you only got where you are because you were sleeping with your superiors.'

Natalie grabbed the pictures, tore them up. 'These aren't proof. Just you and me walking from a flat. Could be anywhere. An investigation.'

'If someone was able to take these, what else have they been able to take? How long have they been following us? How much more do they know?'

'What? You think there is more?'

'Rudd asked me to take a new job. Counter Terrorism Security Advisor.'

'You never mentioned it.'

You're not my wife, Danny thought. Though she still doesn't know either... He looked away.

'What has this got to do with anything? You won't be my boss anymore...'

'I had to meet with MI5.'

She stared at him. He could see her frown as she linked the threads. 'You think they're spying on us?' She looked around. 'Could they have bugged my flat!'

He looked up, scanned the corners of the room, the furniture and wall hangings. 'We have equipment to check in the station.'

Natalie stood, folding her arms. 'Why are you here?'

He stood as well. 'It's over.'

She didn't say anything for a time. Just stared at him. He couldn't read her at all.

'Then you better leave.' She finally said.

'You're an excellent detective.'

'I am.'

'But I won't be recommending you for promotion. Not unless I'm asked. I will give you an excellent reference.'

She turned away. 'I said you should go.'

He looked at the pieces of photos. 'Do you want me to dispose of them?'

Natalie shook her head. 'They'll have copies.'

'They will.'
'I'll handle it.'
He left.

CHAPTER TWENTY-FIVE
Weaponry

The quality of the road was the first giveaway. An unused base would not have required a wide and smooth surface such as the one he drove on towards Acaster Malbis airport. Had he made a wrong turn? His research had shown the former RAF base had been decommissioned in the 1960s having been used to store ammunition and explosives following the end of the war.

He slowed as he saw a turn off for the entrance to the base. The checkpoint confirmed he was in the right place but had been wrong about the military base being abandoned.

It paid to have a cover story for such situations and Philippe had been glad his was more than a superficial one. He had started his Abandoned Bases blog when he first moved to the UK, recording his explorations of decommissioned RAF and Army bases round the country. This very public log allowed him to make contact with former military personnel who were often eager to discuss what their lives had been like when stationed at these bases. While mostly boring and of no value, sometimes these conversations and visits had revealed insights into the military mindset that Philippe intended to exploit.

Only one sentry was on duty in a small hut, watching him as he drove up to the gate, no-one else visible. Philippe casually looked around taking in the details of the nearby buildings and hangers while the sentry walked over to his car. Philippe wound down his window.

'What's the purpose of your visit?' The sentry asked.

'I must have made a mistake, I thought the base was no longer in use,' Philippe told him. 'I was hoping to do some research for my blog.' He fished in his pocket for a business card and handed one to the sentry.

'Abandoned Bases?'

'That's right, you can check it out. It's quite popular with military personnel.'

'Well, as you can see, we are very much in use.'

The sentry stepped back and Philippe knew his time was limited.

'Was the base decommissioned in the 1960s?' Philippe asked. He saw the sentry frowning in thought.

'I don't know.'

'It would be fascinating to find out. If so, it would be the first abandoned base I'd found that was later re-commissioned. My readers would love to hear about that. Would there be someone on the base I could interview?'

'I... I'll pass your request on.'

'That would be really helpful,' Philippe smiled. 'My name and contact number are on the card.' He knew it was time to leave. 'Should I just reverse here?'

Philippe waved as he drove off, seeing the sentry examine his card. You never knew whether the lure would hook a catch but regardless of whether anyone contacted him the trip had revealed something valuable—a military base that wasn't showing up in the public records. Now that was interesting...

~~~

'The AK-47. Nothing else comes close.'

'Heckler & Koch MP7. Far superior in close combat situations and designed to penetrate body armour.'

'How about the Uzi?' Zafar suggested.

Mohammed and Philippe looked at him in disdain.

'An Israeli gun?' Asked Mohammed, his tone derisory.

Zafar tensed.

'It is an effective weapon,' Tariq reminded them.

'The AK-47 will penetrate body armour as well,' Philippe directed at Mohammed.

'But it is so bulky and noisy! Difficult to aim accurately.'

'You think the MP7 is more accurate? I've seen recruits empty a clip and fail to hit the target.'

As the discussion quickly moved on, Zafar told himself to relax. Philippe and Mohammed obviously had more experience with guns than he did and he would need to trust all of his men for their plans to succeed. This was the first of several sub-meetings to deal with specific elements in greater detail. Tariq had requested this meeting first as he had an opportunity to meet with an arms dealer and had recommended Philippe and Mohammed as experts.

'We will be in close combat while we're taking the city,' Mohammed replied. 'The MP7 is far superior when there is less room.'

'Close combat? We're not going to be going room to room!' Philippe laughed in derision. 'We'll be fighting in the streets, if we fight at all. And what about defensively? The AK-47 will be far more useful when we have clear lines of sight down a street.'

'Not at long distance. Even skilled warriors need a rifle with a scope to accurately hit targets at a distance.'

'Where did you train? I was taught to fire the Lee-Enfield accurately over 500 metres with no scope.'

Mohammed sighed. 'We will not all need to be snipers.'

'We will if we want to defend the city for any length of time. There may only be a few major roads into York but there are dozens of routes the army and police could use to infiltrate the city.' Philippe took a map of York that was lying to the side and spread it out over the tablecloth. 'Look here. There is no defensive wall, just a stretch of river that special forces could swim down and climb out at any point.'

'So we block it up with trolley carts or something.'

Philippe sighed in frustration. 'The point isn't that we stop people swimming down the river but that defending the city will not be easy. Especially for longer than a few days. Zafar, you know we will not be able to hold the city forever, don't you?'

Zafar saw that they all were looking directly at him.

'Zafar...' Tariq spoke. 'How long will we hold the city for?'

He had been thinking of nothing else for days but had had no opportunity to share the thoughts going round his head. Not being able to write things down was proving a struggle, especially not being able to use a spreadsheet to organise and plan. 'We follow the same model used to establish the Caliphate. We subdue a city, give them the option to convert or make them pay the jizya and then move onto the next.'

Tariq nodded, whether in approval or agreement Zafar couldn't tell.

'We must be able to move at short notice,' Zafar continued. 'But will have to hold the city for a few days at least. Philippe, you are right to identify threats and weaknesses in the city defences. We will need to allocate extra resources to defend those areas. What would you recommend we need in terms of weapons and equipment?'

Philippe gestured towards Mohammed. 'The MP7 is a good gun. In the right hands it can be used effectively. But it is not a long distance weapon. We would also need rifles and I am conscious that we will find it difficult to effectively train enough people especially if we have to train them to use multiple guns. I believe we will need very little equipment. Too much and inexperienced men will become confused and hesitate. We will need explosives to help block some of the roads but much of that can be done effectively by simply forcing people out of their cars. I propose that most of the men are simply trained to effectively use one gun. One that is suitable both for close combat and distance use. We identify men who have additional skills who can be trained as snipers and also those who can be trusted to plant explosives.'

'Mohammed?' Zafar asked.

'I still dislike the AK-47 but if the men can be trained only to fire single shots it becomes much more accurate. Philippe is right about inexperience.' His eyes took on a distant look as he continued. 'I lost three men on a raid when one of them dropped a grenade he was about to throw and tried to pick it up instead of warning the other men to run for cover. We also need to ensure that everyone knows where everyone else is supposed to be. The last thing we want is our own men firing on each other.' Mohammed paused while he thought. 'I can identify and train men to use explosives. We should also plan to set traps for the inevitable assault that will come. How long do you think we will have before they send in the army?'

'I am working on a contingency plan that will hopefully slow the infidels down,' Tariq answered. 'You will forgive me that I don't explain what that is.'

'What about the citizens of York,' Philippe said. 'Is it our plan to kill those who will neither convert nor pay the jizya?'

'The Quran has always been clear that we are to fight against those who will do neither,' said Zafar. 'They will be given the option, but if they refuse, it will be on their heads.'

CHAPTER TWENTY-SIX
The King's Judgement

'I can't believe you didn't go and see Mary this week.' Cynthia stared straight ahead. Danny couldn't read her expression as he glanced at her then returned his attention to the road ahead. He slowed as they approached the narrow gate that granted access to St Andrew's Parish church on Fishergate.

'Rudd had me chasing my tail. I lost two full days and couldn't spare the time.'

'She's your God Mother...' Cynthia tailed off as he pulled into the small car park. The only benefit Danny could see to arriving early was that he didn't have to use a car park half a mile away. 'We'll talk about it later,' she continued.

'I'm sure we will,' Danny replied. He ignored her look as he turned the car and parked. The fact that Cynthia refused to argue with him when they were at church normally irritated him, but today he found himself relieved that she was so willing to drop the "discussion" for a couple of hours.

Cynthia opened the church building and she and Danny set out the chairs in silence. He hadn't been convinced that spending so much money on ripping out the old pews and buying new chairs was a good idea, but they were a lot more comfortable, and the building was in use during the week now that they had the space.

So much had changed since he had come here as a boy, he reflected. He'd seen two Reverend's come and go, the latest seemed only half his age. There had been a time when he'd enjoyed the weekly visit to church, the singing especially. When had that changed? Danny looked towards the front where a drum set stood surrounded by cables used by the rest of the worship band. Was it a sign of age that he missed the old hymns? That he thought some of the songs they now sang had little, or no, relevance to what he had always understood worship to be.

He helped Cynthia finish setting up the building and then left her to stand at the front door. Tony usually arrived quite early himself and he intended to have a quick chat with him about Mary.

Forty minutes later, Danny was checking his watch every few seconds and had moved to stand out on the street. He'd said hello and good morning to over eighty people as they'd filed past him into the building, all the time looking past them for Tony's car. Tony hadn't answered his two phone calls or responded to his texts and he realised he was starting to worry about him.

'What are you doing out here?'

Danny started at the sound of Cynthia's voice behind him. He turned and saw she didn't look as worried as he did. 'Tony's late. Very late. Is this normal?'

'No, but I'm sure he'll be here soon.'

'How do you know? He hasn't answered my calls or texts.'

Cynthia actually laughed. Danny gave her a puzzled look.

'He never takes a mobile phone with him to church. Don't you know that?'

He shook his head. 'Why…'

'He says he's worried it might go off in the middle of his sermon, but actually… I think he just doesn't want to be distracted from God. Sunday morning's really important to him.'

Danny checked his watch. Three minutes to ten. 'Maybe I should drive back to his house…'

Cynthia shook her head. 'He'll be along soon. We can start without him.'

'Can you?'

'Can we, Danny. The answer's yes, by the way.' She took his hand and gently pulled him towards the building.

Danny couldn't tell if anyone else was concerned by Tony's absence. The worship team started the service on time and hearty singing soon echoed from the ancient stone walls. A full ten minutes after the worship had started, Danny finally turned and saw Tony was standing at the back of the church. He looked out of breath but was still joining in the singing. Tony noticed Danny looking at him and inclined his head in acknowledgment.

As the worship ended, Tony made his way to the front. 'Thank you to the worship team as always,' he said. 'And my apologies for my late arrival.' He held up his hands and Danny saw they were filthy. 'As you can see I've had some manual labour this morning, courtesy of a flat tyre. I wasn't sure whether to try and replace it or make a run for the church and in the end did both!'

A woman with a young child stood and offered Tony a packet of wipes which he took gratefully. Then, making his way to the lectern, he opened the heavy bible and found his place.

'Thank you, Ellen. The reading this morning will be from Luke's Gospel, chapter nineteen, verses twelve to twenty seven. Therefore Jesus said: 'A certain nobleman went into a far country to receive for himself a kingdom and to return...'

Danny listened with half an ear. Tony could deliver some good sermons. He had a flare for the dramatic and Danny had so far been unable to fault his logic. It had made coming to the church more interesting after the previous vicar had retired, though Danny was aware that there was an edge to some of what Tony said from the pulpit. Interesting was being tempered by something that made Danny uncomfortable and had made it easier to stay away.

Tony's voice was rising as he read about the king's judgement over the wicked servant. 'You knew that I was an austere man, collecting what I did not deposit and reaping what I did not sow. Why then did you not put my money in the bank, that at my coming I might have collected it with interest?'

Why not indeed, thought Danny. Would be nice to have some money in the bank to collect interest on. He smiled at the thought as Tony rounded off with: 'But bring here those enemies of mine who did not want me to reign over them, and slay them before me!'

Tony's ending shout echoed round the small church and Danny quickly glanced round. Hard to tell from the backs of their heads but from Cynthia's expression, he was sure Tony had made an impact. Perhaps he would manage to pay attention to the rest of the sermon.

~~~

'What is Jesus telling us through this parable?' Tony was striding back and forth at the front now, notes held loosely in his left hand while his right gestured with every point. 'It is difficult to pin down and I think that was intentional. I didn't read the verse before the parable, let's look at it now.'

Danny watched Tony walk smartly up to the lectern and smiled at his theatrics. Stop, start, skip back. His sermons were never dull.

'He spoke another parable...' Tony paused and looked up. 'Why? Because he was near Jerusalem and because they thought the kingdom of God would appear immediately!' Tony started striding again. 'But that begs another why. It doesn't really answer our question. To understand "what"

Jesus is telling us through the parable, it is sometimes, not always, but sometimes important to understand "why." And I believe this is one of those times.

'Was Jesus simply trying to distract the people? Give them something to think about so they wouldn't start a riot? Perhaps he was sending a message that they should not be so quick to desire his Kingdom. The parable is one of Jesus darker stories and one to think long and hard about. Or was Jesus actually speaking directly to anyone who desired his Kingdom to start and explaining to them what he was going to be looking for?

'Jesus describes his future Kingdom in many ways. The Kingdom of Heaven is like a mustard seed, The Kingdom of Heaven is like a lamp on a hill. But here, he says his Kingdom will be like… a kingdom! It will have a king. And some people will not like that king. And some people will resent that king. Others will respect the king and be rewarded for their faithfulness with… What? By being given small kingdoms of their own. This parable could easily be turned into a soap opera, an episode of Game of Thrones.

Tony stopped his striding and walked slowly down so he was in between the first rows. Those sitting there had to turn their heads to see him. 'Jesus is telling us that his future Kingdom will be very much based on what happens now. Rewards for those who are faithful, punishment for those who hate Him. In the end, in this parable, those who hated the king lost their heads! No more gentle Jesus meek and mild!'

Danny shifted uneasily in his seat.

'Jesus talks about Hell elsewhere in several situations. It would be a terrible mistake to simply write it off and think that our loving Lord would never send anyone to Hell, especially us. But I digress.' Tony smiled. 'A topic for another day, and one I'm sure you all will be as fascinated as I am to explore. What we do and how we act now has consequences in eternity. Are we miserly and fearful towards God now, or are we willing to take risks, to use the small gifts that God has given us?

'Jesus wants us to be risk takers, to be bold in our prayers, to ask him and believe for impossible things. To do small acts of charity whenever they are available for us to do. To forgive the unforgivable, to extend hands of friendship to those who are despised by the world. To stand up for the oppressed, and also, always, to stand up for the name of Jesus.'

Danny watched, captivated, as Tony bowed his head for a brief instant, then looked up and smiled at them. 'Let us pray.' Tony lifted his hands. 'Father, protect us as we leave this place, guard our hearts and our minds. Whatever has been from you this morning, let it grow in us and strengthen us. Let us say the grace together…'

~~~

'Danny! I've been wanting to talk with you.' Tony took Danny's hand and gave a firm shake.

'I was wanting to talk with you, Tony. About Mary. Would you have a few minutes now?'

Tony examined Danny closely, his grip around Danny's hand steady. 'I think we will need more than a few minutes, how about this evening?'

'I could see you this evening. Shall I come round to your house?'

'How about a more neutral setting,' Tony smiled. 'Perhaps The Walnut Tree in Heworth, first round on me. Are you on duty tonight?'

'Not tonight, no,' Danny said, taken aback at the offer.

'That's settled then. How about eight o'clock?'

'I'll see you then...' Danny said hesitantly, suddenly uncertain what he had just agreed to.

CHAPTER TWENTY-SEVEN
The Walnut Tree

The taxi dropped Danny off outside The Walnut Tree and he stood for a moment looking to see where the tree that had given the pub it's name had stood. It hadn't been all that mature a tree he recalled, only fifty years old or so yet it had still made the front page of the Evening Press after being hit by a lorry and needing to be cut down.

He saw Tony walking up looking calmer than Danny felt. Easy now, he told himself. Neutral ground was probably a good idea after all.

'Good to see you, Danny. First round on me, remember.'

'If you insist, Rev.'

Danny ordered a pint of John Smith's with Tony following suit then they carried their drinks outside onto the patio.

'That is a good pint,' Danny said downing almost a quarter of his glass in one go.

'Very good,' Tony agreed, setting his own glass down. 'It always puzzles me how some pints seem to be almost perfect, then they change the barrel and something is lost. Do you get much of a chance to unwind from your job?'

'Not often, no. To be honest I don't even like taking a holiday. Always feel like I'm needed.'

'I know what you mean. It's difficult stepping away.' Tony took another drink. 'How long have you been a Christian, Danny?'

'I, uh…' The question threw him off balance. 'I suppose most of my life.'

'You must have made a decision at some point though?'

He hadn't thought about that in years. 'I guess when I was a child.'

'You guess?' Tony gave him a broad smile. 'Most people are quite certain when they decided to follow Jesus. Have you been filled with the Holy Spirit?'

'I'm not used to being on the other end of an interrogation...'

'Do you feel this is an interrogation?' Tony asked.

'Strangely enough, yes.'

'I see. I just thought we were getting to know each other. You know, we haven't really spoken since I started here.'

'We've talked before.'

'Well, said hello… Exchanged small talk… Not spoken though. Do you feel you know me?'

Danny studied the man sitting opposite him. He looked relaxed and at ease even while wearing his dog collar and drinking a pint. 'No, I suppose I don't.'

'Well, what would you like to know?'

Danny took another draught of his pint. It really was a good batch. 'Okay, why did you want to become a vicar?'

Tony laughed. 'Good question. I mean, why would anyone want to become a vicar! Except, for me, once I became a Christian I couldn't imagine wanting to do anything else. If part of being a Christian is serving God, then it seemed the logical thing to actually give my life to serving the church. How about you, Danny? Why become a detective?'

Danny started to answer, then realised he wasn't sure what he wanted to say. 'I suppose it's similar,' he said hesitantly. 'In a way. I can't really remember when or why I decided I wanted to join the police, but I always remember being drawn to the idea of being a detective.'

'It seemed like you were made for it?'

'Or it was made for me, maybe.' Danny took another drink and then set down his glass, placing his hands on the table. 'Look, I have to say, it seems… Cruel, what you did to Mary.'

'I see.'

'She's given her whole life to the church, almost like you, except it has been her whole life. She's in her Sixties now.'

'I haven't given up on Mary and you need to understand that I gave her every chance to repent.'

'But what did she need to "repent" of?'

'There is so much I don't really know about you, Danny. I know you have a senior position, but do you have anyone working underneath you?'

Danny felt himself tense at Tony's choice of words. 'I have a team that report to me.'

'Then how would you feel if a member of your team, behind your back, actively tried to get you fired? Would you laugh it off? Would you ignore it?'

'No, but that's…'

'Different? No, it isn't. In fact, it's much worse what Mary did. This is God's church and the one thing Jesus was absolutely insistent on was that we should make every effort to be one body. It would utterly destroy your team if you had a person acting like Mary did. Could you keep working with them?'

'I'd have it out with them.'

'Of course. But if they kept doing it. Kept trying to undermine your authority and turn your team against you…'

Natalie could do that, Danny admitted to himself. She had a reason. Maybe it would bring down her career as well, but if she wanted she could whisper in ears, make suggestions and punish him in some way for dumping her. Or any of them could, people he considered friends. People he had entrusted his life to. And if they did… There was no easy way to deal with it. You would have to have it out with them however ugly that turned out. And if they continued, you couldn't just fire them. That would require a disciplinary process that would prompt the question—why couldn't you deal with your team? Aren't you capable of resolving conflict? It could kill a person's career. Maybe you could get that person transferred, but if so, what if they didn't stop? What if they kept on trying to undermine you. You would have lost control of the ability to discipline the person… He realised Tony was sitting back, watching him. 'Thankfully I've never had to deal with that.'

'You realise I am having to deal with it?'

'But this is Mary…'

'I know, and she is very important to you and to Cynthia and to many of us at the church, yes, even to me, Danny. You know Cynthia came with me when I went to speak to her?'

'She said.' Danny didn't want to think back to what Cynthia had said.

'Do you understand why I excluded Mary from the church, Danny?'

'As I said, I think it's cruel.'

Tony looked down at his glass, now half full and then picked it up. Held it up towards the sunset. 'You never answered my question before. Have you been filled with the Holy Spirit?'

'What has that got to do with…'

'You know it's a free gift, right,' Tony interrupted. 'The Holy Spirit. God wants every one of his children to receive the gift of his presence.'

'Okay, so I've not received the Holy Spirit, so what?'

'God doesn't hold back his gifts from us. We choose not to receive them. Forgiveness, salvation, peace, hope, joy… these are all ours for the taking. But we do have to let go of sin, let go of whatever idol we're clinging onto otherwise we can't take hold of what God is offering. It's like this glass. If it was full of water, I couldn't pour any of this fine beer in. And, even if it was only half full of water, any beer you poured in would be diluted.'

'So you're saying that I'm…'

'I thought we were talking about Mary.'

Danny shook his head. 'It still seems cruel.'

'I can't make Mary repent, Danny, just as I can't make you or anyone else in the church turn from whatever sin you might be holding onto. But that doesn't mean it is kind or loving or compassionate to allow someone to carry on doing what they're doing. Excluding Mary from the church was the hardest decision I've ever had to make and my prayer is that it will allow her to realise just how wrong her actions have been and for her to choose to repent.'

'But leaving her on her own like that…'

'She's not on her own, Danny. God is still with her—if she'll listen to him. I'm praying for her as I'm sure you and Cynthia are doing. In fact, we should pray for her this evening, but before we do I really wanted to ask you one question tonight. Who is watching your back, Danny?'

'What do you mean?'

'You are a Christian in one of the most high pressured jobs in the country. You deal with evil every day. Who do you have praying for you, supporting you through what you have to deal with?'

Feeling like someone had just pulled the ground from under his feet, Danny heard himself say: 'No-one's ever asked me that before.'

CHAPTER TWENTY-EIGHT
Encounter

'Mr Thomson, do you have a minute?' Zafar asked as Douglas Thomson put his phone down.

'Mr Thomson? Very formal, Zafar.' Zafar mentally kicked himself as Douglas continued. 'How can I help?'

Zafar held out an envelope containing his resignation letter. 'I've been offered a job,' he said as Douglas took the envelope.

'I see,' Douglas said looking first at the envelope, then up at Zafar and finally looking round the office. 'Let's get a meeting room, shall we.'

He led Zafar to an empty room off of the main office and sat opposite Zafar. For a moment he studied Zafar while tapping the unopened envelope on the table. 'This is…' he asked holding the envelope up slightly.

'My letter of resignation.'

'I see.' Douglas restarted the tapping before laying the envelope down and leaning forward. 'I wasn't aware you were unhappy here.'

'I wasn't, I mean… I'm not.'

'Could we offer you anything to stay?'

Zafar took a deep breath then shook his head. 'No.'

'It must be a really good job offer.' Douglas looked at the envelope as if it held the details.

'It is.'

'Who is it with?'

'Croydon Group.'

'I've not heard of them, what do they do?'

'A mixture of property investment and import, export.'

'Quite different to here.'

'Well, it's still accountancy at heart.'

Douglas nodded, adjusting the position of the envelope. 'What are they offering you?' He asked bluntly.

Tariq had told him he would receive £4,000 a month. It was over a fifty percent increase on his current salary which was enough to be reluctant to turn it down, but within reason for a consultant on a short term contract. He told Douglas who raised his eyebrows at the amount.

'Is there a pension on top of that?' Douglas asked.

'No. It's a consultant role. Just for six months.'

'You're giving up a permanent job here for a six month contract? That's quite risky, isn't it?'

'It seems like too good an opportunity to pass up.'

'Is it just about the money?'

'I'll be based abroad for several months, Europe and America.'

'That could be… exciting.' Douglas' tone sounded flat. 'It just seems out of the blue…'

Zafar held Douglas' gaze, feeling uncomfortable as Douglas let the moment draw out. Eventually he felt he had to say something else. 'Ever since… Things have not been the same since my wife…' he trailed off.

'I understand,' Douglas nodded.

Zafar felt himself bristle at the look of pity Douglas gave him. He tried to hide it.

Douglas picked up the envelope and opened it. Frowned as he read the letter. 'One week's notice!'

'I've hardly taken any holidays this year.'

'We'll gladly compensate you for them, but one week, you need to give us at least a month's notice.'

'I am.'

'Not if you take your holidays before you leave. We won't have time to recruit anyone to replace you.'

Zafar didn't respond. He was thinking about a couple of years before when the company decided to "rationalise" and had ended up making a hundred people redundant across the country. Two people from his office had been given notice and as he remembered it, they had not been given a chance to negotiate their leaving date.

Douglas pressed him and tried to get Zafar to show some flexibility but Zafar stuck to Tariq's advice and held his ground saying as little as possible until eventually Douglas gave up.

~~~

She woke without remembering the dream, felt closer to normal than

140

she had in days. Rachel had left before she woke and Emma busied herself getting ready to go out. She redid her nails, put on her makeup, checked herself and decided she was ready.

The clock on the wall showed half past nine. Time to get a coffee on the way, she thought to herself.

The summer was turning out glorious, the blue sky lighting up the city as she walked into York. Emma turned the corner intending to stop at Costa Coffee and halted in shock. He was there, walking towards her. Dirty blond hair down to his shoulders. An unkempt beard of the same colour. He was wearing an overcoat despite the warmth in the air. Underneath he had a suit on, a charcoal that was closer to black than grey. A pullover under the suit jacket with a shirt collar not quite sitting straight.

His eyes were a light blue flecked with grey. The sun was full in his face and his eyes seemed to reflect the light. He was looking in her direction, but hadn't noticed her.

Just before he was about to walk past she held up her hand to stop him. 'Please…' she said.

He looked then but she saw no recognition in his eyes. 'I've nothing to give you,' he said.

She wasn't ready to talk to him, not that she had ever known what she wanted to say. Are you him? Are you the one who found me? Images from Rachel's description flew through her thoughts.

His eyes narrowed. 'I don't want any trouble.'

'I fell, Monk Bar. A man found me. Last week. Are you him?' She was rushing her words, almost stumbling in her need to make him understand.

He was searching her face now, eyes flicking back and forth and he stepped back. 'You, I thought you… I didn't think he answered. You're alive!' He grasped her arms and gave her a broad smile. 'You're alive!'

'Of course I am. I only bumped my head.' Why would he say that?

His expression turned quizzical. The smile remained but softened. His eyes seemed less intense.

'Forgive me,' he said. 'It must have been a shock for you.'

'Knocked me out cold.'

Again that questioning look passed across his face and then was gone. She noticed he was speaking slower now that he had calmed down. Every word considered.

'I see.'

He was looking past her now. Emma tried to focus, worried he might just walk away. 'I just wanted to ask a few questions. You didn't stay.'

'A woman attacked me. Seemed to think I was hurting you.'

Emma felt her mouth dry up. She forced the words out. 'Were you?'

Now he looked hurt.

'No. Of course not.'

'What were you doing?'

He was solely focused on her now. She felt as if the world was telescoping in on itself.

'Praying for you.'

'Why… What…' She didn't know how to form the question. Rachel's words still fresh in her memory. 'Were you on top of me?'

'I was.'

'Why?'

He sighed, long and drawn out. 'I think we should find somewhere to sit down. I would offer you a coffee but…' He held out his hands and gave her a rueful smile.

'I was going to buy a coffee, I could buy you a coffee.'

'I'm not usually welcome in most cafés.'

'Aren't you? Why?'

'You ask a lot of questions.' He stepped to one side and gestured for her to walk with him. 'I'm homeless.'

'So?'

'So we tend to be shunned by some who want to maintain the illusion that York is a prosperous city. Some deserve to be excluded of course, no-one likes being near someone who doesn't wash or make an effort to dress in half decent clothes.'

Emma looked him up and down again. His clothes were old but clean. Although his hair was a dirty blond and looked uncombed, he could have had a shower that morning and just not bothered to use a comb. Or a brush. Assuming he had a comb or a brush and Emma doubted he did.

'Do you sleep on the streets?'

'Sometimes. If it's dry and not too cold. Otherwise I look for shelter. There is a hostel for the homeless. Sometimes I make use of it.'

He stopped outside Costa Coffee. 'You can get coffee to take away here.'

'You're not coming in?'

'I'll just sit over there.' He pointed to a bench underneath a tree.

She hesitated, worrying that if she went inside he would walk away and she'd never see him again.

'I'll have a tea. White with two sugars. I don't drink coffee anymore.'

'Tea?'

'I'll wait.' He gave her a gentle smile as if he knew what she was thinking.

Emma watched him turn and walk over to the bench and forced herself to go into the café. She ordered two teas and once she had paid, watched him through the window. He was still, not looking about, not fidgeting. She'd had the same sense from him while he answered her questions. At least, after he had calmed down.

Her phone buzzed just as the Barrista brought the teas to the counter. Emma swiped to reject the call without looking. She grabbed some packets of sugar and balanced one cup on top of the other to allow her to open the door.

'Here...' she said as she offered him the top cup. 'I got some sugar, oh!'

'What's wrong?'

'I forgot stirrers.' She looked back at the café.

'Don't worry about it.'

'Are you sure?'

He held out his hand for the sugar and she gave him the packets. He set his cup on the bench and emptied two packets in, slipping the others into a pocket of his coat. Then he set the lid back on the cup, put his thumb over the drinking hole and shook the tea cup.

'Doesn't that hurt?'

He didn't answer. Just put his thumb to his lips to remove the tea.

'You can sit down,' he said. 'I won't bite.'

Embarrassed, she sat next to him. She took the lid off her own cup and sat looking at the hot liquid. Why had she bought herself tea? The weather was too warm. She never drank tea when it was warm. Coffee sure, but not tea.

'You asked me what I was doing?'

She nodded.

'You said you bumped your head?'

She wanted to say that was right. I bumped my head... banged it, knocked it, hit it. She searched his eyes which seemed to be doing the same to hers. Questioning her, asking...

'What happened to me?'

'When I found you, you had no pulse. There was blood all round your head. You looked like you had fallen from the wall.'

'No! That's not possible. There was no wound. They didn't find a wound.'

'I prayed for you. At first I didn't really believe it would help but...' He looked away. Was he remembering? 'I called out to God and he answered. I felt I needed to lie over you, like Elisha did when he healed the boy.'

An image of him straddling her filled her thoughts. It made no sense.

'God brought you back. It wasn't me, I know it wasn't me but he heard me and he healed you and even though I didn't know, he saved you.' He put a hand on her arm. She felt herself stiffen.

He withdrew his hand. 'I'm sorry. You don't know who I am.'

'I thought you could tell me what happened. Explain what you were doing. But nothing you say makes any sense. What has God got to do with any of this? What do you mean he brought me back? I hit my head, that's all.'

The man sat back and set his tea down beside him. 'If that's what you want to believe, I...' He shook his head.

'It's not what I want to believe, it's what happened!'

He didn't disagree with her, just held her gaze.

'It is what happened, isn't it?'

'You asked me what I was doing. You asked me why. When I found you, you were not breathing. You had no pulse. Do you need me to say it?'

'I think you'd better!'

'You were dead.'

'No. No! That's impossible. That just doesn't happen.'

'With God all things are possible. I'd stopped believing that but seeing you...'

'No,' she interrupted. 'Don't say that. I'm not getting conned by you. I, I need to go.' She stood abruptly and walked away, scared to turn round in case he was following her.

CHAPTER TWENTY-NINE
Fallout

Calvin watched her go without making any effort to stop her. He hadn't had time to think, had just been so shocked to see her and then the realization she didn't know what had happened... He didn't want her to be hurt again.

And now she was gone and he didn't even know her name. Why hadn't he asked? It had been too much. He had been completely unprepared for her to walk up to him, full of life, so beautiful. He had not been able to explain to her. How could he have? How do you tell a person they have been brought back from the dead? Someone who has never known God, someone who has no understanding of God's power?

He whispered a plea for God to protect her, to guide her, to lead her to Jesus. He could not go chasing after her. She owed him nothing. He had been obedient and she was well, that was all that mattered.

Except, it wasn't all. There was another...

~~~

'MI5 sent back good feedback on your training day.'

Danny nodded politely at Rudd, the images from the photos fresh in his mind.

'Based on your service record, the feedback from the ARGUS group and from MI5, you show the ability to take control of difficult situations, to ask probing questions, to take the lead in building relationships and also that you are able to grasp the complexity of the problems faced. So let me be clear, Danny. I believe you would be an excellent asset in the role of CTSA. You should see this as a promotion with a much higher profile. It also comes with an increase in salary and better working hours. There's a lot to like about the role.'

'I'm a detective, Sir. That's just who I am.'

'And you can put your skills to excellent use in this role. What do you say?'

'To be honest, I don't think this is the role for me.'

Rudd's smile slipped slightly. They looked at each other for a while, Danny expecting Rudd to say something, anything, but the silence stretched out.

Finally Danny felt he had to try and justify himself further. 'I'm happy where I am, Sir. I feel this is where I make the best contribution. I'm sure there would be a better candidate for this role.'

Rudd put his hands together, leaning on the table and resting his chin against his fingers. 'I believe you are the ideal candidate. But perhaps you're right. Who else would you recommend? Someone from your team?'

Was this a trap, Danny wondered. Was there someone else he could recommend? He didn't want to lose anyone from his team. 'I would need to give that some thought.'

Leaning back, Rudd sighed. 'Very well. I would still like you to accept the role. Think it over this week and either let me know if you accept or who from your team you would recommend. That'll be all.'

Dismissed, Danny mentally kicked himself as he walked back to his office. What had he been thinking? Why hadn't he just refused the offer straight out? Now Rudd was expecting him to either accept or give him a suitable candidate.

Natalie was typing up a report as he walked into the office.

'Someone steal your balloon?' She asked Danny, shooting a look at Alan.

Danny stonewalled her and sat down.

'Boss is touchy today. Better not get in his bad books.' Natalie said to Alan. Alan raised his eyebrows at Danny who shook his head. They both carried on with their work while Danny ran through his options.

It wasn't too late to tell Rudd no. Though what the implications of that would be he wasn't certain. Would Rudd be capable of holding it against him? Danny had to admit he wasn't sure.

He could nominate someone but that would have to be someone who actually was suitable, otherwise it would definitely reflect badly on him. Out of his team Natalie would be his first and, to be honest, only recommendation but there was no way he was going to give her up. She belonged as a detective and was destined to outrank him someday. Yet... Would they be able to keep working together after he had broken up with her? It wouldn't hurt her career any more than his to become a CTSA. If the fight against terrorism was here to stay, she would have the chance to shine.

Should he at least discuss the possibility with her?

And what about Cynthia? He slumped as he realised he'd never even mentioned it to her. What would she think? Danny had a suspicion that maybe she'd prefer him to keep more regular hours and be around more. He didn't want to have that discussion.

~~~

Arriving back at the flat, Emma heard banging from inside. She checked the door: locked. She opened it quietly and shouted in: 'Rachel?'

The banging stopped and Rachel walked into the hallway. 'Where have you been? I waited an hour for you. The Union rep abandoned me after thirty minutes. Why didn't you answer your phone?'

Emma stepped in the hallway feeling that her composure was on a knife edge.

'Well? What's going on?' Rachel demanded.

'I met the guy from that night. Walked into him on my way to the hospital.'

'Just bumped into him?'

'Yes, as a matter of fact, I did!'

'So what's his name?'

'I… I don't know. It wasn't first thing on my mind to ask him, okay?'

'Why not? That's the normal thing to do? Say hello, introduce yourselves. Kind of a given. You do realise that I needed you there today? I was counting on you!'

'I didn't plan this!'

'And that's supposed to make me feel better? You didn't plan on falling off the wall and getting me fired. You didn't plan on not turning up for the meeting that might just get me reinstated. Well I planned on you being there and now I don't know what's going to happen. If the Union decide we're just a couple of wasters then I don't know what other options I have, Emma.'

Rachel put her hand up against the wall. Emma realised she looked tired.

'Why didn't you answer my call? You do know that when you reject a call it doesn't go to voice mail? Just cuts off. Dead. Is that what I am to you?'

'No! Of course not!'

'I thought you understood how much I needed you today. I guess I was wrong. I hope I was wrong, but I don't know that I've got the energy to care any more.'

'I'm sorry, Rach…'

Rachel cut her off. 'Don't bother. I'm going to lie down. You need to decide where your priorities are.'

Rachel went into her room and shut the door.

Emma turned and walked out of the flat.

~~~

How could she have been so stupid? Spending all that time looking for that man and then the moment he turned up he tried to sell her some story about bringing her back from the dead. And to forget the meeting with the Union after she had promised Rachel...

Emma let the thoughts rattle round her head as she speed walked back into town. Just one meeting, that's all it would have taken. Told them her side of the story. Backed Rachel up. What had she been thinking?

She hadn't... Hadn't been thinking at all. Wrapped up in some crazy search for... She halted causing a passing cyclist to swerve slightly at her abrupt change in motion.

He had said the words she had been avoiding for days. No! She started walking again. Tried to let her anger at letting Rachel down overwhelm the voice of doubt that was crying to be heard.

She cut across Monkgate after a car had passed, keeping a wary eye on Monk Bar, then turned onto Lord Mayor's Walk. She hadn't consciously chosen this direction and hurried on, not wanting to look back to where her life had... She shook off the thought of what the man had said. Even though she was three hours late, she was going to find the Union Rep if it was the last thing she did.

~~~

Standing outside room 218, Emma self consciously brushed her dress down. She knocked and before she heard an answer tried the door.

'Hello, sorry for interrupting,' she said, looking round into the room. An older man, balding, with threads of hair combed across his head was sitting behind a desk, opposite a young Nurse who looked as if she had been crying.

'What do you think you're doing, barging in here like this?' The man half rose.

Emma held up her hand in apology. 'I'm sorry, I'll wait outside.'

She retreated outside and carefully pulled the door shut behind her. There were chairs against the corridor wall. She sat in one, leaned back and closed her eyes. Could it get any worse?

Ten minutes later the door opened and the Nurse walked out, followed by the man. He waited until the Nurse had left the corridor before turning on Emma. 'Why would you interrupt a private meeting?'

Emma stood. 'I didn't realise you were in a meeting. I'm sorry.'

The man turned to the door of the room and sighed. 'Property still haven't fixed the do not disturb sign.' He shook his head and turned back to Emma. 'Don Welsh. I only have ten minutes before my next appointment.'

'I'll be quick.'

Emma followed Don back into the room and shut the door.

'Has Mr Cole dumped her then?' Emma asked.

'I'm not here to listen to rumour or gossip. As I said, I've only got ten minutes and I would rather type up my notes than have any more time wasted.'

'Did she tell you they've been sleeping together for the last year?'

'No. That's irrelevant... How would you know that?'

'Everyone knows.' Emma shrugged. 'Surgeons, they're all at it. Is she pregnant?'

Don sighed again. 'Did you actually have something you wanted to talk with me about?'

She took a deep breath and then let it out again slowly. It didn't help.

'I missed my appointment with you and Rachel Phillips this morning.'

He stared at her for a moment and then frowned. 'Emma Hunter?'

'Yes.'

'I can maybe fit you in next week.'

'No! That would be too late.' She continued more slowly. 'Rachel really needs to get this sorted out.'

'You should have thought of that this morning. I have a full schedule in York today and I'm not back until next week.'

'I need you to understand, I hit my head. I didn't know what had happened.'

He was frowning at her again. 'This morning?'

'No... Last week. When I fell off Monk Bar. Didn't Rachel tell you?'

He shook his head then glanced at his watch. 'You have three minutes.'

Emma looked frantically about the room. 'I missed the appointment this morning... I found the man who... who... resuscitated me.'

'What are you talking about?'

'Don't you know why we've been suspended?'

'If you had turned up you could have told me.'

'They said I faked my death but I think I may have...' She forced herself to say the words. 'I really did die.'

'Okay. I've heard enough. Do you want an appointment next week or not?' He opened the diary and began flipping pages.

'He said I had no pulse. I wasn't breathing!'

'Yes or no?'

'Yes!'

'Next Thursday at 3pm. I'll give you half an hour. I suggest you consider coming up with a more plausible reason for explaining the events if you want me to take your case forward.'

There was a knock on the door. Don opened it and smiled, ushering in another Nurse. 'Come on in, Ms Hunter was just leaving.'

Emma stared at the Nurse for a second and then squeezed past her and hurried down the corridor.

~~~

Back in the flat there was no sound from Rachel's room and Emma didn't want to risk disturbing her. Instead she quietly shut herself in her own bedroom and sat in her bed, pulling her duvet up around her until she was cocooned.

It had been a disaster. The Union Rep hadn't wanted to listen to her. Why hadn't she gone straight to the meeting?

But if she had, she would never have met him. She had a sense of stillness then. Quiet, like he had been. No rush, no sense of hurry. Just relaxed.

She hadn't intended mentioning meeting the man to the Union Rep, still less repeat what he had said, yet now that she had...

Why did it scare her so much? She had seen people brought back before. Had helped do so carrying out chest compressions and assisting with a ventilator until the heart had sparked back to life again and resumed its normal rhythm. People died all the time in A&E and often they were just on hold. Paused for a moment while the nurses and doctors kick-started whatever had ground to a halt.

Except... she didn't remember dying. Didn't even have any proof it had happened at all except for the strange new scar and now a homeless man who claimed she had no pulse, that she wasn't breathing. And then there was the blood...

What had he said? Blood all round her head. Blood on her clothes that they had cut off and thrown away. Where had that come from? Not from her, not when her blood pressure was normal and she hadn't even needed a single pack of plasma.

But something happened. Something that had freaked Rachel out. The paramedics certainly thought something had happened, but not death. Serious trauma; head injury.

She took a sharp intake of breath and put her fingers in her hair, feeling the roughness of the scar. Testing its length, the ridges that spurred off from the centre line.

He had been so delighted when he recognised me. You're alive, he had said. So did that mean that for a moment I wasn't? That I was bleeding? My heart and lungs still?

She still wanted to resist the thought. It wasn't possible, to be dead one minute and then alive the next without anyone doing anything. And what had he said? He'd prayed for me? God answered him? Was this some witchdoctor thing, some voodoo? Am I just a corpse brought back to life? She shivered.

'Do you exist, God?' She asked quietly. 'Is that even how I...' She eased her hands out from under the duvet and made quotation symbols. '... pray to you?'

Nothing. No answer. No thunderbolt nor lightning. She sat for a minute, not so much waiting as resting and then a question occurred to her.

Emma pushed the duvet away and rescued her laptop from the floor. Opening the lid it flashed up the battery running low message. The battery was always running low. Could you replace the batteries on laptops, she wondered. She rooted about and found the power cord, jamming it in the hole and then leaning precariously out to turn on the wall switch.

She opened Firefox and began typing in the Google search box: "back to life."

A quick scan of the results did not look promising. Music videos on YouTube and song lyrics. Emma scrolled back up and changed the search term, adding "dead" at the start.

This was more interesting. Emma scrolled slowly down past the newspaper headlines of babies and adults coming back to life. She didn't want to click on any of these and was about to click through to the next page when she noticed a link right at the bottom, under related searches: "I was dead and came back to life."

Her throat seemed to close up but she clicked on it anyway. More of the same. Except there were a couple of links that she found herself both drawn to and repelled from: "Experiences of people who were clinically dead and came back to life" and "Woman comes back to life after being dead for 17 hours."

She tried the second and quickly read the story. It didn't seem relevant to her, a woman who had a heart attack, attempts to revive her failed, yet after they stopped life support she recovered. Emma went back to the search page and clicked through to the link promising experiences. It was a mistake. Immediately she regretted even beginning the search. What had she been looking for? Emma closed the lid and laid the laptop back on the floor.

She curled up again and pulled the duvet back around her and stayed like that until she finally fell asleep.

~~~

'I must confess, I didn't expect to see you again so soon, Danny,' Tony said as he led Danny through to his living room.

'No, it's a surprise to me as well.'

'Please, have a seat, are you sure you won't have a tea or coffee?'

Danny took the offered armchair but sat perched forward, reluctant to relax. 'No, thank you.' He waited till Tony had sat opposite him. 'I've been offered a promotion.'

'Fantastic news!'

'Not really, no.'

Tony examined him for a moment. 'Why is that?'

'It's complicated.'

Tony nodded. 'You know, Danny, people who come to me for advice usually know deep down what they want or need to do. I think God made us to need each other to talk with, to listen to. Sometimes the only way to get our heads clear is to share whatever is going on, not so someone else can tell you what to do, but so we can work it out ourselves.'

Relaxing slightly, Danny explained the position Rudd had placed him in.

When he had finished, Tony looked away, his expression thoughtful. 'So, your Chief Inspector is expecting you to either accept the new role or find someone else, which would mean you would lose a valuable team member. Why can't you... Ah, yes, turning down a promotion is never a good long term move. Why don't you want the new role?'

'Why would I want it? I'm doing the job I've always wanted. I've got no ambitions to move on from being a detective, no desire to move up the ranks.'

'God made you a detective?'

'Yes,' Danny said without thinking, then with a shock, he realised it was true.

'Well, you know what you need to do then.'

'And face the consequences...'

'Of course. Whatever you choose, there will always be consequences...' Tony again had that thoughtful look. 'Do you know the story of Joseph?'

'The guy with the fancy coat?'

'That's the guy. One of my favourite parts of the bible. Joseph didn't choose to have his brothers try and kill him, didn't choose to be sold into slavery, didn't choose to have an affair...' Danny tried not to react, but felt himself tense. '...didn't choose to be falsely accused and thrown in prison, yet in every choice he didn't make, God brought something good out of the circumstances Joseph found himself in. In the end he saved his family and the whole of Egypt from the famine.'

'What are you saying?'

'I'm not saying anything, just reflecting that sometimes choices are made for us and it's up to us to make the best of the situation since it might be that God has a plan he hasn't yet told us about.'

CHAPTER THIRTY
Four Angles

Emma waited until she heard Rachel switch on the shower before leaving her room. She was tempted to sneak out of the flat, but she had to at least tell Rachel she had arranged a new meeting with the Union rep. A week and a half away... Rachel was going to be furious. Again.

She made a pot of coffee and set two mugs out on the counter then pulled ingredients out of the cupboards and started mixing them together in a bowl.

Emma stood nervously behind the counter when Rachel came out, rubbing her wet hair with a towel.

'You made waffles?' Rachel stopped, an expression of mock astonishment on her face. 'It's going to take a lot more...'

'I got us another meeting,' Emma interrupted. 'It's not till a week Thursday, but it was the best I could do.'

Rachel walked over. 'You went to see the rep?'

'Straight away.'

'Next Thursday? That's another week and a half of not knowing whether I'm going to be fired or not.'

'I'm really sorry, Rachel.'

'Sorry enough to make waffles...' Rachel wrapped the towel round her hair and sat down on a stool. 'Pass me a plate then.'

They ate in silence for a few minutes.

Eventually Emma couldn't hold it in any longer. 'I don't know what we're going to say to him.'

'The Union rep?'

'Yes. I told him I'd met the man you told me about, that he'd tried to resuscitate me…'

'Resuscitate?' Rachel interrupted. 'That's not what it looked like to me.'

'Well, whatever. He didn't want to know, told me to come up with a better explanation for what happened.'

'Sounds like a good idea.'

'I don't have a better explanation!'

'Well, you need to think of one. Fast.' Rachel laid down her fork and pushed her plate away.

'I'm not telling them this was a hoax.'

'Don't be stupid, of course not.'

'What then?'

Rachel took a drink from her coffee. 'You really met that homeless bum that attacked you?'

'He said he didn't.'

'Emma…' Rachel gave her a look of exasperation. 'Why would you not just run away when you saw him? How do you even know what he looks like? You were out cold.'

'He said I was dead.'

Rachel's eyes narrowed. 'He said that?'

'He said I had no pulse. That I wasn't breathing.'

Rachel put up her hands. 'No. It's irrelevant.'

'It's not irrelevant, this happened to…'

'It. Doesn't. Matter.' Rachel took a deep breath. 'Even if you have met that guy, no-one's going to believe what he says. You would need someone reliable, someone…'

'What?'

'The police said they were going to look at the CCTV.'

'They said that to me,' Emma remembered. 'I asked if I could look at it.'

Rachel shook her head. 'I don't know if you really want to do that.'

Emma stood and went to get her phone. 'If the police have evidence that we didn't make this all up then I have to see it.'

~~~

'Boss, we've had a call from Emma Hunter, asking if she can view the CCTV footage of her accident.'

Danny looked up at Natalie. 'We'd all like to view that footage. Still not turned up?'

Natalie shook her head. 'I'll call them now.'

'Tell them I'll be down there this afternoon to bash some heads together if it hasn't been delivered. This is the second week.' Danny leaned back in his chair. If he took the CTSA role he wouldn't miss the frustration of trying to gather evidence, though would the frustration of trying to win a war—one that Danny suspected was currently unwinnable—be worse?

A uniform walked into the office and laid mail on Alan's desk.

'Anything interesting?' Danny asked.

Alan sorted through it and brought some envelopes over. Top of the pile, a lab report. Danny opened it and examined the form it contained. Toxicology report, Emma Hunter, nothing found.

He checked the figures. No alcohol, no trace of drugs in her system.

Natalie was on the phone, arguing with someone about the CCTV feeds. He waited until she was done and then showed her the form. 'What's wrong with this?'

'Nothing?'

'Zero alcohol, zero drugs.'

'That can't be right. They took the blood samples while I was there, less than five hours from the incident. She herself said she had at least ten units to drink. No way that was going to clear out of her system that quickly.' Natalie groaned. 'Could they have mixed up the samples?'

'I'll need you to check. What's the deal with the CCTV?'

'Apparently we have it. They sent it last week.'

Danny restrained himself from swearing. 'Right, I'm going down there.'

~~~

'Sergeant.'

'Detective Inspector...' Sergeant Davison smiled. 'How can I help you today?'

Davison was far too cheery for his own good, Danny thought. Stuck in a basement office that served as evidence storage and video library for ongoing investigations, he didn't seem to mind the lack of interaction with colleagues. Though maybe that was why he always seemed pleased to see you. If he'd held up the Hunter investigation, Danny was going to be furious, still, always best to stick to the facts. 'I've been waiting on some CCTV footage from Monk Bar. Apparently it was sent over last week.'

'Nothing from Monk Bar. Hmm...' Davison tilted his head to one side. 'I did get some DVDs in from the Council. No paperwork with them. Haven't had a chance to review them yet.'

'Could I take a look?'

'Certainly. Pull up a chair.'

There was only one desk in the room, the rest of the space taken up with shelves. Mostly the police now dealt with video files stored online, but they still received and had to send hard copy DVDs as part of the evidence chain.

Davison retrieved the DVDs and loaded the first one in. 'Three files, each thirty minutes long.' He copied them onto the server and then loaded the second DVD. 'One file also thirty minutes.'

He started the first video. Fast forwarded until figures appeared and then spun back to just before they entered the frame and played.

'Has her family been informed?' Sergeant Davison asked after they had watched the ambulance pull away.

'What? No.' Danny tore his eyes away from his computer screen.

'You haven't filed a fatality report yet?'

'No. No, I haven't. Look, is it possible to play all these feeds at the same time?'

'All four of them?'

'Yes.'

'It'll take a few minutes.' Davison began opening each video file and minimizing the display until all four were arranged on the screen. Danny watched as he forwarded and rewound each until the time stamps were in sync. 'All you need to do now is play all.'

'Go for it.'

Davison started the videos and they watched as Hunter and Phillips made their way to Monk Bar, Hunter tip-toeing her way on the parapet, then as she turned from Monk Bar, stumbled and fell. He paused the videos after a few more seconds.

'Such a waste of life.' Davison said.

'Don't pause it, keep them playing.' Danny told him.

'What are you looking for?'

'Just play them.'

They watched in silence as Rachel Phillips pulled out a phone and then Davison leaned in closer to the screen. 'Who's that?'

A homeless man came running up from under the Bar. He seemed to check Hunter's pulse and then spoke to Phillips.

Danny flicked from video to video, trying to decide which view gave the best angle until Davison swore.

'What's he doing!'

'Keep playing.'

The man hovered over the girl, almost appearing to kiss her three times and then Phillips appeared from off camera and threw him off, kicking and punching him until he ran.

'Can you pause just that feed?' Danny asked, pointing at the lower right video. There had been a glimpse of the man's face as he ran back under the Bar.

'Sure.' Davison paused the video. 'What about the others?'

'Keep watching.' Danny allowed himself a smile at Davison's confusion.

A minute later an ambulance came into shot. The paramedics taking over the scene, supporting Hunter, moving Phillips back. A neck brace was attached and she was moved onto a board. Then a drip was set up.

'She survived?' Davison looked incredulous.

'Not only survived, no sign of a head wound. Well, no sign of any recent head wound or internal injury. Henderson interviewed her the following day.

'She's conscious!'

'Released. The chief surgeon was ready to throw her out of the hospital himself. Believes it was all an elaborate hoax.'

'No way. Almost enough to make you believe in miracles.'

Danny pushed himself away from the desk and stood. 'Could you save all those files onto the server and send me the link this afternoon?'

'Will do.'

'And that one we paused, I think we might have the man's face. Can you try and grab a still image and blow it up.'

~~~

School had been as boring as usual. It had been good to catch up with her friends, but that didn't make up for a whole day spent listening to mind numbing lessons. Najwa decided to walk through the park on her way home. Maybe she would stop and read for a bit, she knew as soon as she got home her mum would ask her to do some cleaning.

The blossom had all but faded from the trees in the park, the fallen petals had blown into piles around the trunks. She had gathered up some of the early petals, marvelling at their delicacy, then allowed them to fall in a breeze, watching as they had spun and twirled in the wind.

It was a sunny day and there were many people in the park, mothers and their children, people walking and others sitting, enjoying the day or reading. She walked on looking for an empty bench and then saw her neighbour, the old woman they had passed on the street. She still looked sad. Then Najwa saw she was holding a book, the words Holy Bible on the cover. Walking up to her, Najwa asked: 'Have you read it?'

The woman looked up, her sadness not quite replaced by confusion.

'The Injil, have you read it?'

'I'm sorry, I don't...'

Najwa opened her rucksack and pulled out her Injil and showed it to the woman. 'I was enjoying it but then it started getting boring.'

The woman reached out and Najwa handed over the book.

'The Injil?' The woman asked.

'Yes.'

The woman opened the book near the end and carefully ran her fingers over the text. 'This is a bible…'

'Why does it say Good News on the cover?' Najwa sat down beside the woman.

'Why do you call it the Injil?'

'That's what we call the Christian book. How far have you got?'

'You ask a lot of questions.'

'My mother says that as well.'

The woman handed the book back to Najwa. 'It says Good News because of Jesus, because he is God's good news to us.'

'We're told the stories about Jesus have been corrupted.'

'Who told you that?' The woman looked shocked.

'Everyone knows it. I haven't read about Jesus yet. If it's about Jesus why doesn't it mention him?'

The woman shook her head. 'Who are you?'

'We're neighbours, don't you recognise me? We live at 81. I'm Najwa.'

'Pleased to meet you,' the woman said hesitantly. 'What did you ask me? How far have I… What have you read?'

Najwa took the Injil back and flicked through the pages. 'I read the first book, Genesis. I liked that, mostly. It had some stories I hadn't heard before. I started Exodus and it was okay, but then it stopped being a story and was just about rules and laws and I kind of gave up.'

'It's worth reading more,' the woman said slowly. 'It's not really meant to be read like a normal book though. You won't find Jesus until near the end but there are some really good stories in between.'

'What sort of stories?'

'Well…' She thought for a minute. 'There was Ruth who left her family and home to worship a foreign God. Esther who saved a nation from being slaughtered. Deborah who led Israel into battle and victory.'

'There are stories about women in the Injil?'

'Of course, many of them braver and with more faith than the men, even the Marys, whom I'm named after: Jesus' mother and Mary who washed Jesus feet.'

'The Quran has the story of Jesus' mother. I've not heard of the others.'

'They were all brave women. They risked everything to know God, to be obedient to him.'

Najwa nodded, looked away at children who were running and shouting on the grass. She used to have that freedom, would never have it again. She sighed and stood, placing the Injil back in her rucksack. Her mother would worry if she took too long walking home. 'I better go,' she told Mary and walked away.

~~~

Mary watched the girl as she walked away. Such a strange conversation. She had tried to remember the girl while they had been talking but couldn't place her among the Muslim families on the street. She was a Muslim, wasn't she? Mary tried to remember if the Quran was the Muslim holy book. Or was it Hindu, there were Hindu families as well. She hadn't spoken to any of them in all the years she had lived there and here was a young girl coming up to her and asking about the bible of all things. What had she done? Rambled on until the poor girl had fled.

She stood slowly, conscious of how tired she was. Every night she delayed going to bed then lay staring at the ceiling until she finally couldn't avoid sleep. Within a few hours she was scrabbling to wake up, the same dream torturing her night after night. If it wouldn't stop she might have to go to the doctor yet could she bring herself to risk telling a doctor that a dream was plaguing her? They might just lock her up and be done with her.

Is that what you want, Lord? She asked. Are you punishing me like the Reverend?

It occurred to her that she was standing. Where was she going? Her heart sank as she remembered she had been going to the hospital. She had tried twice the previous week. The first time she had made it inside before turning around and heading home. The second time she had stopped outside the entrance. Today she had set out determinedly again only to end up sitting in the park for an hour.

A shuddering took her over as she breathed in and she realised she wanted to cry. Turning towards home she found the strength to walk, determined no-one would see her break down in such a public place.

~~~

A man walked into the reception area of the Police station and held his hand out to Emma. 'Miss Hunter. Good to see you up and about.'

'I, uh…' Emma hesitantly shook his hand. 'Have we met?'

'You were out cold last time I saw you, wasn't sure if you were sleeping soundly or in a coma. My colleague interviewed you when you woke up, Detective Henderson. I'm Detective Inspector Daniel Martin.'

'Yes, I asked for her. Is she here?'

'She's out at the moment but I can help. You asked on the phone about viewing the CCTV of the… incident?'

Incident? Was that what they were calling it? 'That's right.'

The Detective looked intently at her. 'May I ask why you want to see the CCTV?'

Several thoughts burst at once: Why did she want to view it? Why shouldn't she want to see the CCTV, she had a right to know! She didn't want to see it. Images from her dream of the man she'd met on the street. She had to know...

It was only an instant but she wondered what the Detective was thinking as she stood there, her mouth slightly open and no words coming out. She swallowed and looked away from his eyes which had seemed to her to be the colour of brushed steel.

'I just feel I have to see what happened,' she managed to say.

He nodded. 'The CCTV footage is... disturbing. I won't stop you from watching it, but are you sure you are ready to see it?'

She nodded and looked him square in the eyes. 'Yes.'

'Very well.' He nodded to the Desk Sergeant. 'I'll take her through.'

He led her through two corridors, up a flight of stairs and then along another corridor and into a small office with four desks. 'My office. You can take my seat.' He pointed at the desk furthest from the door.

Emma sat, taking in the piles of files on the desk, floor and on top of filing cabinets. The desk itself was mostly clear and had a large flat monitor with keyboard and mouse in front of it. The Detective carried round another seat then leaned over and adjusted the monitor so they could both watch it and pulled the keyboard and mouse till their cables were taut and he could reach them while sitting down.

'If you want me to stop the feeds just let me know.'

'The feeds?'

'The CCTV feeds.'

'There's more than one?'

'We have four different angles.'

She wasn't sure what she had expected. Four different angles! She held her hands tightly together in her lap and kept her head held high. 'Okay.'

The Detective nodded and adjusted the mouse. Emma saw the screen divide into four rectangles. Each with a fuzzy yet recognisable view of Monk Bar. She felt herself take a sharp intake of breath as she saw her own figure clearly discernible in two of the pictures. The pictures changed slightly and Emma realised they were now playing back. She leaned in, her eyes flicking back and forth from movie to movie.

There she was, balancing on the parapet of the wall, Rachel following behind her, no-one else in sight. Emma put a hand to her mouth as she realised how high up she had been. She watched as she stepped over the gap wondering what had possessed her to be so reckless. Why hadn't she seen the danger and there... oh! It happened so fast. One second she had been turning back and then she was falling and now she realised both her hands were by the sides of her head.

She was only visible in one movie now and from a distance so it was hard to make out the detail but... the way she had fallen... she resisted moving her hands back to where her head had hit the ground. She was vaguely aware of Rachel gesturing wildly in two of the movies and then the homeless man appeared from under the Bar. It wasn't just a dream...

He looked up at Rachel, she seemed to be talking to him and then he put a hand to her neck. He shook his head. Emma looked over at the Detective at this and saw he was watching her and not the movies. Embarrassed and a little annoyed, she turned back and saw the man seem to straddle her and...
'What is he doing!'

'We don't know, Miss Hunter.'

It was just as he'd described. Emma looked in horror as the man knelt over her, almost kissing her three times before sitting up and then Rachel appeared, running from the side—Emma hadn't noticed her leave her position on the wall—grabbing the man and throwing him off her. Then she was punching him, kicking at him as he struggled to get up and get away.

One of the movies now showed flashing lights approaching and an ambulance pulled to a halt near her and Rachel. One of the paramedics holding her head while the other took Rachel away, then together they put a neck brace on, checked her pulse and breathing and manoeuvred a board under her before lifting her into the ambulance.

On one feed only, the ambulance receded into the distance, flashing lights getting smaller. The Detective reached out and stopped the movies playing.

Emma swallowed. Everything Rachel had said had been true. Everything the man had told her, even the thing she really could not think about now, with the Detective watching her.

'Can I get a copy of these, this...'

'CCTV feeds. We'll talk about that in a moment. I would like to ask you some questions. Do you feel up to that?'

No, she wanted to get up and walk away. Maybe scream. Throw something. 'Could I get some water?' She asked instead.

The detective nodded. She could see pity in his eyes. She didn't want his pity. Didn't want to answer his questions, but if she stormed out now, what would he think? Would he be suspicious? Does he wonder whether this is a hoax?

The Detective brought her a small plastic cup and carefully placed it in front of her. She wanted to drink but was worried her hands would shake and she'd spill it. 'I'm sorry, I've forgotten your name.'

'Detective Inspector Daniel Martin. You can call me Danny.'

Danny. Does that mean he doesn't think it's a hoax or he's trying to get me to drop my guard?

'As you may know, we've had a complaint against you. That you are responsible for creating an elaborate stunt that has wasted NHS resources and police time. So, Miss Hunter, was all this a stunt or a practical joke?'

Emma felt a tear form in her right eye. She tried to blink it away but it ran down her cheek. She quickly put up her hand to wipe it away then shook her head no.

'Good. Has seeing the video feeds helped you remember anything that happened?'

Looking back to the monitor, Emma thought back. It was so unreal. She could remember waking up in the hospital and some of what had happened in the club. The memory of what she'd just watched was now fresh in her mind, but it was as if she was watching a stranger. An actress playing her.

'No.'

'Okay. Will you contact us if and when your memories do come back?'

'Yes.'

'Do you know the man that...' The Detective corrected himself. 'The man shown in the CCTV?'

'I...' Emma felt her chest constrict. It was like she wasn't getting enough air into her lungs. She hadn't been going to mention him, but... 'I met him, the other day, on the street. I'd been looking for him, Rachel told me... She... I had to find out and... He said I died.'

The detective didn't respond. He was frowning as he looked at her.

'Why would he say that?' She asked.

Again, he didn't answer. He turned to look at the monitor, went to move the mouse and then stopped. 'You met him? I just had Henderson put a picture of him out to officers on patrol.'

'What was he doing to me?'

Shifting in his seat, the Detective looked away again. 'We interviewed the Paramedics and they reported your clothing had not been removed. Nothing was stolen from you.' He looked back at her. 'At the start he seems to be checking your pulse...'

It had looked like that. Or had he been caressing her neck? She instantly regretted thinking of it like that. But then... 'After that? What is he doing after that?'

'Initially—based on Rachel's testimony—we wondered if he was… if his motivation was sexual. We can't discount that possibility.'

Emma felt her hands clench.

'However, the way he almost bows over you. It seems to be like a person grieving. A father throwing himself on a child who has… who has hurt themselves. A husband praying over his wife…'

'He said he prayed for me, but you wouldn't do that for a stranger! You don't grieve for someone you don't know!'

'He said he prayed for you?'

'He said something about Eli… Eli…' She couldn't remember.

'Elijah, Elisha?'

'Yeah, something like that. He said I had no pulse, that I wasn't breathing. Why would he say that?'

'Miss Hunter…' He paused and seemed to consider what he wanted to say. 'You saw the CCTV footage. You say this was not a hoax. I watch it and I see a fatality. Yet you're sitting here with me now, perfectly well. I've never experienced a miracle, but… Maybe you have.'

'That's impossible.'

'Then give me an explanation that makes sense.'

'I hit my head, knocked myself out. This guy, he's homeless, he didn't know how to check my vital signs.'

'Did you have any bruising or scratches the next day.'

Emma didn't want to answer, but eventually shook her head. She grew more uncomfortable as the detective studied her.

'Do you think this man attacked you?'

He hadn't hit her, had almost caressed—that word again—her neck… 'I can't say.'

'Do you want to lodge a complaint against him?'

'A complaint?'

'Miss Hunter, at the moment I have a very strange case which has no rational explanation. Nothing I've seen or you've said suggests that this man has tried to harm you, yet you need to decide for yourself if you want to press charges. I have to say though, as much as I would like to know what really happened, in my experience, sometimes that simply isn't possible.'

Her thoughts seemed to all jump and whirl about her head like a tornado. She tried to focus and order them but they refused to stay still. 'I don't know,' she eventually said.

'Very well. If you want to speak to myself or Detective Henderson about what happened at any time, do call us. Now… The complaint against you…'

Emma focused on the Detective. She had completely forgotten about

Cole's complaint.

'Before the police can bring a formal charge against you, we have to be satisfied there is proof a crime has been committed. Now while there are inconsistencies between the evidence we have and your testimony and that of Ms Phillips…'

'Inconsistencies?'

'You said you'd been drinking that night.'

'I was.'

'Not according to our toxicology reports. Not a trace of alcohol in your system. Then there's your insistence you only "hit" your head…'

'What are you saying?'

'It's a very strange case. I think Mr Cole and I need to have a talk.'

~~~

When Natalie arrived back at the Station, Danny showed her the CCTV feeds. After they ended, Natalie didn't respond for a moment. Danny let her process it while he read a report.

'Boss,' she said. 'I think we need to bury this as quickly as possible.'

Danny moved his chair round and leaned back. 'Okay. Tell me why.'

'It's a lose/lose case. We could spend weeks on this and never get to the bottom of what happened.'

'Go on.'

Natalie held up a hand and started pointing at her fingers. 'The toxicology report was negative. I'm checking to see if the bloods could have been mixed up, but I've got a feeling that's a dead end. Hunter's testimony of how much she drank is consistent with her friend's. Could she have been drugged with something we don't test for? Maybe, but is it even relevant? There's no way to prove whether alcohol or drugs caused her to fall. Testimony of her friend is that she slipped and the CCTV backs that up. Whether drugs could have caused her to get up on the wall in the first place is another matter, but not one we can prove.'

She took a breath. 'Then there's the homeless guy. Okay,' she said holding up a hand. 'I'm assuming he's homeless. He appears, does something really weird and then runs for it.'

'Because he's being kicked and punched by Phillips.'

'Even so, what was he doing to her? Was he on drugs? What could he be charged with? Molestation maybe but the CCTV isn't conclusive and we know he certainly wasn't raping her. But the final kicker is that she's unhurt. She fell, she has a rock hard skull which somehow managed to avoid even getting bruised. The Surgeon's complaint of a hoax is a reasonable one but that footage… There is no way that was a hoax. Not unless someone with a ton of money managed to fake the whole thing and why would they do that?'

'So what did happen?'

'It's not important.'

Taken aback, Danny asked her to explain.

'Weird stuff happens on the job. She's okay, that's all that matters.'

'You don't want to know why she's okay?'

Natalie placed a hand on his thigh then quickly removed it. She stood, obviously embarrassed. 'We could waste forever trying to answer a question that can't be answered. There are more important things in life, you of all people should know that...' She walked past him and left the office.

~~~

It was just before 6pm when Anthony Cole called again. Danny was in the office on his own and took the call.

'Why haven't you updated me?'

'This case is proving more complex than we'd expected.' Danny said, restraining himself.

'What's complex about it? Two girls pull a stupid stunt. Surely you don't need two weeks to investigate.'

'Mr Cole, we only received the CCTV yesterday. We've had to request the toxicology report is double checked.'

'You have the CCTV, why do you need a toxicology report?'

'Perhaps it would be helpful if you came to the station and viewed the CCTV footage...'

'Detective, I don't have time for that. Do your job. And if you can't then I'll have to speak with Chief Inspector Rudd. He's a personal friend of mine.' He hung up.

I'm sure he is, Danny thought to himself as he carefully laid the phone back on the receiver.

CHAPTER THIRTY-ONE
An Inspiration

Aamir found a spare seat at the back of the packed university meeting room. Students he recognised and many he didn't were joking and discussing and fooling about while several men stood at the front, concentrating on a laptop. He hadn't been sure whether he wanted to attend and had even let his friends leave without him as he intended to study, then changed his mind at the last minute.

No women were there he noted. Not surprising as events were frequently segregated. Loud music suddenly boomed out of speakers and Aamir saw a film had begun playing, projected onto the wall at the front of the room, before both the sound and the film stopped.

One of the men at the front appeared to make some adjustments on the laptop and then he and another left the stage leaving one man standing alone.

'Welcome, brothers. I am Zafar,' he began, looking briefly down at a notebook. 'Thank you for allowing me to speak this evening. We know Allah is a God of peace. We know this but sometimes we forget that in order to have peace we must bring peace. Islam is currently under siege from the Government, from the media, in the streets. Our parents are not safe. Our sisters are not safe. The police pay lip service to the idea of justice. Our Mosques are attacked and they do nothing. Our families are attacked and investigations take place but no-one is brought to justice. Our brothers are killed but the murderers cannot be found. If we do not protect them, then who will?'

He did something to the laptop and the film began playing again—low, mournful music filled the room while a green flag with a white crescent fluttered in a breeze.

'We wanted to share this documentary with you. To show you what we as Muslims are facing throughout Britain.' He walked to the side and stood watching the film.

Aamir watched in increasing horror as interviews were shown interspersed with actual footage of attacks taking place. He heard several students exclaim as the face of a young woman was shown, large purple and black bruises the backdrop for two long scars across her cheek and jaw. Footage was shown of groups of white men marching and training, while a narrator explained how far right groups were systematically working to expel all Muslims from Britain, the strategies they were using, the attacks they were believed to have been responsible for.

He knew the situation had grown worse over the last few years, but to this extent…

Finally the film faded to black, the narration and music ceased and Aamir became aware he was almost rigid with tension. He looked around and saw faces as stunned as he felt, became aware of the utter silence in the room.

Zafar walked back to the centre of the stage and Aamir could see tears run down his face yet he did not even try to wipe them away. 'We have relied on the police and government for too long to protect us. It is clear they either cannot or will not. So what should we do? Sit back and watch while these attacks continue?'

Several people shouted: 'No!'

Zafar nodded in acknowledgment. 'Can we wait while those we love suffer?'

Aamir heard more responding, one man even standing as he did so. He was aware that anger was building inside him as well.

'Of course we cannot wait, we will not cower in fear. It is our duty to protect our people and we will do this by establishing defence militias that will allow our families to go about their business in peace.' Zafar walked down off the stage and stood at the front looking, Aamir felt, straight at him.

'I wish I did not have to ask you this…' He trailed off.

For what seemed like an eternity, no one moved or spoke. Then, without prompting, one student rose from his seat and excused himself past the others in his row. He walked to Zafar and Aamir watched as they shook hands and whispered something to each other. Zafar then embraced him before the student walked down the room, though instead of returning to his seat, he made his way to the back where Aamir saw him receive what looked like a business card.

Turning back, Aamir saw a queue had formed at the front with others now walking down the aisle. He looked at the man next to him and suspected he was thinking the same. Aamir stood, joining what seemed to be the whole room and while a fire burned in his stomach he waited to speak to Zafar.

~~~

'How was he?'

'Passionate. He certainly is able to inspire a response.' A long sigh.

'You can speak freely.'

There was a pause and then: 'Are you sure he is the right one to lead the operation?'

'He came to me with the idea.'

'That's not quite how I understood it.'

'Very well, he came to me to discuss the vision he had. I was able to lead him to see that he could act on it.'

'A vision is one thing, will he be able to hold the course after he's had to... What is it they say, the first cut is the deepest?'

'I believe he will.'

'You are putting a lot of faith in a man who is untested and untried. Have you discussed tactics with him?'

'Of course.'

'I'm talking about the realities we will be likely to face. We will need shields. We will need to act decisively. You know we can't afford to hesitate if we face resistance.'

'I believe Allah sent him to me. Remember I know him from childhood, I know how he thinks and feels. He knows what is at stake. Are the other rallies organised?'

'Two at the end of this week and then one a day next week and the week after.'

'Good. I'll be back later tomorrow and can join you in London. There will be no time to waste.'

'There will not.' Another pause. 'If he hesitates...'

'Then he will become a glorious martyr whose story will inspire millions to join the cause.'

CHAPTER THIRTY-TWO
Unwelcome

Calvin looked up at the imposing hospital building, a wall of concrete and glass rising twelve stories high. The last time he had stood looking at the building had been three years previously and he had only stood looking, afraid to do more. After meeting the girl he had begged enough money to pay for a bus ticket only to have the driver hesitate about accepting him on the bus. Calvin had stood silently as he was looked over, conscious of the queue behind him, knowing if he spoke it would only make things worse. In the end the driver had let him on without saying a word.

The journey had been slow, winding its way South, other passengers avoiding looking at him. That was fine by him. He had looked out the window at countryside remembering journeys he had taken before.

His stomach rumbled reminding him he hadn't eaten in over a day but he willed himself to ignore the desire for food. You had no choice but to learn to control your hunger when you lived on the street yet even though he could have begged for or found food, he wanted to be hungry, wanted to fast. He needed to be punished, he needed to suffer. It wasn't complicated. Maybe his penitent behaviour, his rejection of status and acceptance of suffering had finally earned him absolution. It was this hope that had driven him down here to see if he could finally atone for his crime.

He asked God for strength, something he had not done since long before the accident. Long before his time in the city. He asked God to bless him as he sought the patient. Hospital staff were no better than those on the bus for judging the homeless. He would not be naturally trusted. Surely God would not judge him over one lie.

He adjusted his rucksack and walked through automatic doors which slid slowly sideways to let him past. Décor that had seen better days was half hidden by posters advising him to wash his hands, to get checked for prostrate, breast and bowel cancer. Patients or relatives or friends sat in rows, faces sombre. Some glanced up at him, most were lost in their own world.

He made his way to the back of a queue at reception. Shuffled forward until he was faced with an overweight woman who appeared to be in her fifties, her hair tied back in an untidy pony tail, glasses balanced on her nose.

'How can I help you?'

'I'm looking for my brother. I've been told he's in a coma.'

The woman looked him up and down. 'Coma patients are in Ward thirty.'

'Thank you.'

He looked around for directions and saw a sign pointing the way. It led him through and under the hospital and out the back. Down an empty corridor past signs for Care of the Elderly wards and named general wards. A Nurse came out of one ward and looked at him suspiciously but didn't challenge him.

There was no name for the ward, just a sign giving the number. Looking through the door he could see the ward corridor was also empty. The nurses' station was half way up the corridor with rooms off both sides.

The lie he'd told at reception wouldn't work here. He had no right to visit the patient and if he was challenged they would quickly call security.

He eased the door open and walked silently into the ward checking the first room on his left. Thick curtains covered the windows but in the light from the corridor two beds were visible, women in each bed. He backed out and tried the next room along which was on the right. Two more beds but this time with men. He recognised neither. He tried to remember how many doors he had seen looking down the corridor. He thought there had been two on each side before the nurses' station. Maybe the same again after.

Assuming they had men on one side and women on the other, the odds were against him finding who he was looking for before he would have to walk past the likely occupied nurses' station. Of course there were two assumptions there, both of which could be wrong. It was looking like they had men and women in separate rooms but there was no guarantee one sex was more likely to be in a coma than the other. The rest of the ward could be filled with women. Also why should all the rooms be filled with patients? Could some of them be empty?

While he was thinking this through he heard movement out in the corridor and moved to the side, out of sight unless someone came into the room. Someone walked past the door. Calvin thought it sounded like they had gone into the room he had just exited. He decided to risk looking out.

There was no-one visible in the corridor. He quietly walked up the corridor, keeping as far to the right as possible, out of sight of the nurses' station until the last minute. He edged the final step, leaning over to see if anyone was there. It was empty.

Quickly he looked round for the white board that usually had patients' names written on along with the room and bed they were in. He found it and scanned down the list of patients. There! He checked the corridor again and then moved as quickly as he could to the room. He could worry about leaving later. Or maybe not, depending on how things went…

The patient was on his own. Calvin pushed the door closed behind him, holding the handle down to prevent it making a loud click. Enough light spilled through glass panels to allow him to see.

'Give me enough time,' he asked God. He set his rucksack on the floor and took off his coat, stood looking down at the man whose life he had all but ended years before. Calvin remembered him having longer hair, maybe they cut it short to make it easier to wash. His eyes were closed but he wasn't sleeping. There was no monitor by the bedside and he was breathing on his own but there was a drip feeding into his arm.

Calvin kneeled by the bed and took the man's hand.

'Father, you led me to the girl and you saved her. Please father, do the same for this man. Send your Holy Spirit. Show me what to do, I ask it in Jesus name.'

Calvin waited. The power hadn't come instantly when he'd found the girl. He tried to still the voices in his head, doubts that raged, worry he would be disturbed.

'Father, give me faith. Help my unbelief.'

He slowed his breathing so he could hear Jon Thomson. The man he had knocked down and left for dead.

~~~

Thomson had a slight wheeze. Every second or third breath rasping. His hand was clammy. Calvin resisted the urge to squeeze Thomson's hand.

There was nothing. No sense of God's presence.

'Jesus, heal this man. Heal Jon Thomson. I confess I am responsible for his accident. I put him here, in this coma. In your name, I ask forgiveness. You said Jesus that as you could forgive sin you could heal. Show me that you have forgiven me, heal this man now. Wake him from his sleep.'

You couldn't force God's Spirit. Calvin knew that just as he knew that sometimes God could be pushed, could be persuaded.

'In Jesus' name, Jon, be healed. Wake. Rise up.'

How long had it been? Was the Nurse checking each room? Would she find him here?

He remembered how he had sensed God telling him to act as Elisha had, stretching himself out over the girl's body, mirroring her and breathing life into her. Should he do that again? It had been such an unusual impulse. His father had relied on ritual long after the power had left him and Calvin desperately didn't want to follow that road. There was no point in acting unless the Holy Spirit directed him to do so. Jesus had never told his disciples to do anything unusual except heal the sick. That in itself astounding, but there was no mention of them ever doing anything other than commanding the sick to be healed.

But what did they do when nothing happened? Or had that never happened? Had everyone that Peter and James and John and the others had commanded to become well been saved from their sickness?

Was it just his lack of faith, Calvin thought. Had he not prepared himself enough? Jesus said that some demons could be cast out only through prayer and fasting. Was this coma demonic? No, how could it be? It had been the accident, nothing else.

But then, why the girl? Why her when Calvin had done nothing, had all but given up on God? Why had God's Spirit come with such power then, telling him, urging him to act?

'Lord God, why? Why her? Why not this man?'

He'd rushed down here almost without thinking. Focused single mindedly on saving Jon Thomson. Undoing the wrong he'd done. He'd never considered asking if this was what God wanted.

No, that was just doubt. He needed to believe.

'Jesus, help my unbelief!'

He tried to listen, to wait for God's prompting but he couldn't still the thoughts that crowded his mind.

The sense of urgency grew, to do something, anything.

'Jon Thomson, in Jesus' name be healed,' he commanded. 'Wake up from this coma!'

Calvin stood and looked down at him. He... Behind him he heard the door to the room open.

'Who are you?' A woman's voice. Calvin began to turn.

'What are you doing with my husband?'

He saw Marie Thomson, Jon Thomson's wife. The woman who had sat in the courtroom each day of his short trial. Who had said not a single word to him, had barely showed any expression except—when he was finally sentenced—a tight, restrained smile which quickly faded leaving her eyes cold and dead towards him.

'You! Nurse!' Marie Thomson backed out of the room, looking down the ward. 'Nurse, come quick.'

Calvin looked back at Jon Thomson. There was no change. He grabbed his rucksack and walked out of the room as the Nurse came running up, an older Asian woman. She looked from Marie to Calvin, confusion in her eyes.

'What's wrong?' The Nurse asked.

'This man has no right to be here. Call security now.' Marie told her.

The Nurse looked with worry at Calvin and then backed down the ward to the nurses' station.

'I'm sorry,' Calvin told Marie. 'I had to try.'

'Try what? Finish the job? Why couldn't you have just killed him at the time? Why did you have to leave him to suffer? Me too…' She broke off, choking back a sob.

What could he say? How could he explain? Calvin looked down the corridor and saw the Nurse looking back at him, she was talking into a phone, the extension pulled taut.

He told her he was sorry one last time, then turned away and walked down the ward. He didn't look back as he turned out and away from the main body of the hospital, hoping to find an exit. Behind him he heard a shout. He started running. Ahead of him the corridor ended up in a blank wall. There was a ward to the left and as he got near he saw an exit door to the right.

He burst through it and back out into sunlight. He looked around. Where to go? He headed away from the hospital which rose behind him like a giant tombstone. A road curved past the wards and he followed it down. There was another shout but not as close. He kept running until he was out of the hospital grounds and onto the main road, a row of houses opposite and along the street a junction led up another road. He ran for the junction, his lungs now protesting. Reaching the corner he looked back. No-one was chasing him, but still he ran.

~~~

'Emma!'

Emma tried to ignore Rachel but she kept calling out her name and knocking on the door. In the end she shouted out: 'Go away!'

She heard the door open and sat up in bed. 'I said go away!'

'You are awake then,' Rachel replied, looking round the door.

'What part of "go away" don't you understand!'

'No need to get so worked up, I just wanted to see if you were alright. Did you go to the police then?'

'Get out!'

'No need to shout, I can hear you just fine.'

'Get out!' Emma screamed at Rachel.

Rachel's expression hardened. 'No need to be such a...' Her voice was cut off as she closed the door.

Emma realised she was shaking. She put her arms round herself then moved a hand round to the back of her neck. It wasn't possible. She couldn't think about it happening to her and tried to imagine she had been watching someone else fall. The way the head had... No, she couldn't do it even though the CCTV was playing in a loop round her mind. She lay back down and pulled the duvet over her, curling up into a fetal position.

The words of the homeless man were like a voice over to the image that now seemed etched in her memory: "You looked like you had fallen from the wall... No pulse, blood all round your head... Do you need me to say it? You were..." No! She resisted the thought. I wasn't. It's not possible, it's not possible... She repeated the words like a mantra, searching for a way to explain what had happened. Anything to make sense of what she had seen.

~~~

Penniless, homeless, hunger gnawing at him from inside, Calvin used his internal map to circle back to the bus station. He'd never begged in this area but unless the local council and police were especially tough on the homeless the usual tactics worked anywhere. He fished an empty cardboard coffee cup out of a bin and found a section of street that was fairly busy with coffee shops and cafes on the road leading to the bus station. He hid his rucksack as people generally were less generous the more possessions you seemed to have.

He sat down, crossed his legs and set the coffee cup in front of him. You didn't need a sign to tell people you were begging, just the courage to look up and ask if they could spare some change.

On a scale of one to ten where a one was hostile and ten would go and buy a sandwich and bring it to you, there was a good chance that enough people with compassion would walk by to enable him to afford some food. Where to buy it was another matter, not everywhere would sell to the homeless but that was not something to worry about. Jesus' words about worrying made a lot of sense to the homeless.

'Would you spare some change?'

The lady walked on, her head turned away.

'Would you spare some change?'

He looked at Calvin, embarrassment in his eyes and quickly shook his head.

'Would you spare some change?'

The young business man slowed, rooted round in his pocket and dropped some coins in Calvin's cup.

'Thank you.'

Calvin turned to look at the man as he walked away. Just like me once, except I was never so generous. The man turned a corner and then the street was quiet.

Calvin used the time to check the cup. A couple of pounds, the young man had been generous! Calvin fished the large coins out and put them in his pocket. You never left too much money in case people saw it and stopped giving or in case someone grabbed the cup and ran off with it.

Looking up and down the street there was no-one else walking by. Calvin shifted to try and get comfortable. He felt himself warm and checking upwards saw clouds move and then the sun was directly in his eyes, he put his hand up to shade them.

Time seemed to stop as he waited for someone else to walk by. Had he misjudged the location? There had been people in the cafés and coffee shops. Was it just the wrong time of day?

He was beginning to sweat in his coat so he used the quiet as an opportunity to stand and move about as he shrugged it off. Sitting back down he kept an arm up shading his eyes.

Why didn't you heal him? Calvin silently asked God. A part of him wanted to hope that maybe he would be healed, after Calvin had left, like with the girl. But Calvin knew it hadn't been the same.

God didn't respond. As silent as he had been in the hospital.

Why give me the power to heal but not let me use it?

Calvin squinted up at the sky wondering how long until the sun dipped below a building. There seemed to be no clouds heading towards it.

Why is this man less important than the girl? What was the point in even asking the questions? There would be no answer. There never were any answers.

I get it was my fault, he told God. I put him in hospital. Why couldn't you let me help him? Is there some law that says you can't heal someone you hurt?

Nothing.

Across from him the street was in shade. He could move and sit there, out of the glare. Only problem was that most people, given the choice, would walk on the sunny side of the street. And all the cafes and coffee shops were on this side.

He looked round again and saw a van slowly moving towards him. It was plain white, it's driver holding a conversation with himself. The van drew up next to him and stopped, directly blocking the sun. Calvin was able to let his arm down and as he did, it was almost as if he had given a secret signal. People started walking out of the coffee shops and cafes onto the street.

'Would you spare some change?'

'Would you…'

'Would…'

'Spare some change, please?'

There were too many of them, walking both directions, everyone looking straight ahead, not a single one stopping to drop a coin. It was as if he was invisible.

Overwhelmed, Calvin stopped trying. He sat looking at all the wealth passing by him. Wealth he used to possess, used to strive to gain. He had lost it all through one stupid, reckless decision and now was utterly dependent on others to provide for him.

Why am I here? Calvin asked himself. What am I doing? I don't know anyone here or how it works. I came down here on a foolish whim and now what am I going to do? I need to relearn where to beg, where to sleep. A new place and chances are I'll anger someone by encroaching on their patch. I didn't plan to stay here, didn't plan anything. Just got down as fast as I could. And for what? So God could make a fool of me?

That thought stung him. God didn't need to make a fool of him, he'd already done enough himself. He apologised, then addressed God directly. Why? What was it all for? If you didn't want me to come down here, why did you heal that girl? Why let that man and his wife continue to suffer?

His anger expressed, Calvin relaxed. People continued to walk by but Calvin hardly noticed them.

His thoughts drifted and then, from somewhere in his past, words from Job focused: Will the one who contends with the Almighty correct him? Let him who accuses God answer him!

Calvin didn't ask himself where in his memory the words had appeared from. He'd heard his father preach on Job many times. He knew their meaning only too well.

You're not getting off that easily, Calvin answered. Why do you heal some and not others?

Everything under Heaven belongs to me. More words from Job.

Of course it does. But Jesus healed every single person brought to him. Except, that wasn't true was it? Calvin remembered reading about Jesus' time in his home town where he'd only been able to heal a few people. Their lack of faith prevented him doing more. His father had not preached that passage.

Then there had been the disciples, unable to heal the possessed boy. Jesus had told them prayer and possibly fasting was required before the deliverance could happen.

So are you, or are you not, all powerful? Which is it?

Calvin didn't need an answer, he knew who God was. It had been drummed into him again and again until he had rebelled against his father and God. But the rebel carries around the very thing he is fighting against.

So where does this leave me? My fault, my failure, my lack of faith, my lack of fasting and prayer?

A deep sadness filled him.

I wanted to help him. I wanted to make it right, but if you won't help me then what can I do? Don't you want him to be healed?

Of course God did want to heal him. He recalled a picture from a Sunday School book, Jesus standing by a round stone that blocked up a tomb. Tears running down his face, Jesus wept. For a friend, yes, but still, Jesus had compassion, compassion that made him weep again as he stood over Jerusalem knowing the people were about to reject him and knowing what the ultimate cost of that rejection would be for them.

What do you want for this man? Is that the question I should have been asking? What do you want? Do you want to heal him? Do you want him to remain in this coma? Or do you want to take him? Is this his time?

Something broke inside Calvin and he remembered the woman's words, why didn't you just kill him?

I didn't want to kill him, I don't want to be responsible for his death.

But I am responsible, he answered himself. I did kill him. Condemned him to unconsciousness for the rest of his life. What life is that? Is it his time to die? Do I need to let him go?

He wished he could be somewhere else, scream to the sky, cry and sob openly but he was stuck on a crowded street, his thoughts silent, only his tears visible.

Is this what I need to do, let him go? Give him up? Is this what you want?

Calvin sensed it was and quietly began to whisper: Father, take Jon Thomson. I give him over to you. I let him go to you. I'm sorry I hurt him. Sorry I took his life, took him away from his family. If you want to heal him then heal him. If you want to take him then take him. He belongs to you, not me. You are God. You alone are God. I release him to you.

As Calvin looked up, the van moved away and sunlight flooded his eyes. Really? He asked God. Do I have to put up with this the rest of the afternoon?

He sensed God telling him to look down. His cup was full of change. He hadn't noticed a single person throw money in but it was almost ready to spill over.

Calvin looked around. The street was once more empty. Alone again he started to laugh, laughter that broke quickly until a person watching could not have told whether he was laughing or crying.

CHAPTER THIRTY-THREE
The Gates of Dawn

Two weeks without work from Archer and he was reduced to this... William used his bolt cutters to clip through the padlock, then carefully pushed open the door. As he expected—no alarm sounded, though it was always possible the owner had a silent alarm installed.

William pulled the door shut behind him and only then used his torch to look around the workshop. Laptops and desktop computers were arranged along one workbench, mobile phones and more computers on a shelving unit. Opening his rucksack, William quickly placed the mobile phones inside. All of the equipment in here was in to be repaired which implied that it either had been repaired or could be. Either way, it was worth something.

There was no point in trying to move the desktop computers, they were worth next to nothing nowadays, but the laptops could still fetch fifty pounds apiece. He unfolded a large durable bag and began placing the laptops in that. He was bent over in the act of placing one in the bag when he froze.

There had been no sound, no movement he was aware of, but he picked up the bag and without hesitation left the storeroom leaving behind the remaining laptops. He pushed the door closed behind him and adjusted the padlock back in its hasp so the door stayed closed.

He walked away at a normal pace down the alley that ran behind the shop units and as he approached the end of the block he saw a man turn into the alley from the street side. Not police, he noted immediately. William nodded at the man and saw the man look him over as they passed. His senses now on high alert, William listened to the sound of the man's steps to see if the man had stopped after he walked by. No, the man still seemed to be walking on.

William turned at the end and increased his pace as he was no longer visible from the alley. He had left his van a block away and one street down. Not ideal if he needed to leave in a hurry but always better to avoid association with a burglary, replacing a van was expensive.

Now moving at a brisk walk, William headed for a snicket that would take him off the street. The sooner he was out of sight the better.

Had the man been the owner? He might never know though he would be checking the paper for the next couple of days. Burglaries frequently made the papers and it was always interesting to read what had been revealed and what had been left out. Also to see what his competition was up to.

Not for the first time William wondered what had warned him he needed to leave. Maybe the man had driven to the front of the shop and walked round to the back and he'd heard the sound of the engine. Yet he was certain there had been no cars passing by on the street. Not at three in the morning.

In his view, stealing from a shop was only a little less worse than stealing from someone's home. Small shops like this were lifeblood to the owner who might not have adequate insurance to cover the loss. Warehouses were his preferred target. He would be happy doing over a larger retailer but the security was usually too risky unless you had someone on the inside and for that you needed the range of contacts that Archer had.

The temptation to call him was getting stronger but William knew he needed to wait it out. Archer would call. He had to.

~~~

'How did you get my number?'

Tariq looked away from the arms dealer and quickly scanned the restaurant. 'You supplied weapons to a friend of mine.'

'Which friend?'

Tariq held the man's gaze for a few seconds. 'The weapons were delivered to Libya in August last year. My friend said you were a professional.'

'Ha!' The arms dealer barked a short laugh and casually looked round the restaurant himself. 'I recall the delivery. So, how can I help you?'

Tariq saw the waiter approaching and held up his hand, smiling at the waiter.

'Are you ready to order?'

'What soup do you have today?' Tariq asked.

'The special today is carrot and orange.'

'I will take that, thank you. And do you have green tea?'

'Yes sir.'

'A pot of that as well.'

'And you sir?'

The arms dealer ordered lemon sole with new potatoes and a glass of apple juice. Tariq was impressed, dealing with men who did not respect Islam often meant having to put up with customs he found distasteful. Eating with someone who thought bloody meat or bacon was an acceptable choice to have with a Muslim was one of the prices he had to pay.

After the waiter moved away Tariq pulled out a notepad and pencil. He tore out a page and began writing. The arms dealer waited patiently and then took the offered paper and read it carefully.

'This will be expensive. It will require multiple deliveries and time to source.' He folded the paper and laid it on the table, his hand resting on it.

'How expensive and how much time?'

The arms dealer leaned forward and spoke in a hushed voice. 'One thousand rifles will take approximately two weeks to source. I should be able to provide them at 1,200 Euros each. The more specialised rifles will be 5,000 Euros each but will take an extra week. Ammunition will be available immediately. The quantities you are looking for...' He thought a minute. 'You're looking at an easy quarter of a million.

'The plastic will be expensive. One hundred kilos at 1000 Euros each kilo. I can source this immediately. Body armour...' He looked up at Tariq, a slight crease between his eyes. 'Not something I get asked for very often. Two hundred units at 300 Euros each. I'll need a couple of weeks to source them.'

He sat back. 'Secure delivery on top at 300,000 Euros. All in I should be able to source everything within three weeks. Delivery will require an additional two weeks of staged deliveries, three in all. I recommend we use multiple sites. Total cost...' He put a hand to his mouth and stroked his beard. 'I can provide everything for two million Euros all in. I will need half in advance. The remainder to be paid in equal installments on receipt of each delivery. Is this acceptable?'

Tariq nodded. 'I will arrange for the first million to be transferred tomorrow.'

The arms dealer slipped the paper off the table and placed it in the inside pocket of his suit. He then took out a small card and slid it over to Tariq. 'My account number. Will you be in Vilnius for long?'

'Unfortunately not.' Tariq waited while the waiter approached again with their meals.

They thanked him and both tasted their meals. The soup was excellent, neither too sweet nor tart.

'I may walk down to see the Gates of Dawn before I leave.'

'It is worth viewing.' The arms dealer took a bite of his fish. 'I realise the portraying of images is not... universally approved of but the intricacy of the icon of the Virgin Mary is spectacular.'

Tariq smiled and nodded. He had no interest in idolatry but had been curious to read about the gate in a tourist guide as he had traveled to Lithuania. While different from the Bars of York, it also had some similarities to them. He wanted a chance to study a gate without worrying about CCTV cameras recording him doing so.

~~~

'I'm home,' Danny shouted to Cynthia. Silence greeted him. He stood for a moment, the lack of noise an almost physical sensation, then busied himself putting his things away.

He found Cynthia in the living room, the room deathly quiet as she sat still on the sofa. He saw her bible next to her. Always praying, he thought. He sat down. 'Can we talk?' He noticed her eyes seemed brighter than normal as she turned to look at him. Had she been crying? She didn't answer, just looked at him with those too bright eyes. 'Rudd's recommended me for a new role,' he said.

Cynthia looked at him in puzzlement. 'What does that mean?'

'There's a position opened up, it's called a Counter Terrorism Security Advisor. Rudd feels it would be a good opportunity for me.'

Cynthia shook her head. 'Counter Terrorism? What has that got to do with police work?'

Danny sighed. 'More than you'd suspect, we get weekly briefings now. For the last five years we've been receiving training on how to identify potential terrorists, how to prevent people from becoming radicalised. Every year it seems to become a bigger part of my job.'

'But you're a detective... Why should that be part of your job?'

'I meet with people in the community, sometimes vulnerable people who could easily get caught up, groomed in a way to become a terrorist.'

'You've never mentioned any of this before.'

'It was just part of the job. They show us training videos, we have to attend courses. You know what that's like. You take it for granted.'

'When does Rudd want a decision?'

'Friday.'

'Friday!' She stared at him. 'When did he ask you?'

Danny held her stare. He could see she felt hurt but there was nothing else for it. 'Last week.'

It took her a while to respond. All the time she sat there she kept looking at him and he desperately wanted to look away.

'Why are you telling me now?' She eventually asked.

He was thrown by the question. 'What do you mean?'

Again she didn't respond straight away but kept studying him. 'You said Rudd asked you last week. Maybe that was on Friday which means you had the whole weekend to tell me and didn't. But maybe he asked you on Monday which would mean you waited a week and a half. Either way, if you've waited all this time, why tell me now?'

'I thought you should know.'

'I should know? Not you wanted to discuss it with me, not ask my opinion, just thought I should know.' Her voice was strangely calm. Danny would have preferred if she was shouting at him.

'I should have told you.'

'Should have? Out of a sense of duty? Maybe.' She picked up her bible and stood. 'Maybe when you've decided what you're doing you should tell me.' She walked out of the room.

'Cynthia…' He called after her, stood but then remained where he was.

CHAPTER THIRTY-FOUR
The Fifth Angle

His Sergeant had arranged an appointment with the Chief Surgeon at 4pm. Danny turned up early at York District Hospital and asked at reception where he could find Mr Anthony Cole. His office was on the third floor, a view of The Minster's twin towers visible over the houses in between.

'Thank you for seeing me, Mr Cole.'

'Thank you, Detective? Have you good news?'

'Of a sort... I have the CCTV footage.' Danny handed over a DVD Davison had burned for him.

'I told you I didn't have time, Detective.'

'It will speed things up tremendously if you would just watch the footage. It's very short. Less than ten minutes.'

'Very well, you have ten minutes.' Cole took the DVD and inserted it in his laptop. Danny walked round Cole's desk to watch with him.

The four CCTV images started to play and Danny watched Cole as he first frowned, then almost tried to look away and then shook his head. 'What is this?'

Danny checked. The ambulance had not arrived yet. 'Keep watching.'

As soon as the short movie ended, Cole reset it and leaned in, studying the views intensely. Danny waited and watched Cole who eventually sat back.

'I don't know what you're trying to show me.'

'You have accused members of your staff of perpetrating an elaborate hoax and wasting valuable NHS resources.'

Cole's eyes flicked to the now still CCTV images, stopped as the ambulance drove off camera.

'My team requested the CCTV feeds immediately after the incident was reported to us. We've checked them thoroughly and there is no obvious discrepancy between them. The footage checks out exactly with the testimony of all parties involved and so unless you are also accusing the telephone operator; your Paramedic staff; and the staff who run the Video Surveillance Unit of all being involved in this elaborate hoax, then I think we have to assume this was, on the face of it, at worst a foolish accident that could have been a lot worse.'

'It's not possible.' Cole fumbled about with the controls on his Laptop and finally managed to restart the movie but at a slower speed. He pointed at one CCTV feed. 'Look here, the angle of her fall. That would break her neck. Would have killed most people instantly. Those that survived would be paraplegic. No movement below the neck. But then, the way she hits, that would have cracked open her skull as well. Massive trauma accounting for the blood and the spinal fluid observed in her ears.'

'Yet she was discharged within two days with you yourself giving her a clean bill of health,' said Danny. 'I met her yesterday. Apart from some memory loss, which suggests some trauma, she appeared perfectly healthy. I told you yesterday that we had some questions about the toxicology. We had wondered if the blood samples had been mixed up, but then we got the DNA analysis back on the blood and fluids found at the scene. I'm not a doctor, would you…' Danny handed over a folder.

Cole skimmed the forms, then read them properly before laying them on the table.

'Blood samples taken from her hair are a DNA match. Same with the spinal fluid. It might be possible to extract and store your own blood but not spinal fluid.'

'I was told she has a scar on the back of her head…'

'There is evidence of an old head trauma. Scarring of the skin and the MRI revealed healed bone damage. Nothing in her records though. No, this makes no sense. We need to look deeper into what happened.'

'I believe she is… I don't like the term lucky… Let me say fortunate. Let me ask you. We are both professional men who deal with traumatic situations on a daily basis. Have you never come across a situation that defied explanation?'

'I'm a scientist, Detective. There is an explanation for everything.'

'My scientific discipline is forensic and I disagree with you. Some things cannot be explained. I am closing this case, Mr Cole. If you wish to make a formal request to my superior for additional information, that is your prerogative, but I strongly advise you that pursuing this in any way could have a detrimental effect on your own career.'

'Are you threatening me?'

'I am warning you that the evidence backs up Ms Hunter's story. What little of it she can remember. I will release this footage to Emma Hunter. I will give her full access to any information she requires to defend herself including, if necessary, transcripts of testimony obtained.' He hesitated before continuing. 'I'm warning you that if a copy of this was to leak out onto YouTube and it was made public that you are leading a witch hunt against this girl, she will become a celebrity while you become a villain.'

'You are threatening me! How dare you!'

'Neither I, nor anyone in my department will in any way smear your name, but I cannot speak for Ms Hunter or her friends. I understand you had her and her friend suspended?'

'Of course.'

'From their perspective, neither she nor Ms Phillips have done anything wrong and yet you have made it your personal mission to ruin their lives. Tread very carefully around this case. As you have kept stating, it is not just NHS resources that are being wasted but police resource also, though not as far as I can see by Ms Hunter or Ms Phillips. My advice—you reinstate them, quietly apologise, and pray that they don't decide to sue you, because if this footage ever sees the light of day, your career is over!'

CHAPTER THIRTY-FIVE
Watchman on the Wall

Mary opened her eyes, the images of death still fresh in her mind. Why Lord? Why am I having these dreams? She let the words fade away and allowed herself to lie still, wondering if she could just drift away herself, let go of this life and just be at peace.

May their blood be on the head of the watchman… The thought appeared at the front of her mind like the remembering of a task that had been forgotten. It was from Ezekiel, she knew that instantly. A book that she avoided reading as it always made her feel uncomfortable. How did it go? You are the watchman, if you warn the people, their blood shall be on their heads. If the watchman does not warn them, their blood shall be on the head of the watchman.

She knew it was symbolic, that Ezekiel had been told to warn the people of Israel that if they did not turn from their sin, destruction would take them yet that destruction had been literal. The Babylonians had conquered Jerusalem and those that were not slaughtered were taken into captivity.

This dream she had been having, how could she have not realised this before, what if it wasn't a torment for her but a warning? What if she was the watchman?

She sat up. But who can I tell? She asked God. The Reverend has forbidden me from speaking to the church and if I was to tell them this now, they would just think I'm crazy.

May their blood be on the head of the watchman. The thought wouldn't go away. Is this from you, Lord? What should I do, who should I tell?

She waited and when there was no answer she finally cried out in exasperation: 'You are so infuriating!'

Even this didn't seem to warrant a response so she made to get out of bed. She finally looked at the clock and realised it was after 6am. A normal time to wake up for once. Had she actually had more than a few hours of sleep?

She pulled on her dressing gown and headed downstairs where she suddenly realised who she should talk to.

~ ~ ~

'Sir, I've decided to accept the role.'

'Excellent. That's the right decision, Danny.'

'I have a few conditions.'

Rudd sat forward, placing his elbows on the desk and hands pressed together, almost as if he was praying. 'I see.'

'I want a two month handover. I still have several live cases and want to support my team while they progress them.'

'That sounds reasonable.'

'Also, I am only committing to the role for one year, two at the top. I will invest in the role, but I'm still not convinced it's where I'll be of most use. I would like an assurance that should I decide I'm not in the right role after that time, I will be able to return to my current role.'

It seemed ridiculous that at his age and with his experience that he should be this nervous about negotiating over a role, but as he sat in Rudd's office, it occurred to Danny that he'd only ever had one real interview— when he'd applied to join the force. He'd been clear at the outset that his aim was to make detective and while he'd had interviews leading up to each promotion, they had all been informal. He'd already known going in what the outcome was going to be.

Eventually, Rudd nodded. 'It's not unreasonable. I've pushed you to take the role of CTSA. However, if you're still uncertain now then perhaps you should recommend someone else…'

'I've given it a lot of thought, Sir. The training day was useful and I'm wondering if I can set up a network in York that will prove useful both in combating terrorism and fighting crime.'

'But you have doubts?'

'As you said, Sir, this wasn't my idea. I can see potential and possibilities in the role. Maybe I will grow into it. I would like to know that if I'm not the right fit, that I will be able to come back to a job I love.'

'Very well then. One year in the role and we can review it at that point. But only a one month handover. You'll find your workload increases dramatically over the next month as you start getting the briefings through.'

It was as good a compromise as he could have hoped for. Danny thanked Rudd, they shook hands and he left hoping he had made the right decision.

~~~

The phones ringing woke her but Emma turned over and ignored it. She heard Rachel answer it, a muted conversation and then a short silence. She was starting to drift off again when her door opened.

'Are you awake?' Rachel asked, loudly.

Emma peered over the duvet and shook her head.

Rachel sat on the bed and pulled the duvet down slightly. Emma tried to pull it back but then gave up and put a hand over her eyes to block out the light. 'What?'

'I'm tempted to leave you to stew in here but I've got to talk to someone.'

'You're making no sense.'

'You're off the hook. Well, almost. I still think you're a cow and I'm not sure if I'll ever trust you again. But you're off the hook.'

'Off what hook? What're you talking about?'

'They've re-instated us. That was HR, they want us in Monday morning. The suspension has been lifted, we'll be paid as if we'd been working. Everything has been dropped.'

'Why?'

'Who cares why! We've got our jobs back. What more do you want?'

'I don't… I'm sorry. Does this mean I can go back to sleep?'

'No! You've got to get up. We're going to celebrate!'

Emma waved, gesturing Rachel out of the room. 'Let me get dressed then.'

She watched as Rachel left and closed the door and then pulled the duvet around her again and closed her eyes. She knew she should feel happy but instead she just wanted to shut the world out.

~~~

'Daniel! I didn't think, well thank you for coming so soon! Come in.' Mary stepped back from the door and let Danny into her house. He and Cynthia had been invited round for a Sunday dinner a few times, many years ago, but as Mary had become more cantankerous and he had become busier, they had stopped accepting the invitations. He thought that, until the expulsion, Cynthia was still meeting up with Mary for coffee occasionally, but realised with some shame that he wasn't sure.

'Can I get you some tea, Daniel?'

'Danny, please Mary, no-one calls me Daniel. No thanks, I just have a few minutes. You were saying you had something important to tell me?' He noticed Mary wringing her hands together.

'Well, yes. Please come and sit down.' She led him into her sitting room. 'You're named after a great man, you know. An honourable one. You should not be ashamed of your name.'

'Danny is fine,' he said, sitting down. 'Now, you wanted to tell me something?'

'Did you know your uncle?'

Danny sat back and studied Mary. Perhaps she really had flipped.

'Daniel Carter. Your father and mother had a high regard for him. One of the elders in the church when you were born. He led your father to faith.'

Daniel Carter, had he heard that name before? Danny cast his mind back and tried to recall if his parents had mentioned why they had named him Daniel. He couldn't remember ever asking them or them mentioning a specific reason for choosing his name. He had always been Danny, as long as he could remember.

'I can't remember them mentioning him.' Danny tried leaning forward. 'Anyway, as I said, I don't have a lot of time. You wanted to tell me something?'

'Oh yes. The dreams.'

He felt himself go rigid. Dreams!

'I didn't know who else to talk to. I can't go to the Reverend, not after everything he has done.'

He has done? 'Perhaps you could talk with Cynthia. I'm sure…'

'Cynthia? But Daniel, this is important!'

'Dreams?'

'Yes.' She stared at him and Danny noticed dark circles under her eyes. She looked exhausted.

'Every night for two weeks, the same dream. I think… something terrible is going to happen.'

Danny began wondering if he should call a doctor, or psychiatrist.

'I wondered if maybe you could do something. If there's a way to stop them?'

'Them?'

'The men that are going to attack York.'

He stood up. 'I don't have time for this, Mary, I think you need help.'

'Daniel!' She stood as well. 'Sit down!'

'I'm not going to be bullied by you, Mary.' He said in a soft voice.

Her expression said it all, confusion. Had no one ever stood up to this woman?

'I… Detective Inspector, I believe some men are planning to attack

York, can I tell you what I know?'

Where had that come from? She looked broken, fragile even and yet somehow she had managed to say the only thing that gave him no choice but to listen. Danny slowly sat himself back down. He fished out his notebook and pen from his coat pocket. 'Okay, tell me what you know about this plan to attack York.'

~~~

He drove on autopilot on his way back to Fulford Road. How could she have known he had just accepted the CTSA role? Had Cynthia told her? No, he hadn't even told Cynthia yet! He groaned, he was not looking forward to that. Cynthia had asked him to see her, maybe if he'd gone sooner... But what would he have said, have done? He still was uncomfortable with Tony's expulsion of Mary, yet even before he'd talked with Tony, even though he still didn't want to admit it, at some level he agreed with what he'd done. You couldn't go around trying to undermine your leadership.

Maybe if he'd had some plan of what to say to her before he'd gone, but when she'd called that morning, sounding desperate, telling him it was urgent... What a complete waste of time! Oh yes, he'd taken the notes, assured her he would look into what she had said and left as soon as she had finished. In the end, he had felt sorry for her. She looked completely broken. Obviously not sleeping, unable to handle the thought that the church she felt so passionately about no longer wanted her.

Tony had been right in starting the discipline process. Even a church needed to set boundaries at some point. Trying to get Tony removed, that was going too far. Maybe if someone had spoken with her earlier...Maybe if he had... He didn't want to go there, she had been getting worse for years. Her attitude had been increasingly dismissive, she had become unapproachable. He would have to tell Cynthia, Tony as well. She needed help. Maybe even to be admitted for a while until she could cope again.

A terrorist attack? Where had that come from? A nightmare that she had latched onto. Except, what had she said? It had gotten worse, the same dream, night after night. Could that actually happen? The same dream again and again.

Danny tried to remember the last time he had dreamed. What was it they said? Everyone dreams every night, we just don't remember most of the time. It certainly would make her feel important, special. God giving only her a warning. Something to latch onto after being kicked out of the church. Except, she had no-one to share it with... Was that why she was so distraught?

How could he investigate a dream? He'd be a laughing stock. Besides, if

God was really going to intervene wouldn't he have spoken to someone who could do something about it?

He pulled into the police station on Fulford Road. Locking the car, he decided he would ask Cynthia to try and speak with Mary. As for his promise to investigate a possible terrorist attack… It would be better for everyone if that was forgotten!

~~~

'I went to see Mary.'

Cynthia turned round from the hob setting down the spoon she'd been using to stir a pan.

'You did?'

Danny felt slightly hurt by the shock evident on her face.

'I said I would.'

Cynthia raised her eyebrows slightly but didn't say anything in response.

'Anyway, I think we need to get her help, maybe take her to a doctor.'

Cynthia's hand flew to her mouth. 'Is she sick? Has this all been too much for her?'

'No, not like… The old bat still seems fighting fit, no, it's her mind.'

'This is your God Mother, don't call her an old bat!'

Danny took a deep breath. 'She's cracked, Cynthia. Maybe all this trying to get Tony removed is just part of some dementia or something. She was telling me about these dreams about a terrorist attack on York.'

'Dreams?' Cynthia tilted her head slightly.

'Yes, she was fixated on them, believes God's trying to warn her.'

Danny expected Cynthia to respond, but she continued to look at him, an expression he couldn't read on her face.

'Maybe he is,' she eventually said.

Danny gave a half laugh. 'You're kidding, right?'

'God's spoken to me in dreams before.'

He felt a gulf between them as the words registered. 'You've never…'

'Never what, Danny?' She turned back to the hob and started stirring the pan again. 'Never spoken to you about the dreams I've had? When would I do that? When you peck me on the cheek before rushing out the door in the morning. Perhaps in the few minutes I see you on an evening. When exactly would be a good time for you to sit down and actually listen to me?'

He took a hesitant half step towards her. 'Why would God tell Mary about this? Why not me?'

'Maybe he used Mary to tell you.'

'Are you saying you believe her?'

Cynthia turned to him again. 'I'm saying that God has spoken to me in dreams. Who am I to say he hasn't spoken to Mary?'

'I can't act on the dreams of a mad old lady.'

'Remember who this is you're talking about!'

'She's gone insane! Do you want me to throw away my career for this?'

'Well, if your career means so much to you... I had always thought you cared more about the people you were serving than your career. Is this why you've been considering this CT... CST...'

'Counter Terrorism Security Advisor and you should know I've told Rudd I'll do it.'

'You weren't going to tell me?' He could see the hurt on her face.

'Of course I was going to tell you.'

'Not before you told Rudd.'

'This isn't...' He tried to regroup. 'I needed to tell you about Mary. No-one is going to take me seriously if I start talking about dreams.'

'Then don't talk about them! You can investigate what she's told you without revealing your source can't you? You can even say that you are not sure how reliable it is? You do have that, don't you? Unreliable witnesses that sometimes turn out to be right.'

'Yes,' he grudgingly admitted. 'But it's hard going to investigate something with no evidence and no suspects.'

'What was it you said once? If it was easy they wouldn't need you to do it! I don't know if Mary's dreams are from God, but perhaps you should try asking him yourself before dismissing what Mary has told you!'

~~~

Najwa sat very still and listened for sounds outside her room. The normally bustling house was quiet with her two younger brothers and father at the Mosque for evening prayer and for once, none of her cousins or their friends hanging about. Her mother was downstairs watching TV and Najwa had excused herself saying she wanted an early night. For maybe an hour she had some privacy.

With younger brothers who were as nosy as they were disrespectful she had learned long ago how to hide anything she did not want stolen. She retrieved the Injil from it's hiding place and made herself comfortable on her bed. She started flicking through the pages, searching for any mention of Deborah. Ruth and Esther had been easy to find, both had whole books to themselves! Esther's story was far more exciting and Najwa had been unable to stop thinking about what she'd had to do, wondering if she would have been willing to risk her life to save her people... No wonder Mary had called her brave.

Ruth's story didn't strike Najwa as all that brave. If she had married a foreigner she had already turned away from her own people. Maybe she would have found it hard to get married again. Though as a foreigner in Israel, Najwa supposed Ruth might have found it equally hard.

The index didn't show any book called Deborah so she could not have been as important as Ruth or Esther and there were no books called Mary either. Did Christians believe these women were more important than Jesus' mother who was even mentioned in the Quran, or was this part of the corruption of the Injil as she'd always been taught? She kept flicking pages hoping that the name might jump out to her. It had always seemed strange to her that the Injil could have become corrupted. Why would Allah give his word to the Jews and Christians and then allow them to change it? If the Quran could have been kept unsullied, surely the Injil could also have been saved.

'Najwa!' She heard her mother call. 'Could you come and help me?'

She groaned and slid the Injil under her pillow in case her mother came up, then lay down and pretended to be asleep.

Her mother called once more, but then was silent and before long Najwa wasn't pretending.

CHAPTER THIRTY-SIX
A Tent Peg

Najwa had slept in as was usual on a Saturday and when her mother asked her if she had plans for the day she knew she had better do something or she would end up spending the afternoon doing chores. She told her mother she had library books to take back which wasn't a lie, she always had books to take back though she usually read them so fast she had weeks before she needed to return them.

The day was colder than it had been but was sunny, so Najwa decided to walk through the park on the way into York. When she was younger her parents had taken her to play on the slides and swings and she stopped to watch the children running and shouting. One day it will be my children playing here, she told herself.

Getting cold from standing still, Najwa walked on. Almost out of the park she saw a woman—dressed like Mary—walking in front of her. Najwa ran to catch her up.

She reached the woman, but had to catch her breath. '…Mary?'

The woman stopped and turned, it was her!

'I couldn't find the story of Deborah, or Mary,' Najwa told her.

Mary didn't respond and Najwa realised she had a confused look.

'I like the story of Esther,' Najwa continued. 'Ruth was boring though.'

'You're the girl,' Mary said. 'You spoke to me last week.'

Najwa bit back a sarcastic response. 'So where are the other stories?'

'Other stories…' Mary's frowned. 'Oh. Deborah I don't know exactly, her story is in the book of Judges. Mary is in the gospels.'

'What are they?'

'The gospels? They're the books about Jesus—Matthew, Mark, Luke and

John. The first three have Mary's story, though there are other Mary's mentioned. Excuse me, I don't know your name.'

'Najwa. Okay, I better go.' She turned away and started walking on. Judges... She would have to look that up when she got home.

~~~

Mary stared after the girl as she hurried away. Twice the girl had asked her about the bible and what had she done this time? Only directed the girl towards one of the most violent books in the bible! Then gone on about her namesakes, no wonder the girl had rushed off.

What had her name been? Najwa? What must Najwa think of her, Mary wondered. Probably the same as Daniel who despite taking notes and assuring her he would investigate had looked at her like she was crazy the whole time he was with her. She had hoped that the nightmare would have stopped after telling him but no, that night she had been woken up as usual, if anything the pictures more vivid than they had been.

How could she talk sense to anyone when she was this tired?

Lord, she prayed in silence. I am a failure. How can I reach anyone for you? Please, by your Holy Spirit, speak to this girl. May she hear from you.

A gust of cold air made Mary shiver and she started walking again. She really needed advice, but the Reverend had made it clear she was excluded from the church. Should she even be speaking to the girl without her mother there? The girl had sought her out but even so... Yet how could she turn her away?

Mary turned towards her home. She had wondered about trying to go to the hospital again but she obviously needed to rest. Maybe next week...

~~~

Deborah wasn't that brave, Najwa thought. Fortunately she hadn't had to read far through the book of Judges before she found the story. Jael was the real heroine of the story, killing the commander of the enemies army like that. What must it have been like, to stand boldly in front of your enemy and invite him into your tent? Father would have a fit if I did that, she thought. Then to drive a tent peg into his skull... Najwa imagined herself kneeling with a long spike in one hand, a hammer in the other. She shivered.

It wasn't that Deborah wasn't amazing, it was just strange that Mary had said it was Deborah's story, not Jael's. Here it was saying Deborah was a prophetess—making her almost equal with Mohamed. Najwa had never heard of a female prophet and not only a prophet, but the leader of all Israel. Not just the women, but the men too.

It went against everything she had been taught, that men were the leaders, that a woman's role was that of servant. Was this part of the lie that had corrupted the Injil? Was this why Mary thought Deborah was more important than Jael—because Jael simply killed her enemy while Deborah was a leader and a prophet?

Who could she ask about this? No-one in her family. No-one in the Mosque. She got up, unrolled her prayer mat and bowed down. 'Allah, hear my prayer. What should I believe? Should I read more of this Injil or is it full of lies? You sent your prophet to us. Did you also send this woman, Deborah?'

She waited, silence buzzing in her ears. A memory of Mary's words from earlier came to her—the books of Jesus. She sat up. Jesus was a prophet, the Quran even said he was Messiah.

She got back on her bed and looked for the books of Jesus. Finding the book of Matthew, she started reading.

CHAPTER THIRTY-SEVEN
A Hidden Army

Tariq set a kettle onto boil. He slapped his face and rubbed his eyes to wake himself up then walked round the small kitchen to get his blood flowing. It had been a productive week. After returning from Lithuania he'd attended two of the recruitment meetings observing Zafar and the response to him. He was a natural born recruiter and they already had more men signed up for their defence league than they needed at each university. At this stage though, more men could only be an asset as he was certain they would not be able to rely on all of them to progress to the second stage.

He had managed to get five hours sleep the previous night. Not enough but it would have to do, there were calls to be made this morning. Zafar had had no idea how extensive his network was and had protested when Tariq had laid out his own timeline for their project. The fact was that he already had men in place throughout the country who were potential leaders. He now intended to activate them to begin setting up the informal defence groups and identify men who would be unsatisfied with passive defence.

There was so much that could go wrong at this stage, the risk increasing as they started to recruit their army. Every individual a potential security risk, exponentially increasing the chance of someone doing or saying something that would alert the security services and result in the whole operation being uncovered before they could act. Fortunately his network was made up of men who were highly motivated and with his experience of recruitment he was confident he could minimize the risk.

What he was less sure of was the hope of inspiring a true revolution. Would they really see a British Spring? He had the backing to enable an armed uprising in all of the major cities but would his brothers actually be willing to fight or would they cower in their bedrooms?

The kettle was now boiling but Tariq left it as he allowed his thoughts to flow. The reality was as Raj had intimated. Throughout the Islamic world the masses were usually content to put up with dictatorships rather than fight for true Islam. Even the revolutions of the past few years had only replaced one form of dictatorship with another. Yet perhaps this was the only way through. The Islamic world was in turmoil at present. A boiling pot that Tariq believed was purifying the believers, was causing them to turn back to the Quran, back to the teachings of Mohammed.

Tariq switched off the gas and moved the kettle off the hob. He readied a teapot with green tea and poured in the steaming liquid.

Together with Zafar they had estimated they would need two hundred people to capture and hold York. A small number for such a large task but no hostile action on this scale in the UK had ever been attempted. Two hundred people to recruit, to train, to deploy... All without raising suspicion.

If their attack was to have any long lasting result there was a need to double that number as soon as possible. To recruit a second army that could be dispersed throughout Britain and strike at the moment of greatest confusion, show his brothers and sisters this was not just an extravagant but isolated event. Show them this was the opportunity to rally together, to not just preach peace but to bring peace, to bring true Islam to Britain.

Tariq poured a cup of barely coloured liquid into his round, handleless tea cup. Water. He then quickly poured the liquid back into the teapot, mixing the water and releasing more flavour from the tea before pouring it out again. Mud. Tariq again poured the liquid back into the teapot and lifted the pot to give it a gentle swirl before pouring for a third time. Tea!

The ritual complete, Tariq lifted the scorching tea to his mouth and took a sip. It would taste better with jam but that was a luxury he would not allow himself.

He would need someone to lead this second, hidden army. Someone organised, with a broad imagination. It would mean losing their input to this first phase of the operation but if the first phase was to have any lasting meaning there would have to be further attacks. Tariq poured himself another cup as he sat in silence, his mind thinking through the next steps he would have to take.

CHAPTER THIRTY-EIGHT
Security Risks

At 09:50 Emma and Rachel walked into the hospital's HR reception area. Emma let Rachel speak to the receptionist while she sat down, she felt really on edge and a little light headed and was trying not to let it show.

Rachel sat down, chatting away as she had on the bus over. 'We're meeting with Katie Harper, have you met her before? I think I spoke to her once about shift pay,' she continued without waiting for an answer.

Emma tuned her out and focused on her breathing, giving the occasional murmur and nod as Rachel kept speaking. Emma wasn't sure if Rachel was excited or nervous. She'd certainly been far more relaxed around Emma over the weekend, talking enough for both of them which had been useful as Emma had not felt like talking. Instead she was able to zone out as she was doing now, not really thinking about anything and especially not about that...

'Right, thank you for coming in. I'm Katie Harper... Have we met?'

Emma looked up and saw Rachel stand.

'I think you helped me a couple of years ago.'

'I thought I recognised your face.'

Emma stood as Katie smiled at her.

'You must be Emma, good to meet you. Come on through.'

Emma followed Rachel and Katie who led them into a meeting room.

'We're eager to get you both started back right away,' Katie said as soon as the door was closed. 'Unfortunately though we had to fill the slots on A&E while you were away.'

Emma and Rachel exchanged a glance as they sat down.

Taking a seat herself, Katie breezed on: 'We have shifts available on several wards including General ward's 3 and 4; Elderly ward 12 and Psych' ward 15. Which would you prefer?'

'We'd prefer to go back on A&E.' Rachel said. 'Wouldn't we Emma?'

Emma gave a non-committal shrug. Even with a whole weekend's warning she hadn't even considered she might actually be going back to work.

'We can certainly put you on the waiting list for slots.' Katie smiled at them both. 'As you'll know people do move about and I'm sure it won't be long. In the meantime we will need to find you a different area.'

'Maybe we should speak to the Union Rep,' Rachel suggested.

'Oh, I'm sure that won't be necessary. I'll see what I can do to make sure you're at the top of the waiting list.'

Rachel sighed in defeat and looked at Emma who had yet to say a word. 'What do you reckon? A year of jostling to get on A&E and we're away for a couple of weeks only to be bumped off. Can you cope going back to a General ward again?'

Emma looked away.

'I'm sorry!' Rachel put a hand on Emma's arm. 'That came out wrong.'

'It's okay. Actually, I'm not sure I'm ready to go back to A&E anyway.' Emma gave Rachel a quick smile and turned to Katie. 'I don't mind doing a Psych' rotation. You can put me down for that.'

'Rather you than me.' Rachel gave a fake shudder. 'Put me down for one of the General wards. But keep me at the top of your list for A&E.'

~~~

Zafar paced up and down near the front of the hall rehearsing in his mind what he would say. He had notes ready, bullet points he and Tariq had worked out and which he had used during the first couple of "Stage Two" meetings they had held, but he knew he would make more of a connection with the men if he spoke from the heart rather than a script.

The hall was filling up fast and it looked like every seat might be taken. Everything was moving so quickly he couldn't quite comprehend how they were managing to keep on schedule. Tariq had asked him to give out business cards at the first meeting. There was a phone number unique to that meeting on each card and everyone who called or texted the number was sent a text giving a link to a website Tariq had set up solely for their operation. The website asked for contact details and asked the respondents to complete a questionnaire that was in itself fairly innocuous but which had allowed them to identify suitable recruits to progress to "Stage Two."

This was the riskiest stage of their operation, the point where he would begin to reveal their intention. While the response had been overwhelming during the first meetings, he knew that not everyone would be enthusiastic, yet he had to try and win them over.

Zafar saw Raj walk into the hall, close the door and give him a nod. It was time. He walked to the front.

'Brothers…' He held up his hands and waited for the chatter to die down. 'I had hoped I would have good news to share with you tonight, but it seems that at every attempt to defend our people we are being blocked and impeded by our government. We had hoped to begin the first defence patrols within a few weeks but have been informed that if we do, the police will arrest us.'

There were angry murmurs at this news.

'The same police that turn a blind eye when our people are cut down, the same police that fail to investigate crimes against our families—they will not allow us to defend ourselves.' Zafar could see anger building and continued. 'Our holy lands have been corrupted by the West. Dictators propped up by the UK and US so they can steal our oil. When the people rise up to reclaim their land, they are brutally cut down. When we protest here we are called terrorists when the real terrorists are the UK Government who attacked Afghanistan and Iraq, who sent their soldiers into Libya and Syria.

'There are some who believe we should wait, that we should accept what is done to us, that time is on our side. Those people say that over hundreds of years we have traded with the infidel, have lived among them and that we have outlived them to let our children worship Allah in safety, extending the Ummah. They forget or are choosing to ignore the many times we have had to fight to survive, the wars we have fought to ensure that Allah and his prophet would not be blasphemed.'

Zafar stopped, seeing the rage he was feeling expressed in the faces fixed on him.

'We set out to defend, to bring peace. To do so lawfully, but if we cannot…' He hung his head for a moment. 'I know you want to live in peace with our neighbours and so do I, but it is our neighbours who are attacking us. I will not ask any of you to do something that would make you a criminal, but I will not stand by any longer and watch the people I love live in fear. I intend to fight for our families but this will make me a target for the authorities. So, I must ask you to make a choice.' He looked slowly round the room, meeting the gaze of as many as he could. 'If you are not willing to do whatever it takes to protect our people then leave now. If you stay then I am asking you to commit to a cause that is greater than each one of us. A cause that will demand sacrifice, will demand that we serve a higher law than that imposed by the infidels. Make your choice now.'

There was silence as the men looked uncertainly around. In both of the previous meetings men had left at this point and as one man stood near the back of the room, Zafar wondered that more did not join him in walking out.

'There is no shame in making a choice.' Zafar told the room. 'It is better to weigh up now what you are willing to do for Allah.'

No-one else stood.

'Very well, you have chosen and it is a choice you will look back on and be proud of. I ask you now to all stand with me and swear allegiance, to commit to our cause.'

As they recited after him, Zafar examined them. In the eyes of some he saw hope, but in most he saw only fire and death.

~~~

Aamir had sat through Zafar's speech with increasing doubts, disturbed at the change in tone from the first meeting he had attended. The first presentation had affected him deeply as he'd felt a surge of anger at the way his brothers and sisters were being treated and found he had a desire to do something. However he had never considered violence to be the answer.

What he had expected he now didn't know, but knew that breaking the law was only going to make their lives worse. Hadn't there been enough violence in the world?

Outside the room he saw a man reading a book. The man looked up and gave him a sad smile. 'It is not for everyone.'

Aamir shook his head in agreement.

'Would you like me to call you a cab?'

'Yes, thank you.'

The man dialled a number on his mobile. 'Where are you going?'

Aamir gave him his address and the man recited it to the cab company.

'It'll be about five minutes. Would you like a seat?'

'I'll just wait outside.'

The air was moist after a fresh rain fall. Low clouds above reflected lights from the city giving the street a dull orange look. The cab arrived and Aamir eagerly got in, wanting to be away from the place as fast as possible. It took fifteen minutes to get to the house he shared with three other students. He had left two of them at the meeting while the other, Naqid, had shown no interest in going to either of them, instead opting to study.

Letting himself in, Aamir knocked on Naqid's door wishing he had made the same choice but there was no response. Naqid sometimes went to the University library to study in the evenings to get away from the noise of their neighbours. He would talk to him in the morning, share his concerns and see what Naqid thought.

~~~

Katie had asked Emma if she could have a word alone with her after they'd agreed which wards they'd be assigned to.

'I've read the report on what happened,' she'd said. 'I don't want you to feel we're rushing you back. Are you sure you feel up to returning to work?'

Emma hadn't seen any choice and anyway, she needed something to take her mind off that... Telling Katie she was fine, in fact raring to go, was a gross exaggeration, but it was too late now. At least she was assigned to the night shift starting that evening. Katie said it was a preferred shift as the patients were often sedated but more importantly it meant that Emma had an excuse for going back to bed for the rest of the day. She didn't hear Rachel go out to begin her afternoon shift but almost jumped out of bed when the alarm went off an hour before her shift started.

She grabbed a quick sandwich and coffee, showered and dressed and was walking towards the hospital with half an hour to go, more than enough time. For the first time in a fortnight she found herself enjoying an evening walk. The sky was just turning from deep blue to black. A couple of stars gave the street lights competition and when she could see the horizon, there were a few stray clouds showing a reddish tinge.

She was due to start the shift handover at 21:30 and was at the entrance to the Psych ward ten minutes before. Katie had given her the key code for the entrance and Emma let herself in and found the nurses' station. There was no-one about so she took off her coat and checking in the staff room, found a kettle and set it to boil.

'Making yourself at home?'

Emma turned and saw an older Nurse setting a bag down on a seat.

'Expecting a long night. Emma Hunter.' She offered her hand.

'Sister Joan Cairns.' Joan shook Emma's hand then stepped back and appraised her. 'Have you worked on a Psychiatric ward before?'

'A few times before I started in A&E. Not for a couple of years. I mostly worked on General wards before and the usual rotations during training.'

'You'll know what it's like then, in many respects much the same as your other wards. Patients are ill, they need treatment. Some patients are confused, others angry, some are fairly passive. I'm sure you've seen your share of interesting patients over the last three years?'

Emma nodded, thinking of situations she would just as soon forget.

'Well, we treat every patient with respect, just as I hope you'd treat a relative with similar symptoms.' Joan checked the clock on the wall. 'You can get a drink later. Let's meet the previous shift for the handover and find out what's been happening.'

Emma gave the kettle a longing look but turned it off and followed Joan out to the nurses' station.

The handover was similar to hundreds of others Emma had taken part in. A tired team of two male nurses and Sister quickly updated them on each patient's status, recent history if relevant and any changes there had been that day. Unlike most other handovers they did not tour the ward as some patients suffered from paranoia.

About five minutes before the shift was formally going to start and just as the handover was ending, a Nurse walked briskly into the ward and up to their group.

'Late again, Tanya?' Joan commented.

'I never understood why the handover has to take so long,' Tanya said, shrugging off her coat and laying it over the desk counter.

'Emma Hunter, Tanya Cooper. You'll be working together tonight,' Joan introduced them.

Emma shook hands with Tanya who seemed more interested in one of the male nurses.

The handover finished and Joan gave Emma and Tanya each a pile of clipboards. 'Check and assess each patient now and then I'll review them with you in half an hour.'

Most of the patients were in bed though one man was wandering around his room, gesturing and muttering to himself. Emma skimmed the notes and made sure she was aware of each patient's medication and when they had last received a dosage.

Joan found her as she was looking in on her last patient, an elderly woman who was curled up tightly on the bed, her fists clenched together.

'Diagnosis?'

'She needs regular physio. If she doesn't get help to move she's just going to end up getting bed sores and infections.'

'I agree. Unfortunately, that tends to be the role of the day shift and they are often understaffed as it is.'

'But it's a no brainer, it costs far more to treat someone with secondary infections.'

'Well, I would be delighted if you could persuade our short sighted Government to change their policy. Talk me through the rest of your patients.'

Emma summarised her observations and the status of each patient's medication as they walked back round the ward. Back at the nurses' station Joan set the clipboards back on the counter. 'Think you'll do alright. Get the kettle back on and we will plan the rest of the shift. Mine's a white tea with two sugars. Now, where's Tanya got to?'

~~~

Emma had made herself and Joan cups of tea when Tanya popped her head round the door.

'Oh good, you boiled the kettle. Can you make a tea for one of the patients?'

'Sure, which one? And how do they take it?'

'Michael Irving, bed eight. White tea, no sugar.'

'Joan's looking for you.'

'I know.' Tanya winked and her head disappeared back out.

Emma heard Michael before she reached his room.

'Don't go out. No, of course you're going out. Don't drink. No, of course you will, how could you not.'

Emma walked into the room and saw the man she had first seen carrying a sandwich board, Michael. She hadn't known his surname. She forced a smile and laid the plastic mug of tea down on Michael's bedside table. The tea was lukewarm, less than 70 degrees when the teabag went in and under 50 after the milk was poured. Foul stuff, but not knowing if the patients were as likely to throw the tea as drink it, what could they do?

'How are we doing tonight, Michael?' She asked.

He looked troubled. 'I can't, how can I...' He started but seemed to run out of words, looking up past her to the ceiling above the door.

'What can't you do, Michael?' Emma asked, trying not to dwell on her role in having him assessed. It was the right thing to do, wasn't it?

'You mustn't go out. Mustn't... Stay in.'

'No one's going anywhere, Michael. Don't you want to get to sleep?'

'Such a long way down. So cold.' He shivered.

Poor guy, Emma thought. He really did need help. The conversation wasn't going anywhere and she wasn't sure how best to encourage him to lie down.

'Michael, I've brought you a cup of tea. I'll check on you later.'

She was about to turn away when he looked straight at her.

'Stay off the wall, Emma. It's dangerous on the wall.'

A memory of falling came back to her, looking up at Rachel, trying to grab her hand. Emma turned and half ran out the room. She slowed but kept walking through the ward, round corners and past rooms with open doors. These were Tanya's patients, but Tanya wasn't around.

Emma checked the sluice room, the patient's bathroom, the day room. All empty, no sign of Tanya. She checked back round her own patients to see if Tanya had looked in on any of them. No sign. Joan was visible in the small office, tapping away on a computer. Emma walked past and went into the staff bathroom. Tanya was there, checking her makeup in the mirror. Emma let the door close behind her.

'I took Michael his tea.'

'Thank you.'

'Did you think it would be a laugh, telling a patient about my accident?'

Tanya turned and looked at Emma with a puzzled expression. 'Accident?'

'You wanted to get a rise out of me, you succeeded. I've got no time for people who think they've got a right to spend their days winding other people up.'

'I really don't know…'

'Save it! As low as so called practical jokes are, I never thought I'd meet someone who thought they had a right to tell a patient about a colleague's personal life.'

'What are you talking about?'

Emma studied Tanya's expression. Was it genuine puzzlement she saw? There was a hardness there as well.

'I'm here to work. You deal with your patients, I'll deal with mine.' Emma turned and left before Tanya could respond. She heard Tanya say: '…get stuck with all the…' before the door closed and cut her off.

Walking back into the staff room, Emma felt herself shaking. She wrapped her arms around herself for a minute until she had calmed down and then set the kettle to boil again. She needed a cuppa more than ever.

'Not made the tea yet?'

Emma looked up and saw Joan walk in followed by Tanya.

'I was just about to.'

'I take mine black, one sugar,' Tanya said as she sat down, looking steadily at Emma as she did so.

Emma acknowledged her with a stiff nod and turned to Joan. 'You were saying about planning the shift?'

Joan sat down and laid several clipboards beside her. 'If you're comfortable working night shifts then we'll get you regularly assigned to this team. It's not for everyone but most people find they handle a consistent shift pattern better rather than rotating from days to nights. Normally we assign each person to a group of patients for the whole shift. You're more likely to be aware of changes that way, but I'm sure you already know that…'

Emma realised Joan was looking for a response. 'Consistent care by one individual increases likelihood of identifying changes in a patient's health. Miller,' Emma quoted.

Joan nodded while Emma saw Tanya roll her eyes. Behind her the kettle came to boil and Emma turned to make the teas.

'Since this is your first shift, we'll swap round the patients after three hours—at 1am. I'll expect you both to provide a full report on observations. Emma at 2am, Tanya at two thirty. Do ask for help when you need it or if you have a query about a patient. Any questions?'

Emma handed Joan her tea. 'No.'

'On general wards there is sometimes a slack time during the night shift and staff can take a short nap. Unfortunately on this ward we often get patients who are unusually active during the night. Pace yourself, okay?'

'Okay.' Emma handed Tanya her cup and then sat down with her own. It was going to be a long night.

~~~

Outside the back of Aamir's house, Philippe picked the door lock. The cab driver had been a member of Tariq's team for several years and had confirmed where Aamir had been dropped off. Each person that had left the meetings early had been similarly followed and had met with a different fate.

Tonight Aamir would be suffocated before the house was set on fire. The authorities would assume he died of smoke inhalation but would be unable to confirm through an autopsy as the body would be too badly burned.

Each potential security risk had been contained just in case someone decided to tell the authorities what was being planned. It would not do to give advance warning.

CHAPTER THIRTY-NINE
The Watcher

Emma's shift had started eight hours previously at 21.30 with the handover from the evening shift. Now, with half an hour until they would begin their handover to the day shift, she was exhausted.

Molly Cartwright had pulled her catheter out three times during the night and managed to either leak or wee enough urine to overflow the absorbent mat and soak her sheets.

Carol Thaw started screaming at 2am and woke up three other patients. Eventually they had administered a sedative which had calmed her down enough to go back to sleep.

There had been a parade of events throughout the shift, Helen and Neil getting up and wandering until they were gently steered back to bed, Sylvia waking up confused and scared and needing to be reassured, then around 4am, John asking for his breakfast. Tanya—who never seemed to be around for the real work—had made him some toast and tea while Emma dealt with Molly's latest flooding.

Not having heard from Michael Irving since she had checked on him earlier, Emma decided to take a quick look on her way back from the sluice room. She found him looking obviously terrified, tightly pressed into the corner of the room and the head of his bed. His hands were wrapped round his knees and he was staring upwards to the opposite corner of his room.

'Mr Irving?' He didn't respond.

'Michael, what's wrong?' Emma moved into the room so he could see her.

His eyes flicked towards her but then went straight back to the darkened corner of his room.

'Is there something there?' She asked.

'He's watching me, always watching me.'

'Who is, Michael?'

'The eyes, so many eyes.'

Emma glanced over at the corner, caught herself doing so and looked back at Michael. 'Look at me, Michael.' She said firmly.

Michael slowly turned his head towards her but his eyes kept flicking back and forwards between her and the corner.

'There are no eyes. Michael! Focus on me. There is nothing in the corner.' Emma saw his eyes stop flicking and settle on her. 'I believe you can see them but they are not there. Now if you want, I can get a sedative to help you get back to sleep or if you prefer, I can get Tanya in to get you up and you can sit in the day room.'

'No,' Michael managed. 'I'm okay.' He gave a hesitant smile. 'Thank you, Nurse.'

'Okay.' Emma gave him a long stare. He seemed to be beginning to relax. 'I'll check on you before I go off shift, alright?'

Michael nodded and Emma gave one more glance at the troubling corner before leaving the room.

~~~

Almost as soon as the Nurse was out the door, Michael's eyes again fixed on the giant spinning wheel that had kept him up half the night. It's every surface was covered in eyes, blinking at different times so that no matter what, it could always see him. Michael pushed himself back into his corner and hugged his knees close.

~~~

Joan gathered Emma and Tanya by the nurses' station at 05:45 'Morning shift will be here in quarter of an hour. If any of the patients are awake then we normally get them up to help out.'

'Michael Irving is awake, though I'm not sure he's slept at all.'

'Neither have we.' Tanya stifled a yawn.

'He hasn't slept much at night since he was admitted. Seems to nod off during the day according to the other shifts. Okay, anyone else?'

Tanya shook her head.

'Emma, you get Mr Irving up and change his bed. Tanya, check on the other patients then see if Emma needs help.'

Emma fixed her smile in place as she went into Michael Irving's room. He had shown no sign if he knew she had been the one who caused him to be admitted. She carried bed sheets in and laid them on the meal table. 'Going to get you up now and change the bed, Mr Irving. Can you get up and sit in the chair while I do it?'

He was still hunched up in the corner, sitting on the bed with his knees pulled up to his chest. His notes had shown he needed a sedative to sleep but that he was refusing medication. Was lack of sleep part of the reason he had turned to delusion? He had been muttering as she walked in the room but he had stopped and she realised he was looking at her with wide eyes. Emma quickly looked away, feeling uncomfortable. She was still unsure whether Tanya had told him about her accident. He couldn't just have guessed that, could he? Randomly created a fantasy where she fell? She adjusted the chair so it was facing more towards the bed, then stepped back to give Mr Irving room to get up.

She watched Mr Irving slowly relax his legs and stretch them out until his feet dangled off the edge of the bed. He then slowly shuffled forward until he was able to stand and move into the chair. Emma forced herself to let him do this on his own though she wished he would hurry up.

She gave him a quick smile and then began to strip the sheets. She had just begun to tuck in the new sheets when he said it again.

'Don't go on the wall, Emma. Don't go on the wall.'

Emma froze, one hand under the mattress. Stay cool, she told herself. You don't need to get wound up by a nut job who only last week was carrying sandwich boards round the centre of York.

'Who told you that?' She asked him, slowly continuing to make the bed.

'It's dangerous, you need to stay away.'

'I know, Mr Irving, but who told you about the wall?'

'Don't go on the wall. Mustn't go on the wall.'

It was no good, Emma felt a panic start to rise as she felt the same sense of falling as the first time he'd told her. She remembered her dream of falling, of waking up in hospital. She told herself to leave, walk away, but stayed where she was.

Turning to look at Mr Irving, her voice beginning to rise, Emma asked again: 'Who told you what happened on the wall, Mr Irving?'

His jerky glance, above and behind her, made her follow his gaze round to stare at the blank wall. Something inside her snapped and she turned back.

'It's too late, okay? I already fell off the wall so stop telling me to stay away from it!'

Despite her anger, Emma quickly grew concerned at the reaction Michael Irving had to her outburst. He began to shake, his eyes grew even wider and he seemed to try and draw back away from her.

When he whispered: 'Are you a ghost?' she tried to take a step back but felt like she was losing her balance. Mr Irving seemed to be walking away from her which was strange as he was sitting down but then the world seemed to tilt and she was falling and though she felt cold, it was almost a relief to let go.

CHAPTER FORTY
Witness

She wasn't aware of opening her eyes. Just of a round picture that seemed to be a long way away. As she looked at the picture, details started to come into focus and it became more like she was looking out from a tunnel. It did not seem to make any sense though, even when someone's face came into view.

They were opening their mouth and that was when she started to notice the ringing. Maybe it was a loud buzzing but it was getting louder and slowly the round picture was getting bigger and then Emma could just hear that Tanya was saying something but why was she looking at her like that and Emma found herself trying to yawn to clear the noise in her ears and then very quickly it all seemed to focus and the ringing faded and Tanya was asking if she could hear her.

'What happened?' Emma asked.

'I found you lying on the floor. Did you slip? You can get compensation for that.'

'No. Don't think so.' Emma tried to sit up.

'Hold on, are you sure you're ready to get up?'

'I'm okay. Just need to sit down for a minute.'

'You were already on your back, did you faint?'

'No I…' Emma realised there was a bed beside Tanya. 'Is this a patient's room?' She tried to remember what had happened but it was hazy. 'Whose room is this?'

'Steady.' Tanya held onto her shoulder as Emma swayed. 'Did you hit your head?'

Tanya looked round at the back of Emma's head and roughly pulled her hair back in a few places. 'Can't see any blood.'

'Whose room?'

'Michael Irving. He didn't attack you did he?'

Emma remembered she was going to change his bed. She felt a wave of nausea and swallowed it down. She slowly shook her head. 'You can't tell Joan!'

'Your funeral.'

'Tell me what?'

Emma saw Joan standing behind Tanya and groaned. Tanya turned and moved aside so Joan could crouch down.

'Lie back down,' Joan ordered Emma.

'I'm fine,' Emma protested but lay back down. As she did, the room seemed to shift beneath her and she closed her eyes, feeling light headed.

'Far from fine, I would say.'

Emma felt Joan move and adjust her legs until her knees were raised up. She opened her eyes to see two Joans looking concernedly down at her.

'You're white as a sheet,' Joan murmured. 'Just lie still for a few minutes. Tanya, where is Mr Irving?'

'I, uh…'

'Go and find him.' After Tanya had left, Joan turned back to Emma. 'Can you remember what happened?'

Emma thought back but her brain seemed sluggish. 'No.'

Joan checked her watch. 'The morning shift will be here soon. Do you think you can make it to the staff room?'

Emma nodded.

'Okay, let's get you up. Slowly.'

Joan helped Emma stand and then walked with her to the staff room where Tanya found them.

'He's in the day room. Still in his pyjamas.'

'We'll just have to leave him there. Emma, how do you feel now?'

'Better,' she lied. During the walk to the staff room she had felt faint again, tunnel vision threatening to suck her down and the buzzing in her ears had started up again.

'Lie down on the couch. After the handover I'll take you over to A&E and get you properly checked out.'

'No, I can't. They won't let me back to work.' She could tough this out, couldn't she?

'Emma, you fainted on duty. I've a legal responsibility to you and to the patients to report this. I can't force you to go to A&E but if you don't, I'll have to report you to HR.'

Joan stood but before she walked out, hesitated. 'In all probability you just started back too soon. A night shift probably wasn't the best choice either. Tanya...'

'One minute.' Tanya waited until Joan had left and then walked up to Emma. 'What accident?'

Emma looked away. 'I fell. Was off work for a couple of weeks.'

'You fell? Oh!' Tanya drew out the exclamation causing Emma to look back.

'You're famous. I didn't know your name but everyone was talking about you. I don't get it though, they said you were suspended, that it was all a big hoax.'

'I don't want to talk about it.'

'Did you really fall off the Bar?'

'Yes.'

'Lucky to be alive then.'

'Yeah, real lucky.'

As Tanya walked out, glancing back at Emma with curiosity etched over her face, Emma remembered the words that Michael Irving had said.

'I'm not a ghost.' She whispered to herself, even as she curled up on the couch. 'I'm not a ghost.'

~~~

Emma almost died from embarrassment during the half hour shift changeover. She was curled up on the couch when the first Nurse came in.

'Long night?' She asked, throwing her jacket on one of the other seats. Not waiting for a reply, the Nurse left. A few minutes later another Nurse and the Sister came in.

'Don't mind us,' the Nurse joked and Emma considered trying to sit up but quickly decided against it. It seemed to take forever for the handover to end and Joan and Tanya to come back in. Tanya left quickly without saying anything but Emma saw the way she was looking and suspected there would be a whole new round of gossip starting that morning. She hadn't considered that anyone would have been talking about her.

Joan walked her out and over to the A&E department and explained what had happened—as far as she knew—to the receptionist, then she sat down with Emma.

'You've got more colour in your cheeks,' Joan said.

'Are you going to let me go home then?'

'No, you need to get checked out. HR told me about your accident. I was surprised you were being let back to work so soon afterwards, but it seems you were insistent and as you had no sign of trauma, well... You know as well as I do that losing consciousness after having had a head injury needs to be taken seriously.'

Should she tell her? Emma knew that it had been Michael Irving's words that had shocked and scared her, yet what did that say about her fitness to work? A patient's rambling pushing her over the edge. If she had to take some more time off because they thought she had a head injury, that was preferable to being classed as mentally disturbed.

'You're right,' Emma sighed. 'I guess I didn't want to believe I was really injured.'

'You hear about hairline fractures, not always easy to spot. Definitely best to take another look.' Joan stood. 'I was pleased with your work last night. I would be happy to have you back on my team. How did you get on with Tanya?'

Emma thought for a minute. 'Okay. Didn't really spend much time with her.'

'Some shifts are like that. I'll let HR know what happened and when you're ready to return to work, give me a call.'

Emma thanked her and resisted the urge to follow her out the door.

~ ~ ~

Emma waited in A&E for two hours—almost nodding off several times—before a junior doctor took her through to a cubicle. She told him she had collapsed, that she had fallen two weeks previously and that she had a scar from that fall.

The junior had a sceptical look after he finished examining the back of her head but made no comment other than to recommend she was kept in for observation and to get an MRI scan.

It took another hour for her to be allocated a bed on a general ward. She climbed into the bed and, despite the noise and bustle, fell asleep within minutes.

A Nurse woke her up and took her through to get scanned. Even though she was exhausted and forced to lie still in the donut fronted machine, Emma couldn't sleep with the banging sound it produced. Neither the Technician nor the Nurse would tell her what the results of the MRI were— if they had seen a fracture or anything else. Not that Emma thought that could have caused her to faint but it was slightly preferable to the alternative.

Back in the ward she tried to sleep again but her thoughts kept her awake. Thinking about the scan, the night shift, wondering what rumours Tanya would be spreading. None of it was in her control but she couldn't let go of it, the same train of thought on an endless loop round her head.

'Would you like some company?'

Emma looked round and saw an old woman. She appeared to be in her Seventies with her wrinkled skin and pure white hair.

'I was trying to sleep,' Emma said giving the woman a wary look over. On General wards they occasionally got "do-gooder" visitors coming in and spending time with the patients, usually religious but mostly the patients seemed to appreciate having someone to talk to.

The woman seemed to sag and Emma recognised a confusion in her expression, mingled with a sadness that for some reason, as the woman started to turn away, made her call out: 'Wait!'

The woman turned back and Emma also noticed a deep tiredness in her eyes.

'You look like maybe you belong here as much as me,' Emma told her.

Taking a hesitant step forward, the woman gave a tired laugh. 'Maybe I do. Too many nights without sleeping...' she trailed off.

Emma sat herself up. 'Why can't you sleep?'

The woman made as if starting to say something several times, but for some reason couldn't seem to find the words. 'You wouldn't believe me,' she eventually said.

'Try me,' Emma said, thinking that nothing could be stranger than her own life at the moment.

'Do you mind?' The woman said, gesturing at the chair beside the bed.'

'Why not? I'm Emma, by the way.'

'Mary.' She sat down and fussed with her handbag for a minute.

'Well...' Emma prompted. 'Why can't you sleep?'

Mary had a look of desperation as she turned to Emma. 'I keep having the same nightmare. Every night for two weeks. I wake in a... I can't get back to sleep. I don't want to go to sleep because I know I'll dream the same awful dream again. I wondered if maybe it meant something, but... Do I sound crazy?' She looked pleadingly at Emma.

In her mind Emma pictured a blonde haired man reaching out to her, a dream she never seemed to think about when she woke and yet how many times after the fall had she dreamed of him? Not since she had met him on the street, not since he had told her... 'No, that doesn't sound crazy. Well, no more crazy than...' and Emma told Mary everything—all that she knew and all she had been told, right up to being asked if she was a ghost and waking up on the floor of a patients room. 'Now all that is crazy, right?'

But Mary wasn't looking at her like she was crazy, instead she was staring intently at her.

'What do you really think happened that night when you fell?' Mary asked.

Emma shook her head and pulled her knees up so she could put her arms round them. 'I don't know. I must have hit my head but… It doesn't make any sense. There was blood at the scene. Both Rachel and the paramedics reported spinal fluid in my ears. Yet by the time I got to the hospital I had no sign of recent injury. Only a scar on my head that I'm certain wasn't there the previous day. I was unconscious for six hours, but I may as well have been asleep. There was no sign of bruising or bleeding, internally or externally apart from the blood in my hair.' She realised her arms had become rigid and that she was shaking slightly. She looked again at Mary. 'He said I was dead, the homeless guy, when I found him. That he… Prayed for me and God answered him. Why would he have said that?'

Mary didn't answer for a time, just seemed to study her until Emma felt uncomfortable.

'Do you think you died,' Mary eventually asked.

'I don't know… When I saw the CCTV… I don't want to believe it. You work in a hospital for long enough and you'll see someone flatline, we just take it for granted. Their heart stops and you try and restart it.' Emma put both her hands to the back of her head, easing through her hair until she could feel the scar. 'What the CCTV captured… the way I fell… you don't just wake up the next morning with a healed scar.'

'When you have eliminated the impossible, whatever remains, however improbable, must be the truth,' Mary said almost to herself.

'But this is impossible!' Emma insisted. 'Me sitting here, walking around for the last two weeks, all of that is impossible.'

'With God all things are possible,' Mary spoke quietly, almost reflectively.

Neither of them spoke for a minute and then Mary asked: 'Do you know the story of Jesus?'

'Sure. Christmas, Angels, a Manger. We had a nativity play in our school.' Emma saw Mary frown slightly at this.

'Christmas is only a tiny part of Jesus' story. He brought several people back to life.'

'Did he?'

'He did, but his real achievement was to return from death himself. Easter is really the main Christian celebration. Jesus offered himself as a sacrifice to wipe out all the debt we owe God. He allowed himself to be killed on a cross. He clearly died but on the third day after his death he returned to life.'

Emma shuffled uncomfortably. 'Why would God think we owed him anything?'

'We owe God everything. Our lives, this world we live in. And we are guilty of breaking the law.'

'What law? I haven't broken any law.'

Mary looked like she was going to respond but then she hesitated and looked troubled.

'What's wrong?' Emma asked. Mary was now looking worried, even upset.

'Someone told me that I'd hurt them recently,' Mary said, looking at the floor. 'Accused me of gossiping, of trying to stir up trouble. I didn't want to believe them, I still don't, but...' She looked up at Emma, her eyes pleading. 'What if they were right? What if I had no right to say what I said?'

Emma had no answer. She'd never heard anyone admit to something in this way.

Mary stood in a hurry. 'I'm sorry. I thought I could do this, but...'

Not knowing what to say, Emma watched as Mary started to walk away. Half way to the door, Mary stopped and then came back to her bed. Opening her handbag, she pulled out a small black leather book. Without saying anything she stood there holding the book for a moment which stretched until Emma almost asked her what the book was. Then Mary offered her the book which she felt obligated to take.

'What is this?' Emma asked, looking at Mary rather than the book.

'You said it was impossible, what happened to you,' Mary said. 'A lot of people are afraid to read this but you shouldn't be. It's honest and real. Says things straight where they need to be straight but also can be mysterious and poetic. I recommend you read the book of John, chapter eleven.' Her eyes had an intense look as she continued. 'What happened to you can't be impossible because it happened before. Also, since you're a nurse, you might find the book of Luke good to read after.'

Not sure how she wanted to respond, Emma remained silent.

Mary adjusted her coat and handbag. 'May you find the answers you're looking for. Goodbye.'

'Bye.'

Emma watched her walk out of the room, her movements stiff as if she was struggling in some way. Once Mary had gone, she looked at the book in her hands. The words Holy Bible could be faintly seen on the cover and as she opened it she saw the pages were dog eared and worn. How many times did someone have to read a book before it looked like this, she wondered. The last time she'd held a bible was in High School when the Gideons had been handing them out. That had ended up in the bin eventually, unread.

Book of John, book of Luke, wasn't the bible one book? She found a table of contents and scanning down eventually found Luke and John, one after the other. Sure enough, when she had found the start of John it was described as a book. She flipped pages noticing that almost every one had at least some words underlined and on some Mary had written notes along the edges. She reached chapter 11. There was a heading: The death of Lazarus.

Laying it on a bit thick aren't they, she thought after reading the first few sentences. A bit further on she stopped and had to re-read a passage—it just didn't make sense.

She tried reading it out loud, conscious of the other patients in the ward. 'Now Jesus loved Martha and her sister and Lazarus. So when he heard that Lazarus was sick, he stayed where he was two more days.' No, she still didn't get it. How could Jesus love someone, then just ignore them when they were ill? Why not go to them straight away?

The passage made her feel very uncomfortable. She shivered as she had a flash of falling, pain and then someone talking softly to her. Was this a memory? A dream? She remembered that first shower after she woke in the hospital, washing the blood out of her hair. How could she have blood in her hair but no wound. A scar that just appeared?

If she had died she certainly didn't remember a tunnel or any bright lights she needed to stay away from. The images from the CCTV were mixing with her dreams, was that making her think she could remember falling?

Emma turned back to the bible and read further. She noted how the writer had talked about sleep instead of death. Did that make it easier to stomach? Despite the archaic language and unusual style she found herself being drawn into the story. It wasn't just a story about Lazarus, one of the guys—Thomas—was talking about going with Jesus to die. It put a new perspective on the earlier bit where Jesus had delayed leaving. Was Jesus scared? What changed his mind about going? There were no answers. Then when Jesus arrived he found Lazarus had been in the tomb for four days. It conjured up images of dark and gloomy crypts.

Reading on, the images were banished with the description of a funeral, friends gathering afterwards for the wake. Then there was a strange conversation: Martha said to Jesus that her brother would not have died if Jesus had been there. Jesus responded with what could have been a throwaway comment, 'Your brother will rise again.' Again, Emma found the concept a bit creepy picturing figures clothed in bandages walking slowly from darkened doorways. Too many zombie movies, she thought.

And what about me? The thought came unbidden and brought with it a sinking feeling in her stomach. Feeling queasy, she forced herself to read on.

Martha gave a statement that sounded, Emma searched for the right word, pious, yes, that was it! But then Jesus' response! Emma felt herself take a breath at the force of it: "I am the resurrection and the life. The one who believes in me will live, even though they die; and whoever lives by believing in me will never die. Do you believe this?"

Emma didn't want to answer that question. The question wouldn't go away though. Do you believe this? What did she believe? Something happened to me and I can't explain it.

Emma laid the bible down, tears springing to her eyes, her thumb keeping her place. She closed her eyes and held her head. 'God, if you're there, I just don't get this. Please, help me!' She reached over for a tissue and tried to compose herself. Why am I so emotional? She asked herself.

Feeling a bit better, Emma tried to read some more and found the words hard to take in. Boring, somewhat repetitive. But suddenly, Emma was glad she had persevered. Two words. Two simple words. How many times had she heard friends laughing or cursing as they said them. Jesus wept.

He did care, he had loved Lazarus. Emma felt relief mingle with a shared sadness that this man had had to die. Had he felt the same as her? She read on, forcing herself to concentrate, eager now to find out if and how he was brought back to life. Then, having read the whole story, she read it again and then sat there with tears flowing freely down her face. It was such a strange story! She wanted it to be real, wanted to know that someone else had experienced what she had experienced. In the end, it seemed so different, she just could not conceive of having been dead for so long and then being brought back. Physically, his body must have gone through some major changes. Yet, aside from warnings that the grave would smell when they opened it, there was no sense of horror.

No horror at a dead man walking out his grave and no real sense of what it had been like either for Lazarus himself or for those who were there. She read on, hoping for some glimpse of what Lazarus must have felt like, only to find a short passage saying that the leaders had plotted to kill him to stop people believing in Jesus. How must that have felt? To be brought back to life only to have people try and kill you straight away. More like a zombie movie than she cared to admit.

Emma shook her head and laid the bible beside her on the bed. She was not a zombie and no-one was trying to kill her. She lay back in her bed and stared at the ceiling. All Jesus had done to raise Lazarus from the dead was to tell him to come out of his grave. Is that what the homeless guy had done? Just tell her to sit up? As she thought about it, the sense that it really was that simple began to take hold. She couldn't quite place what she was feeling, except she was alive and that was okay! Why hadn't she been able to accept that before?

It had been a difficult week and for the first time since that night, she felt that maybe life could be normal again. Emma grabbed the box of tissues on the cabinet beside her bed. There were going to be more tears, but that was okay. She wasn't sure she was going to get any more answers but maybe she wouldn't need them after all.

~~~

Stepping out into sunlight, Mary stopped so suddenly that someone bumped into her from behind, fortunately grabbing her arms otherwise she might have fallen. A man came round to face her and she realised he was asking if she was alright. Nodding at him didn't seem to satisfy so she brusquely told him she was fine. He backed away slowly then seemed to have had enough and turned to continue walking on.

Taking several deep breaths, Mary remembered why she had stopped. She almost turned round and marched back into the hospital. Why had she left her bible with that girl? Not just left it but given it to her! What had possessed her to do that? It had seemed the right thing to do at the time, but why had she ever thought that was a good thing to do?

It wasn't just a book, a book could be replaced. She had been given the bible by her own mother, one of the last gifts she had received from her over thirty years ago. It was now underlined in many places where she had been comforted or challenged. Her handwritten notes could be found on the narrow margins throughout, personal thoughts, prayers even. How could she give it away like that?

She became aware that people were looking at her as they passed by. She could return to the ward, apologize, ask Emma to give her bible back. She would understand, wouldn't she? No. How would she understand? As Mary thought back to what she had said, how she had poured out her own troubles instead of taking time to listen. What must Emma have thought of her, thought of her questioning herself, worrying about what she had done to the Reverend?

As she thought of this she gave a low groan causing a passerby to look worriedly over at her. Mary held up a hand and shook her head to indicate she was okay. Mary began to walk on, seeking somewhere to sit down, somewhere she could think without worrying about other people interfering.

Was she just tired, so exhausted that she had started to doubt herself? She had been utterly certain that the Reverend was wrong and yet in an instant, listening to Emma deny she had broken God's law, she had heard herself protesting. The cast iron certainty she'd had in her motives was now shattered, all those words she'd used to bolster her belief in the need to remove Anthony Wright seemed so hollow. Other words that she knew inside and out were now further eroding her confidence: "If we claim to be without sin, we deceive ourselves and the truth is not in us."

Lord, she pleaded, help me! I don't know what to think. I thought I was right, I thought I was protecting your church.

Round and round her thoughts three words trampled over what was left of her assurance: "…we deceive ourselves…"

~~~

Heading home for lunch, Najwa cut through the park hoping she would find Mary. She had looked for her on Monday needing to talk to her about what she'd read. She didn't have a lot of hope she would see her neighbour there but checked each park bench and examined every woman in the park just in case… There! She was just sitting on a bench, looking off into the distance and didn't respond as Najwa sat down.

'Hi.'

Mary started, placing a hand to her chest. 'You startled me. Najwa, is it?'

'Are you okay?' Najwa asked.

'I… Not really.'

Najwa realised that Mary looked quite upset. She had a handkerchief in one hand. Had she been crying? Feeling uncomfortable now, Najwa hesitated but her need to talk won over. 'I wanted to ask you, why do Christians say Jesus died on the cross?'

Mary gave her a strange look. 'There is a story,' she began slowly. 'That Abraham was told by God to sacrifice his son. Abraham was about to do this when God stopped him and showed him a lamb to use in place of Abraham's son.'

'I know this story,' Najwa told her.

Mary nodded. 'God told people to sacrifice animals and that the blood would take away their sin. But God did not really want people to have to keep killing animals. He wanted us to serve him and be obedient and be free. In the end God sent his only son Jesus to become a sacrifice for us, to take the place of the lamb with Jesus blood taking away our sin for all time.

'When God told Abraham to sacrifice his only son, he was really testing him to see if Abraham would be willing to be obedient. But God also knew that one day he would do what he had ordered Abraham to do.' Mary sighed and her voice broke as she said: 'I believe Jesus died on the cross so that my sin could be forgiven, washed away by his blood.'

Najwa saw tears roll down Mary's face. She looked away, embarrassed.

'The Quran says that Jesus did not die on a cross.'

'I've not read the Quran.'

'It has a lot about Jesus.'

'Does it? I didn't know.'

'Why would people have changed the Injil to say Jesus died when he didn't?'

Najwa looked again at Mary and saw she was looking at her.

'I don't believe the… the Injil… was changed,' Mary said. 'The bible, Injil, doesn't make any sense unless Jesus died. Everything Jesus did, everything he said… If he didn't eventually die for us and rise from the dead, it was for nothing.'

'But if the Injil wasn't changed…' Najwa trailed off. She couldn't say the thought that followed.

There was a long silence between them. Najwa's thoughts seemed to be stuck. It was like there was something blocking them.

'Najwa,' Mary said after some time. 'I don't know if you've read about Jesus in the Injil, but he was always clear that following him would be difficult, that not many people would be able to.'

Mary was looking at her again, her expression sad. Najwa looked away, now deeply uncomfortable.

'You're a Muslim,' Mary said.

'What difference does that make?' Najwa suddenly felt defensive.

'Jesus warned people that if they followed him they would suffer, like he did. They would eventually receive eternal life, but the cost would be high.'

'Why are you telling me this?'

'Why would anyone change a book to make people less likely to want to read it, let alone do what it says?'

'I don't know.'

'Neither do I. You're very intelligent, Najwa. Read about Jesus. Decide for yourself whether the Injil has been corrupted. Then, there's a passage I think you should read next…' Mary's lips moved silently as if she was trying to recall something. 'Corinthians. Chapter eleven. I can't remember the verse, but well, you'll know it when you read it.'

Uncertain she wanted to read any more, Najwa stood. Mary was looking up at her, trying to smile, but she couldn't hide that sadness. Najwa turned abruptly and walked away.

~~~

I shouldn't be allowed to speak to people, was Mary's initial thought as she watched Najwa walk away. What had possessed her to place so many obstacles before Najwa? The girl was showing a clear interest in the bible and all she had done was warn her about suffering. Certainly she had heard many stories about people being rejected by their families when they turned to Jesus from Islam, but did that mean it would always happen? What about those families who then followed the lead of the first person to follow Jesus?

Yet how could anyone follow Najwa unless she first shared her faith in Jesus and to do that would involve risk... What should I have said, Mary asked. And what about Emma? Almost breaking down in front of her like that...

Mary wiped away tears from her face. There was no point in feeling sorry for herself, she knew what she had to do, maybe had known it for two weeks. It would certainly explain why she hadn't been sleeping, maybe would even explain the nightmare she'd been having, her mind trying to tell her that something was wrong.

She stood and adjusted her coat. It was time to make a call.

CHAPTER FORTY-ONE
Paying Your Debts

'This is Tony.'

There was silence on the other end of the line, but before Tony was able to speak again he heard what was unmistakably Mary's voice: 'Reverend Wright.'

With those two words she managed to convey a lot of emotion, the sound of a person trying very hard to maintain control but whether she was upset or angry he couldn't tell. Tony had walked over to pick up his cordless phone and decided to remain standing rather than returning to his desk.

'Mary? Are you okay?'

He heard her take a deep, sobbing breath.

'Is now a good time to talk?' She said in a rush.

Tony looked over at his desk where he had been preparing his next sermon. 'Of course.'

Her breathing sounded ragged and instinctively he began asking God to help her.

'I know I should speak to you in person but I... I hope you'll listen to me now.'

Tony took a deep breath and braced himself. 'What is it, Mary?'

'I think... you were right.'

The brief silence that followed her words seemed to surround him like a presence. Had he heard her correctly?

'I was... was wrong to... try and turn people against you.'

Tony held back from responding. He knew he needed to let Mary continue.

'I've never thought of myself as a gossip before, but... I'm still uncomfortable with the idea of Inter-faith meetings, but... I don't know how to reach people. I've been trying yet every time I have an opportunity I seem to say the wrong thing. People need to hear about Jesus, how do I tell them?'

She genuinely seemed to be asking him the question and it would have to be one of the hardest questions to answer, even for a Reverend...

'It is difficult, even if you have a natural gift for reaching out to other people. God doesn't expect us to be someone we're not though. I do believe that each one of us can find our own way to share about Jesus.'

'I feel that all I've done is push people away.'

Restraining his natural response, Tony gave Mary time to continue.

'I want to learn... how to tell people about Jesus.'

'I would love to help you do that,' Tony said.

There was a long silence and then: 'I'm sorry... Tony.'

He had never once heard her use his first name. He was so taken aback he didn't respond as he knew he should.

'I'm starting to realise why you had to exclude me from the church, I don't know how I can ever go back after what I said... I hope maybe you can forgive me but...'

'Mary, wait!' Tony knew he couldn't let her go on. 'I forgive you. I do forgive you,' he emphasized. 'We can work through this. Together. Over the phone isn't... It would be better if I, if Cynthia and Philip and I could come round?' He said as a question.

'Would you do that?'

'Of course, Mary! Of course.'

~~~

Emma was released that evening. Rachel came back after her shift had ended and had a mini freak out in the kitchen when she heard Emma had been admitted again.

She calmed down when Emma explained she thought it was just shock at Michael calling her a ghost.

'You are definitely not a ghost, Ems.' She poked Emma in the arm. 'See... Ow!' She cried out as Emma responded in kind.

There was an uncomfortable silence for a moment.

'What am I then?' Emma asked, harsher than she'd intended.

'What kind of a question is that?'

'You said it yourself, you said I died when I fell off that wall. So what am I?'

'There's no need to shout at me,' Rachel said putting her hands up and taking a step back.

'You won't talk to me about what happened? I saw it, okay! I went to the police and saw the CCTV!'

Rachel put both her hands over her mouth.

'You said I died. Well you were right. I got to see it from four different angles.' Emma realised her hands were clutched round the back of her neck. 'There's no way I could have survived that fall so how... How is it that I'm walking round with a scar that wasn't there the day before and couldn't possibly have healed in a few hours?'

Rachel was shaking her head.

'Why won't you talk to me about it?' Emma asked.

'I can't.'

'Why not!'

'I just... I can't, okay?'

'No, Rachel.' Emma shook her head. 'That's not okay. I need to understand this. I have to find out what happened.' She left Rachel standing in the kitchen, her arms wrapped around her. Retrieving the bible Mary had given her, she headed out.

~~~

One of the many benefits of living in York was that coffee shops stayed open late to cater for the thousands of tourists who thronged to the city. Emma ordered a large mocha and found an armchair to curl up in. Once settled she turned to the Table of Contents and found the book Mary had recommended. Mary hadn't said why Luke was a good book to read if you were a nurse, but she had definitely felt better after reading the story of Lazarus. Better than after another argument with Rachel...

Emma found the first few pages difficult to read. Whether it was the language or style or just the strangeness of the customs, it was hard to see how it was relevant to her. Yet in spite of this, or maybe even because of it, she kept reading phrases that resonated with her. One in particular stood out to her: "To shine on those living in darkness and in the shadow of death, to guide our feet into the path of peace." She felt that she had lived in the shadow of death ever since waking up in hospital that first time. If this book could guide her into peace it was worth persevering.

As she read on, she struggled to work out who Jesus was supposed to be. It was like he wanted to pick a fight with the people in charge. When he spoke he seemed to be deliberately trying to confuse people, talking in riddles. Everywhere he went he kept healing people—fevers, leprosy, paralysis...

She kept reading until one sentence made her stop: "As he approached the town gate, a dead person was being carried out..." Emma forced herself to read on. All Jesus did was speak to the dead man and he came back to life. Had he just been in a coma? Even so, people in a coma didn't just sit up and start talking because someone spoke to them. And if he had been in a coma, wouldn't they have written that? Dead people didn't breathe. Surely they would have known the difference, even back then.

This was the second time Jesus had brought someone back to life. Emma kept reading but before too long she put the bible down with a thump on the table in front of her. Why did it keep talking about sin? Jesus was always forgiving sin, the authorities were angry that Jesus claimed to be able to forgive sin. Why did they keep going on about it, wasn't God supposed to be all about love?

She glared at the book for a while, then got up to order another coffee. She'd just got too involved in what she was reading, that was all, she thought to herself while waiting for her order. But as she sat back down and sipped at the steaming mug she felt that wasn't right. There was something specific about that last story that had annoyed her. Really annoyed her.

She took another sip of the coffee then set it down and picked the bible back up. Re-reading the story she felt herself tense as she read. Right from the start the woman in the story was described as a sinner. It didn't say what that meant, but everyone else, from the host to Jesus and the other guests, seemed to know it as a fact.

She was a sinner, she is a sinner, her sins are many... Wasn't there any other aspect of her character they could have used to describe her?

Then on top of that there was the way the woman debased herself to Jesus, weeping over him, washing his feet with her tears—how hard was she crying anyway—then she actually wipes his feet with her hair before kissing them! Emma had to look away for a minute. She kissed his feet... Why would you do that? Why would anyone do that to someone else?

Of course the answer was right there in the story. No riddles this time, no attempts to confuse or even pick a fight, she did all this because Jesus had forgiven her. Forgave her debts, wasn't that what Mary had talked about—forgiving debts. What debts the woman had, the story didn't say, so was it important?

It didn't seem to help that Jesus had then laid into the host, pointing out that he had failed to treat him as an honoured guest while the woman had honoured him. The assumption seemed to be that what the woman had done with her tears and kisses was a normal reaction to having your sin forgiven. Or at least to having many sins forgiven.

Emma knew she wasn't a big fan of feet but that wasn't the point, was it? Was sin really that bad? Could I ever be that grateful? Emma didn't want to answer that question. She decided it was time to call it quits and picked up her coffee trying not to think about what would make a woman so desperate.

CHAPTER FORTY-TWO
Crossroad

The green lorry slowed as it approached a tight corner. The driver had made this journey many times in the past and no matter how many drivers behind him tooted their horns or flashed their lights he was not going to risk taking the corner too fast.

He didn't know what cargo he was carrying, he knew not to ask questions like that. If he knew what he was carrying he would be unable to look customs officers in the eye when they questioned him. He was not a curious man, one of the reasons he'd survived in this job for so long. He was a generous man though, sharing the many notes he'd been given along the way, spreading good cheer among the poorly paid border guards. He himself would be handsomely rewarded for his efforts but he did not dwell on the reasons a simple cargo of Blu-Ray players could be considered so important.

Blu-Ray players on the manifest, that was all he needed to know. Shipped from China along the Silk Road. Stated destination: Belgium. Ultimate destination: unknown.

The lorry trundled slowly round the corner and the driver kept his speed down after the road straightened up to allow some of the drivers to overtake. A few tooted their horns as they passed, whether to say thanks or to express anger he did not care. He gradually sped up until he began to approach the next corner. It was a satisfying job. He got to enjoy stunning views all the way from Ukraine to Central Europe. Once he had even driven to Spain, through the Pyrenees. Now they had been beautiful mountains.

~~~

Emma woke early the next morning and, despite her desire to avoid

Rachel, decided to make a point and established herself on the sofa with coffee and the bible, ignoring Rachel as she busied herself getting ready for work. Rachel seemed happy to avoid Emma as well and left quickly without saying a word.

Although she had opened the bible, she wasn't able to concentrate on reading while Rachel was in the flat. Once Rachel had left she carried on from where she'd left off, trying not to dwell on the story of the "sinful" woman. She read quickly, skimming the stories until she read about a young girl who was dying. Okay, so not dead yet but on her way. Emma read on, suddenly gripped by the story. Someone slowed Jesus down, a different woman who was healed just by touching Jesus cloak. It was like something from science fiction—Jesus talking about power going out of him.

But it was too late. Whether the other woman delayed him or there wouldn't have been time anyway, the girl died. Emma couldn't help but notice the parallel with the story of Lazarus. At least, she hoped it was…

Sure enough, as she kept reading she found Jesus didn't accept this and this time said the girl was asleep. Was that Jesus referring to a coma then? Or was he just saying that because it made it easier for the parents to accept their daughter back from the dead?

She was starting to see a pattern—get the person something to eat, don't tell anyone what happened. Except they never kept silent and then they wrote a book about it!

Had she been hungry after she woke up?

She couldn't remember. Did dying make you hungry?

She kept reading and slowly became enthralled by the stories. Jesus was an enigma. He seemed to delight in confusing almost everything he said. He spoke in riddles and yet even the riddles seemed to have a clarity about them. When he seemed to speak clearly it was almost as if he was in the same room. And what he said made her increasingly uneasy. Her whole life she had been taught that self-fulfillment was all that was important. What was it people said—nothing really matters. You're born, you live, you die. All that really mattered was what you managed to squeeze out of this life in the middle. Yet Jesus challenged every single thing she had ever lived by.

He kept telling people to repent, to give away their possessions. Money was unimportant, helping the poor was vital. Okay, he seemed to agree with her view that friends were important, even praised a crook who wangled his way out of being fired by writing off his master's debt. But had she really lived believing that friends were important. Fun to be with, some of the time. Company when you were lonely. A shoulder to cry on. But did it run any deeper than that? Would any of her friends forgive her seven times in one day if she kept doing the same stupid thing over and over? Would any of them bail her out if she was broke? She didn't even know what Rachel would do if she could not pay her share of the rent.

But as easy as it was to wonder about her friends, Emma couldn't help returning to questions about herself. Did she have it in her to forgive her friends constantly? Would she share everything she had with them? And then Jesus kept on going on and on about sin usually telling people to repent of their sin. Every time she read that she thought of Paul and Jennifer. What did repent actually mean? She reached for her phone and Googled repent and saw: "To feel such sorrow for sin or fault as to be disposed to change one's life for the better."

That fit—go and sin no more. Emma mulled it over. What I did was wrong. I seduced him. I knew it was wrong, knew it would damage his relationship with Jennifer, knew she would hate me for it but I did it anyway. Okay… I know I don't want to do that again.

It wasn't enough.

I'm not going to do that again.

Right. That's sorted. She kept reading.

Although she kind of knew how the story ended it was still a shock. Suddenly all the hints Jesus had dropped were revealed not so much as subtle but as blindingly obvious. First he was betrayed, then falsely accused, then sentenced to be crucified. She had never given it any thought. Some people wore crucifixes at work, a couple with a little silver Jesus. Every year Easter came and went and she had picked up facts without considering them. Suddenly all that information fell into place and she was able to picture Jesus being nailed to the wooden cross, lifted up and then left to hang until he died.

She had treated enough patients with emphysema to know that being unable to breathe was a horrible experience. Hanging like that with nails through his feet, he would have been unable to support himself for long, if at all, and would have gradually been pulled forward, restricting his lungs.

And so the man who had been able to bring people back from the dead—cure blindness and dropsy and madness and deformed limbs—died himself.

Was it just poetic licence that had made the writer state the land went dark for three hours and the sun stopped shining?

Emma read on, knowing what happened next but wanting to read it even so. Jesus wasn't found in the tomb. His followers didn't believe the reports initially. Typical men, dismissing what the women said! But then they started to see him as well. He was alive, he could be touched, he could eat. So many words had been written about Jesus before his death that it was an anti-climax to find herself at the end. Was it really all about that one big event? Everything that led up to his death and return to life? Emma found that too simplistic.

She felt a hunger pang and checked the time. 'How did it get so late?' She murmured. She made herself a sandwich and another coffee and then started reading the next book.

~~~

Mary opened the door and stood back allowing Cynthia, Philip and... Tony... to enter. She followed them through to her sitting room where they all stood awkwardly for a moment before Mary asked them to take a seat.

'Thank you for letting us come round,' Tony said as she sat down, trying to hide the fact she was trembling. She gripped her hands tightly together and nodded in acknowledgment. She didn't trust herself to speak.

'Mary, I told Cynthia and Philip what we discussed over the phone. It would be helpful if you put in your own words what you want to say.'

She looked from Cynthia to Philip and then back to Cynthia who, Mary suddenly noticed, was also shaking slightly but trying to smile and look at ease. Mary now felt ashamed at how she had treated Tony, but to have hurt Cynthia... Her eyes began to well up. She put out her hand to Cynthia who took it with a fierce grip.

'I'm sorry,' Mary said reaching for a tissue to dab at her eyes. 'I mean...' She realised she had just apologized to Cynthia and turned to face Tony. 'I am sorry, Tony... Reverend Wright...'

'Tony is fine.'

She glanced at Cynthia and then offered her the box of tissues as she saw tears running down her face as well. Mary noticed Philip and Tony both were looking increasingly uncomfortable and had to bury an inappropriate thought towards them. Get on with it, she told herself.

'What I said, what I did—going behind your back, trying to turn the church against you... It was wrong. I...' Her voice broke and she tried to recover. 'I never thought of myself as a gossip. I've always despised...'

'Mary, it's okay. I said it before and meant it. I forgive you.'

Mary gripped Cynthia's hand tighter as her trembling intensified. She saw that Tony's smile and expression were genuine yet could not let go of the fear inside her. 'It's not that simple though, is it?'

Tony sighed deeply, looking down at the ground.

Mary shook her head. 'I've been such a fool! You said it right, Tony... I've never led anyone to Christ. I tried and all I've done is push people away, those poor girls... I should never have tried to go to the hospital.'

She saw Tony look uncertainly at Philip and Cynthia who both shook their heads.

'The hospital?' Tony asked.

Mary let go of Cynthia's hand and dabbed at her eyes again. 'I thought maybe... I've visited friends many times there. I thought it was something I could do. But I couldn't. So many times I almost went in... I should have given up. Then I wouldn't have babbled on about the nightmares. What must that girl have thought of me...'

'Nightmares?' Asked Cynthia.

'Just stupid dreams...' Mary was interrupted by her phone ringing. She gazed stupidly at it for a moment and then turned to the others.

'If you want to get it...' Tony said.

'Probably just someone trying to upgrade my boiler,' Mary said, standing and walking over to the still ringing phone. The tension broke as the others laughed.

'Hello,' Mary said into the receiver then turned in shock as she heard the voice at the other end. 'How did you get my number?'

'It was written under your address, "If found, please return to..."' Emma said. 'I thought it would be rude to turn up at your doorstep.'

Mary put a hand out to the wall to steady herself. She didn't know what to say.

'Weell,' Emma said after a few seconds silence. 'I read those books you told me about. I've got a few questions.'

Cynthia was looking at her with concern evident while Tony and Philip were frowning. Philip mouthed—are you okay.

'I see,' Mary managed to say. 'That's good. Now isn't the best time...'

'Oh. Right. I'm sorry.'

'Maybe... Tomorrow?'

'Sure. Anytime. I've been signed off work. Got a lot of time on my hands.'

There was something she needed to... 'What's your phone number?'

'Yeah, that would be sensible.' Emma told her and Mary wrote it down on a pad she always kept next to the phone.

'I'll phone you tomorrow then.' Mary said and then said goodbye. She replaced the receiver and stood for a minute, still in shock.

'Boiler being upgraded tomorrow then?' Tony asked with a confused laugh.

'That was Emma, the girl I gave my bible to.'

'You gave your bible away? Mary!' Cynthia exclaimed.

'I was going to leave, but she said she'd died and someone prayed for her and brought her back and I just thought she needed to read about Lazarus.'

'And this—Emma—she just called you.' Tony said. 'What did she want?'

'She has questions.'

Tony studied her until she felt uncomfortable. 'If this girl has questions then you should try and answer them,' he eventually said.

'But I don't know what to say. What if I break down again or put her off?'

'Mary, we're here because I believe you have chosen to repent. God uses people who repent, God mainly uses people who repent... He doesn't ask for us to have the right words—he gives us the right words when we need them. God must have brought you to this girl and if she is reaching out to you then God must still need you to help her.'

She made her way back to her chair, holding onto the armrest to steady herself as she sat.

'Now,' Tony continued. 'There are two things I would like you to do before we can put this matter behind us...'

~~~

The green lorry was getting low on diesel and the driver had started looking out for signs to service stations. He didn't like the German Autobahn. The cars drove too fast for his liking and his lorry simply wasn't able to maintain the speed the roads required but that was the route he had to take.

He didn't need to start slowing down when he saw the next sign. The off ramp was long enough that he could ease off without having to worry. He pulled up to a pump and filled the tank. He paid in cash and drove a short distance to the larger complex where toilets and cafes were.

He made one phone call from a local pay phone, back to his wife in Lithuania, then bought himself a sandwich and tea and filled the cup with three sugars. It was only another 8 hours to Belgium but he'd been driving for 14 hours and needed to sleep. He locked himself in the cab of the lorry, rolled out his sleeping bag on the long seat and was out within ten minutes. He woke when there was a noise outside but ignored it and was asleep again shortly.

~~~

Najwa walked into her room, closed the door, threw her bag on the floor and herself on the bed. Why did she have to go to school? She stared at the ceiling for a while trying to still her emotions and unwind. It didn't help. She wanted to lose herself in a book, but unfortunately she had not managed to go to the library at lunch time. She only had the Injil still out on loan and after meeting Mary the previous day she didn't know if she wanted to try reading it again.

After a bit, curiosity over Mary's suggestion eventually won over and Najwa got the Injil from where it was hidden. Mary had said she should read a passage from Cor... Corthians? She looked up the table of contents and towards the end found not one but two Corinthians. Mary hadn't said which one.

Najwa found the first book, apparently a letter to the Corinthians, and then chapter eleven. After reading for a bit she stopped and checked she was still reading the Injil, it was so different to what she'd been reading. "But every woman who prays or prophesies with her head uncovered dishonors her head—it is the same as having her head shaved. For if a woman does not cover her head, she might as well have her hair cut off..." This was just like Islam! Rules about how you should pray, women being treated differently to men. Was this what being a Christian was really like? It just didn't match with Najwa's perception of most Christians she had gone to school with, or with Mary, though then she remembered that she'd sometimes seen Mary wearing a hat. Was this something to do with praying? What was she trying to say?

Najwa read on: "For when you are eating, some of you go ahead with your own private suppers. As a result, one person remains hungry and another gets drunk." Are all Christians so ignorant they need to be told how to eat? "For those who eat and drink without discerning the body of Christ eat and drink judgment on themselves." After reading further on, Najwa put the Injil down with a feeling approaching revulsion. She didn't want to read about eating Jesus body or drinking his blood.

What was this to do with Jesus? Jesus who treated women as equals, who ate with sinners, who challenged the corrupt authorities. Once you got past that, was it all rules and judgements? Najwa sat despondently for a few minutes until it occurred to her that there was another letter. Did it have a chapter eleven?

Najwa carefully turned the delicate pages of the Injil. She had almost read the whole of Matthew's book, his account of Jesus life. It had been a revelation to her. That Jesus had been so open, so kind, yet also had such authority. Nothing like the Mullahs who preached in the Mosques. And the Mullahs of Jesus' day had hated him, had conspired to kill him. It was no wonder the Mullahs taught them not to read about that Jesus. But the rest of this book... Najwa was now uncertain as she found the second chapter eleven and began to read.

Again, this seemed to make no sense. Why had Mary wanted her to read this? "I promised you to one husband, to Christ, so that I might present you as a pure virgin to him." What? What! It was only because she had been taught from an early age to respect her elders that Najwa persevered now, hoping there was something Mary had wanted her to read, that made sense out of the strangeness. And then she read: "Five times I received from the Jews the forty lashes minus one. Three times I was beaten with rods, once I was pelted with stones, three times I was shipwrecked, I spent a night and a day in the open sea, I have been constantly on the move. I have been in danger from rivers, in danger from bandits, in danger from my fellow Jews, in danger from Gentiles; in danger in the city, in danger in the country, in danger at sea; and in danger from false believers... have often gone without sleep... have known hunger and thirst... have been cold and naked..."

Najwa felt her whole body shiver. The last part of this chapter was suddenly as clear as the rest had been confused. Was this what it meant to be a Christian? And Najwa suddenly knew it was, for her.

She knew of other girls who had been beaten, for a variety of reasons but mainly spending time with boys. They did not like to talk about it but every Muslim girl knew the rumours about others that had been killed, for losing their virginity and also for threatening to leave the faith.

What was she doing? Najwa suddenly closed the Injil. She couldn't keep it in the house any longer, she would need to take it back to school. Grabbing her school bag, she forced the book down to the bottom, underneath her school books.

Zipping up her bag she sat still, listening for anyone walking by her room. The house was quiet. She didn't want to be on her own anymore, hurrying downstairs she found her mother in the kitchen. 'Can I help?' She asked.

CHAPTER FORTY-THREE
Discovered

'Najwa.'

The sound of her name barely registered. She resisted responding to it, attempting to stay asleep.

'Najwa.'

It was too loud. She pulled the covers over her head.

'Najwa!' Someone banged on her door.

She opened one eye and saw cotton sheets. 'What?' She called back.

'It's quarter past eight. You're going to be late it you don't get up.'

Both eyes were now open and, far faster than normal, she was awake. She untangled herself from her sheets and grabbed her phone. 'Nooo,' she moaned. Why hadn't her alarm woken her?

Rushing, she grabbed a towel and wrapping it round her, went out to the bathroom. It was locked. Banging on the door, she shouted: 'Hurry up!'

'Just a minute,' came the response. Her youngest brother, Abrar.

'You better be, or I'm going to hide your blanket!'

The door opened revealing Abrar dressed only in his pyjama bottoms, toothpaste foamed round his open mouth, a look of horror on his face. Najwa pushed past him and then pushed him out.

'Finish in the kitchen,' she told him.

She washed and dressed in record time and then hurried downstairs, dumping her schoolbag in the kitchen as she went to make breakfast.

'You made it then?' Her mother said in an exasperated tone. 'What time were you reading till last night?'

Najwa ignored her as she tore off a chunk of bread and shoved it in her mouth. Why did the kettle have to take so long to boil?

'I thought you wouldn't have time so I made you lunch.'

Najwa turned to see her mother pulling her school books out of her bag with one hand, a lunchbox in the other. 'Thank you,' she mumbled through the bread.

'How many books do you have in here, this can't be good for your…' Her mother's voice drifted to silence as she leaned over Najwa's bag. She pulled out…

'Still here?' Her father smiled at her as he walked between Najwa and her mother into the kitchen.

Najwa put her hand to her mouth, a feeling of dread sucking all warmth from her as she saw her father's expression change to one of puzzlement as he looked at her, then turned to her mother who was holding up the Injil.

Her father took the book. Najwa saw a look pass between her father and mother. She hated that, what were they secretly saying to each other with a look?

'Where did you get this?' He asked, his voice far calmer than she would have expected.

'The school library. We're studying Christianity in RE,' she said in a rush.

'Are you?' He nodded, a strange expression on his face.

'I was taking it back today.'

He nodded again. 'You didn't need to, you know.'

'Well, I kind of do, it's a school book.'

'No, I mean, you didn't need to borrow one. We have one.'

Najwa looked from her father to her mother and back. 'You have an Injil?'

'Of course. If you want to read it, you just have to ask.'

Najwa had no answer. She could only stare as her father handed the book back to her mother who set it on the table.

Her father put on his coat and kissed her mother before placing his hands on her shoulders. 'Are you ready for school?'

She nodded and he kissed her forehead.

Najwa watched him leave and then turned back to her mother whose arms were crossed.

'Why didn't you tell us you were reading the Injil?'

Najwa looked away. 'It was for school.'

'Najwa…'

'I thought… I thought you'd be angry.'

'Why would you think that?'

Because you're standing there with your arms crossed and a strange expression on your face. Najwa couldn't think of anything she wanted to say.

'Well, here's your lunch.' Her mother put everything back in her bag, placing the Injil at the top. 'You should not place a holy book under anything else.'

She handed Najwa her bag, then gently put a hand on her cheek. 'Peace be upon you,' she said.

'And to you be peace,' Najwa replied automatically.

Her mother's expression looked sad but she smiled, then left the kitchen calling up to her brothers to come downstairs.

Feeling utterly confused, Najwa looked at the oven clock and groaned. She was definitely going to be late now.

CHAPTER FORTY-FOUR
Listen

Danny looked up at the minarets of the mosque and tried to quell the unease he felt. It wasn't as if he hadn't met with Mullahs before, or Swamis or other faith leaders, but it had always been in the course of investigation. This meeting, his first official meeting of the handover, was different.

It was ironic, he thought to himself, that he had so little faith and yet he was uncomfortable about his role requiring him to provide support to leaders of other faiths. Or was it because his own faith was so weak that he felt threatened by exposing himself to Islam?

He would just have to suck it up. No matter how foolish he felt the government's policy of encouraging multiculturalism was, he had a job to do and ultimately that job was about keeping the peace—about preventing conflict and that had to be a good thing, right?

He saw Roger Harbrook standing outside the entrance, a briefcase in one hand, and walked over.

'Danny Martin, right?' Harbrook asked, shaking his hand.

'Yes. We attended a WRAP session over the winter.'

Harbrook nodded. 'I remember. Though they all tend to blur into one. Glad to hear you will be taking the role over. Are you happy for me to take the lead on this one?'

'That's probably a good idea.'

Harbrook led the way into the Mosque, talking as he did. 'I'm sure you already know this but a large part of the job is just about building relationships. If people trust us they'll talk to us and hopefully we can work together to prevent problems before they start.'

Harbrook led him down a corridor and knocked on a door. As the door opened, Harbrook smiled. 'Mullah Waazi al-Rasheed, thank you for agreeing to meet with us.'

Danny followed Harbrook in and shook the offered hand as Harbrook introduced him.

'This is Detective Inspector Daniel Martin. He will be taking over from me in a few weeks.'

'You are very welcome, Detective Inspector,' the Mullah said.

'Not for much longer... The title I mean,' Danny said quickly as he realised how that could be interpreted. 'People who know me call me Danny.'

'Then I hope I will get to know you, please take a seat.' He showed them to a sofa and Danny took the opportunity to look around the room— obviously an office with a desk and book shelves but large enough to accommodate a sofa and two armchairs, one of which the Mullah took as they sat.

Harbrook took out a brochure from his briefcase and gave it to the Mullah. 'This is a follow up from the workshop on raising awareness of the government's Prevent strategy.'

'Quite a mouthful,' the Mullah interjected.

'Indeed,' Harbrook agreed. 'We wanted to ask if you would be willing to host a workshop for the worshipers at the mosque.'

The Mullah nodded thoughtfully. 'There has been resentment at the Government's handling of recent events. I'm not sure how well such a workshop would be received, yet...' He stood abruptly, walked over to the door, opened it and checked outside.

'My apologies,' he said after closing the door and sitting down again. 'I am...'

Danny exchanged a glance with Harbrook.

'Are you worried about something?' Danny asked.

'We are a close community, forced closer together by the attacks we've seen taking place around the country. I am not bound by confidentiality as Catholic priests are, but to break a confidence has ramifications, you understand?'

Danny nodded. 'Our role is to build relations between the local community and the police and government, I appreciate the lines can get blurred at times.'

'You hear about young men and women running off to Syria but don't think it would happen here,' the Mullah said clasping and unclasping his hands. 'If the family had expressed concern I would have reported it...'

Danny resisted the urge to pull out a notebook. 'Has someone gone missing?'

The Mullah shook his head. 'I don't know. The family won't talk to me about it. Their son—Kazim—stopped attending prayers. In itself it would be unusual but not unheard of. He is a teenage boy. Sometimes they rebel, sometimes they just get distracted.'

'But you think it is more than that?' Danny prompted.

'I asked some of the young men if they had seen him and they had not. They didn't know where he was.'

'Would you like us to try and find out what has happened?' Danny asked.

'Perhaps the boy is sick, or they have sent him to stay with relatives—these things happen, but yes, if it is possible it would set my mind at ease. I could not understand why they—his parents—avoided me. I thought, hoped, they would have come to me if something had happened to him.'

Danny took out his notebook and took down details about the boy, his family and school.

'Is it a terrible thing to hope I am wasting your time, Danny?'

'Not at all. Hopefully he will be found safe and well, but it's far better we check. If he has been radicalised…'

'There were no signs in his behaviour,' the Mullah interrupted.

Danny took a breath. 'When there has been, if we can find out how, we can put a stop to it.'

The Mullah opened the brochure and scanned it. 'Perhaps I must have this workshop after all.'

~~~

'What do you think?' Danny asked as soon as they were clear of the Mosque.

Harbrook looked back at the Mosque. 'I hope for the family's sake the boy hasn't tried to join IS.'

'Do they distrust us so much the parents wouldn't have reported him missing?'

'Not everyone. But it must be difficult when there is so much anger and hatred directed towards them. The way things are going, it wouldn't surprise me if the family were targeted if news leaked we were investigating.'

'What have we come to?' Danny pulled out his phone. 'I'm going to call it in.'

Harbrook held out his hand. 'You handled the situation well,' he said as Danny shook hands. 'I'll see you on Monday morning.'

Danny said good bye and called Natalie as he walked to his car. She didn't answer so he left a voicemail asking her to call him back.

He was on the A64 before his phone rang and he hit the speaker button.

'What's up, Boss?'

'I'd like you to run a possible missing person check.'

'You were just at a Mosque?'

'That's right.'

'Give me the details.'

Danny held up his notebook and reeled off the details in between checking the road ahead. Natalie said she'd pass the details onto Alan as she was out of the office. Danny thanked her and hung up.

He'd known Alan was in the office today, catching up on paperwork, yet had still called Natalie. He wasn't going to be able to keep relying on her, would have to stop thinking about her…

He pulled into Fulford Road half an hour later and found Alan on the phone.

'…uh huh. I see. That was when?'

Alan wrote something down and Danny leaned over to look. The notepad had the following:

No passport

No driver's licence

No unidentified matches in morgue

Has not attended college in four weeks

Another student missing

Alan hung up the phone. 'Sadiq Osman. Stopped attending college at the same time as Kazim.'

'Four weeks ago?' Danny asked struggling to believe no-one had called the police in that time.

'That's right. I got the boy's details, let me just check to see if I get a hit on a passport… Nothing. Hard to believe two young men of Middle Eastern origin could just walk out of the country without passports.'

'Unless they're using forgeries now.'

Alan tapped his pen on his desk. 'Facial recognition. The college will have photos, probably the Student Union as well. I'll get them passed over to Border Control and see if they find a match. How much time should I spend on this?'

Danny looked up at the blank spot on the wall. 'This is our number one priority.'

'Four weeks is a long time, can we really do anything about it now?'

Danny shook his head. 'One person going missing maybe not, but two kids disappear and no-one says anything? I'll call Leeds. I'll need them to send out officers to the parents.'

~~~

'They're all different—all the books about Jesus. Some of the stories are the same and some of them are similar but mostly they're just… different.' Emma picked up the large round cup in front of her and took a sip of cappuccino. Across from her, Mary sat very properly with a pot of tea next to her cup.

'Why wouldn't they be?' Mary asked.

'What do you mean?'

'Each account of Jesus was written by a different person, you wouldn't expect them to be the same, would you?'

'So, why are there so many books? Why not just make one?'

'They did!' Mary laughed. 'That's what you have in your hand.'

'But…' Emma shook her head in frustration and laid the bible she'd been holding in her left hand onto the table. 'That's not what I meant.'

'You meant, why not roll them all up into one story?'

'Yes! Wouldn't that have made more sense?'

'I don't know. Maybe. But maybe there is something valuable in these four accounts. I've heard some people say that each book is almost aimed at a certain type of person, like the four main personality types. Often people will say they empathise more with one book than the others. Did you find there was one book that you enjoyed more or could relate to better?'

'Well, I guess I thought John was the best. I don't normally like poetry but it was like the whole book was like, so deep. It was all about love as well. You can't go wrong with that. The other books were more… challenging.'

'That's a good word to describe them.' Mary took a sip of her tea.

'Why did you give me the bible?'

For a moment Mary looked like a deer caught in headlights then she gave an embarrassed shrug. 'I hoped you might meet Jesus.'

'Meet Jesus? In a book? Isn't he supposed to be in Heaven right now? Right hand of God and all that?'

Mary sat up straight, holding Emma's gaze. 'I believe God speaks to me when I read the bible. That's what I mean, that you might hear Jesus, sense him speaking to you through the bible.'

Emma picked up the bible again and sat back, placing her hand on it. Had God spoken to her when she was reading it? No. And yet… she had responded to what she read. Her decision to never again cheat with anyone's boyfriend had just been the start. After she had read through John she'd flipped back and started on Matthew and Mark. She'd felt slightly cheated when she found out there were only four books about Jesus. It didn't seem anywhere near enough to capture all that he had been and of course the books seemed to repeat each other. Then they teased by mentioning all the other things that Jesus was said to have done. Why not just write it down then? Why leave us guessing? She'd found Matthew especially hard going. Pages of Jesus words that seemed to cut through her, lay her bare and cause her to question things she had done, said or thought.

'How can anyone be good enough for Jesus?'

'Oh, we can't. None of us can be good enough. That's why Jesus gave himself up, became a sacrifice.'

'It keeps saying that but I don't understand. Why would he do that? If he was God why couldn't he like just wave a magic wand. Everything is sorted.'

Mary sighed. 'People more knowledgeable than me have asked similar questions for centuries. We don't know is the honest answer. Except, it does make sense. If justice exists, if crime has to be paid for then all debts have to be paid. But not all debts can be paid. How do you pay when someone has died? Or when the crime is so terrible no-one wants to forgive? If God is absolutely holy, if he cannot have anything to do with evil or sin, then how can he have anything to do with us? But God isn't just absolutely holy. He is also absolutely kind and so he made the ultimate sacrifice, taking our debt, our punishment on himself. His kindness allowed him to die in our place so that his holiness could not be tarnished by our sin.'

'I don't really get holiness.'

'I think you have to experience it to really... get it. I'm not sure I understand it either. There are several stories in the bible about prophets who came face to face with the holiness of God and fell down unwilling or unable to look at him. One time an angel took a burning coal and touched a man's mouth to cleanse him. I've read that story dozens of times and thought it was symbolic, but only just talking to you I wonder if he was burnt by the coal. There are numerous times when we're told that our sin will be burnt away. We try not to think about that as being a real experience but maybe it will be. I think holiness is total goodness. Pure gold, white linen, absolute light—all symbols for holiness. Sin cannot be in the presence of holiness without wanting to flee.'

'That doesn't make any sense though. Jesus dies so that we can be holy but I'm not. I read it all. I think I believe it but I'm not any different and I'm not sure how I can be any different. And what is this power from on high business?'

'Power from on high?' Mary looked away, her eyes searching. 'Stay in the city until you have been clothed with power from on high?'

'That's it. What does it mean?'

Emma noticed the "caught in the headlights" look was back.

'Jesus was talking about the Holy Spirit.'

'And what is the Holy Spirit?'

'Well, God's presence. The first disciples were told to wait in Jerusalem until God sent his Holy Spirit to them.'

Emma tapped the Bible. 'Is that what John was talking about, writing about? Jesus sending the spirit of truth?'

'That's right.'

'And did he?'

'Yes.' Mary took a sip of her tea. 'The Holy Spirit did fill those first disciples.'

'Fill them?'

'I don't really understand it myself. I've never experienced it.'

Emma couldn't make out Mary's expression. Was it regret or was she somehow ashamed?

'I'm sorry, Emma. I can only tell you what I've read and seen. Even then, I'm not sure that everything I've seen can be trusted.' Mary picked up her handbag and began sorting through it. 'Maybe we've talked enough for today.'

Her look was apologetic but Emma saw a hint of desperation in her eyes, eyes that suddenly looked very tired.

'Can we meet again tomorrow?' Emma asked.

'Of course.' Mary was still fidgeting with her bag.

'Would you like to come round to my flat? I could make you lunch.' The words were out of her mouth before she realised what she was asking.

'Well, if that would be no bother?'

Emma gave Mary her address and then watched as she hurried out the café. There were still too many questions running round her thoughts. She'd hoped Mary could answer them and to an extent she had except her answers just seemed to provoke more questions. Then this one question had rattled her. Why had talking about the Holy Spirit spooked her so much?

~~~

Najwa's father handed her a piece of bread he had just broken off from a loaf. She took it silently, avoiding his gaze.

Both her father and mother had said very little to her since she had come home from school. She'd gone straight to her bedroom. Normally that wouldn't stop her mother coming to check on her, but not today. The usual chat around the table was absent. Her brothers didn't seem to notice, Abrar shoving Parvez who was laughing at him.

Najwa ate slowly, pushing rice around her plate more than she picked it up. Finally she had enough. Looking up at her father, she asked: 'Why do you have an Injil in the house?'

He looked at her mother before answering. Another of those looks she wished she understood.

'Why shouldn't we have an Injil in the house?'

She shook her head in frustration. 'Papa!'

'Sometimes, when all my children have gone to bed, I like to take it out of the secret place we store it… and read it!'

Najwa couldn't believe it when both her father and mother laughed. She looked in confusion at them.

'You haven't answered my question,' her father reminded her. 'Why shouldn't we have a copy of the Injil?'

'My friends…' she trailed off, feeling silly.

'Your friends? Did they tell you the Injil is a terrible book, filled with lies? Did they tell you what happens to girls and boys who turn away from Islam?'

She nodded.

'Najwa, words only have power if we let them. If you read a story about… What is it you girls are into now? Vampires, Zombies?' He shook his head. 'You don't believe what you read because you know it is a story.'

'Is that the same with the Injil?'

Her father thought for a minute before replying. 'We are taught that the story has been changed. That it is no longer to be trusted.'

'Do you believe that?'

Again he looked at her mother, a long look this time. Eventually her mother said: 'Say what you want to say.'

'I don't believe everything I read in the Injil,' he said. 'But much of it I do. Jesus was very like Mohammed and very different from all the other prophets. I think if Jesus was to be alive today, I would like to spend time with him.'

'You believe Jesus died?'

'Of course he died. How he died… Well, that is something I can't answer.'

'Not on a cross?'

'That is what the Quran says.'

'What do you say?'

'It puzzles me.'

'What does?'

'I can understand men following a person because they have been deceived. I can understand them following a person because they expect to gain great wealth and power. I can't understand why anyone would follow someone who promises they will suffer and die. Every single man who followed Jesus in the beginning is said to have died a similar death. Why would Christians write such a story? Who would believe it? We Muslims follow a warrior, one who promises wealth and power here and now. That is something I can understand.'

Najwa couldn't resist: 'Do you feel you have wealth and power, Papa?' She purposefully looked around the room.

He laughed, then her mother joined in and even her brothers, though she doubted either of them understood why.

After the meal she asked if she could read the Injil.

~~~

Interpol got a tip off about the lorry while it was in Germany. The licence plate had been scanned as it crossed the border into Germany and again as it drove out. The lorry was picked up by CCTV cameras in Belgium and a tail placed on it with a team mobilized to intercept. The lorry casually made its way to a warehouse registered to an electronics import/export company. It was stopped before it drove into the warehouse, the team surrounding the vehicle, and guns readied at the driver who looked around in alarm.

His door was opened for him and he was ordered out and to lie down on the dirty concrete. He took his time kneeling, his knees were beginning to show the first signs of arthritis.

Two team members were assigned to watch the driver with a third assigned to over-watch. The final member and team leader opened the loading door at the back of the truck, the team leader pointing his weapon and torch inside. As they'd been tipped off, the truck contained thirty crates. They checked the cargo manifest and impounded the vehicle.

The truck was driven to a customs warehouse at the port where there was scanning equipment while the driver was taken in the back of a police car to a holding facility nearby. Led in handcuffs by two officers to an empty room, he was uncuffed and ordered to undress. When he protested he was told all prisoners were required to undergo a strip-search.

'Am I under arrest?' He asked.

'Are you refusing to submit to a strip-search,' was the response, accompanied by the withdrawing of the officer's baton.

The driver looked at the baton and for the first time in his career wondered if the extra money he received for looking the other way was worth it. He took off his coat.

Twenty minutes later the driver grabbed the offered orange jumpsuit and dressed quickly, glaring at the two officers as he did. Led into a cell that already held six other men, he avoided eye contact and sat down wondering what had been in the crates he had been carrying.

~~~

Mary walked to the bus stop that would take her home to Clifton. Forgive me, Lord. She prayed in silence. Why that question? Why is it after all these years you've never allowed me to experience what they experienced? Am I so evil that you cannot bear to be close to me? And yet you've placed this girl in my path. Then there are these dreams that plague me—are they from you? If so, I don't understand, what is it you're trying to say to me? Why can't you speak clearly?

I know I shouldn't doubt you. There must be a plan. But I need to sleep, don't I? Every time I close my eyes I see them. Are they demons? Are they men? Is it a symbol or are you really going to send giants to fight against us?

What am I saying! You wouldn't send them, would you? I know we are an evil people but, oh, I don't know. You do talk about sending destruction. You sent enemies to destroy Jerusalem. If you could discipline your chosen people you could discipline us. But what should I do?

Mary continued her one sided conversation as she rode on the bus to her house. Continued while she changed and did some housekeeping. Continued while she prepared her supper and as she readied herself for bed.

'I don't know what I'm going to say to this young girl tomorrow, Lord,' she said out loud while on her knees by her bed. 'She needs you, not an old woman who has no answers. How can I help her when I've never known your Holy Spirit?'

There didn't seem to be anything left to say. Exhausted, she laid her head down on her duvet and rested. One by one, her questions and concerns drifted away until she was almost asleep. A part of her tried to assert that she needed to climb into bed but she quashed that thought. It was peaceful where she was and although she didn't want to think about it, trying to sleep might only bring on the dream again.

She relaxed and a thought popped into her mind: you need to listen.

But I do listen, she protested.

There was silence.

Memories of her afternoon and evening surfaced. A constant stream of chatter. All of it worthwhile, all of it directed at her Heavenly Father and yet with no gaps, no spaces for him to reply.

'I'm sorry, Lord. I…' She cut herself off. 'Forgive me.'

A thought focused in her mind: you are forgiven.

Almost immediately a doubt challenged her. You're just making this up, having a conversation with yourself. Voices in your head, first sign of

252

madness don't you know!

Trying to ignore that doubt, though it refused to back away, Mary shifted her knees. 'How can I help Emma…' Again, she cut off a flow of questions that wanted to overwhelm her thoughts.

You need to listen.

Listen? I was listening, Mary objected. She waited but there was no response. I need to listen? Okay. I don't know how that will help but I will listen.

She had a sudden thought. 'Will you let me sleep?'

The response—it was a response, wasn't it—was instant.

Yes.

She didn't trust herself to wait any longer. 'Thank you,' she said, then crawled into bed. Sleep came quickly.

Although she did not dream of the giants, although she woke the next morning less tired than she had in weeks, she woke knowing they were still walking towards her, towards York.

CHAPTER FORTY-FIVE
Boarding the Rollercoaster

Natalie pushed back from her desk and stood up. 'Boss, you should take a look at this.'

Danny looked up and saw the concern on her face. 'What's up?'

'I ran a check to see if anyone else had gone missing. I didn't get any direct hits, but the search flagged some other reports I found suspicious.'

Danny saw Alan stand and walk over to Natalie's desk. He joined them and saw she had a simple spreadsheet open on her monitor. 'What am I looking at?'

'Eleven names. All Middle Eastern, North African or Asian origin. All Muslim. All died within a two week period around the same time our two boys went missing.'

'Hardly a pattern,' said Alan in a dismissive tone.

Danny agreed but held back from joining in to see what Natalie had to say.

'Do you know the statistical likelihood of this many deaths occurring so close together?' She retorted.

'Half a million people die in the UK each year. Quite high I'd have thought.'

Danny suspected Natalie was restraining herself from giving the answer she'd have liked to have given. Her eyes narrowed as she looked at Alan. 'Three million Muslims in England, roughly five percent of the population. Total deaths in 2015 for fifteen to twenty four year old males—1,500. Five percent of that is 75.'

'There you go then, eleven is nothing.' Alan smiled at Danny who started to wonder if he was winding Natalie up.

If he was, she took the bait. 'Total deaths! Annual. Didn't you ever do basic arithmetic?'

'I don't remember that being a compulsory course at training college,' Alan replied in a bemused tone.

'One and a half deaths a week! That's the average for a Muslim male in that age range.'

'Half a death a week…'

'That's in poor taste, Alan.' Danny quickly interrupted.

Natalie finally clocked what Alan had been doing and punched him in the shoulder.

'Abusive behaviour, Boss,' Alan said, stepping away quickly.

Danny gave him a warning look but let it pass. 'Okay,' he said to Natalie. 'How could so many young men die without this being all over the news?'

Natalie used the mouse to select a range of names. 'There's little clustering by location. These nine are all from different towns and cities spread throughout the country—Manchester, Birmingham, Glasgow… Each one might have made local news but none were picked up nationally. The only two that were in the same city were both in London and they had over one hundred homicides last year so two deaths in the same week would just have been business as usual…'

'Are these all homicides then?' Alan asked.

'No. None of them. Which is really why I'm calling it out. I'd almost find it easier to believe there had been a rise in racist murders than random deaths of young men.'

'Suicide?' Danny thought he should check.

'One suspected suicide. One car crash, what may have been a drowning, or a bad fall where the man ended up in a canal, an asthma attack, two muggings gone bad, two drug overdoses and three house fires.'

Danny thought for a minute. 'If you'd showed me this a couple of days ago I would have told you to get on with some real work. We see spikes all the time, what would be more unusual would be a regular pattern pointing to a serial killer.'

'What if the two from Leeds didn't go missing? What if they were killed and the bodies haven't turned up yet?'

'It's a stretch. Is there anything that links it all together?'

'Religion and ethnicity… and the short timescale.'

Danny shook his head. 'You'll need to contact each investigating officer, ask them to follow up a closed case.' He sighed. 'Open a case alongside the rest. Don't spend too much time on it.'

~~~

Emma got up to an empty flat, had some breakfast and then went back to bed. She woke for the second time that morning and was staring at the ceiling when she remembered. Jumping out of bed she checked the time: just after eleven thirty… 'What was I thinking…' she muttered to herself as she threw on her clothes. She sped round the flat, picking up clothes and magazines until it seemed presentable then checked the kitchen.

It was a disaster zone. The dishwasher was full of dirty pans and plates from the previous day. She'd forgotten to set it running and it seemed Rachel hadn't noticed either. Emma checked the time—quarter to twelve. What time was Mary coming round? She'd said for lunch but couldn't remember saying a time. Emma knew she was usually starving by noon when she was on a day shift. She checked the fridge and winced when she saw a block of mouldy cheese and some shriveled lettuce. There were three slices of bread in the bread-bin. Why didn't I go shopping yesterday, Emma thought to herself.

Okay, stop panicking, she told herself. It's not like your Gran is coming round… Though, Mary was a similar age… What would Mary likely eat?

A picture of cucumber sandwiches popped into her mind. Emma shook her head to clear the image. Not in a million years, she told herself. She looked again at the clock. Ten minutes to noon.

There was no time. She couldn't go out to Morrison's in case Mary arrived while she was out. Couldn't order in… Wait, pizza… Emma pulled out her phone and speed dialed. Five minutes later she checked the app on her phone and was reassured to see the pizzas were being prepared.

Okay, she thought. Feet up for a few… She glanced at the sink and groaned. She couldn't leave that mess of plates and bowls sitting there. She had just washed the last bowl when the door bell rang.

'She's here,' Emma whispered to herself. Why was she whispering? She didn't know. She looked round the flat, decided it would have to do then went and opened the door.

'Delivery for Hunter.'

Emma looked at the pizza delivery man. 'That was fast,' she said.

'Two medium half and halfs.' He pulled the boxes out of his insulated bag and handed them over.

'Wait,' she said as he turned away.

Emma found a pound in her pocket and handed it over. 'Sorry it's not more,' she said.

She closed the door and took the pizzas through to the kitchen and checked the clock. Twenty past twelve. She ran a cloth over the surfaces then put out two plates and put the kettle on to boil.

Then she waited.

At quarter to one Emma wondered if she should phone Mary.

At one o'clock exactly there was a knock on the door. Emma rushed to open it. Mary was standing there, handbag clasped by both hands in front of her.

'Come in!' Emma ushered Mary inside and offered to take her coat.

Mary stood in the middle of the small living room and looked round.

'Not very big, is it?' Emma smiled. 'Take a seat.' She said, pointing at the stools next to the breakfast bar.

Mary raised an eyebrow at the high stools but carefully sat on one while Emma reheated the kettle and opened the pizza boxes.

'I wasn't sure what to get, I hope this is alright.' Emma said, gesturing at the pizzas. 'I've got cheese, ham and pineapple, pepperoni and vegetarian... Actually, that was probably a mistake putting vegetarian with pepperoni... Do you eat meat?'

'You didn't have to go to all this trouble. I don't usually eat much at lunch-time... But I do like pizza.' Mary took a plate and helped herself to a slice of ham and pineapple.

Breathing a sigh of relief, Emma turned to the kettle.

'I'm sorry I... I rushed off yesterday,' Mary said.

The boiling kettle had reached a crescendo as Mary spoke and Emma had to raise her voice. 'Not a problem.'

'You asked about the Holy Spirit.'

'Yes. Jesus kept on referring to... It?'

'I'm no expert.' Mary shook her head, made to pick up her pizza slice but then put it back down. 'I don't actually know if I've experienced the Holy Spirit.'

'Do you believe it's all real? Jesus coming back to life, the power he had, that he was God?'

'Oh yes! I just don't know if what I've experienced is the same as what I read in the bible.'

'What have you experienced?'

'I've never seen anyone healed. Never spoken in tongues...'

'In what?' Emma interrupted.

'Oh. Did you read the book of Acts?'

'No.'

'You must. After the Gospels: Matthew, Mark, Luke and John, the book of Acts tells the history of what happened to the apostles after Jesus went to Heaven.'

'Oh-kay. And what are tongues?'

'Languages. When the apostles first received the Holy Spirit they all began speaking in different languages. People around them from different countries heard and understood them praising God.'

'But you've never done that, never spoken in a different language?'

'Only at school. Not everyone seems to be able to do it. I don't know why, whether we just don't have enough faith, or if it is a gift God only gives some people and not others.'

Emma noticed Mary still hadn't eaten. 'Please, don't let me keep you from eating.'

Mary picked up her pizza slice and hesitated. 'I'll just give thanks,' she said.

Emma studied her as Mary quickly thanked God for the meal and blessed her for her hospitality. 'Do you do that every time you eat?' She asked.

'Most times.' Mary answered.

'Why?'

Mary finally took a bite from her pizza and waited till she had swallowed before answering. 'Lots of reasons. God has provided us with everything good so it seems right to thank him.' She paused to take another bite and for the first time since she had entered the flat seemed to relax, a smile playing on her face. 'There are also stories of the apostles eating food that had been poisoned and being unharmed. Their faith that God would protect them was so strong. Thanking God for food is in some ways a tradition remembering back to that. Of course, I'm sure this food is all fine.'

Emma gave an uncertain laugh. 'I see. Would you like cyanide or arsenic with your tea then?'

'I'm allergic to both. Just milk will be fine.'

Emma poured tea for them both. She ate a slice of pepperoni and took one of the vegetarian. 'I don't like these dips,' she said. 'Why don't they just offer ketchup?'

'I don't know.'

'I don't know what to do with all this. I started out wanting to find out what happened to me. I still don't know for certain but even if I never know, what do I do with all this… About Jesus, the Holy Spirit?'

Mary looked as if she wanted to quickly fire back an answer but she pursed her lips, frowning at Emma.

Emma waited uncertainly.

'You've read all the gospels…' Mary began.

Emma eventually nodded.

'What do you think Jesus is telling you to do with it all?'

'He's not though.'

'Imagine the gospels are a letter. A series of letters from Jesus to you. What is he saying?'

'Follow me. Which makes no sense because how can you follow someone who's been dead two millennia?'

Mary nodded slowly. 'Except he came back to life.'

'There is that, I suppose.' Emma sighed. 'Though how do I know?'

Again Mary sat silently, frowning at Emma. Then she put her head to one side. 'What did Jesus say about that?'

'What do you mean?'

'Jesus said he wouldn't always be with the disciples…'

Emma looked away, recalling what she'd been reading. 'He said he would send the Advocate, the Spirit of Truth.'

'The Holy Spirit.'

Emma stood suddenly and walked out of the room. She found Mary's bible in her room and returned with it. 'It was in John's book. Wait a minute…' She opened the bible and began flicking pages.

'Here: "the Holy Spirit… will teach you all things and will remind you of everything I have said." So, if Jesus sends his Holy Spirit, it's like he is with you?'

'I think so, yes.'

'Okay then. I want it.' She smiled at Mary. 'You look terrified. What's wrong?'

'I don't know how it works. I don't even know if I've received the Holy Spirit myself. I want to help you but I don't know how.'

'But Jesus said how, didn't he. "Ask and it will be given to you." How did it go? "How much more will your Father in heaven give the Holy Spirit to those who ask him." Or something like that.'

'How much more will he give the Holy Spirit to those who ask him,' echoed Mary. 'But when you ask, you must believe and not doubt. Oh God, forgive me my lack of faith!'

'So all we need to do is ask, right?'

'I'm scared, Emma.'

'It's good though? Getting the Holy Spirit? If he can convince me I'm not mad, I'm up for that. So, how do we do this?'

Mary had a look of desperation as she clasped her hands together. 'I was always taught to put my hands together, bow my head and pray.'

'Seriously? No offence, but why?'

'I think to stop distraction.'

'If God is real then he probably can cope.'

'I meant us being distracted.'

'I'm sure he can cope with that as well. Okay, shall I lead off?'

Mary nodded.

Emma found herself suddenly less certain than she had been. She looked across at Mary who still had her hands clasped but was looking back at her, her doubt mirrored.

'God. Wait, Jesus said Father. Father in Heaven, I don't know what hallowed means and I'm not convinced you want us to say the same words every time we talk to you but we're here to ask you for the Holy Spirit. We don't know how this works, or really what we need to do but... Give us the Holy Spirit. Thank you.'

Emma had found herself looking all over the room, glancing upwards mostly, then looking back at Mary who was frowning. 'Now what?' Emma whispered, feeling that to speak loudly would be somehow wrong.

Mary unclasped her hands and placed them palm down on the counter. Her frown was fading and she looked more curious.

'You've read through the gospels. What did Jesus say to do if your request isn't answered?'

'Keep asking.'

Mary nodded. 'May I?' She asked Emma.

'Okay.'

Mary licked her lips then looked upwards. 'Lord, you know how frustrated I get not understanding why things don't happen or do happen. But Emma is right.' She looked at Emma. 'You don't make this complicated. You said you would send your Holy Spirit. Lord, I don't even know if I have received your Holy Spirit. If I have then I'm sorry I haven't understood, haven't believed. We ask you will send your Holy Spirit to us. Fill us. Give us your comfort. Give us your truth. In Jesus name we ask. Amen.'

Emma noticed a change in the room. It had gone quiet like all the electricity had gone off.

'Your turn,' Mary said.

Very aware of the room's silence, Emma looked around her. Her earlier impulsiveness had faded and she felt like she had just strapped herself into a rollercoaster.

'Father. Jesus said he wouldn't leave us alone. Please don't leave us alone.' She felt her eyes welling up and rubbed the tears away. 'Jesus said... He said if two people ask for something in his name you would give us it. He said he would send the Holy Spirit. He said if we believe it would be done. We're asking in Jesus' name, send the Holy Spirit to us. I don't know about the last bit. How do we believe? Jesus kept on talking about children.

Children ask and just expect to get, until they get that knocked out of them. I hope you're not that kind of father, who stops his children from expecting the best. I don't think you are. I want to believe. Help me, help us to believe.'

Emma looked across at Mary who held up a finger and shook her head. She was looking around, searching for something. Suddenly Mary reached across the counter and took Emma's hands.

'Do you receive the Holy Spirit?' She asked.

'I guess so.'

'No guessing. Do you receive the Holy Spirit?'

'Yes.'

And as she said the word, Emma felt a warmth start to spread from her head down through her body. A gentle tingling heat that remained as it flowed down through her legs and her arms. As the heat spread to her hands she in turn clasped Mary's hands.

Mary gasped and looked down at her arms and then up at Emma. 'It's happening. Oh God, thank you!'

Tears started to run down Mary's face and then she started laughing. Emma didn't feel like laughing but she did feel at peace. No, it was much more than that. Was this what joy felt like?

They sat without speaking for a time. Then Emma felt she needed to move about and stood up. 'What now?'

'I don't know.' Mary shook her head slowly. She was still smiling.

'I feel so alive. I want to go out, do you want to go out?'

Mary thought for a moment. 'Yes! Let's go out.'

Mary put her coat on while Emma waited. They were about to leave when Emma heard a key in the lock and the door opened.

~~~

Rachel opened the door to the flat relieved she would finally be able to put her feet up. Early shifts were sometimes worse than late ones.

'Hi!' Rachel said as she saw Emma.

'We were just going out.'

'We?'

'Oh, yeah, Rachel, this is Mary. Mary, Rachel.'

A woman Rachel had never seen before reached round Emma and offered her hand.

'Hello…' Rachel shook Mary's hand uncertainly. 'Is everything okay?' She asked Emma.

'Oh yes, couldn't be better. There's pizza on the counter. Be back soon.' Emma squeezed past Rachel and waited for Mary who stepped back to allow Rachel into the flat.

Rachel heard them begin to chat animatedly as the door closed. Something about an experience. She sniffed the air hoping she wouldn't smell drugs but there was only the smell of pizza which she found sitting out as Emma had said. Rachel decided to avoid eating the pizza.

She had a shower and changed but before she could start preparing something to eat the door to the flat opened and Emma and Mary burst in, chattering and giggling.

Rachel could only stare at them as Emma grabbed a slice of the cold pizza and filled her mouth with it.

'Oh my, this is so good,' Emma mumbled as she ate.

Mary seemed to be slightly more in control of herself, but then she started to smile and then chuckle and then Emma joined her and the two of them burst out laughing.

'What's going on with you?' Rachel said, feeling like she'd turned into her mother as she realised her hands were on her hips. She folded her arms instead but that also felt wrong. 'Well?' She demanded. 'What have you been smoking?'

The two of them looked at each other and started laughing again, Emma actually doubling over.

'This isn't funny,' said Rachel, then realised that was the worst thing she could have said. She turned away and pulled a couple of pans out of the cupboard and then a bag of pasta and jar of sauce. Behind her the laughter gradually subsided.

'Maybe I should go,' said Mary.

'No, stay and eat with us,' Emma replied.

Rachel ignored them, only responding when Mary said goodbye. She turned and acknowledged her, but then carried on preparing her meal. She heard the door open and close and then Emma walk back into the kitchen.

'Hasn't it been a great day?' Emma said.

Rachel turned and saw Emma was looking out the window. 'Have you been drinking?'

Emma looked at her, placing her head to one side. 'No.' She gave a huge grin.

'Are you on some sort of drug?'

'Nope.' Emma emphasised the P and then began repeating the word, turning the P into a popping sound.

'That's not terribly reassuring.'

'I'm not on drugs, Rachel. Though now I think about it, that is a pretty good description of how I feel right now. I am high!'

'Oh, no. Did that woman give you something? Weirdest pusher I've ever seen but...'

'No. No she didn't, but...'

'But? But what?'

Emma moved over to the breakfast bar. 'Something amazing's happened, Rachel. I know God is real. Jesus is real!'

Rachel did a double take. 'You've become a Jehovah's Witness? Is that who that woman was?'

'No.'

'A Mormon?'

'No.'

'What then?'

'I don't really know that I've become anything. I just know God is real.'

Rachel studied Emma for a moment. 'That's wonderful, Emma. Really.' Then she turned back to the hob, her heart beating far too fast. She heard Emma start to sing. A thought forced it's way into her mind: I'm losing my best friend.

~ ~ ~

The tip-off had advised bomb making materials and weapons were being smuggled into Europe resulting in the case being elevated to highest priority for the national police forces involved. It took a full day to x-ray each of the crates, verify they were safe to open and finally open and unpack each of them. A total of twenty six officers were involved in four countries working over 450 hours between them.

Thirty hours after the lorry was stopped, the driver was released without charge, a senior police commander drafted in to offer a full apology for the misunderstanding, inconvenience and any offence caused.

Scans of the crates had shown each crate was full of electronics matching the cargo manifest which ruled out weapons. Unfortunately every crate had to be opened and each box fully examined in case an attempt had been made to smuggle devices or explosives hidden within the genuine Blu-Ray players. Sniffer dog teams were called in to check for signs of explosives but no such sign was found, either from the cargo or the lorry.

A sample of boxes from each crate were opened and dismantled, checked and then reassembled before powering them up and checking they worked. Eventually the lead investigator called a halt to the work convinced the whole thing had been a waste of their time. In that regard he was absolutely right. While his team had been scouring the lorry and the cargo, two other lorries had openly made their way to ports on the Northern European coast, one carrying assault and high end sniper rifles that had been swapped over for the Blu-Ray players in Germany, the other carrying 100 kilos of semtex.

As the explosives were divided into two smaller shipments and loaded onto separate fishing boats, an enquiry was ordered into the source of the tip-off. The source though had disappeared.

CHAPTER FORTY-SIX
Away Day

Carrie tried to tune out Jack's constant questioning: 'What's he doing, Mummy... Where are we going... Can I have a sweetie?' His push chair bumped along as she negotiated the cobbled market square. It seemed like a dozen tourist buses had all disgorged their passengers at the same time. The place was heaving with them, all milling about in different directions and taking in the sights, sounds and smells of York's farmers market.

Carrie fished a toffee out from a packet in her coat pocket and unwrapped the golden paper. It was bad for his teeth but he would be getting a new set over the next few years, unlike her with more fillings than teeth it sometimes seemed. She sighed and let the sweetie wrapper drop unnoticed to the ground. They always swept up the market before the next day. Kept someone in a job.

She pushed on looking for a stall that sold a socket block. Her Mum had given her—well, given Jack really—a Wii. Mum had brought it over last night, second hand of course. Ask me no questions and I'll tell you no lies, nudge nudge, wink wink. Still, it worked fine and Jack had loved it. Carrie tried not to think about what it would do to the electric bill. They would manage somehow.

Problem was, there was only one socket on the wall and the TV, video recorder, DVD player and set top box already took up one four socket extension. They had unplugged the DVD player last night, after accidentally unplugging the set top box and video recorder which had both reset, but Carrie wanted to be able to have them all plugged in together rather than having to reach behind the TV and mess about with the dusty cables.

'Mummy, can I have an ice cream?'

'Not now, honey.'

Jack ignored her and started singing: 'I want an ice cream, I want an ice cream.'

Carrie took a deep breath and trundled the push chair on. 'Mummy can't afford it, honey. Maybe next time.'

Jack carried on singing. Carrie spied the stall she was looking for, mobile phone covers decorating the sides, signs for batteries, watches and there, a row of extension sockets!

Carrie excused her way past a group of older women who were clustered round the opposite stall looking at children's tops. There were four and six socket extensions but she only needed a three socket block and she couldn't see one.

'Hi,' she said, catching the attention of the stall holder who was re-arranging bejeweled phone cases. 'Do you have any of those three socket blocks?'

'I don't get many people asking for those nowadays, most people want the four or six socket strips. They're a lot safer.'

And a lot more expensive, Carrie thought to herself. 'I just need an extra socket,' she said.

'What's it for?' The stall holder asked.

'What are you, an electrician?'

'Just looking out for you. You know those socket blocks are dangerous, right? They can overheat if you stack them together.'

'I don't need you trying to sell me something I don't want.' She realised her voice was raised and looked down and saw that Jack had stopped his singing. He was looking up at her with that expression he often had when he was about to start crying. Just what she needed! She looked back at the stall holder. 'Do you have one or not?'

'I stopped selling them a few years ago. The four socket extensions are only £4.99…'

'No thanks,' Carrie said abruptly. She manoeuvred Jack's push chair around and walked away. There were usually a couple of stalls in the market selling electrical goods and if she couldn't find a socket block here there would always be the pound shops…

~~~

Zafar huddled in a doorway realising he was actually scared to move. He looked at the other members of his team who were all looking back at him, waiting for his instructions. He couldn't remember a single name from the group. Not surprising when he'd barely had a chance to get to know any of them since arriving at the agreed location. No, wait, one of them was Kadar.

'Let's go,' he shouted, trying to convey enthusiasm rather than fear. His team charged out the door, Kadar clapping him on the shoulder as he ran past and Zafar found the courage to turn and follow them out.

They were scattering, each finding cover and he could see two of the team taking aim and firing. Zafar felt something wiz past him and he flinched, then realised he was an easy target standing up. Ducking down, he scuttled to join Kadar behind an overturned crate.

'They've got three men trying to flank us on our left,' Kadar shouted. 'A fourth seems to be acting as a sniper at our right, over by the tower. If he gets up there then we're going to struggle to move from this position.'

Zafar risked a quick look round the crate pulling his head back quickly. He looked at Kadar. 'I can't see anything!'

Kadar laughed. 'Follow me!'

He led Zafar to their right, crouching down but moving quickly from obstacle to obstacle. Shouts from their own team and their opposition were interspersed with the muffled phuts of guns being fired.

A paintball exploded against a brick wall near where Kadar stopped. Zafar looked at the spatter marks which had almost reached his own feet.

'What now?' Zafar asked.

'The sniper is twenty feet away, near the ladder of the tower. We should have some cover from the others on their team.' Kadar paused, breathing heavily. 'We split. I'll go round the right, you go round the left. He can only shoot at one of us leaving the other with a clear shot. Just pump as much paint at him as you can. Maybe he'll hesitate but so long as one of us reaches the ladder without being shot, then we take the tower and use it to try and take the others out. Okay?'

Zafar nodded.

'On three?'

'Sure.'

Kadar grinned widely. 'Three!' He pivoted towards his right and Zafar had no time to worry, he split left, turned and rose pointing his own rifle towards the tower. He wasn't aiming, he was just spraying the bottom of the tower as he ran. He then saw his opponent rise and now directed the flow of paint in his direction. Kadar had been right, the two of them approaching from different directions caused him to hesitate and Zafar saw the man get hit, whether one of his or Kadar's he didn't know.

The opponent lowered his rifle as Zafar rushed by and began climbing the ladder. He realised Kadar wasn't with him, looked back and saw Kadar had also lowered his rifle, paint smeared across his chest. There was no time to think though, he climbed up into the tower—the floor of which was only at head height—and scanned the arena. He saw the two others in his team were pinned down by their three remaining opponents.

He chose a target and fired a couple of shots at him. The feedback even at this distance was excellent, Zafar could see where his shots were hitting— a metre away from where he'd aimed. He pulled the rifle in closer to him to steady it and adjusted up and to his right. Still not quite right but he'd got his target's attention. The guy dropped down out of sight.

Zafar shifted to another target and adjusted his aim again. This time the target almost instantly responded, turning to fire a wild shot back at him before ducking behind a crate. He moved to the third who was trying to move forward. Zafar had a clear shot and took it. He hit the guy's leg. The rules were simple enough, if you were hit in an arm, you were supposed to stop using that arm. Hit in a leg, you were supposed to stop moving. Hit anywhere else you were dead.

The guy didn't stop moving. Angry, Zafar adjusted his aim again and this time hit the guy on his arm, then kept firing until the guy had several paint spatters on his side and head. He watched the guy chuck his rifle down on the ground in disgust.

Two left. Zafar felt a thud of paint hit the wall of the tower and ducked himself. Now what was he supposed to do? If he lifted his head to try and take a shot would they just shoot him? He scooted forward and jumped down, crouching before anyone saw him, then moved as quickly as he could up the arena to try and flank the remaining opponents.

He ducked as he scurried past a low wall and then crawled a section to some drums until he thought he had moved behind them. His goggles had started to steam up and he lifted them to allow them to clear. He heard shouts but couldn't tell who or what they were saying.

Stop hesitating he told himself. Taking a deep breath he looked round but couldn't see anyone. Okay, keep moving towards where you last saw them. His sense of sight and hearing seemed to be magnified as he stood, raising his gun level with his line of sight. He walked forward, scanning left and right, sweeping his gun back and forth.

Ahead, near their team entrance he saw movement and thought it was one of his team. He waved. Instead of waving back, the man pointed his gun at Zafar and starting firing.

Zafar crouched and ran to the nearest crate. Where had his team moved to? There was no secondary goal in this game, just wiping out the other team members so his team could be anywhere, trying to get a better position as he had.

Well, his opponents knew where he was now so he had to move before they surrounded him. He crawled back and then right, trying to get as far away from where he'd been spotted as he could. He rounded another crate and came face to face with one of his remaining opponents.

The guy was looking straight at him but his gun was pointed away. Almost without thinking, Zafar pulled his own trigger. Paint splattered across the guy's chest. Only one left.

He could continue crawling round the arena hoping to bump into him like this but what if the other guy did the same and they never came near each other? No. He'd had enough. Maybe if he drew the guy out, one of his other team members could take him down. Skulking around on his knees wasn't fighting like a warrior. He stood up, turning to where he thought the other opponent might be. He couldn't see him but started walking in that direction anyway.

'Are you going to fight me like a man?' Zafar called out. 'Or are you hiding like a woman? Too scared to face me?'

He kept sweeping his gun, back and forth as he looked left and right... There! The final opponent rose up, his own gun pointed at Zafar. Right, all he needed now was one of the remaining members of his team to shoot and the game would be over. Zafar kept walking forwards but no-one else shot. His opponent seemed frozen, hesitant. He wasn't firing at Zafar. Just standing there as Zafar walked closer.

Were they the only two left?

Zafar stopped. There was only about twenty feet between them. Their guns pointed directly at each other.

The arena was silent but in the distance Zafar could hear shouts from other arenas. He half let out a breath and fired a single shot. Whether his opponent fired after him or not, he couldn't tell but he felt the stinging impact of a paint pellet against his own chest almost at the same time as he saw his opponents chest turn red from his own pellet.

Game over. It was a draw. Zafar heard clapping and turned, reaching up to remove his face mask and goggles.

'No! Keep them on,' shouted Philippe who had been observing them. 'Remember you should never remove the face gear in the arena.' He waved the others over and waited till they were gathered round. 'We'll debrief in the arena. Remember we are in a public place and everything you say can be overheard. Take no chances. Right, both teams tried to capture the tower. What happened?'

'I couldn't climb the ladder. Zafar's team pinned me down. If I'd tried to get up they'd have shot me in the back.'

'They shot you in the front anyway. Nice flank, Zafar,' Philippe told him.

'It was Kadar's idea.' Zafar confessed.

'It was a good one.' Philippe nodded at Kadar. 'Storming the tower like you did was a gutsy strategy. Was it worth it?'

'Of course, Zafar took the tower,' Kadar replied.

'But you were shot. We're not sending you out with suicide vests. We can't afford to lose people every time we take an objective.'

'There's not going to be any resistance when we take the city,' said Kadar.

'You don't know that. All you need is some local hero with a golf club and you not paying attention and that'll be you down.'

'Okay, so we watch out for mad dogs.'

'And the police, and the army. And you can count on it that at least some of the locals will have access to fire-arms and given a chance will use them. When we first attack we will have the advantage, but if we lose key people early on that will make it far harder to retain the city when the inevitable assault happens. Zafar... You took the tower but then abandoned it. What happened?'

'I got pinned down. They knew I was there and if I'd stuck my head up I'd have been shot.'

'But why did you duck down anyway? You had the strategic advantage. If you'd kept on firing you could have kept them down and given your team the chance to overwhelm them. As it was, once you abandoned the tower they took out the rest of your team before you'd made it half way across the arena.'

So that was what had happened—why his team hadn't been supporting him. He looked apologetically at them, not that they could see through his face mask.

'And as for you...' Philippe rounded on the others. 'You had the advantage, two to one. Why didn't you use that?'

'We didn't know where he was.'

'Zafar didn't know where you were yet managed to flush you out. Gutsy move by the way,' Philippe said turning again to Zafar. 'Stupid, giving yourself up like that but gutsy. Don't let me see any of you copying it though. You can die in this arena as many times as you like, but we're not trying to teach you to die, we're trying to teach you tactics and strategy so you can survive and lead. The initial assault is just the beginning, we're going to start a fire that will consume this country! Now, let's shuffle up the teams and go again...'

~~~

Thomas put down the phone, shaking his head. Always at the last

270

minute… He hoped Karl hadn't… The phone rang. He picked it up.

'That's the hotel booked.' It was Karl. Too late…

'You're not going to believe this. I just had a call from Johnson.'

'He wants to come now?'

'He does.'

'What is he like!'

Thomas heard Karl sighing.

'Okay, I'll see if I can book another room.'

'He could always sleep in the coach.'

Karl laughed. 'You know, maybe I should just forget to call the hotel back. Every single year he does the same thing… Why do we put up with him?'

'He helped found the club.'

'Yeah, that. He always enjoys the competition—why can't he just sign up with the rest of us.'

'I reckon he's just looking for attention, a few weeks of half the club telling him he should go.'

'He wants attention he should get a dog.'

~~~

The fishing boat was fifty miles out of Grimsby when the storm blew up. Within ten minutes the stars had disappeared, blocked by a dark cloud that left the crew with only their running lights to see by.

Wind forced the waves higher and higher until the boat was driven up and over the increasingly steep swell. The crew moved quickly and locked everything down before they were fully in the grip of the storm. The captain knew that when you're riding thirty foot swells, there's not a lot you can do except point the bow into the wind and pray.

Not that the captain or the crew were much into praying. They were used to sudden storms and there was no fear. They imported bricks of drugs from the Netherlands to England two to three times a month. Usually only a few boxes, small enough loads where the individual bricks could be hidden under the catch of fish they would aim to unload on arrival. Their tax free profit for transporting the drugs sometimes more than they received for their catch on the occasions they had transported larger quantities: a full cubic metre of weed; once even 10 kilos of heroin.

They'd been told the bricks they were carrying below were unprocessed heroin, a full 50 kilos. Not as high value as the processed commodity, but still sufficiently valuable that as he tried to see ahead through the rain spattered windscreen, the captain was wondering about buying a bigger boat.

Out at sea, engines have to be reliable in extreme weather conditions. While the captain had maintained the boat's engine, he'd neglected to ensure the fuel tank was regularly decontaminated. Over a number of years a layer of silt and debris had built up on the bottom. As the sea became rougher, the fuel sloshing around in the tank dislodged some of the silt which got sucked in through the fuel pump and blocked the injectors.

The captain noticed the engine spluttering but had no time to react before the engine cut out. He shouted down to the boat's engineer: 'Have we lost fuel?'

The engineer was already at the engine. 'It's probably the injectors,' he shouted back as he started to bleed the fuel line.

Had the boat been in calmer conditions he could have cleaned out the fuel line, the injectors and the pump in half an hour and had the engine restarted, but it only took two minutes for the boat to start to broach, the rudder not able to maintain the heading without the propeller thrust.

'Get your survival suits on,' the captain shouted as he realised the danger they were in.

The engineer heard him as he was uncoupling the fuel pump. The angle of the boat was wrong and it only took him a split second to decide to abandon the engine and he raced to grab his suit.

As the boat dropped down one swell it turned beam on and as it hit the bottom of the trough was shunted sideways. Down in the hold, unsecured boxes of fish began to slide across the steep deck making the boat even more unstable. Carried up the other side of the trough the cargo slammed back against the inside of the hull and the boat began to roll.

The water flooding over the deckhouse triggered the auto-release for the lifeboat. For the first time in their lives each crew member found themselves thrown into the freezing North Sea.

The emergency beacon activated on the lifeboat and provided the only light source for miles in every direction. Despite being disoriented and terrified, the engineer struggling to stay afloat as tried to finish zipping up his suit, that flashing light gave the men hope. Swimming for their lives, the four crew each reached the lifeboat and scrambled aboard.

The lifeboat was pushed away from the upturned hull which seemed in the strobing light to be sinking. The Captain hoped it fully sank. He didn't want to have to explain himself if a salvage crew managed to recover the boat.

He wasn't worried about the men who'd arranged the drug shipment. It was a lot to lose, but that was the risk they'd taken. He was oblivious to the fact that his cargo was far more deadly than heroin. Once secure in the lifeboat the only concern on his mind was a suspicion he might have missed the last insurance payment…

CHAPTER FORTY-SEVEN
Greater

Mary arrived as late as she could to St Andrew's, wanting to avoid speaking to anyone before the service. When Tony had told her what he wanted her to do, she had had a moment of panic. Then she realised as he continued that he had said he wanted her to do two things and as he spoke she forgot to breathe. Then, when he kept speaking and told her why, she was mortified and had silently told God it wasn't worth it.

Now as she looked at the open doors to the church, hesitating to go in, she remembered a sense she'd had when Tony had finally stopped talking and she'd started breathing once more—not a picture as some people called it and certainly not a vision—just a sense that God was looking at her with one eyebrow raised slightly.

I'm still not sure, she sent up at him, but stepped forward nonetheless.

Jim was standing in the entrance and couldn't hide a double take as she walked in. When he said: 'Good to see you, Mary' it wasn't as convincing as she might have hoped. She took the hymn book he offered and steeled herself as she entered the sanctuary.

For once she was hoping the back rows would be empty so she could slide in unseen but to her great discomfort there were people sitting in almost every row until one half way up the aisle. She hurried forward keeping her eyes down and ignoring everyone to either side. As she settled herself, she heard Tony welcome everyone and risked looking up only to flinch as someone sat next to her.

'I thought you could use some support.'

Mary looked round at Cynthia who took her hand.

'I don't know if I can do this,' Mary whispered to her as the rest of the church stood around them.

'Would you like me to go up with you?' Cynthia whispered back.

'Can you do that?' Mary didn't dare to hope.

'Of course.' Cynthia squeezed her hand. 'Do you feel up to singing? It might take your mind off it.'

Mary nodded and they stood. Singing didn't take her mind off what she was going to do, but as she joined in with the worship she felt her resolve growing even if her trembling didn't stop.

They reached the end of the song, sat down with everyone else and Mary felt the fear grip her as Tony began to speak.

'We recite the story of the prodigal son so often that I wonder if we fail to appreciate what it means. There is rejoicing in Heaven over one sinner who repents. One sinner…'

Mary wondered what they must all think of her as Tony paused briefly.

'Easy to cast a stone at someone else and ignore the burden of sin that we carry around,' Tony continued. 'Easy to judge another while covering over our own tracks. All have sinned and fallen short, all we like sheep have gone astray, if we say that we have no sin, we deceive ourselves…'

Father, I don't want to do this, Mary silently prayed.

'We are all sinners saved only by God's grace and mercy through Jesus. Those of you who were here a few weeks ago will know I shared that I had decided to discipline a sister in the church, to exclude her from meeting with us. Some of you were understandably concerned about this and I thank you for coming to speak with me. To discipline a brother or sister is and should be one of the hardest decisions a leader ever has to make. The only reason for doing so is to encourage them to repent and to seek reconciliation and forgiveness. Cynthia, Mary, would you come up to the front.'

Mary looked round at Cynthia in surprise.

Cynthia leaned in. 'Tony suggested I come up with you.' She smiled. 'I was going to anyway, but it was good of him to ask.'

Mary stood with Cynthia and managed to walk up to the front, next to Tony.

Tony leaned in. 'You're shaking, we'll make this as quick as possible.'

She nodded gratefully.

'May I take your hands?' He asked.

She let go of Cynthia's hand reluctantly and tried to control her trembling as she let Tony hold her hands. She steeled herself and looked into his eyes.

'Mary,' he said in a voice that carried round the sanctuary. 'I forgive you and I welcome you back into fellowship with us.' Then in a softer voice that was only for her, he asked: 'Are you okay to continue?'

There was no way she could go through this again. She nodded, not daring to speak, knowing that she was going to have to.

Tony released his gentle hold on her hands and turned to the church, placing one arm around her. She couldn't look out at the church but studied the carpet instead.

'I believe meeting with leaders from other faiths is something God has called me to do—a responsibility I have to witness to them, to pray for them and to declare and demonstrate as Elijah did that our God is the only true God, worthy of our worship.'

Mary tried to calm herself as Tony spoke. Again she told God that she didn't want to do what she'd been asked. There was no response. Then she prayed two words: help me! Immediately she sensed God telling her: I am with you. And although her trembling didn't cease, it seemed to lessen.

'Yet, no matter how convinced I am of my calling, it would be wrong of me to ignore the warnings in God's word about worshipping other Gods and just as importantly the counsel that I should hold myself accountable to you and that I should place no stumbling blocks before you. So… I felt it appropriate to ask Mary to accompany me to an Inter-faith meeting—to give her an opportunity to hold me accountable and I extend that request to you all. That if you have any concerns about my involvement in meeting with leaders of other faiths, that you join us. Either your concerns will be eased, or it will give you an opportunity to challenge me based on what you have witnessed rather than what you imagine. If you still have concerns then we can decide together how we should proceed.

'And finally…'

Mary shut her eyes tightly.

'…I've asked Mary to pray for me now. Would you join with us as we pray.'

Mary looked up at Tony who was smiling encouragingly at her, then out at the church. Some of her friends had their heads bowed, but others… She saw Ethel smile at her and Arthur was nodding his head. She knew what she needed to ask, turned and placed a hand on Tony's shoulder and began to pray.

~~~

Jack giggled as he jiggled his Wii controller and watched his cow jump and land on a scarecrow. 15 points! Carrie smiled as her son's cow bumped her own off the track and she had to tilt her controller to try and catch up. Her eyes flicked towards the clock. 'Oh my! Better get you ready for bed,' she said to Jack.

Carrie helped him get the controller strap off his wrist and then switched off the TV and put the controllers in their stand to charge. She didn't notice a crackling from the new socket block that didn't quite fit next to the other plugs. Fetching a plate of biscuits, she took Jack upstairs and followed a routine that seemed to be helping him to drop off to sleep. Pyjamas on, supper and a story. No matter how difficult the day had been, she looked forward to these few minutes when she could cuddle up next to Jack in his bed and he'd listen attentively as she read to him.

Whether it was the routine or the sound of her voice or having to sit still for longer than ten seconds, Jack pulled his blanket to his chin, stuck his thumb in his mouth and closed his eyes. She sat with him for a few minutes, stroking his hair and wondering when she would be able to wean him off the thumb and blanket. Not tonight, anyway.

She checked her watch. Tommy would be in from his shift in a couple of hours looking for his dinner. She had ironing to do before then and realised that now she had a spare socket, she could watch TV while she ironed without having to unplug anything. She kissed Jack, switched off his light and left his door just open in case he called out.

$\sim\sim\sim$

'The boat sank! What was it carrying?'

'Explosives.'

'We've lost the explosives?' Zafar took a step back and sat down.

'Only half. I always insist on shipments being split.'

Zafar looked up at Tariq, still reeling from the news. 'Half?' He shook his head trying to focus. 'You don't seem worried.'

Tariq shrugged. 'These things happen. It's not the end of the world, it could have been worse.'

'How?'

Zafar couldn't believe it when Tariq actually laughed. 'One of the couriers could have been caught. Now that would have been bad. It's unlikely it would have been linked back to us but if the authorities knew someone was trying to smuggle this quantity of explosives into the country... Everything would be locked down. No, for all that could have gone wrong, this was a minor setback.'

Minor... Zafar told himself that Tariq had more experience but even so... 'Is there time to get more?'

Tariq shook his head. 'No. We're looking at two weeks minimum for delivery and by that time... Well...' Tariq held out his hand to him.

Taking his hand, Zafar pulled himself up.

Tariq placed his hands on Zafar's shoulders. 'We're going to war,

brother. There will be setbacks and losses but Allah is on our side.'
Zafar steeled himself. 'Our God is greater.'
Tariq nodded. 'Allah Akbar.'

CHAPTER FORTY-EIGHT
Minimal Security

Danny turned over onto his back and opened his eyes. Sleep just wasn't happening. Another fight with Cynthia the previous evening and he'd been unable to stop churning it around in his head after the shouting had ended in a stony silence.

He looked over at her. She was lying with her back towards him. Ever since he'd broken up with Natalie, Cynthia had seemed far more distant. Or was it that he was actually around now to notice? He'd always avoided arguments in the past, but over the last few weeks several had boiled over.

Would it only get worse when he was full time as a CTSA? Better working hours had been one of Rudd's selling points. Less time on the job would mean more time at home… Right now he couldn't think of anything worse.

They must have fought before yet Danny couldn't remember a time when his relationship with Cynthia had been this bad. Yes they had grown apart, both living their own lives, but Cynthia had seemed happy. Ever since he'd broken up with Natalie though… Did Cynthia know somehow? Had she sensed what was going on? Danny thought back. It had all gone down hill since Rudd had offered him the CTSA role. If Rudd had not recommended him then MI5 would not have investigated him and he would still be seeing…

It was a dangerous line of thought and he cut it off. He'd known as soon as he saw the photos that it was over between them. He couldn't have that hanging over him whether he had decided to risk rejecting the CTSA offer or take the jump into the unknown.

Did it have to be this difficult though? Yes he'd been—he resisted the word—unfaithful… But he'd ended it. So why had life with Cynthia suddenly become so much harder?

Dwelling on it wasn't helping him sleep. He turned over, away from Cynthia—and closed his eyes again, tried to empty his mind. It was no use. Case after case cycled through his thoughts. The string of burglaries along Tang Hall Lane, the suspected arson case in Heworth, a sexual assault in Clifton, the missing boys…

Why was he even investigating that? Leeds was well outside his jurisdiction… Except it wouldn't be, would it. His area of responsibility was going to expand massively and he would somehow have to avoid getting drawn into every potential issue he came across. Not that he would be able to ignore something like this case if he came across it, but he would have to hand it over and let the locals deal with it, even though that could cause it's own problems…

Had Natalie found something in linking the missing boys to a national series of deaths? She was intuitive and he'd always encouraged that, but was she just wasting time that could be better spent investigating crimes locally?

Manchester, Birmingham, Glasgow… what had that to do with…

He sat up in bed. There was something there, he'd had it for a split second… No, he couldn't lose this. He quickly got out of bed and pulled on his dressing gown. Heading to his study he kept reciting the list over and over: Manchester, Birmingham, Glasgow… Manchester, Birmingham, Glasgow…

He shut the door to his study and turned on the light, blinking as his eyes adjusted. He pulled down a road atlas from a shelf and opened it to a page giving a full UK map then began putting pins in each of the locations Natalie had identified the deaths, finally putting two pins near the square that marked Leeds.

It was hardly conclusive and yet Danny knew it was important and as he looked down at a map it reminded him of the one Barnes had shown him on his wall. Connections that might have led to nowhere and yet which had seemed to be linked in some way he wasn't then able to see.

He could see a link here. A tenuous one and yet one which made him pick up his phone to wake both Barnes and Natalie. Every single death had occurred near a major university.

~~~

'Will!'

William recognized Archer's voice on the phone. 'Hello, Archer.'

'I have a job for you tonight.'

'Okay…' It had been over three weeks since he'd had the run in with

Archer. Normally he would have had work every week or fortnight. Archer was obviously annoyed that Will hadn't delivered the full two pallets he'd expected.

'There's a shipment of high end Blu-Ray's being delivered to a warehouse in Acomb this evening. Minimal security. These are next-gen devices—they'll record High Definition.'

'Right. What's the value?'

'Five hundred per unit—retail. I should be able to shift them at one hundred a piece. I've been told there will be 135 per pallet with four pallets in total. Can you manage that quantity?'

He could fit four pallets worth of goods in his transit, that wouldn't be a problem, but not on the pallets. There was only floor space enough for two. He'd have to manually stack the other two which would take longer...

'Is there a loading bay?' If there was, he could back the van up, wheel over the four pallets, push two pallets in and would just have to quickly stack the other two.

'Yes.'

Okay, Will calculated: 270 units, say ten seconds each to stack, 2700 seconds... Drop the zero and divide by 6 to get minutes... 'Forty five minutes plus five to move the pallets plus ten to enter the building. That's a full hour.'

'Can you do it or not?'

An hour on site was a long time for any job. But with minimal security... 'No guards?'

'None.'

'What would my cut be?' Will asked.

'Twenty percent.'

He ran the numbers—not even the full value of one pallet. Still, ten thousand would come in very handy and if this meant Archer was willing to trust him again... 'I can do it. Give me the details.'

~~~

Rachel found the end of her shift dragged on. Patients needing one thing after another, little jobs that had to be done but with no real sense of achievement. Shift change over, she changed out of her uniform and then just sat down.

One of the bank nurses came in. 'Tiring shift?'

Rachel didn't answer but stood slowly, got her bag and walked out. It had been a tiring shift but that wasn't the problem she admitted to herself. She just didn't want to go home.

It was a nice evening so she decided to walk, it would give her a chance to think if nothing else. Ever since Emma had had her "accident" things just hadn't been right between them. Sure, Emma had been irritating and sometimes downright annoying before but she'd also been fun and outgoing and it had worked well sharing the flat.

But now?

Now she wasn't sure if she could trust Emma. She hadn't seemed to care at all that she had almost got them both fired, had missed the meeting with the Union and now she was hanging round with this strange old lady becoming what? Some sort of Jesus Freak?

She'd seen her reading that bible, even though Emma had tried to hide it. What was so interesting about an old book anyway?

They couldn't hang out with Jennifer and Paul anymore. At least not all together like they used to. Rachel clutched her coat closer to her. Take away all the fun and partying and Emma seemed to be just another selfish cow.

As she reached the entrance to the flats Rachel wondered if maybe she should start talking to some of the other nurses about sharing a flat together.

There was the muffled sound of loud music emanating from their flat as Rachel reached the door. 'What is she doing now?' She muttered.

Opening the door it was as if she was stepping into a night club. She hung up her coat and dropped her bag in her room before walking into the living room. Emma was dancing in the kitchen, two wooden spoons in her hands, pretending to bang on pots on the stove as if they were drums.

Emma turned and saw her. 'Hi!' She shouted over the music.

Rachel went and turned the music down.

'I thought you liked that song?'

'I'm not in the mood,' Rachel said. 'What are you doing?'

'I felt like dancing.' Emma pretended to bang her pot drum again. 'Making pasta.'

'I see that. Why are you so happy?'

'Don't know. Just am.' Emma grinned at her. 'I'm going back to work next week. Called up HR today. Got to have a check up but that should be okay.'

'Alright for some.'

'Yes it is. Do you want to go clubbing tonight?'

Rachel put her hands up. 'No, I don't want to go clubbing! What is with you? You're up and down like a yoyo!'

'I know, I have been. Why can't you be happy that I'm feeling better?'

'I just need some stability. You keep freaking me out.'

'I'm sorry.'

'And what is this with you saying sorry? You never say sorry!'

'Is it a bad thing?'

'It's just not you.'

Emma looked at her until she felt uncomfortable and had to turn away.

'When will the food be ready?' Rachel asked.

'It's ready now.'

Rachel got plates and cutlery out. They ate mostly in silence and after they'd tidied up she went to bed early. As she got changed the same thought went round and round. It's just not working out.

CHAPTER FORTY-NINE
Warehouse

William drove round the industrial estate slowly as if looking for the right address. He felt slightly on edge but couldn't tell if it was related to feeling the need to deliver to Archer or was flagging a warning. As with most industrial estates there was only one entrance which meant only one exit, yet there was no activity visible at any of the other units so he was hopeful he wouldn't be disturbed. Police occasionally drove into these estates, but less often than the unit owners probably suspected. He'd asked Archer if there was private security patrolling the area and had been assured there wasn't.

Google Street View had once again been useful allowing him to examine the area closely before he set out. William found it hard to believe such a system was widely available to the general public. He'd made extensive use of it since first hearing of it, always careful to use a pirated wi-fi signal or pre-paid data connection to avoid the certainty of some force somewhere tracing his search back to him.

He'd seen a fire exit on the ground floor to the rear of the building which he'd discounted immediately—they were often chained from the inside. A broken window at the rear on the first floor next to a drain pipe was the only other access point to the rear but that would have been dangerous on too many levels. Someone parking a van outside a warehouse could have several legitimate reasons. Climbing a drain pipe at two in the morning had none and if you were to slip and break a leg... Well, it would be a long wait until people started arriving for the morning shift in the morning.

As he drove up to the front of the warehouse he checked windows for lights—all were dark. The three loading bays were shuttered and free of parked vehicles. The main entrance was also shuttered. He headed for the bay on the far right, turning so he could reverse in. Handbrake on, engine off, lights off, seatbelt off. Grabbing his carry-all, William climbed out and walked briskly round to the shuttered bay door. It was locked with a key at both sides of the door. Setting down his carry-all, William took his drill out and drilled out both locking mechanisms. He slid the door upwards ignoring the clatter.

Taking a torch from his utility belt, William switched it on, scanned inside and realised he had a problem. He'd assumed when talking to Archer that he'd be able to reverse up to a raised floor and wheel two pallets straight in his van but the floor of the warehouse was level with the ground outside. He'd have to manually stack the full four pallets. He cursed but had no time to waste. Archer had informed him there was an alarm keypad located near the front entrance. He had sixty seconds to enter a keycode or the alarm would be triggered.

He ran across to the entrance, the beam of his torch jerking wildly. He found the keypad and entered the code Archer had given him then started counting. If Archer had given him the wrong code he'd have to bail and would have no hesitation in letting Archer know what he could do with his jobs in future.

He allowed himself to reach fifty before deciding the code had worked. His heart beating faster than he'd have liked, he took a proper look round the warehouse. The whole ground floor was open with no supporting pillars to break up the space, a row of offices and rooms—two floors high—spanned the rear wall with a steel staircase leading to a second floor. A transit sized van with jacks under the front axle and no front wheels sat at the right. Empty pallets were stacked a dozen high in neat rows at the left beyond the entrance and some crates were laid out in the centre. He looked again taking more time but couldn't see any pallets with boxes anywhere in the warehouse. Was it possible they were in one of the rooms at the back? William thought it unlikely but didn't have time to waste pondering it.

He walked over to the crates and examined them. Plain wooden board with no markings anywhere. He set his carry-all down, retrieved a crow-bar from it and started to jimmie the top off a crate. Taking care of the long nails that had been used to secure the top, he lifted it off and saw crumpled up newspaper that was presumably being used as packing. It was an odd thing to use and as he shone the torch in one of the boxes, William realised the writing wasn't English. If the recorders had been sent directly from abroad, that wasn't all that surprising, but why use crates when you could stack more on a pallet?

Putting his torch between his teeth he pushed aside the newspaper only to step back in horror. Drugs! Had to be. He forced himself back to the crate and pushed away all of the newspaper to reveal eight brick like shapes of a solid grey substance, each thickly wrapped in a tough transparent plastic. He pulled out one of the bricks and found another underneath. He threw the brick away and heard it make a satisfying thump against the wall then checked another crate. More grey bricks. Had Archer known this was going to be here? It made no sense, Archer knew how he felt about drugs.

Desperate to retrieve something he could actually take, William turned to a third crate. This one took less time to open as either anger or fear gave him a surge of energy. He levered up the last side and let the top clatter to the concrete floor of the warehouse. Shining his torch inside, his heart sank. This one had no newspaper to hide the three... six... no, twelve guns that were carefully held inside a wooden matrix. Not just pistols either, but large rifle like weapons.

William only scanned them quickly, his mind was now racing. He looked at the remaining crates and knew he didn't want to open any more. He'd heard news reports of police seizing drugs and been astonished at the quantity recovered, but never heard of gangs using these sorts of guns. It was something he could imagine finding in America or Russia, but not here in the UK.

He looked over at the offices then checked his watch. He'd already been in the warehouse five minutes. He had rules. If the job went bad, leave, get out. Your life is always more important. Never touch drugs. Never use a gun.

He hesitated. He had to at least check the offices, right?

The office on the left had a window and William ran over and shone his torch inside. Desks and filing cabinets. He quickly moved on. A door to the next room along opened easily and William found shelving with car parts and some boxes. He opened them only to find paperwork—invoices and delivery notes.

The next room was empty and when he opened the final door he discovered a sink and what had to be two more doors leading to toilets.

Shaking his head and knowing it was foolish he ran back and climbed the staircase to the first floor. He was going to give Archer an earful, but needed to know, 100 percent, that he'd checked the whole warehouse.

There was a passageway at the back of the building with three doors and what seemed to be a kitchen at the far end, at least he saw a sink unit in the beam of the torch. Opening the first door he found an old sofa opposite a large flat screen TV. The TV didn't interest him and he moved on to the next room. More filing cabinets. Only one more room to check. He pushed the door open wide and swore loudly as his torch found a large man standing in the corner—they'd left a guard!

William froze, picturing the guns he'd seen in the crate. If the guard had one, he'd be torn to shreds if he tried to run. He waited for the guard to say something, scared to make any sudden movements. When the guard made no movement himself, William began to wonder if he had a gun. The man hadn't even said a word since he'd burst into the room.

His torch still shining on the man, William gradually became aware that the man had a blanket draped round him. Focusing on his peripheral vision to avoid looking away, William saw there wasn't any furniture in the room, not even a chair. Why would a guard spend his time in an empty room when there was a sofa and TV down the hall?

Then he began to notice the floor was covered in rubbish. Coffee cups, wrappers, plastic bags… The place was a mess. He moved the beam of the torch up and saw an unkempt white beard, long dishevelled hair and wide eyes staring back at him.

'Who are you?' William asked.

The man opened his mouth to speak but only manage to make a rasping sound. He cleared his throat. 'Please, could you shine that away from my face.'

William examined the man for a moment longer then lowered the beam. Whoever the man was, he wasn't a guard. Moving into the room, he walked slowly over to the window that looked into the warehouse, keeping his distance from the man and risked a look down. The warehouse was dark with only a wedge of light from where he'd opened the shutter.

'I don't want any trouble,' the man said.

William walked back towards the door. 'If you don't want trouble you better find someplace else to sleep tonight. Those crates downstairs, I opened them and found drugs and guns.'

The man moved to the window and looked down. 'Oh, no,' he said softly. Then he turned to William. 'Follow me,' he said with urgency and pushed past William who watched him move swiftly towards the room with the sink.

Despite being worried about letting the man out of his sight William returned to the window only to feel his stomach drop. Where the warehouse had been empty only a few minutes before there were now two men with what had to be hand guns carefully walking towards the crates.

A rough hand grabbed his arm and whispered urgently: 'Come on!' William was pulled backwards and had to back pedal to allow himself to turn.

'Let go of me,' William hissed trying to shake the man's grip.

'Do you want them to catch you?'

It was happening too fast. 'Follow you where?'

'There's a drain pipe at the rear of the building, outside the kitchen. That's how I got in. Come on, we don't have much time.'

The man led the way down the corridor and pushed open the broken window before climbing out. 'You afraid of heights?' The man asked, half out of the window.

'I'll be fine.' William looked back down the hallway. He'd left his carry-all next to the crates. All his tools and his van…

'What are you waiting for?' The man called from outside.

William shook his head and followed him out the window. The man was already on the ground. He quickly shinned down the pipe, relieved it was securely fastened to the wall.

'Took your time,' said the man when he reached the ground.

William gave him an irritated look as they both started jogging away from the warehouse. 'Is that the thanks I get for saving your life?'

'Thought I was saving yours.'

William decided to save his breath. The man was heading off to his left and William realised he'd spotted an escape route in that direction while researching earlier. He risked a look back as they approached a neighbouring unit and saw a figure silhouetted in the window they had climbed out of. 'They've seen us!'

Then something ricocheted off the ground near them and William heard a crack that could only mean one thing. He started running for the side of the unit. There was another ricochet, this time from the wall in front of him and again that piercing crack. William realised the man was ahead of him and he forced himself to go faster.

They rounded the unit and William allowed himself to slow, his breathing ragged.

The man looked back. 'Don't stop now,' he shouted at William. 'You think after shooting at us they're just going to let us go?'

He hadn't thought about it, was struggling to focus on what he should be doing, but the man was right. William tried to catch up with the man who seemed to be exerting little effort compared to himself. 'D'you know where you're going?' He shouted.

'There's a housing estate after the next warehouse.'

'How does that help?'

'Lots of places to hide.'

William wasn't sure a housing estate offered much in the way of protection but he had no better ideas. 'You know this place well then?'

'Well enough.' The man didn't elaborate.

William decided he really could not afford to keep talking and concentrated instead on putting one foot in front of another. Behind him he heard the sound of tyres squealing. He exchanged a look with the man and they both sped up.

The ground around the final warehouse was landscaped and William stumbled as they went up a grassy slope. He felt the man grab his arm and lift him, keeping him upright.

There was the sound of a vehicle braking behind them as they reached the back of the unit and without needing to discuss it, they both headed round out of direct line of sight of the road. Ahead of them was a tall chain mail fence, easily nine feet high with a shorter wooden fence just beyond. William knew if they didn't get over both fences before they were caught they would have nowhere to go. He ran full pelt and jumped to reach as high as he could, scrambling up the fence until he was able to swing his leg over. As he turned he realised the man wasn't beside him. William looked down and saw him struggling to climb. 'What's wrong?' He called down.

'My coat, it's caught.'

'Leave it, there's no time.'

William held down his hand. The man shrugged off his coat and took William's hand almost pulling William off the fence. He clung desperately with his other hand until the man was able to let go and pull himself over, then without waiting any longer, William lowered himself to the ground and turned to the wooden fence. He was able to reach the top without jumping and walked himself up the side.

Once again poised with one leg over he looked back and saw men running round the unit. There was a flurry of motion beside him and the man almost seemed to vault himself upwards, grabbing hold of the top of the fence and rolling over it. William followed him down into a garden and together they ran past the house and out into the street.

CHAPTER FIFTY
Hide and Seek

Crouched down behind a shed and trying to catch his breath, William watched as the man he suspected was a squatter peered round the side.

'I think he's gone,' the man whispered.

'Give him another couple of minutes,' William replied, keeping his voice low. His mind was racing, trying to think of a way out. So far they'd only seen two men but each of them had guns.

'I don't think we should wait,' the man said.

William agreed, apart from the part of him that wanted to stay crouched here until dawn. Grow a pair, he told himself. 'We should split up,' he said.

The man seemed to study him. 'If you think so. Which way will you head?'

He hadn't been able to stop thinking about his van and tools left at the scene—could they be traced back to him? While he didn't think so and these guys chasing them were unlikely to go to the police and get them checked for fingerprints, he'd never left anything behind on a job. Not once. 'Back to the warehouse. They won't be expecting that.'

'Your funeral,' the man said bluntly. 'I probably should thank you for leading them away from me. Doubt I'll get the chance later.'

Suddenly the man grabbed his shoulder. Before William could react, he'd said: 'May God protect you,' then he turned and scurried round the side of the shed. William stayed put, listening for shouts or gun shots. There was nothing and he forced himself to follow.

Keeping low as he moved down the side of the house to the driveway, he tried to forget the words the man had said. The last thing he needed right now was being distracted by some Jesus Freak. He risked a quick glance out along the road in both directions. Clear. Bracing himself he stood slowly and looked round. There was no-one visible in the dull street light.

He set off walking at a brisk pace. Nothing was more suspicious or likely to draw attention than a running man. Even at this time of night you had people returning from night shifts and while it was odd to see someone walking, innocent people rarely ran.

As he retraced their steps back to the warehouse his irritation at the man's parting words grew. Why did people put their trust in a God they couldn't see, who failed you when you really needed him? May God protect me? He gave a silent laugh, doing a bang up job tonight!

Cutting through the garden they'd landed in when they jumped over the fence, he forced himself to focus. Fortunately the house didn't have a motion sensor on any outside lights which would have advertised his arrival. Reaching the fence he'd climbed less than an hour before, he peered through the slats.

Taking his time, he checked to each side before studying the back of the unit. A slightly darker shape stood out near the middle and as his eyes adjusted he knew they'd left someone to keep watch. He had seen two men searching for them and now one here. Was it possible there were only three and they had left the warehouse unguarded?

He'd studied the map of the industrial estate that evening and recalled the layout of the buildings and surrounding streets. He could work his way round so he could enter the industrial estate unseen by the sentry but it would be slow going and increased the risk of drawing attention to himself if he chose the wrong house to sneak past. All he'd need would be a motion sensor to be tripped or worse—the owners to have a dog—and he might as well start setting off fireworks.

As he tried to think of a better way, he suddenly saw someone else walk round the unit. A fourth man? He heard muted voices in a language he didn't recognise and then the sentry and the other figure both walked to the side of the unit and then out of sight.

William turned his back on them. He had a clear run into the estate now but it was pointless. He wouldn't be able to risk approaching the warehouse now in case one of the men was taking up post there. His only option was to try and clear the area without getting caught. He shook his head in disgust, the job had been an utter disaster. Had Archer known what he was sending him into? If he found out he'd been deliberately burned…

While the industrial estate only had one road in and out, the housing estate had three main exits and since he was on foot, several dozen more if he was willing to chance exiting via a garden. William headed North up the street that paralleled the industrial estate as he decided on his fastest route that would also avoid CCTV cameras. Last thing he needed would be to become a Crimewatch person of interest as he tried to make his way home.

He ducked into a snicket, crossed one road and was about to enter another of the alleyways that joined so many of York's streets when a sound made him halt. Easing forward until he could see down the alley, he saw a man walking away from him almost at the other end of the snicket. He immediately pulled back. It might not have been one of the men that had chased them but… Turning, he set off at a smarter pace back down the street. It was now in the opposite direction to where he wanted to go but the curve of the street would take him round hopefully without bumping into that man.

Before he had gone another 100 yards he saw a man exit a snicket ahead of him looking, fortunately, the other way. William immediately hid down, pushing himself into the hedge he had been walking beside. The man looked his way but gave no sign he had seen him. He stood still for a moment, then raised something up to his face. William heard him speak in the same language the other men had been using and then the squelch of static followed by a curt reply told him the man was using a radio.

Remaining motionless was all he could do while the man carried on a discussion. If the man turned towards him and walked by, he would be seen, of that William had no doubt. If he could have forced himself through the hedge he would have but it was a solid mass of twigs that would take a chainsaw to cut through. It was too risky to squirm backwards in case he made a noise or attracted attention through his movement. He lay still, his heart hammering away, cursing at his foul luck.

Eventually the man put his radio away and looked again up the street towards William. He tensed, determined that he would at least put up a fight if the man found him but after checking down the street, the man crossed over and headed down another snicket. William began crawling backwards until he reached a gate. Unwilling to risk a loud squeaking by opening it, he stood and vaulted himself over into another garden.

Motion sensors were tripped constantly through the night by wandering cats but a light flashing on could be seen a couple of streets away due to the short terraces that made up this housing estate. Four houses long, the same pattern had been used throughout York during the forties and fifties with an alley between the centre two houses and wider gardens for the end giving easy access to the rear. Sneaking through gardens in the dead of night was utter foolishness yet William felt he had no choice as he navigated past vegetable patches and trampolines and discarded toys that looked as if they'd been left deliberately to trip him up. Staying out on the street felt too exposed. Twice now he'd almost run into one of the men searching for him.

He kept going, crossing streets in a hurry and then cutting through gardens hoping the searchers would stick to the streets and snickets. A loud squeal and sudden motion almost stopped his heart as he jumped down into one garden. He'd almost landed on a cat that sped away in a blur.

Easing past a shed he sensed rather than saw a form rising up but before he could react, a hand was over his mouth and he was being turned round, forced to the back of the shed.

'For a thief you make so much noise I'm surprised half the neighbourhood isn't awake,' whispered a familiar voice.

William felt a pressure ease from his chest where his jacket had been grabbed and, in the shadow of the shed, made out the face of the squatter, one finger raised in front of his mouth.

'Decided to follow me out of here?' The squatter asked now lowering his finger and removing his hand from William's mouth.

'They'd left a sentry behind.'

'You couldn't find a way round him?' The man's tone was mocking.

'I felt sorry about leaving you behind.'

'Of course you did. Calvin,' the man said.

'What?'

'My name. Figure since we're going to be spending so much time together we should introduce ourselves.'

'I don't do introductions.'

'Well, that's just rude. So what am I going to call you then?'

William shook his head and moved past the man, Calvin, to look round the shed.

'I think you look like a Bill.'

Turning round in shock, William glared at the man. 'Don't call me that,' he hissed.

'Why ever not?'

'I hate that name.'

'Then I think we've got a keeper. Unless you want to share your actual name…'

'I'm quite happy to ditch you again.'

'Of course, you were doing so well on your own. Only took you half an hour to catch up with me.'

'Calvin? That's your name right?' The man nodded. 'Why don't you shut up?'

He saw Calvin smile, a broad smile that William felt an urge to punch.

'In a minute,' Calvin said. 'Someone I need to talk to first.'

William could only stare as Calvin began muttering to himself. 'Are you alright in the head?' He asked.

The muttering stopped. 'I'm praying. Think you can handle that?'

Anger flared inside him. 'Like the big man hasn't got us in enough trouble already tonight.'

'What?'

'Well, tell me something that hasn't gone wrong, for either of us?' William spat out.

'We're alive.'

'Yeah, but for how long? Your God is not going to give us a 'Get out of being hunted' card.'

'Well, I'm asking and he will deliver.'

'Can he send some pizza while he's at it then? I'm starting to get hungry.'

'Very well.' Calvin took a step back and raised his hands upwards. 'Father, we need a quick way out of this. Provide us with transport... And some pizza for Bill.'

'Perfect,' William muttered. 'I'm on the run with a lunatic.'

'Come on.' Calvin pulled on his shoulder and headed round the side of the shed.

'Where are you going?' William hissed after him.

'It's time. We need to go.'

'Time for what? You can't just go running out there!'

'I didn't say we were going to run.' Calvin held up a hand. 'Listen...'

William bit back a retort and tried to listen. 'I don't hear any...'

'Come on. Now!' Calvin turned and hurried down past the side of the house.

Against his better judgement, William followed, hanging back just in case.

A driveway at the side of the house was empty and open to the street. Calvin stopped just inside the driveway, crouching down. Willam joined him, looking both ways for signs of their pursuers.

'What's your rush?' He asked.

'Just wait.'

'For what?'

'I said wait... You hear it now?'

William was going to say no when he realised he could hear a vehicle engine. He risked a look up the street and saw a small van driving slowly towards them.

'I take it you have no problem with stealing?' Calvin asked him.

He shook his head.

'We'll need to be quick.'

'It's not going to stop...' But then the van did stop just beyond where they crouched. William pulled back as the driver got out and walked round to the back. He heard the rear door being opened and closed. The engine was still running.

'You drive,' Calvin said, easing forward.

'Do I get a choice?'

'No. Come on!'

Calvin started running for the van. William followed, heading for the driver's side. He opened the door and flung himself into the seat just beating Calvin who had had to run round the other side.

'What took you so long?' William shouted as he kicked the clutch and rammed the gear stick forward. He let off the handbrake, revved the engine and released the clutch and felt the van jump forwards. William saw the driver in the rearview mirror as he changed gears, chasing after them but rapidly losing ground as he quickly moved up to third gear.

'God forgive us.'

William glanced over at Calvin who was turned around, looking backwards. 'Didn't you ask your God for transport? Make up your mind.'

Calvin didn't reply. He just stared ahead as they reached the end of the street. William turned right, accelerating as fast as the van would allow, working out in his head the quickest way out of the estate and away from the men who'd been hunting them. He kept checking the mirrors for any sign they were being followed.

'Look!'

Calvin's shout drew his attention forwards and he saw Calvin pointing ahead at a man who was jogging towards them. The man stopped, staring at them as they drove past and William saw a radio in his hand. Checking the mirror, he saw the man lift the radio up to his head.

'They know we're in this van,' Calvin said.

'They're on foot, what can they do,' William replied. He tried to move into fourth gear but the lever stuck.

'What's wrong?'

'Gears are shot.' William released the clutch and tried again. The lever slid home into fourth. He noticed Calvin muttering beside him. 'That's not helping,' he said and was pleased to see Calvin stop, obviously irritated, then his expression changed.

'No!'

William turned to look ahead. They were approaching a junction and a white transit van was exiting the junction onto their road at speed, heading straight towards them. William swerved round the back of the transit but it clipped the back of their van knocking them into a spin. They ended up facing towards the road the transit had exited. Without hesitation, William changed down gears and headed straight on, back towards the centre of the estate. He forced the van up through its four gears until they ran out of road and this time took a left, narrowly missing a car parked on the opposite side of the road.

Next to him, Calvin had turned round to stare through the rear windows and gave a running commentary as he drove through the housing estate. 'It's turned into this street, almost up on two wheels there. Picking up speed. I think you're getting away though. Can't see them now, no, there they are. There!' Calvin shouted and pointed ahead. 'Turn right there!'

William looked at a line of parked cars. 'Where?' He demanded.

'After the green car, the snicket.' Calvin kept pointing and William had to slap his hand away.

'You sure?'

'It used to have a bollard but it got knocked down.'

'Figures.' William still couldn't see it but braked as he approached the green car and prepared to turn.

There was a gap just after the green car—a Renault, worth £500 to the right person—William noticed as he turned. He saw the stub where a bollard had been and then a narrow road leading through between the houses, high metal chain fence on either side.

'Its narrow but should be wide enough to get through.'

'Here goes nothing.' William shoved the gear stick into first and floored the accelerator pedal. The vans wheels skidded as he let out the clutch but he kept the van from hitting the fence at either side. Ahead, where he expected to see the snicket end on another street, the lane curved slightly to the right.

'Isn't there another street behind this one?' William had to raise his voice over the sound of the engine.

'Not here,' Calvin shouted back. 'This leads behind a school. It should take us two streets up.'

'Stroke of luck.' William chanced a look in the mirror as he approached the curve. Behind them he saw the white van pull up and stop. 'They're never going to get up this.'

Two holes appeared in the top of the windscreen, the sound of glass being shot out from behind and in front registering a millisecond later. William ducked instinctively.

'They're shooting at us!' Calvin shouted.

William put the van into second gear and gripped the steering wheel tighter as he tried to take them out of line of sight. To the left he could now see an open grassy area next to what had to be the school building. The bicycle lane continued to curve away from the school. Just a few more seconds, he thought. The thud of more bullets hitting the metal frame at the back of the van made him flinch. The drivers mirror broke off as he hit the fence on his side, then the passenger mirror followed suit as the snicket narrowed. 'If this gets any tighter, we're going to get stuck!'

'We'll make it.'

They reached the apex of the curving lane and William couldn't stop the van dragging on the fence at either side, a terrible sound of tearing metal drowning out the sound of the engine. They were approaching a line of houses. 'Is this the end?' He asked.

'Yes.'

William had a sudden thought. 'There's not another bollard at this end is there?' He gave Calvin a quick glance and registered uncertainty in his expression.

'I, uh… I don't think so.'

William cursed and started to slow the van. Fortunately as they came into view of the exit, the way was clear. Trusting his sense of direction, William turned left out of the snicket, heading for the city centre once more. He managed to get the van into second gear before the engine violently stalled.

'What the…' William gasped as he was thrown forwards. He managed to avoid banging his head on the steering wheel but heard a thump beside him and knew Calvin had not been as lucky. He didn't have time to worry about it though. He turned the ignition off, put the clutch in and tried to restart the engine. It turned over once but sounded terrible and immediately died. He tried again but noticed smoke starting to rise from the bonnet.

'Out! Out of the van. Now!' William reached over Calvin and opened his door for him, then shoved him to emphasise the need to move. He clambered out himself as fast as he could, ran round to the other side and helped Calvin out and they backed away as a lick of flame made its way out the front grill.

'Could this night get any worse?' William almost shouted in frustration.

'That house is on fire.'

William turned to Calvin wondering if he'd banged his head on the dashboard. 'No, it's the van. The van's on fire.'

'No, that house is on fire.' Calvin pointed across the street and William turned to see a mid-terrace that had smoke coming out of a ground floor window.

CHAPTER FIFTY-ONE
Burnt

'Bill! Bill!'

William registered someone was trying to get his attention and slowly turned his head towards… Calvin. It was Calvin. The squatter that he'd found at the warehouse. Where they had started running. He felt himself wobble and put out his hands to steady himself.

'Are you okay?'

'Just a second.'

'What happened to you? You seemed to shut down.'

William shook his head and tried to focus. 'Where are we?'

'I don't know. It doesn't matter.' Calvin looked across the street. 'I'm sure that house is on fire. We need to do something.'

William looked over and felt a wave of dizziness rock him. There was smoke coming out of a window. He pulled his mobile out of his pocket and looked at it. It was Pay As You Go, but if he used it now there would be a trail. Records that potentially could link him to this street and this time.

Cursing as he did, William handed his mobile to Calvin. 'Call 999. Then start knocking on doors, see if anyone knows who lives there and can help.'

'What about you?'

William gave Calvin a resigned look. 'I'm a thief. Breaking into places is what I do.'

William ran across the street and opened the waist high gate to the front garden. Dark smoke was obvious behind the living room window, some escaping out of a section of window that had been left open. He knocked hard on the front door, opened the letter box and shouted inside. There was no answer. He tried the door handle with little expectation it would open, then headed for the alley through the middle of the terraces.

It was a standard mid-terrace red brick house. Same as hundreds in York and similar cities. Two or three bedrooms inside, living room at the front, kitchen at the rear. But many of them had been modified since they were first built in the thirties, forties or fifties. Some still had the old coal cupboards at the side with a door to the outside. Others had had those cupboards modified to become a downstairs toilet or an additional exit door. There was no such door from the alley.

He reached the back and found a typical UPVC door and kitchen window. He hammered his fist several times each on the door and the window and then stepped back to think what best to do. Allowing himself those few seconds seemed to allow his brain to kick into gear. He cursed as he realised there was no point in trying to get in the kitchen. These houses all had the stairs starting at the front door and the only access to the kitchen was through the living room. He ran back round to the front door.

With the fire obviously in the living room, he had to hope the door from the hallway was closed. That there even was a door!

William found his set of keys on his utility belt. They were nothing more than a selection of stiff wires and long, flat strips of shaped metal. There was only one key hole in the door, a standard mortise lock. William selected the correct grade of wire and strip combination and proceeded to manually slide each tumbler into place.

This had been one of the first skills he had begun to learn. One that had taken him several years to master giving him confidence that he could pick any lock given enough time. Right now, he had all the time in the world. He just wasn't sure how much time anyone in the house had. He felt the first and second tumblers move into place.

The door was not warm, a sign that the fire had not yet spread from the living room. The third tumbler aligned with the first two.

William noticed Calvin running up to the house to his left, the next in the terrace. Calvin began hammering on the front door. The fourth tumbler gave way and moved.

He moved the keys a fraction further into the lock and felt for the fifth tumbler, there, he had it. William pulled the door handle down and felt the door open. All of two inches.

Looking through the crack, William saw a chain stretched across. Standing back, he kicked hard and high. The door slammed against the chain but it held. Wincing, William kicked again. Again the chain held.

Third time a charm. William kicked once more and the door flew open. There was smoke seeping under and round the door to the living room. He ran in and up the carpeted stairs. Definitely a council house—everything was simple and the same as dozens of houses he had been in.

There were only three doors at the top landing, one had a picture of a cherubic boy peeing into a basin. Bathroom then. One door was ajar and William pushed the door open. There was a young boy asleep in his bed. Without bothering to wake him, William bundled him up and hurried him downstairs and into the garden.

'Calvin!' He shouted.

William saw Calvin running towards him with another man. 'Here, take him, I need to check the other room.'

Calvin took the boy. 'Shouldn't you wait for the fire brigade?'

'No time.' William turned and ran back into the house. As he passed the living room door, he could feel heat coming off it and forced himself to speed up the stairs. Taking a deep breath at the top, he carefully opened the other bedroom door and stepped back as smoke billowed out.

'Oh, no,' he coughed. Steeling himself, he stepped into the room and immediately felt his eyes sting as the smoke began to irritate them. Forcing them to stay open, he stepped over to the bed and could make out a body lying there. The figure moved and coughed and William lifted the person up until he was able to get a good hold and carry them out.

He banged their leg going out the bedroom door but managed to keep their head away from the frame. There wasn't enough room on the stairs but William twisted himself and was able to carry the—it was a woman—down slowly. Every step hoping they would get down before the living room door gave out.

'Wake up,' he shouted as he eased the woman outside.

Calvin stepped over and helped him ease the woman to the ground.

'Is there anyone else in there?' William shouted at the woman.

The woman was breathing very shallowly, barely conscious as she managed to whisper: 'Jack, is Jack okay?'

'Is Jack your son?'

'Yes.'

'He's okay, I got him out. Is there anyone else?'

'Tommy. Where's Tommy?'

William swore, looked at the house and then at Calvin.

Calvin shook his head. 'It's too dangerous.'

William leaned over the woman. 'Which room? Which room is Tommy in?'

She managed to open her eyes and look at him. 'Mine. Please, what's happening?'

William ignored her. He got up and turned towards the house. Calvin grabbed his shoulder. 'Don't! You've done all you can. You'll never get past.'

William saw black smoke was now billowing up from the front door. 'I can't just leave him. Ask your God to protect us.'

'No.'

'What!'

'It's too late. You can't go in.'

'I'm wasting time.' William broke away from Calvin and stepped towards the house. He could feel a wall of heat as he approached the front door. The smoke was thickening but he could see flames through it. He tried to will himself to jump through, the thought that there was a man in there, the flames reaching higher… The heat was too intense and he finally backed away, turned and ran. Ran past Calvin who was reaching out to him, past the woman and her child, out into the middle of the street where all around, neighbours were standing on their doorsteps, staring at him, at the house on fire.

Inside that house a man was slowly burning to death and he had failed to help him.

Calvin walked over to him and William shook his head. 'No! Stay away from me!' He could feel tears welling up in his eyes and he angrily tried to blink them away.

'It's not your fault.'

'Then whose fault is it?' William shouted. 'Yours? God's? Why did you hold me back?'

'You would have died.'

'How do you know that?'

Calvin didn't answer for a moment, just stared at him, then said: 'God showed me.'

'God? God!' William spat out the words. 'God showed you I was going to die? What kind of a being shows you that but doesn't warn them their house is going to burn down?' He pointed at the house and could now see flames licking up the side of the house from the door. 'Is that your God? Playing dice with our lives, I live but they die?'

William looked up into the sky. 'This is all your fault,' he shouted. 'I was ready to help them. Why couldn't you hold the flames back a minute longer? Or do you just enjoy watching us suffer?'

He noticed Calvin taking a step back, saw his shocked expression and turned on him. 'This whole evening! It's as if I've been cursed. I get sent to… into a trap. That was supposed to be a safe job! Then I get chased half across the city.' He shook his head. 'Everything we did to get away, they just kept on finding us. And that van! Why did it have to die here?' William looked over at the now smoking hulk that had been the pizza van. He became aware of the sound of a siren. It was getter closer.

'We better get out of here,' he said to Calvin. 'They'll have to call the police and I really don't want to be questioned about this.'

'I already did.'

'You did what!' William tensed, his hands forming fists but Calvin drew himself up and stepped forwards until he was right in his face.

'You allowed a man to die tonight and you dare to shout at God?'

'You think you're God now?'

Calvin leaned over and for the first time, William realised how tall he was.

'You shout and curse God, you shout at me, when are you going to realise that you are responsible for everything that happened tonight!'

'I did not start that fire.'

'You stood next to that van for a full minute like you were in a coma. You knew we could do something but you blanked it out. You might not have started the fire but you wasted time you could have used getting that man out.'

William had a flash of running round the back of the house and realising he could not get in.

'How dare you curse God for your mistakes,' Calvin continued. 'For your indecision and fear!'

William found himself starting to look wildly about for some way to escape this abuse. He could not remember why he had felt angry a brief moment before.

'You know I didn't start that fire. It was pure fluke that we landed up here tonight. Being chased by those men...'

'God works everything for good for those who are called by him and chosen by him!'

'And what is that supposed to mean?'

'Nothing happened by chance tonight, everything was a choice that someone made but God has used it for good.' Calvin stopped abruptly and winced.

William stepped back, glad to move away, glad for anything to stop Calvin's tirade, except Calvin straightened and began to keep pace with him as he kept trying to back away.

'God didn't tell you to steal from that warehouse tonight.'

'There was nothing to steal anyway.'

'You walked into a death trap and if I hadn't have been there you would have died.'

'Rubbish! I saved you.'

'I had an escape route. If I hadn't dragged you out you'd have been caught, trapped in that room.' Calvin winced again. 'Who is Archer?'

William stopped backing up. 'You know Archer?'

'What did you do to him?'

'Are you saying he set me up?'

'I'm asking who he is and what you did to him?'

'He found out. He must have. How do you know him?'

'I don't! What did you do to him?' Calvin demanded.

'He was ripping me off. I returned the favour.'

Calvin winced again. 'Why do you steal... William?'

It was the use of his real name which threw him completely. He stopped backing up, the question demanding an answer. Why do you steal... why... why do I steal?

It was a way of life, had been forever. Or had it? Was there ever a time when things were different? He had spent his whole adult life hiding what he did. He was good at it too. You didn't manage to avoid getting caught without being better than most. But for all the times he had justified the lies and the thefts, nothing seemed to stand up against that one innocent question: Why do I steal?

He knew how it started, could remember the circumstances, what he was thinking. It seemed the right thing to do at the time. And all the other times since, when he had planned and prepared and managed to stay one or two or three steps ahead of the people he had stolen from, from the police.

Yet he knew that wasn't what the question was looking for, knew there was a deeper implication. It was as if it had not even been Calvin who had asked, someone else wanted an answer, someone who was entitled to that answer and would not let him rest until he faced the real question.

William felt sick. The question was, would he accept that someone else had a right to ask the question, someone who was not simply asking to get an answer but to draw a line in the sand. An answer was being demanded of him, but could he give it? That in the end was the real question, or perhaps how he chose to answer. He had a choice. William seized on that—a choice! He could answer the question, or not. He could ignore it and hope it would go away. Except, what if it did go away. For some reason, even though it went against everything he'd lived by for years, William wanted to face the question.

'I don't think about it,' he said. 'Why would I? This has been my whole life.'

Calvin studied him. 'You need to stop stealing and start working for a living.'

An almost maniacal laugh rose from within him. 'Why would I do that?'

Calvin seemed to wince again, his whole body twisting forwards from the waist. He reached out and grabbed William's shoulder for support. 'Because if you keep stealing you will die.'

'No.' William tried to move away from Calvin but his grip on his shoulder tightened.

William saw Calvin look past him. His expression changed rapidly, a frown replaced by a look of understanding.

'Your time is up,' Calvin said, grabbing his other shoulder and turning him roughly around.

At the end of the street he saw the van that had been chasing them. He looked back at Calvin and their eyes locked.

'Don't curse God,' Calvin warned him.

He bit back the curse he instinctively wanted to shout. He tried to shake himself loose from Calvin's grip, but the squatter held him firm.

'Remember this!' Calvin said forcefully. 'God works for good for those he loves, for those he calls!'

'My number's kind of busy right now! Will you let go of my shoulders!' William tried to prize one of Calvin's hands off but he was held looking up towards the van which was now slowly driving towards them. 'Look, these guys seem kind of freaked out by all the people and the fire and all, I think this is a good time to make a break for it, don't you?'

'It's time to stop running, William.'

'I think you mean time to start, right?' William was getting desperate, clawing at Calvin's hand and wrist.

'Look...'

'Yeah, that's what I'm saying—look, will you let go?'

'No, look!'

William looked up and saw blue flashes first then the red box shape of a fire engine taking the turn as fast as it was able. A second fire engine followed it and the first let its siren sound for a second as it approached the white van that was blocking the way in the middle of the street.

The van accelerated and swerved to the side allowing the fire engines to pass.

Calvin pulled William with him to the pavement and they stood watching as the white van slowly turned and drove away.

CHAPTER FIFTY-TWO
Interviews

'I could have run. Been a mile away by now.'

Twisting his head to look at William, Calvin sighed. 'Sure, only then you'd have had the police chasing you as well as those men.'

'And this is better? How?' William slapped the back of his hand off the head rest in front of him and looked in disgust round the interior of the police car they had been "asked" to sit in. Outside, the police officer who had requested their assistance was on his mobile phone. 'Probably checking if they've enough free cells for us both.' William swore and punched the head rest in frustration.

Calvin saw the police officer had noticed William's outburst. 'Calm down! Do you want to draw attention to yourself? There was nowhere we could have gone. If we'd have headed back the way we came, the police would have spotted us running and picked us up anyway. Those men will have pulled back, but they'll be watching for us.'

William shook his head. 'No. They'll be long gone. It's too dangerous for them here.'

'The guns!' Calvin started banging on the door window. 'We need to tell the police.'

'Wait!'

Calvin felt William grab his arm but saw the police officer had already lowered his mobile and was moving towards the car.

The officer opened the front door. 'Something you want to tell me?' His blank eyes flicked from Calvin to William.

Next to him, William muttered a curse. Calvin recalled seeing the wooden crates and wondering what was in them. 'One of the warehouses in the industrial estate…' He took a breath. 'There are crates of guns in it.'

The police officer examined them both.

'I want a solicitor,' William said.

'You saw these guns, did you?' The officer asked Calvin.

'I…' Calvin thought quickly. 'I saw the crates and we've been shot at.'

'What about you?' The officer directed at William.

'Like I said, get me a solicitor.'

The police officer frowned. 'What's the address of this warehouse?'

Calvin realised he didn't know. He looked round at William who looked ready to jump.

'You have got to be kidding me?' William said. 'I'm not saying anything without a solicitor present.'

Calvin looked back at the police officer. 'It's okay, I can take you there.'

'Are you out of your mind!' William hissed at Calvin. 'That warehouse is a death trap!'

'Each of those guns will be used to kill someone. That's on your head if you do nothing. I know you're scared, you want to keep running…'

'Are you calling me a coward?'

Calvin did not reply. Just held William's gaze until he turned to the police officer.

'Unit 14,' William said through a clenched jaw. 'Acomb Industrial Estate. You need to be very careful going in there.'

'This better not be a wind up,' the officer said, lifting up his radio mike. 'Control, patch me through to the Duty Officer.'

~~~

Reports of gun shots being heard. One person believed dead and two in hospital following a house fire on the same housing estate where a van had also been reported stolen and may have already been recovered on Castleford Road, burnt out next to the house fire. There had been enough incidents in one evening to keep his team busy for weeks. Not that they'd be his team for much longer…

Danny had woken his team when the initial reports of gun fire had come in. Not one of them an Authorised Firearms Officer but they had a duty to respond regardless… The Firearms Support Unit had been notified and a team of six were on their way from Tadcaster due to arrive in ten minutes. He had been on his way to the street that had been the source of the most calls when the house fire was called in and decided to divert there. It seemed too much of a coincidence to be unrelated.

His mobile rang. Danny waited until he had turned a corner before reaching and pressing the answer button. He was only two minutes away from the house fire now. 'Hello?'

'Detective Inspector?'

'Daniel Martin, yes?'

'D.I., this is Control. I have a Sergeant Gunn on the line.'

'Put him through.' Danny slowed as lights ahead changed to amber.

'D.I., I'm holding two men who were involved with the fire in Acomb. One of them claims he saw some crates of guns in a warehouse within the Acomb industrial estate. He also claims to have been shot at.'

Danny felt a heightening of his senses. 'Did you get an address for the warehouse? Is he saying there is a link between the warehouse and the shootings?'

'Yes to the first: Unit 14, Acomb Industrial Estate. They also warned that we needed to be careful approaching it. They were evasive about any link between the guns and the shootings and I get the impression that both men are hiding something. One of them has requested a solicitor.'

'Okay, thank you Sergeant. Where are the men now?'

'Still at Castleford Road. I was going to take them back to Fulford Road for further questioning.'

'Take them immediately. I'm going to divert to the warehouse. Control?'

'Detective Inspector?'

'Patch me through to Chief Inspector Rudd.'

'You want me to wake him, Sir?'

'He's already up.' Rudd had woken him ten minutes before.

Danny accelerated as the lights turned green and instead of turning into the housing estate, continued on the road that would take him round to the industrial estate.

Control's voice came back on: 'I have the Chief Inspector on the line.'

'Danny?' He heard Rudd's voice. 'Are you on site yet?'

'I'm going to divert, sir. I have a report of guns being seen in a warehouse. Can you arrange a warrant?'

'What's the address?'

Danny told him.

'I'll have it for you within the hour.'

'Thank you. Permission to proceed without a warrant?'

There was a pause on the line. 'Do you have Firearms Support with you?'

'No, I was going to ask if you could re-task some of the team to join me.'

'I'll contact them now. Don't approach the building until they've arrived.'

'Understood, Sir.'

Rudd hung up.

Reports of shootings, guns in a warehouse… He was taking a risk even approaching the building without armed support but he couldn't risk delaying. He ignored a sense that he might already be too late.

Approaching the entrance to the industrial estate he realised he didn't know the layout inside. He called Control back. 'Where is Unit 14 within the estate?'

'Hold on… Where are you now?'

'Just approaching the entrance.'

'Once you've entered the industrial estate, take your first left. The road will loop round to the right. Unit 14 is at the top of the curve in a row of five. If you keep going past the unit there is another left turn which you can use to get behind it.'

Danny thanked Control and slowed as he reached the entrance of the estate. After he turned in, he called Natalie.

'I need you to head back to Fulford Road.'

'Boss?'

He heard the hurt in her voice.

'Sergeant Gunn is bringing in two witnesses. They claim there are guns in a warehouse in the industrial estate. I need you… I need you to get as much out of them as you can. I'm heading to the warehouse to meet up with the FSU.'

'I'm only a few minutes away, I can back you up.'

'We need information, quickly. You're the most skilled interviewer on my team. Please, Natalie…'

There was silence on the line.

'I'd say you owe me but…'

'I'm sure I do.'

She swore. 'Whatever you say, Boss,' she said with a heavy dose of sarcasm and killed the connection.

Above him, Danny saw the sky was turning grey.

~~~

Still fuming at Danny, Natalie braked hard to park her car behind Fulford Road Police Headquarters. She called the reception desk as she walked through. 'Has Sergeant Gunn arrived with the witnesses?'

'Not yet.'

She hit the wall closest to her. What was Danny playing at sending her back here to deal with witnesses when there were people running around Acomb with guns!

Reaching the reception she found it unmanned. She called Control. 'Where's Sergeant Gunn? No wait, I see him.' A car had just parked in front of the building.

She walked out and met Gunn as he got out of the car. In the back she could see two men. 'Tell me what you know.'

Gunn updated her as she studied the two men. A Calvin Smith who was leaning back with his eyes closed, unshaven with long unkempt hair. Homeless but apparently lucid and willing to co-operate. The other was studiously ignoring her, his face set with an obvious twitch in his jaw. He'd refused to identify himself though Gunn had heard him being addressed as William.

'Take William straight through to interview room four and Smith to room three,' she told Gunn. 'I'll need you to sit in with me.'

She watched as Gunn let them out of the vehicle and then followed them in.

Waiting as Gunn seated Smith in room three, Natalie studied William through the one-way glass. Less than two miles away Danny was approaching a warehouse that might be guarded by armed men. He was a colleague, that was all now, but even though she was still furious with him for breaking up with her… She should be there backing him up.

Gunn walked out of room three.

'Let's go,' she told him and walked into room four, sitting down opposite William. She started the tape recorder.

'Tell me about the warehouse.'

William looked at her but did not reply.

'Okay,' Natalie continued. 'Let me lay out what we currently have. You and Mr Smith were in the warehouse at some point yesterday evening or tonight. Either you or Mr Smith claims to have seen crates full of guns. We have reports of guns being fired at several locations between the warehouse and where you were found, next to a burning van and a house on fire. We have initial reports that you saved two people from the house fire. There are possible bullet holes in the van's chassis and we have a report of a stolen van again between the warehouse and the location you were found.

'As you will be aware, the UK is still on high terrorist alert following recent attacks and attempted attacks in the UK over the last year and I cannot ignore a report of a warehouse full of guns.'

'Get me a solicitor and we'll work something out.'

'I don't have to get you a solicitor.' Natalie held William's gaze and saw his face tighten in response. 'A man died tonight…' She saw his jawline twitch at that. 'My Super' has authorised me to hold you here for 24 hours before I charge you and if you continue to refuse to co-operate I'm sure we can get a magistrate to extend this to 96 hours.'

William cursed. 'I know my rights. Get me a solicitor and then we'll talk.'

'Furthermore, if at any point in the future these guns are recovered or if they are ever used and connected to that warehouse, your life as you know it will be over if you do not tell us everything you now know. There is zero sympathy in the courts for anyone found to have helped terrorists and believe me when I tell you delaying us is helping terrorists.' Natalie had leaned forward and remained still with her forearms resting on the table, hands facing slightly upwards as if she was ready to catch whatever was said next.

~~~

Leaning as far back as the metal chair would allow, William knew he was close to losing control. He felt anger at the certainty in this young woman's eyes. But it was the fear caused by his knowing how much power she currently held over him that was the worst. She didn't yet know for sure he had been in the warehouse and certainly didn't know his van had been and maybe still was there. His fingerprints over everything including his tools that he'd abandoned when he'd had to run.

'This is all so simple to you,' he said. 'You don't give a toss about the lives you ruin.'

'It is simple, you're right. Someone tells me there are potentially hundreds of guns waiting to be used to kill people on my streets and I want to make sure that doesn't happen.'

'All I want is a chance to talk with a solicitor.'

'Why are you wasting our time, William? My colleagues are about to search the warehouse. If they are in danger and you refuse to help me now…' She didn't have to expand on her threat.

Through gritted teeth, William replied. 'This is nothing to do with me!'

'Then how did you know the address of the warehouse?' Asked Sergeant Gunn.

'Either you're misleading us by claiming guns are in that warehouse, or you're withholding information which could help us secure them, which is it?' Natalie followed up.

'If you go there, you can see for yourself!'

'But we can't enter the building without a warrant, that would be breaking and entering. Right, Sergeant?'

'Right, Ma'am. And you specifically warned me to be careful going in there. What should we be careful of, William?'

He looked away, just for a second and the Sergeant banged his fist on the table.

'What do we need to be careful of! Are you trying to send our men into a trap! Tell us what you know!'

Natalie put a hand out to Sergeant Gunn's arm while looking at him. 'Can you give us a minute, Sergeant?' She asked with a soft voice.

Sergeant Gunn stood slowly, his expression furious. William stared at him until he had left the room.

'I think you've played the hero at least twice tonight,' Natalie said after the sergeant had left. 'We have witnesses saying you pulled two people out of a house fire and reading between the lines, I think Mr Smith next door owes his life to you. We need you to tell us everything you know because if you don't, I think a lot more people are going to be killed.'

'It's nothing to do with me!' He said in a stilted voice.

'The moment you saw those guns it became something to do with you. Why were you there, William? What are you scared of?'

'Other than being shot at?'

'Were you shot at in the warehouse?'

He remembered the silhouette in the warehouse window, the sound of cracks from behind and ricochets to the side. He shook his head. He couldn't think, the questions were coming too fast. How could he tell them any more without confessing to his own crime? He couldn't make up a story, not with the tape recorder going to allow them to pick it apart one lie at a time.

'Where were you shot at, William?'

It wouldn't hurt to tell them that, would it? Sure, they'll use everything and anything against you. That's what they do. Don't speak, not until you get your solicitor!

'You're not helping me, William. I get the feeling you want to, maybe even that you think you've done enough except, you haven't. Not by a long shot!' Natalie leaned forward again. 'Look at me. We have a homeless guy next door who claims there are crates of guns in that warehouse, the one you identified. The only problem is, he gets really vague every time we ask him what he actually saw. He is one man, one man who may have a history of mental problems, drug abuse, alcohol addiction. And he's the only one telling us anything. I cannot get a warrant to look in that warehouse based on his testimony. I need someone I can trust. Can I trust you, William?'

Setting his elbows on the table and leaning his head into his hands, William sighed with frustration. 'It's not what you think.'

'That's okay, William, what is it?'

'I can't... I wasn't...'

'What did you see, William?'

'There are guns but... There are also cases of drugs.'

'You saw this inside the warehouse?'

'Yes.'

Natalie nodded. 'Okay, thank you.' She switched off the tape recorder. 'You will get a solicitor but you need to tell us everything you know. If any of my men get harmed going in there and you didn't tell us everything...' She left the thought hanging and left the room.

~~~

Natalie called Danny but the call went to voice mail. Ignoring a tightness in her gut, she left a message telling him the warehouse had contained crates of drugs as well as guns.

Taking Sergeant Gunn in with her she interviewed Smith and where William had been uncooperative, Smith was the polar opposite, freely telling them more than she wanted to know. Aware that Danny might even now be meeting up with FSU she kept cutting Smith off and moving him on. After ten minutes she had had enough and thanked him.

Leaving the interview room she called Danny once more. He didn't answer.

CHAPTER FIFTY-THREE
Bricks and Stones

Danny drove past the warehouse and noted there was no activity, no lights and no vehicles. He thought one of the roller doors might be up, but it was poorly lit. Four minutes after he'd turned into the adjacent unit and parked his mobile rang.

'D.I., I have Sergeant Cutter from the FSU,' Control told him.

'Put him on.'

'D.I., this is Sergeant Cutter. Are you in a BMW?'

Danny looked round but could not see a vehicle. 'I am.'

'Hold your position, sir. We've received the warrant and are going in now. Stay on the line.'

Danny barely had time to acknowledge before he saw a Range Rover accelerating up the road. It turned hard into Unit 14 and pulled up to the loading bay. Three figures jumped out, clad in tactical gear, machine guns ready and quickly entered the building. Still holding his mobile to his ear Danny heard shouts of "Clear" along with descriptions of the interior. He imagined the three rapidly moving around checking everywhere for potential threats.

It took less than three minutes before Cutter addressed him once more: 'The building's empty. You can come in now.'

Danny drove round, parking so as to allow the FSU vehicle to leave in a hurry if required. One of the officers was waiting outside, his helmet in his free hand and weapon pointing at him as he exited his vehicle. Danny introduced himself and the officer lowered his barrel.

'I'm Sergeant Cutter, did you see anyone when you drove up,' the officer said.

'No-one. I didn't even pass anyone on the road.'

Cutter shook his head. 'We were too late.'

Danny looked past Cutter to the still dark entrance. With a sinking feeling he walked past Cutter into the warehouse. Pulling out a torch he shone it round. An abandoned transit and piles of pallets were the only things taking up floor space. Of the crates he'd expected to see there was no sign.

~~~

Why had he told her? All he'd had to do was keep his mouth shut and wait for a solicitor, try and cut some sort of deal. He looked ahead into his reflection and didn't recognise himself. Were they standing behind the glass, that female detective and the sergeant who had driven them to the station? Were they studying him, perhaps laughing at how he'd caved so quickly?

He slammed his fist down on the table.

He was free to do that, they hadn't cuffed him yet, hadn't read him his rights, not yet anyway but did that really matter when they'd taped him saying he'd seen guns and drugs in the warehouse? Drugs! He hated them. Would not touch them except to throw them away, like that packet from the crate. He would have happily told them everything to help them catch whoever was dealing if he wasn't terrified of the consequences. Yes, he admitted to himself, I am terrified. Not of Archer—though there would be consequences and maybe Archer should be terrified… Who was he kidding? He'd never threatened anyone. He was a burglar, not a robber.

He ran his fingers through his hair, watching the stranger in the glass copy his movements. Was it too late? Had he effectively signed his confession? He might as well have.

He needed advice. Needed a solicitor. Except, was it too late, had he already told them too much?

~~~

Even without proper lighting Danny could tell that they would get little of value from the warehouse. The warehouse was fairly clean which was the first problem—no dust to show where the crates might have been. It was dry so no mud or water marks to show footprints and the warehouse had obviously been busy in the past as there were marks and gouges all over the floor. He couldn't even tell for sure where the FSU team had been as they'd cleared the building.

He'd asked the team to give him some space while he looked round, hoping he might stumble across some lead that would enable him to continue the chase. He'd circled the warehouse, looping round from the centre outwards, examining the floor closely for anything that might have been left behind. He was now walking close to the wall towards the pallets when he saw the brick lying next to the wall, hard to see in the shade of the pallets, apparently the same colour as the cement floor.

He took a couple of steps on before something clicked and he stopped, looking around. Incongruency—that was what an instructor had once told him to always be on the lookout for: things out of place, that just didn't fit. It could be someone's demeanour—a falseness in their smile, could be an ornament out of place that suggested an attempt to tidy up an incident. The warehouse was clean. It had been well used, and sure, there was an abandoned van at one end but otherwise it had none of the usual odds and ends you might find. No coils of rope, no tins of paint or buckets or even brooms left out against the wall. Just this one brick.

He cautiously approached the brick and crouched down to look at it. His first thought was drugs—a clear plastic wrapped brick of grey. It looked wrong though, the colour and texture… He pulled out a pair of evidence gloves and then thought better of touching it and stood and called for Cutter.

'What do you have,' asked Cutter as he walked over.

Danny stepped back allowing Cutter space to examine the brick. 'I'm not certain but… Have you seen a substance like this before?'

He watched as Cutter crouched down and studied the brick without touching it.

Standing Cutter looked at him. 'You didn't touch it did you?' He asked.

Danny shook his head.

'You need to try and get prints off the plastic wrapping as soon as possible.' Danny saw his face had paled. Cutter continued: 'We'll need to confirm, but it looks like plastic explosive, maybe Semtex… Your witness only mentioned guns?'

Danny felt an icy shiver as he wondered who had the crates and what they were planning to use them for.

~~~

Danny arranged for forensics to attend the warehouse and left the FSU team guarding it. Traffic was building up on the roads as he drove at speed back to Fulford Road, a blue light attached to the roof of his car. He called Rudd and told him of the suspicion they'd found explosives.

It took a few seconds for Rudd to reply: 'Do we have any leads?'

'Maybe one,' Danny replied.

'Anything you need, Danny. Anything. Just call me.'

'Understood, sir.'

Natalie had left him three voice messages. He didn't bother listening to them and instead called her and asked her to meet him in reception. He was only two minutes out.

Walking in he saw her with frosty expression and folded arms. He didn't have time for it. 'Walk with me,' he told her as he walked past, slapping his ID against the scanner.

'What did you get out of them?' He asked when they were in the corridor, turning round to look at her as he walked.

'What's the rush?'

'Just answer the question,' he said abruptly.

'The homeless man, Calvin Smith had been sleeping in an upstairs office for three nights before today. He's been co-operative but useless. He entered through a broken window each night after the warehouse was closed and left early each morning, trying to avoid being seen and avoiding seeing anyone that could give us a description to work with.

'The other man, William has been demanding a solicitor. He's scared and unco-operative. The only thing I've managed to get him to confirm is that the crates contained guns and drugs.'

Danny halted at that and turned to Natalie. 'They weren't holding drugs.' He continued on, reaching the stairs that led down to the interview rooms and cells and started down.

Natalie caught up with him. 'What did you find?'

Danny hesitated. Nothing had been confirmed and yet... 'I think the crates contained explosives. It's all gone, the crates, the guns. I found one brick of a plastic substance. It wasn't any drug I've seen.'

Natalie swore.

'Where is he, this William?' Asked Danny.

'I left him in the interview room.'

'Take me to him.'

~~~

The door opened and two officers walked in, the woman who'd been leading the previous interviews—Henderson—and an older man he'd not seen.

'I want a solicitor,' William stated, looking from one to the other.

They didn't reply. The man laid his mobile on the table and tapped on the screen.

'You said you saw crates of guns and drugs in the warehouse?' The man said.

They had not started the tape recorder. William wasn't sure if that was a question or statement and decided to stay quiet.

'We didn't find drugs or guns in the warehouse,' the man continued. He made a few more taps on his phone then turned it and pushed it towards him.

William glanced down at it automatically and saw one of the bricks of drugs he'd seen.

'Is this what you saw?'

He'd already told the woman, would it hurt to confirm it? He couldn't decide. The mobile screen dimmed.

'We've yet to run an analysis on the contents but I believe this to be a plastic explosive.'

He looked up at the officer examining his expressions, checked the woman. No hint they were being anything other than deadly serious. 'I need a solicitor,' he said. 'Now!'

'This is now officially a terrorist investigation and you are our only witness,' the officer said. 'I can hold you for 72 hours without charge.'

'This is nothing to do with me.'

'What were you doing in the warehouse?'

William didn't answer.

'What were you looking for? Did someone send you there? Who else knew about the warehouse?'

The questions came at him clipped, without time for him to answer even if he'd wanted to.

Henderson leaned over the table. 'You said the crates contained guns and drugs. How many crates contained these bricks?'

He folded his arms. 'Solicitor!'

'How big were the crates?' Henderson asked. 'How many bricks did they contain? That one brick, it would have weighed what... Half a kilo. Do you have any idea how much damage plastic explosives will cause? This isn't some amateur fertilizer bomb, this looks like military grade plastic explosive. A kilo would utterly destroy a house and probably take down most of the properties to either side. Someone sets one of those half bricks off in a crowd... A hundred people dead in an instant.

'We need you to tell us everything. You were in that warehouse and you are now neck deep in this whether you like it or not.'

'I'll talk once I've spoken with a solicitor.'

The other officer leaned forward now. 'This is terrorism, William. Terrorism... Get it into your head! You are holding up an investigation that could prevent a terrorist attack. If one person is hurt as a result of your time wasting there isn't a judge in the country that will have any sympathy for you.'

William shook his head. 'I'm not wasting your time. I don't even know who you are.'

'I'm Detective Inspector Daniel Martin. What are you afraid of, William?'

Archer. William looked over at the door. In the movies he could have overpowered the police, grabbed a weapon and shot his way out of the Station. This wasn't the movies. Why had Calvin opened his mouth? Would it have made any difference? A van burning in the street, bullet holes clearly visible in the back doors. Calvin didn't owe him anything and even if he had, there'd been no time to dream up...

'Snap out of it!'

William started as Martin snapped his fingers in front of his face.

'What were you doing in the warehouse?'

He needed time to think. To work out what to say, but the questions kept coming...

CHAPTER FIFTY-FOUR
Deal

Chenbek stared at the number entered in the mobile. He should have called the contact half an hour ago, but had been too angry to trust himself with the conversation. Beside him Huan drove South in silence, his expression relaxed, a finger actually tapping the steering wheel to some beat only he was aware of. Chenbek ignored the irritation and focused on what he would do.

His men had dispersed taking all evidence of their presence at the warehouse, including the van and bag left behind by the thief. The van would be stripped for parts and sold for scrap. His other operations in York were now on hold until they could determine if it was safe to return. The cost would be huge in terms of lost revenue. He closed his eyes, breathed deeply and tried to centre himself.

It wasn't working.

He rarely trafficked guns and when he did it was usually small arms—pistols and the occasional rifle. This quantity of AK-47's... Had he known he would never have agreed to the shipment. Yet even that did not bother him compared to the discovery they had been used to smuggle explosives into the country. Explosives at a time like this, when the entire security apparatus was on constant alert for terrorist activity. It was beyond understanding.

What was his contact planning? He couldn't imagine York being a staging point for a transfer out of the country which implied...

He had been born in London and while he had never felt totally at home in the country of his birth, it had been a lucrative place to work. For the first time he wondered if he needed to consider seeking an alternative base of operations. Of course this line of thought was not helping him resolve his immediate problem.

The terms of the contract were always simple. Nothing would be shipped that could endanger the courier. The couriers would not open the shipment. All components of the shipment were to be safely transported and stored until needed with full payment in advance.

He had failed to protect the shipment believing it to be secure. The cost saving of not leaving a guard on site was now going to cost him far more than the wages would have done. Allowing someone else to open the package was potentially worse than having opened it himself. If they could have contained the intruders then perhaps they could have moved the shipment without anyone knowing what had happened but… As he had watched the fire engines drive towards that burning van he felt sure the police would have become involved.

Did the thief know what he had seen? The guns certainly, but the explosives? Fortunately he had ordered the shipment moved as soon as he saw the van parked outside, his men rushing to move the crates as he'd run after the fleeing men, the crates that were now sitting in the truck behind him.

The contact was to receive delivery of them in two weeks time. He could just say nothing, hope that if the police became involved that they may not want to advertise a shipment of guns had been found, hope the thief would not have recognized the explosives. Hope… He might as well dress in red and start rearranging his furniture! He had not built his business through hope, no, he would succeed as he had until now through deliberate action.

He had never failed to deliver a shipment. He had suffered losses—shipments damaged in transit and had felt obligated to offer compensation. Having been paid in advance, to fail to deliver would bring dishonour on his name and his business, something he did not want to contemplate.

Yes, he had failed to secure the shipment but having recovered it he could still deliver. But if he did—what would be the consequence? You never asked questions like these about the business partners you dealt with. Never examined their motives or their actions. All was business. All was professional, distant, safe.

But how safe would he be when his contact had dozens of machine guns and crates filled with explosives?

The British had a foolish saying—there is honour amongst thieves. He snorted at the ridiculousness of such a saying. He was no thief, but was he honour bound to keep a contract when to do so would put him at such risk?

This country was worse than his father's for surveillance. He had visited his ancestor's homeland once and even in the city it was only people one had to be careful of—people who could be bribed or threatened. Here there were CCTV cameras at every junction. They only needed to link this lorry to the warehouse at one location and they could trace backwards and forwards until they found it again.

No, it was unacceptable that he could become a target for the authorities for shipping goods he had no knowledge of. While it was still a risk, the truck could be disappeared. The cargo on the other hand...

Terrorism had not been good for business. There was a way the cargo could be disposed of, risky but preferable to allowing it to find an owner willing to use it.

The mobile in his hand was a pre-paid model, cheap and untraceable. He looked once more at the number which he had memorized weeks previously and clicked to call.

~~~

The Sergeant was back in the room. He'd entered, whispered something to the Detective and then taken his place.

William looked at Henderson. 'I want to help you.'

'Start talking then,' she told him.

'Get me a solicitor, allow me to work out a deal.'

Henderson leaned forward. 'You don't seem to be getting this. We own you. We can question you without charging you for the next fortnight. Longer if necessary and if those guns or explosives are used—you will be charged with obstruction and aiding and abetting a terrorist cell. Stop stalling and start talking!'

'I'm not the one wasting time here! You're right. You can hold me forever. Even ship me off in a plane and disappear me. But you think I know something that can help you and every minute you waste is a minute that more evidence might be slipping through your fingers. You delay too long and maybe nothing I know will even exist anymore. The sooner you get me a solicitor, the sooner I can help you, okay?'

He thought for a second the Sergeant was going to hit him but Henderson stood and told the Sergeant to take him to a cell.

'You can't do that,' he protested but the Sergeant just gave a mean smile.

'Are you going to go quietly or do I have to cuff you,' the Sergeant said.

They hadn't arrested him, hadn't charged him but he was their prisoner nonetheless. His anger flared but he knew he was trapped. Reluctantly he let himself be directed out of the room and down a corridor into a cell. To add to his humiliation the Sergeant made him remove his shoes and belt before he went in. For his own safety...

Inside, the iron door securely shut, he collapsed on the cot holding his hands together to stop them shaking. His watch along with his mobile had been taken at reception and he had no idea how long he'd been in the interview room. Interview... More like interrogation! Question after question that he couldn't answer without incriminating himself. Damned if he spoke, damned if he kept silent. Why didn't they just allow him a solicitor?

~~~

'You can't be serious, Natalie?' Danny stopped his pacing to look at her.

'He's not going to talk without one.' Natalie leaned back against the wall of the canteen and took a sip of coffee.

'The solicitor will just tell him to clam up. We'll lose the little leverage we have.'

'We lose nothing. We know he's a thief but do you really care about that?'

Grudgingly, Danny shook his head.

'He's admitted being in the warehouse. His refusal to co-operate is a crime under terrorist legislation. His solicitor will realise this and persuade him it's in his best interest to talk.'

'It's a big risk.'

'The biggest risk is we fail to find out what he knows. Do we have any other leads?'

'No.'

'He said it himself, every minute we waste those crates are another mile away. He's clearly terrified. Not just that we have him, but I'm guessing someone has got influence over him. He was there to rob the warehouse and got burnt. How did he know there was anything there? Did someone tell him? That's who we need to talk to and William is the only lead we have.'

Danny put his hands on a table, the exhaustion hitting him. 'We were so close. If I'd just been a few minutes earlier...' He straightened. 'You're right. It's a good call. I'll tell Rudd. Can you arrange a solicitor? CPS should be able to get someone here in quarter of an hour.'

~~~

The cheap plastic handset smashed against the wall, shattering the casing into a dozen pieces. Tariq gave a scream of rage, venting his fury to the empty room. How dare the infidel betray him like this! The man had been openly insulting, even daring to mock him as he had revealed his betrayal. Tariq swore an oath that he would find the man and kill him. No, not just kill him, destroy him. Crush him until the man begged to be released to face the punishment of Allah.

A movement caught his eye and he looked down at the exposed workings of the mobile. Numbers were scrolling across the grey LCD screen which had survived the impact. With a flash of anger he realised the connection was still live. He stamped down hard on the components feeling a satisfying crunch, then repeated the action until he was sure the phone had been disabled.

Had he been listening? Had he heard the curse promising his destruction? If so, it was good. Perhaps the man would reveal himself in his fear, would make mistakes as he fled.

Struggling to calm himself, Tariq finally tried to contain his anger. He would have to tell Zafar, call the leaders together. It would take weeks to bring the project back on track.

~~~

'Switch off your recorder.' William demanded.

Opposite him he saw Detectives Martin and Henderson exchange looks.

'You said you would talk once we arranged a solicitor,' Henderson said. 'We're interviewing you under caution. Your solicitor should have made you aware that under current terrorist legislation we can hold you for 14 days without charge and apply to extend that period if necessary. If it turns out that you have withheld information that could have prevented a terrorist attack you will be deemed to have assisted, aided and abetted in that attack and will be tried accordingly. There is no limit on the jail sentence that could be applied.'

'Do you know what they do to snitches in jail? Do you!' William slammed his fist on the table. Beside him the solicitor started. 'I want nothing to do with terrorism and I'll help you all I can, but don't ask me to tell you anything about anything else. You aren't sending me to jail to become a life size voodoo doll.'

'We can protect you...'

'You can't do jack squat! Turn it off.' William pointedly glanced at the recorder and sat back, crossing his arms.

Martin switched off the recorder. 'Two minutes. Start talking.'

'I can give you the trail, lead you to the person who put me onto this job, describe everything I saw, but I need immunity.' Will turned to his solicitor. 'Can you guarantee I'll walk out of here in twenty four hours?'

The solicitor turned to the police. 'My client is willing to co-operate and help. He's simply asking that a minor offence be overlooked and that his freedom is restored.'

'This is an ongoing investigation,' Martin said. 'We might need his assistance until it is finished…'

'You have nothing on me.' William interrupted. 'You have the word of a homeless bloke who might have been jacked up counting pink unicorns last night. You have me rescuing two people from a house fire! That's your circumstantial evidence. Give me what I'm asking for in writing now and I'll give you everything. Otherwise you're on your own.' William folded his arms and leaned back.

Martin stood and leaned over, placing his fists on the table. 'Why are you wasting our time? My colleague tells me you said it yourself…'

'Detective Inspector!' Beside him, his solicitor placed an arm between him and Martin. 'Do not threaten my client!'

'Shut up!' Martin all but shouted. 'Every minute you waste those crates are a mile away. You want me to ignore breaking and entering I'll ignore it, but I am not letting you waste another hour persuading a judge to write you a get out of jail letter.'

'You'll let me go?' William said, trying to keep his voice from trembling.

He saw a mix of emotions battle across Martin's face. 'You give me a decent lead, you tell us all you know and I'll let you walk.'

William looked as his solicitor who shrugged and shook his head. Pushing his chair back, William stood. 'Then let's go.'

'You haven't told us anything yet.'

'We can do that later. I only have one contact and I know where he'll be right now. You want to meet him or not?'

~~~

The detective dropped him off outside the row of shops. 'You've got ten minutes. You're not out by then we'll raid the place.'

'If I'm not out in ten minutes I'll probably be dead.'

'I should come in with you.'

William looked up at the windows above the computer repair shop Archer owned as a semi-legitimate business. 'No, I need to do this myself.'

The detective handed him over a mobile. 'My number is selected. Press call and I'll be straight in.'

William nodded and closed the car door. He'd met Archer here on several occasions. Always up above the shop in the office where hard drives from customer's computers were scanned to determine whether they contained information that could lead to a possible job. Even household laptops were sometimes used by small business owners and on occasion they had been asked to recover data from business computers. When Archer had told him this he'd made it clear they never acted directly on what they found. That would have been too risky. But a picture could be built up and occasionally information on alarms or other security systems could be gleaned.

'Archer upstairs?' Will asked as he walked in.

'He expecting you?' The manager asked.

'As always.' William charged up the stairs.

'What are you doing here?' Archer asked, a look of anger on his face.

William didn't try and restrain his own anger. 'Did you set me up?'

Archer's "assistant" stood quickly from where he'd been flicking through a magazine, moving to a position almost between William and Archer.

Archer glanced at his assistant, then leaned forward towards William. 'The arrangement is you call and we tell you where to meet.'

'Answer the question!'

'What're you talking about?'

'Crates of guns and explosives. That's what was in the warehouse. Did you know?'

The look on Archer's face told William he'd had no idea.

Archer swore. 'High-end electronics. That's what I was told.'

'They tried to kill me.'

'Who?'

'Whoever we were ripping off. Chinese, I think. Chased me through Acomb. Right to the police…'

Archer stood hurriedly. 'What're you talking about?'

'Take it you haven't been watching the news.'

'You went to the police? What are you doing here?' Archer and his assistant exchanged worried looks.

'Of course I didn't go to the police. But after half of Acomb got shot up the place was crawling with them. Then there was a house fire…' He trailed off. It was a long story and there wasn't time to tell it all. 'The only word you need to hear is terrorism. I was arrested and the police wanted to know everything about everyone involved.'

'Did you give them my name?'

'Archer, we've had a lousy working relationship. You're a thief, I'm a thief. You rip me off and I do the same to you.'

'Did you tell them my name!'

'No. I led them to your front door. And your back door. I suspect by now there will be dozens of armed officers all over the place.'

'You're a dead man, William Claybourn.'

'The police aren't the enemy here, Archer. You didn't see what I saw. There was enough firepower and explosives to attack a city. Whatever psychotic shipped those weapons into the country isn't going to care who they kill. You think you're going to be able to continue operating in a war zone?'

'You've got big brass ones, walking in here like this. Are you on a wire? Have the police really got the place surrounded?'

The assistant suddenly went to the window.

'No wire,' William said. 'But see that car sitting outside…?'

'Archer!' The assistant gestured. It was the first time William had heard the man speak.

Archer walked over to the window then pressed his face against the glass looking up and down the street. He swore. 'Check the back,' he told his assistant. Turning to William his expression was furious. He went to his desk and retrieved a gun from a drawer.

'You kill me, then you lose any chance at a deal,' William said hurriedly.

'You turned me in.'

'No! I cut you a deal. They couldn't care less about what I was trying to steal, they only want to know about those crates.'

'I'll never talk to the police.'

'Get real, Archer! This isn't about your pride or some stupid code of silence. We're at war. Under attack and you're either on this country's side, or the enemy's side. Do you want to let another bunch of terrorists get away with it? You want that on your conscience?'

'I don't have a conscience.'

The assistant came back into the room. 'I saw at least three cops at the back.'

William pulled up a chair and dropped onto it.

'What're you doing?' Archer demanded.

'You have five minutes. I told them I could persuade you to talk. If I don't call them, or we all walk out to that detective, then they are going to raid the place. It's over, Archer, for me and for you. This is bigger than us. They are willing to offer a deal—if you co-operate. There's even a solicitor in the car.'

'The police brought a solicitor, you're having a laugh!'

William shook his head. 'Three hours ago I had two men shooting at me. In Acomb! The police just want the terrorists. You can help them. But you should put that gun away or they might decide you're one of them and shoot first. I'm giving you a choice, Archer. What will you choose?'

~~~

Terrorism—it was a magic word. Under normal circumstances Danny was sure Archer would have refused to say a word, but the threat of being implicated in a terrorist plot had worked wonders. Danny finished copying down the shipping details that Archer had provided and pulled out his mobile. In a few minutes this would be out of his hands.

'D.I., I'm hearing chatter,' Barnes said in greeting.

It shouldn't have surprised him and yet Danny wondered how and what Barnes knew. 'I need your help. There's a shipment of explosives and guns in the UK, we just missed it in York. We believe it was shipped in via Dover and have a copy of the shipping note. Can you help trace it back to origin?'

'Dover? That would be almost impossible... Do you have the shipping reference?'

Danny read out the reference and key details.

'Okay,' Barnes acknowledged. 'Send me over everything you have—photos, documents, everything and I'll get our guys working on it.'

'We also have a name, a contact at the shipping company who was feeding information on shipments to a criminal gang in York: a Janice Moore.'

Barnes checked the spelling and said they would locate her.

Danny thanked him and hung up. His own team would work the leads as well but he suspected MI5 would be faster. He looked across at Archer who was glaring at him, defiant in spite of the two FSU officers who were guarding him, their MP5s ready.

A third FSU officer came into the room, his radio squawking. 'The vehicle is ready outside, sir.'

Acknowledging him, Danny turned back to Archer. 'Are you sure that's everything?'

Archer looked across at the CPS solicitor then back at Danny. 'I've got no reason to hold anything back.'

'For your sake I sincerely hope not. Take him out,' Danny said to the FSU officer.

'Hold on a minute,' Archer protested. 'We had an agreement.'

'And until your story checks out we'll need to keep you secure in case we need to ask any more questions.' Danny turned away and headed out of the room and down the narrow stairs. It galled him to think they may have to release Archer when it was painfully obvious he was involved in so many crimes but he had to focus on the real priorities. He waited outside while Archer, still protesting, was placed in the car and then got in his own. Following the FSU car back to Fulford Road, Danny called Natalie for an update on the investigation. She kept expanding the perimeter of traffic and CCTV cameras but there was still no lead on the van William had said he was driving or the one that had chased him and Smith through Acomb.

They were living in the CCTV capital of the world—how could two vans vanish without a trace?

~~~

Danny couldn't recall a time when three interview rooms had been in use simultaneously. He supervised a still protesting Archer into room one and then left to find Natalie waiting for him.

'This the infamous Archer then, Boss?' She asked.

'I'll need you to take him back through his statement, try and find anything I've missed.' He handed over his notebook.

'I'll do that now. What about the other two?' She gestured down the hall towards the other interview rooms. 'I put William back in room four. Smith has been in room three since he got here.'

Danny walked up to the window looking into room three. Smith was sitting upright, staring ahead, calm and apparently unconcerned. 'I doubt we're going to get anything more useful out of him but we better keep him overnight, just in case. I'll get him moved down to cells. Has he had anything to eat?'

'I don't think so.'

'Okay, I'll get that sorted.' He moved onto room four and saw a very different picture. The man, who would only and reluctantly respond to William, had his head down, banging slowly on the table. His hands in fists were clenched, also banging in an apparent rhythm. 'We'll keep him here for now. We should verify Archer's statement with him and may need to follow up with him after you've spoken with Archer.'

Danny looked round at Natalie who he saw was frowning. 'What's up?'

'Just a minute…' She walked back to look again into room three.

She moved closer to the glass.

Danny walked over.

'It's him.'

'Who?'

'Calvin Smith. He's your mystery man, from that CCTV clip you showed me.'

Beside her, Daniel also moved closer to the glass to get a better look, resting his hands on the counter that ran in front, almost touching hers, but not quite.

'Well I'll be…' He muttered. Face on in the unforgiving lighting of the interview room the man looked younger than he'd understood the image on the CCTV to be, but the hair, the build, the shape of the face… He stood back. 'Don't release him until I've spoken with him.'

~~~

Danny ended his call with Barnes who had called to say MI5 had picked

329

up Janice Moore and were pouring over the records at the shipping company where she worked. His own team's investigation had been a dead end. They had put a flag against the licence plate of the van William had been driving but had had no hits through the Automatic Number Plate Recognition system. Maybe they had used back roads, maybe they had changed the plates, either way, short of following a lead on every single unmarked white transit van they were out of options. The cargo had vanished.

Danny yawned. He had sent his team home an hour ago, told them to get as much sleep as they could and be in for six the next morning. He only had one more task to do and he was going to head off himself.

All the witnesses had been taken to holding. The cells were in the basement and Danny jogged down the stairs, trying to wake himself up. The duty officer stood, putting down the novel he'd been reading.

'Calvin Smith,' Danny told him.

The officer opened his cell.

Smith was lying down, curled up with a blanket over him. He looked up when Danny walked in, but made no effort to move.

Danny leaned back against the opposite wall.

'A month ago a young woman fell from a wall. Tell me what happened that night.'

Smith frowned then pushed himself up until he was sitting. 'Is she alright?'

'You were there then?'

'Is she okay?'

'I met her the other week. She was looking for you.'

'She found me.'

Danny recalled that Emma had said that. 'Will you tell me what happened that night?'

Smith looked away. 'You'd never believe me.'

'You were captured on CCTV. I've seen the footage.'

'I didn't hurt her.'

'So what did you do?'

His shoulders slumped and he looked down at the floor. 'She was dead when I reached her. No pulse. She wasn't breathing. There was blood on the road, a lot...' Smith stopped and Danny could imagine what he was remembering. Could imagine being there himself, her skin white, eyes unfocused...

'I prayed for her. But it wasn't enough...' He looked up and Danny saw pain in his expression. 'When I was young I was told about a prophet who prayed for a dead boy, how the prophet covered the boy's body with his own. Three times prostrating himself until the boy began to breathe by himself. I hadn't finished when someone started attacking me. I was afraid and I ran.' Danny held his gaze, but felt a cold chill. He'd heard the same story many times. Elijah healing the boy, or Elisha—he always got them mixed up—was a strange and disturbing story.

'Why did you run?'

Smith looked around at the walls. 'I've been living on the streets three years. There's never been a reason not to run.'

'Is it possible you were wrong, that she was just injured?'

'Have you seen a dead body?'

'More than I care to remember.'

'Have you ever been unsure they were dead?'

'How much experience do you have with dead bodies?'

'More than I care to remember.'

'You expect me to believe this?'

'I told you you wouldn't.' Smith sighed. 'Why should I care what you believe? You're the one asking what happened. You say you've seen the CCTV. You tell me what happened.'

Danny couldn't hold his stare. He looked down. 'I can't.'

'Jesus always told people not to talk about being healed. Maybe he knew it would just get them in trouble.'

Danny walked over to the cell door and knocked. 'You're not in trouble,' he said.

As he left, Danny looked back. Smith was lying back down on the narrow bunk.

The duty officer locked the cell door behind him. Danny started walking away then had a thought and dug out his wallet. He had sixty five pounds in cash. 'Would you do something for me,' he asked the duty officer. 'That man, Calvin Smith, he rescued two people from a house fire last night and I think he saved a woman last month. Would you give him this.' Danny handed over the money. 'Maybe ask some of the other officers if they want to chip in.'

'He'll just blow it on drink or drugs.'

Danny shook his head. 'No. He won't.'

~~~

'How could this happen!' Philippe expressed the anger Zafar felt when Tariq finished telling them what had happened.

'We have no explosives?' Raj asked.

'Half were in the boat that was lost,' Tariq said, his voice measured.

Zafar looked round at the assembled men, their faces a mix of shock, disgust and anger. Only Mohammed seemed untroubled by Tariq's news the Chinese had betrayed them.

'Explosives we can make, it's the guns and ammo that are the real loss,' Rani said.

Raj shook his head. 'No, not in the time we have. It would take weeks to make our own explosive and even then we would be rushing, risking raising suspicion.'

'We can still achieve the mission without explosives,' Darius said looking at Zafar. 'Your vision—the men only had guns. We use the enemy's vehicles against them to blockade the roads.'

Zafar nodded. 'Darius is right. The explosives would only make our work easier, it is not impossible without them. How many guns did we receive?'

'Only enough for the first assault.' Tariq slammed his hand on the floor.

'On York? We have enough then?'

'No.'

Zafar studied Tariq. He was missing something…

'Guns jam,' Philippe interjected. 'You don't send men into combat with no backups, no spares. Not if you're intending to start a long campaign. And it wasn't just the guns—the ammunition is just as irreplaceable. And we don't just need the guns for the first assault, we have to arm the teams that will carry out the guerrilla attacks we've planned.'

'Then we've no choice, we have to postpone,' Zafar said looking at Tariq for confirmation. Tariq looked away, his face set in anger. 'We arrange a new shipment,' Zafar continued. 'It will give us more time for training, to recruit others…'

'There is an alternative,' Philippe said in a quiet voice.

The room went still.

'I have a contact I've been working on recruiting. This may be the time to activate him.'

'What contact?' Zafar asked.

'He's a sentry at Acaster Malbis.'

'What is that?' Rani asked.

'A former RAF base near York.'

'Didn't they close all those bases down?' Rani said.

'Most of them. This one's different, they kept an armoury on the base. One they don't want to publicise.'

'Then how do you know about it?'

'As I said, I have a contact.'

'You want to steal the weapons we need from the British Army?' Zafar couldn't hide his astonishment.

'It makes a lot of sense,' Darius spoke up. 'We will end up fighting their army at some point. Every weapon we take from them now is one less they can use against us. We will have to capture their strongholds eventually—far better to do so now while we have the element of surprise.'

'No!' Zafar interrupted. 'If we attack this base we lose the element of surprise! The whole country will be placed on their highest alert. They will respond instantly to our attack and we also risk the possibility they may pre-empt us—if they have somehow uncovered any cell, they will move in. We could lose everything we've planned for.'

There was an uncomfortable silence as Zafar looked round at the others.

'We won't be relying on plans once the fighting begins,' Rani eventually said, his contempt obvious in his tone and expression.

Seated next to Rani, for the first time since Zafar had met him, Mohammed laughed. He slapped Rani on the back. 'We'll miss you, Rani.'

Rani turned in anger 'What do you mean?'

'The warrior who fails to plan is the first to fall. We'll give you a good send off I'm sure.' He laughed again to Rani's disgust. 'It is a good idea, Philippe. Perhaps we just need time to consider it.'

Zafar heard the mild rebuke and stiffened. Was it a good idea? Possibly the only option that would allow them to proceed to the same timescale? Or would it be as he feared—an act of arrogance that would undo all they had prepared for?

Tariq spoke, relieving him of the need to respond: 'Decisions made in anger and haste are rarely wise. Philippe, thank you for your suggestion, we will consider it carefully. I suggest we meet again tomorrow and bring whatever suggestions we have. We have come so far together. These events are just a setback.'

~~~

They gathered at Philippe's flat after Tariq dismissed them. A handshake and whisper inviting Mohammed, Darius and Rani. Each of them looked as sombre as he felt as he welcomed them in.

'Why are we here?' Darius asked as he sat down.

Philippe looked round at them all. 'Do any of you believe we can afford to wait? It could be another month or six weeks before another shipment can be delivered.'

'Our teams are ready now,' Rani said. 'It won't do their morale any good to be sitting doing nothing for that length of time.'

'Untrained men make mistakes,' said Mohammed. 'The risk of someone talking will increase unless we have a strict discipline.'

'Darius?' Philippe asked.

Darius screwed up his face. 'I think Zafar was wrong. The British will be left reeling by an attack on their army in their own country. It will only add to our advantage to then quickly follow up by taking a city.'

'I agree,' Philippe nodded. 'Though I wasn't initially thinking of a full scale attack on an army base—simply that we may be able to get access and obtain the weapons and equipment we need. Now though, I wonder whether it has become imperative that we attack.'

'Why?' Mohammed asked.

'If we delay our plans every time there is a setback, will we ever act?' Philippe saw they all shared his concern. 'If we were to do this, it would force our hand. There would be no turning back.'

Mohammed smiled. 'And if we fail?'

'Then we will meet in paradise.'

'What do you propose,' Rani asked.

Philippe told them.

CHAPTER FIFTY-FIVE
Raid

Philippe recalled the first time he had driven to Acaster Malbis, wondering if he had made a wrong turn. When he had seen the check-point he knew he was in the right place, just that what he had thought was an abandoned RAF base appeared to be very much in use.

He'd had low hopes about being contacted but a few days later he got an email from the sentry—Jamil Travers, sounding him out and asking him what sort of information he was looking for. Philippe had explained he was fascinated by how World War Two had transformed Britain and was planning to write a book on the build-up and eventual decline of Britain's military bases. He directed the sentry to his blog and said that he understood that it wouldn't be appropriate to discuss the base as it was currently used but would the sentry have any knowledge about the base's use during the war?

Slowly he had reeled him in, eventually meeting up with Travers at a local pub where Philippe had gently steered the conversation round to religion and begun the process of trying to convert him. Half the battle in any conversion was simply getting someone to talk. Philippe had found that if they were willing to talk, the rest was only a matter of laying out the evidence. It was then in Allah's hands whether a person would respond or not.

Travers was close, Philippe had sensed that, but even if he had submitted his life to Allah, it would be a radical step for a sentry to betray his country. Fortunately, Philippe's plan didn't depend on that. He had called ahead to tell Travers he had completed a draft of his book and asking if he could drop it off at the gate. A hastily compiled set of print outs from his blog sat on the parcel shelf under a basic title page and table of contents he had prepared months before in case it was required.

He drove past the entrance once, stopping to let Mohammed and Darius out where they could not be seen. Rani was curled up in the boot under a dark blanket. Philippe pulled up short of the gate noting there were two people watching him from inside the sentry hut. One of them exited and Philippe recognised Travers. He lowered his window as Travers approached.

'As-salam alaykum, brother,' Philippe said. 'Thanks for coming out to meet me.'

'Alaykum as-salam.' Travers reached in through the window and shook Philippe's offered hand.

'The draft is in the back. I'll just get out and get it for you…'

'No, wait!' Travers said. 'I'll get the gate opened and you can drive into the car park. We're not supposed to block the gate.'

Hiding a sense of relief, Philippe nodded and waited while the gate was lifted. He had been prepared to act from outside the gate but it would be far easier once inside.

He drove slowly forward into the base and then parked as directed behind the sentry hut. He smiled at Travers as he exited the car. 'I'm so excited to show you this. You know you'll be the first person to read it…' He kept up an excited patter as he opened the boot and took the stack of papers from the parcel shelf. Turning too quickly he lost his grip on the stack and the middle section fanned out over the car park.

Philippe looked in horror as dozens of sheets of paper drifted lazily to the ground.

'Mate!' Travers laughed. 'What you playing at?'

'It's okay,' Philippe said, stooping down to start picking up the pages. 'They're numbered.'

Philippe noted that Travers was standing back, not offering to help. Tactically it was the right decision. Philippe wondered what Travers would be like in a battle, would he be a good man to fight alongside?

Picking up the last sheet he stood and held up the stack of paper. 'That's it. Just need to put it back into order…' He left the statement hanging.

Travers shook his head. 'You better come inside.'

Philippe thanked him and followed Travers inside the sentry hut. Philippe quickly took in the monitors showing a selection of CCTV feeds, a computer monitor and keyboard, an opened thermos flask with steam rising from it and a cup beside it.

Travers slapped his hand on a bench at the back of the hut, opposite the monitors. 'Here you go,' he said, smiling bemusedly at Philippe.

Dropping the stack of papers on the bench, Philippe began sorting them. He was half way through when the other sentry spoke

'Hey Travers, are you expecting anyone else?'

Philippe turned to see Travers and the other sentry looking down the road.

'Wait here.' The other sentry gave Philippe a suspicious look as he opened the door of the hut. 'Watch this one,' he said to Travers.

'Ignore him,' Travers said after the sentry had left.

'What's up?' Philippe asked.

'Someone's walking up to the base. Not something we normally see.'

Travers was looking outside, watching his colleague.

From it's holster at his back, Philippe pulled out a Taser.

He waited until the other sentry was next to the gate then jabbed the Taser at the back of Travers neck, pressing the contact switch. Travers gave a low, agonized grunt and collapsed onto the monitor desk. Philippe pulled cable ties out of an inner pocket and secured Travers wrists together behind his back. Lowering him to the floor of the hut, he then secured his ankles and finally gagged him. Standing once more he saw the other sentry on the ground, Mohammed and Darius carrying out the same actions.

Philippe left Travers and walked out to his car, the boot still open. 'Rani? You can come out now.'

There was no sign of movement and Philippe moved closer and saw the boot was now empty.

'Over here.'

Philippe turned to see Rani stand from where he'd been crouching at the back of the hut, his silenced gun pointed at the ground. He'd walked right past him.

Rani looked round and Philippe saw Mohammed and Darius carrying the other sentry.

'Take him in the hut,' he ordered. To Rani he said: 'Keep watch.'

Inside the hut, Philippe slapped Travers in the face until he opened his eyes. He waited while Travers tried to speak and realised he was gagged. Saw fear in his eyes.

'I need your help, Jamil. I'm sorry it went down like this. You're my brother and I want to believe I can trust you, can I trust you?'

Travers stared at him, uncertainty evident in his eyes.

Philippe reached out to the gag. 'I'm going to take this off. You're not going to shout, okay?'

An almost imperceptible nod.

Philippe undid the gag.

'What are you playing at!' Travers shouted, spitting at the end.

Philippe pushed the gag back down over and into Travers mouth as he tried to squirm away.

'You said you wouldn't shout,' Philippe told him. 'How many soldiers are on duty tonight?' He released the gag.

'I'm not going to tell you that.'

'You are going to tell us. You have a responsibility to help us, we're your brothers now, Jamil.'

'No,' Travers shook his head.

'Where are they? If you tell us we can let them live.'

'You would kill them? What are you doing here?'

'I need in the armoury, Jamil. I need you to help me.'

'I can't do that.'

'You will, Jamil. If you are my brother, if you are a servant of Allah, you will help me.'

'I thought Islam was supposed to be a religion of peace, what are you going to do with what you find in the armoury? Why do you want to get in there?'

'We don't have a lot of time. I need you to answer my questions. How many soldiers are on the base?'

'I'm not a traitor.'

'If you betray Islam then you are. You need to decide who you serve.'

'What, you going to kill me if I don't talk?'

'No Jamil, I'm going to torture you until you do talk.'

Travers swore at Philippe. 'You're evil! Twisted. You lied to me. You're going to burn in Hell for this!'

Philippe replaced the gag, struggling to tie it as Travers resisted. Finally he stood and turned to Mohammed. 'We can't wait for him.'

Mohammed nodded at the monitors. 'There are at least two guards circling the outer fence. Darius and I can take them out.'

'Okay, Rani and I will use their uniforms, deal with anyone that approaches the gate. Be quick, we won't have much time.'

Mohammed and Darius left.

Philippe looked down at Travers. 'You submitted to Allah, my brother. Help me and you can join us.'

Travers shook his head.

'Then you will suffer the fate of all who resist Islam.'

~~~

Zafar was woken by his mobile. He grabbed it and answered, falling back to his bed.

'We've solved the problem,' he heard Philippe speak. 'Meet us now at Barnbow.'

The connection was terminated before Zafar could reply. He held up his phone, staring at it for a moment. Barnbow was to be their staging post— the site of a former munitions factory on the outskirts of Leeds. The plan was to distribute weapons and ammunition there before setting off for York. It was just after 5am. Why would Philippe want him there at this time? What did he mean he'd solved the problem?

Zafar got up and hurriedly dressed. Had Philippe gone ahead with his plan?

Despite his concern, he managed to keep within the speed limit as he drove. It would make no sense to draw attention to himself. Even without speeding it only took him twenty minutes due to the early hour. He pulled up at the gate leading up Barnbow Lane seeing three vans and two cars already parked there. The mood was jovial, he could see Philippe, Raj, Mohammed, Darius, Rani and Tariq turn as he parked.

'You have solved the problem then?' Zafar shouted as he got out of the car.

'Come and see,' Rani said gesturing to the back of one of the vans.

Zafar saw Philippe studying him as he walked over to the open doors. The interior was full of crates. One had been taken out and opened allowing Zafar to see the rifles it contained. It was as he feared. 'How many guns?' He asked.

'More than enough,' Rani smiled.

Zafar felt his focus narrow. 'Philippe, how many rifles did you take?'

'Two hundred.' Philippe strolled over to the next van. 'We also obtained half a million rounds of ammo, three boxes of grenades, two rocket launchers and twenty kilos of C4. All in all a good haul.' Philippe's look did not waver from Zafar.

'Did you meet any resistance?'

'Nothing we couldn't handle,' Rani said.

Zafar ignored him. 'And your contact, where is he?'

'We had to leave him behind.'

'Isn't there a risk he will talk?'

For the first time Zafar saw Philippe's normally arrogant expression slip. 'He's dead.'

The others had gathered round and Zafar glanced at them before continuing. 'And now what?'

'We proceed as planned,' Philippe said.

'Next week?'

'Of course.'

'No, Philippe. We can't wait until next week. Not anymore.'

'Why not?'

'I told you why not. You didn't listen and now we can't afford to delay any longer. The moment the government find out what you've done they will alert the whole country. Every hour that goes by our opportunity to act diminishes. Tariq, how long will it take to gather everyone?'

Philippe held up a hand. 'Wait, we can't just attack today, we're not ready.'

'That's on your head, Philippe. We are now the government's number one priority. They will pour every resource they have into finding us. You want to spend the next week hiding in the hope no-one comes knocking on your door?

'You're over-reacting.'

'Tariq?' Zafar turned to him.

'Zafar is right,' Tariq said. 'We risk too much if we don't move now.'

Zafar stepped back and addressed the group. 'We have already planned which groups will attack which targets. Wake everyone up and get them on their way here.' He looked at his watch. 'It's almost six and we will need to leave here at four which gives us all ten hours to finalise preparations. The attack on York will begin at 5pm.'

~~~

Mary woke as if freed from someone's grasp, her arm was reaching up and she choked back a sob at the nightmare she had escaped from. They were back, the men that had haunted her for long weeks.

She sat up in her bed, catching her breath, wanting to shut out all sense of the evil she had witnessed. As her breathing slowed she had a sense that more was expected of her. Without knowing why or what she was to do, Mary slid out of her bed and onto her knees.

The burden that she needed to fight against whatever the nightmare represented grew as she prayed and while it weighed heavier and heavier, the sense that the Holy Spirit was guiding her also grew.

~~~

Emma woke to silence, an absence of noise that felt palpable. She checked her clock and would have groaned except it felt wrong to disturb the peace that surrounded her. Sitting slowly she pulled her duvet up around her to keep warm and sat for a moment looking about curiously, wondering what was different.

Her stomach growled and she got up to make coffee and toast which she took back to bed, the whole time tiptoeing both so as not to wake Rachel and because she wanted to maintain whatever it was she was feeling. Whatever it was it certainly wasn't down to what she'd been reading the night before. As she carefully munched on the toast she mulled over the fantastical descriptions she'd found in the book of Revelation. Weird just didn't cut it: a sword coming out of a man's mouth, a whore of Babylon, beasts and monsters. Emma had never taken LSD but last night she had wondered whether the author had been on something similar. When she'd asked God if John had been eating magic mushrooms, she got no answer.

She had pressed on, skimming the pages as the vision became darker, determined to find some reason why it had been included in the bible. Her reward was no less mystical than the earlier chapters with a crystal city falling from the sky, yet with the promise of a renewed world, of trees of life that would heal every sickness and disease... Why do we have to wait, she had asked. Why not now?

After reading something so strange she would have thought her sleep would be disturbed and maybe it had been—she had woken far earlier than normal. Yet the sense of peace she was experiencing had been worth waking up to.

She sat in stillness until she heard Rachel get up. The TV was switched on and the sound of the early morning news filled the flat. Emma sighed and got out of bed.

'Hey, you,' she greeted Rachel as she walked out of her room.

Rachel looked over. 'You're up early,' she said, her voice accusing.

Emma sensed the tension and sensed it would be better not to respond. She made herself another coffee, trying to stay out of Rachel's way as she hurried about making her lunch. Retreating to the sofa she pretended to watch the news while wondering what had happened now to make Rachel so annoyed with her. In front of her, images of war cut to a presenter with the headline: Conflict in the Middle East. Was there ever not conflict there, she thought to herself. The economy was still flat-lining. Unemployment was up and down and up again.

She was wondering why Rachel bothered with the news when local news came on and she almost spilled her coffee. 'Rachel,' she gasped. On the TV screen in front of her was a photo of the homeless man she'd found in York, side by side with another man she didn't know. The headline scrolling across the screen read: Local heroes save family from house fire. Emma turned up the volume and looked round. Rachel hadn't heard her. 'Come over here, quick!' She shouted.

Looking back at the TV, Emma saw the presenter was now on the screen with the pictures of the men in the background. 'That's him,' she said, pointing at the TV.

'Who?'

'My man, the homeless man. The one who… prayed for me.' As she said it, Emma had a flash of the CCTV, of the man saying he had prayed for her. Her hand reached up to the back of her head.

'…Police have released images of the two men whose quick reactions saved a mother and her child from the house fire in Acomb on Monday night…'

'Prayed for you?' Rachel's tone was mocking. 'What are you talking about?'

'He was there. That night I fell. You chased him away.'

Rachel leaned in closer to the TV. 'What? This guy, on the left?'

'…The two men are currently helping police with their enquiries…'

'That's him.'

Rachel shook her head. 'You're incredible. You just can't let it go, can you?' She returned to the kitchen where she opened the fridge door then slammed it shut.

'No, I guess I can't,' Emma murmured to herself. She went back into her room and picking up her mobile, pulled up her call log. There hadn't been many in the last few weeks. She found the number she was looking for and dialed it.

'Fulford Road Police Station,' a man's voice answered.

'Could I speak to Detective Daniel Martin?'

'Who is calling?'

'My name is Emma Hunter.'

'One moment.'

The call was put on hold and Emma walked back through to the living room. Rachel had either gone into her room or the bathroom. The TV was still broadcasting local news and Emma walked over to switch it off.

After a couple of minutes the voice came back on the line. 'What is it regarding?'

Her mind went blank. 'I just saw a news report, the fire. I know one of the men. I need to speak with Detective Martin, please.'

'One moment.' She was back on hold.

She walked back into her own room and shut the door then paced up and down until another voice came on the line.

'Miss Hunter, please tell me this is important,' she heard the Detective say. 'I don't have a lot of time this morning.'

'I saw the man on the news, the one from your CCTV.'

There was a long silence. 'On the news… The TV?'

'Yes. It said he was helping you. Please, I… What is his name?'

'I'm not sure I can tell you that.'

'Can I see him?'

'Miss Hunter…' He sighed. 'What if he doesn't want to see you?'

Emma felt tears filling her eyes. 'Will you ask him?'

'What number can I reach you on?'

Emma told him and then he hung up.

She finally sat down, staring at her mobile, willing him to call back. A minute went by. Five. She got dressed. Nothing. She heard the sounds of Rachel leaving the flat. That meant the bathroom was free. She brushed her teeth and checked her face—she looked a mess. She wondered about putting on makeup but for some reason didn't want to. She brushed her hair and then checked her mobile again. Nothing. If she caught a bus, she could be at the police station in half an hour. She went to get her coat.

~~~

The shutter on the jail door clattered back and Calvin saw a pair of jaded eyes checking he hadn't hung himself. 'Calvin Smith?' The shutter was swiped back into place and he heard the discordant rattle of keys against the metal door. The door swung open.

'You're free to go.'

Calvin placed his hands on the metal bench and felt his fingers wrap round the edge. He'd been left alone to sleep most of the previous afternoon, fed and warm in the cell. He'd tried going back to sleep after the officer had questioned him about the girl, but had struggled, his thoughts turning to questions he couldn't answer. He felt no desire to get up.

'Are you deaf? They don't need you for any more questioning. You can leave now.'

Still Calvin did not move. A disturbed sleep had added to the exhaustion he'd felt after the previous night. The cell was warm and reasonably safe. He had been served two hot meals since he was taken in. Why on earth would he want to leave just now?

The officer stood in the doorway, impatience growing more apparent in his expression. They knew he was homeless and Calvin knew that the police would not hesitate to physically throw him out of the building if he refused to walk of his own accord. He closed his eyes and took a deep breath. 'Any chance of one last meal?'

Eyes closed, he heard the officer sigh and take a step back.

'In the circumstances I could arrange it.'

Calvin opened his eyes and examined the officer's face. A hint of resignation with perhaps a trace of sympathy.

'You can use one of the interview rooms. One hour tops. Then you leave, okay?'

Calvin nodded and slowly stood. He had nothing, no reason to keep on going. He would eat and then walk out and he did not want to think about after.

He ate slowly. Bacon, eggs sunny side up and white toast—buttered, with a mug of white tea, two sugars. One of the officers had actually gone to the trouble of cooking this for him. Not just a factory prepared meal cooked yesterday and shipped in this morning. He had only been sat in the interview room for less than ten minutes when the tray had been brought in. Calvin was surprised enough that he had thanked the officer.

Food in the cells was slightly better than in jail and infinitely better than thrown away scraps. But he had never had a police officer cook food for him before.

Eating slowly was a habit. Too many days spent hungry had taught him that it was always a bad mistake to eat quickly when he finally got food. It was also a defence. A mechanical act that allowed him to postpone the future for a few more minutes while he cut the bacon and eggs and chewed them carefully.

Eventually he had soaked up the last of the thick yellow yolk and bacon grease with the toast. He couldn't savour the tea for too long as it would have been spoiled by going cold. Someone had been watching him as the door opened only a minute after he had put the mug down.

'All done?'

Calvin ignored the rhetorical question and stood. The same officer that had come to the cell held the door open while he walked into the plain corridor. The officer then led the way through doors that only opened when a card was passed in front of a scanner.

Calvin followed him out to the front desk and came to an abrupt halt as he saw the girl he'd healed sitting in one of the three chairs near the entrance. She stood as she saw him, her expression guarded.

The officer glanced between them and exchanged his own questioning look with the duty officer. Turning to Calvin he said: 'Mr Smith, thank you for your help with the investigation. We were able to recover some of your possessions from the… Ah…'

Calvin had expected to get his jacket and the few pounds they had taken from him when he was taken in for questioning but was surprised to see the duty officer lift a brand new sports bag onto the front desk.

'Your sleeping bag and clothes, including your jacket, are in here,' the duty officer said.

The first officer also produced a large brown envelope. 'Your money is in here along with...' He cleared his throat. 'Well, the thing is... You and the other man saved the woman and her son and we had a whip round for you last night. It's not a lot but we felt you should get something for what you did.'

Calvin took the envelope and looking inside saw his change and several twenty pound notes, maybe two hundred pounds in all. He looked up and saw the officer had his hand held out. For a second he wondered if the officer wanted the envelope back and then realised he was expecting Calvin to take his hand.

The officer shook his hand with a firm grip. He did not say anything else but Calvin saw something in the man's gaze that he had not seen in years. Respect.

Then the duty officer had his hand out and for the second time in less than a minute, Calvin forgot he was homeless, forgot he had almost no money, no place to sleep that night. Instead of telling him to move on or threatening or arresting him they were treating him like a man.

The first officer glanced over Calvin's shoulder and nodded to Calvin. Still in shock at how he was being treated, Calvin turned to see the girl standing near him. 'Shall we go,' she asked.

Suddenly he felt like he had been set up. There was no "we." Was this all just a ploy to get him out of the station without him causing a scene?

The girl moved closer to him. 'There's a coffee shop just up the road. Could I buy you some tea?'

He searched her eyes and saw barely contained emotion.

He didn't want another tea, was still full from the meal he had had, yet looking towards the glass entrance doors, he had nowhere else to go. Calvin let his breath out in one large sigh. He felt exhausted again. 'Okay.' He realised he sounded ungrateful, like he was being forced, yet that was how he felt.

The girl nodded in acknowledgment and thanked the police officers. She waited while he took his new sports bag and walked him out of the station.

'Why did you thank them,' Calvin asked.

'They treated you like you deserved,' she said without looking at him. 'They didn't have to do that.'

They walked for a bit more and then she said in a rush: 'I'm Emma Hunter. I should have told you my name when we met but... And you're Mr Smith?'

'Calvin.'

'Calvin it is.'

She turned right at Fulford Road and began walking back into York. 'Do you want me to carry the bag for a bit?'

Calvin turned but she wasn't looking back at him.

'No,' he said abruptly. 'I can manage.'

Emma didn't follow up her question and it was only after they had been walking for a few minutes that it occurred to him that she might have been teasing him. He stole a look at her but could tell nothing from her expression.

They kept walking with Calvin feeling a growing sense of discomfort, until they came to a short row of shops with a cafe on the corner. Emma raised her eyebrows as if to ask "Okay." Calvin simply nodded back and he allowed her to lead the way in.

There was no queue and only one white haired man sitting at a table reading The Press, his large bowl shaped cup now empty.

'What would you like,' Emma asked.

Take whatever you can get, Calvin thought to himself. You never know when you'll next eat. Except, he wasn't hungry and looking at the menu with a selection of wraps and paninis only served to remind him of his former life. Memories he did not want to disturb.

'Whatever,' he said shortly. 'You choose.' He turned away and walked over to a small table next to the window, dumped his bag and sat down looking out at the cars travelling in and out of York. Why didn't he just walk out. Lose himself in the snickets and alleyways and find somewhere to hide? If he had saved her life, he didn't owe her anything.

Calvin caught sight of her reflection in the window, her back towards him as she spoke in a soft voice to order. She had on a long black coat and her red hair spilled over the collar. Her skirt or dress, dark grey and muted with black tights and shoes only served to highlight the richness of her hair, even in a dim reflection. He watched her reflection pay and then stand, waiting—but not patiently—while drinks were prepared. Her fingers drummed on the counter. She shifted her feet, her head moving slightly, as if to turn but then stopping.

Eventually the round bowls had been filled and she carried a tray over to the table. Emma set a large cup in front of him. 'Tea for you.' She placed two sachets of sugar next to his cup and a spoon and then sat down herself. Calvin looked at the black liquid in her smaller cup and then followed the steam up to her face.

She was looking at him and he waited for her to speak but she remained silent.

'What are we doing here?' Calvin asked.

Emma picked up her cup and gently swirled the liquid around. She didn't drink it. 'Having a coffee,' she said at last, her eyes flicking from the cup to his eyes and then back again.

Having a coffee. Calvin picked up one of the sachets of sugar, tore the paper and emptied it into the tea. He did the same with the other sachet and then stirred the tea. 'That's all?'

'That's all,' she replied.

Picking up his cup with both hands, he sipped the tea. Not quite enough milk but it was hot and sweet. He took another sip, looked up into her eyes and saw she—Emma—looked as if she was about to cry. He felt his own heart freeze in response.

Are you all right, he wanted to ask. But of course she wasn't all right. She'd reacted badly to what he'd said the last time they'd met. She hadn't believed that he'd helped her. He had tried to forget about her but it seemed she had not forgotten him. He didn't want to have this conversation and yet here they were. What are we doing here? Having a coffee? Why had she come to the station? That was okay to ask, wasn't it?

'Why did you come to the police station?'

She turned away to the window, looking out towards the street. 'Your picture was on the news. You and some other guy had rescued a mother and her child from a house fire.' She stole a look at him. 'I called the police station because they said you were helping them with their enquiries. They didn't call back. But then I just knew I had to come down… I wanted to speak to you.'

There was a part of him that wanted to stand then and there, to walk out and keep on walking away. Calvin suddenly felt very old and tired, his lack of sleep catching up with him.

'Why? Why did you want to speak to me?'

She looked directly at him then. Her eyes looking like they could well up at any moment and yet she held it back.

'I believe you.' She looked away for a moment. 'I didn't before but no matter how hard I tried to convince myself, I just felt it inside. I don't know how you brought me back. Well, I didn't. I met someone and it's all changed. I still don't understand but I want you to know, I believe you.'

She pushed her fingers along, under her eyes, wiping her tears away in that way woman seemed to do without actually letting herself cry.

He tried to put a barrier up, to protect himself from feeling involved but the three words she said: "I met someone" had started to circle round his thoughts. She kept talking and he tried to focus on what she was saying.

'I was dead and you said you prayed to God for me and I came back. I'd never heard of anyone doing that before. I always thought religion was just some superstition, like horoscopes and lucky charms...' Emma stopped suddenly. 'I'm rambling. I'm sorry.' She took a quick drink of her coffee and Calvin could only watch her as she carefully put the cup back on the table.

She caught his eye. 'You gave me a gift. One that you didn't have to do. You saved my life and I have no right to demand anything of you. I do have questions. I have so many questions! But only if and when you are ready. I... I just want you to know that I care about you and I'm here for you as a friend and if you need anything then please, just ask.'

Calvin found himself unable to do anything but stare at Emma. She waited a few seconds and after he didn't respond she gave a little half smile. 'I uh, also wondered if maybe we could start again.' Still smiling in that lopsided way she hesitantly held out her hand. 'Hi. I'm Emma.'

CHAPTER FIFTY-SIX
Missing

Danny was in a meeting with Rudd when his mobile started vibrating. He pulled it out of his pocket and saw Barnes name on the screen. 'Chief, I should take this.'

Rudd nodded his assent and returned to his desk as Danny accepted the call.

'Danny, I need you to drop what you're doing and head to Acaster Malbis,' said Barnes.

'We're in the middle of the most important investigation we'll probably have to tackle…'

'This is higher priority,' Barnes interrupted.

'What can be more important than what's just happened?'

'Not over the phone. Your boss is about to get a phone call.'

Danny looked and saw that Rudd was already on the phone. Danny hadn't noticed Rudd's phone ring… Had he called someone? Rudd was looking at him, a frown on his face.

'What's at Acaster Malbis?' Danny asked.

'It's a former RAF base.'

'And now?'

'You'll find out when you get there. We'll speak then.' Barnes hung up.

Danny looked back to Rudd who had also hung up his call. 'Sir?'

'You're to go to Acaster Malbis. There's been an attack on a military base.'

'Wouldn't Military Police normally deal with that?'

'Danny, that was the Home Office. Take Detective Henderson with you.'

'Yes, Sir.'

Irritation at being kept in the dark nagged at him as he went to collect Natalie. She gave vent to his anger which allowed him to take a step back and consider some reasons Barnes would not have wanted to tell him why he was being sent to this secretive location.

'Enough, Natalie,' he interrupted her. 'We can discuss it on the way. Let's go.'

Danny looked up the location on his mobile as they walked out to the car. Whichever direction they took it wouldn't be direct, the Ouse and A64 both insurmountable obstacles.

'Head South,' he told Natalie. 'Google's predicting 20 minutes.'

They drove in silence until they reached the A64, Danny directing her towards Leeds.

'Is this going to be your life from now on,' Natalie said after a few more minutes of driving. 'Secret missions where you're kept in the dark the whole time?'

'I hope not.'

'Sucks to be you if it is.' She stole a look at him. 'So why did I have to be dragged along? You missing my company?'

'Rudd's orders. The Home Office called him.'

'The Home Office? Where are we going?'

'I don't know. But I can think of some bad places…'

Natalie put on the lights as she took the off ramp at Askham and looped round to Appleton Road. She didn't say anything else and Danny was content to remain silent as they wove their way South.

Military Police had blocked off the entrance to the base with two Land Rovers. Natalie pulled up and they both got out. Danny noticed a soldier covering them with his rifle. An M.P. walked over, his own sidearm unholstered but pointing down. Danny carefully pulled out his badge and introduced himself.

'We've been told to expect you. Who's this?' He asked looking at Natalie.

She showed her badge.

'My colleague, Detective Natalie Henderson.'

'We're not expecting her.'

'Well, she's here. Are you going to let us through?'

The M.P. stood back and spoke to someone on his radio.

Danny exchanged a look with Natalie.

The M.P. finished his conversation and turned to Danny. 'Your colleague will have to wait here. We only have authorisation to let you through.'

'Who did you just speak with?' Danny asked.

'My C.O.'

'Then get back on your radio and tell him we've been ordered here by the Home Office. If you don't let us through in sixty seconds we're heading back and you can explain why we were denied entry.'

The M.P.'s gaze hardened. 'Sir, you have permission to proceed, your colleague...'

'Fifty seconds.'

Danny counted down as the M.P. glared at him. 'Forty seconds.'

The M.P. lifted up his radio. 'The police are threatening to leave if both detectives are not allowed on the base. They are saying they've been ordered by the Home Office.'

There was a long pause during which Danny's countdown reached zero. He opened the car door and got back in.

'Start the car,' he told Natalie once she'd shut her door.

She gave him a questioning look.

'Don't argue, just do it.'

Natalie started the car.

'Okay, let's go,' he said.

'Where?'

There was a thump on the car roof.

Danny saw the M.P. standing over him.

'Your colleague can enter,' the M.P. said.

They exited the car.

'What happened here?' Danny asked.

'The base was attacked last night. Follow me.' The M.P. led the way to the sentry hut. We found one body in here, tied up and shots to the chest and head. We haven't moved the bodies yet.'

'Bodies?' Natalie asked.

'Everyone on the base was killed.'

'Terrorist attack?' Danny asked.

'We don't know. It doesn't fit recent terrorist M.O. but if it is, then it's a major event.' The M.P. opened the door to the sentry hut and Danny looked in, saw the soldier lying on the ground with his legs tied at the ankles, a small pool of blood around his upper torso. He stepped back to allow Natalie to view the body.

'With all due respect,' Danny said. 'Why are we here? This is your jurisdiction.'

'Because of what was stolen.'

Natalie beat him to it: 'What was stolen?'

'C4, rocket launchers, grenades, rifles and ammunition. We're still checking against inventory to work out quantities.'

Danny saw that Natalie looked as concerned as he felt at the news. 'We're investigating a shipment of explosives and guns that passed through York a couple of days ago...'

'The attack on the base here happened last night.'

'Do you have any estimates of how much was taken?'

The M.P. shook his head. 'Enough to start a small war.'

'Do you have any leads we can start running?'

'Three vehicles were taken, Transit sized vans. We've already flagged the licence plates.'

'GPS trackers?' Natalie asked.

'Not standard issue.'

'Anything else?' Danny asked.

He saw the M.P. flinch.

'I need you to see something.'

He led them around and along the front of large hangers. 'There were six personnel on the base last night,' the M.P. said as he walked. 'Three on active duty, three in quarters. We found the bodies of the other two sentries outside. It looked like they had been ambushed. Two of the off duty soldiers were found in their quarters. It appears whoever killed them did so quickly and efficiently.'

He stopped by the open door of one of the hangers. 'The base is now mainly used as an armoury. This is where we found the sixth body.'

He walked inside, Danny and Natalie following and Danny saw dozens of rows of shelving leading off into the hanger, crates and boxes filling the shelf space. Near the entrance, off to one side, there was a rack of rifles with several gaps as if someone had grabbed the guns in a hurry. Danny counted four soldiers with clipboards moving up and down the aisles.

At the right hand side of the hanger an area had been cordoned off and big white screens erected, the sort that usually signified a homicide. Danny could smell several disturbing odours as they approached. The M.P. stopped outside the screens.

'If you can, I'd like you to imagine what you see had happened to one of your own people. I hope it never does.' He hesitated. 'If you need to throw up, please hold it until you get outside the hanger.' He moved aside a screen and Danny felt himself recoil.

The sixth solder had been stripped naked and nailed to the wall. His face and torso showed signs of bruising underneath a sheen of blood and he had been shot in the chest.

Danny felt his breakfast begin to rise and swallowed it down. Next to him Natalie was tight lipped, her eyes flicking from side to side.

'Why? Why would they do this?' She asked.

'What does this look like to you? Danny asked.

'Like the work of some sadistic serial killer.'

'A lone serial killer could not nail a man to the wall like that. It would take two or three people at a minimum. What does it look like?'

'I don't know, what are you asking?'

'It's a crucifixion.'

Natalie tilted her head as she examined the man. 'He's not on a cross. Sure, the arms are outstretched, but…'

'Six men dead…'

'Four men and two women,' the M.P. corrected.

'Sorry, yes, six people dead. Were any of them killed like this man?' Danny asked the M.P.

'One of the sentries was killed using a knife. His throat was cut. The others were all shot. Bullets to the chest and head.'

'The sentry in the hut, he was tied up. You don't tie up a dead man. From what you've described…' Danny nodded at the M.P. 'The base was attacked by people with combat experience. You called it efficient.'

'Yes. As if it had been a team of special forces.'

'Everyone else on the base was killed as a matter of expediency, apart from this one man. Killed in a very particular way.'

Natalie pointed. 'He was shot in the chest.'

Danny sighed in exasperation. 'Maybe they couldn't risk him being found alive, but if he hadn't been shot he'd have died there on that wall.'

'How? Blood loss? Come on, there isn't enough blood to kill someone like that.'

Danny found himself getting frustrated. 'Don't you know this?'

'Strangely enough we never covered crucifixion at the academy.'

'You die from suffocation. Look, the arms are fixed in position, just above the shoulders. It constricts the lungs, makes it difficult to breathe. You can push yourself up using your legs, but eventually your legs get tired and your arms by that point aren't strong enough to support your weight so you sag forward and eventually you suffocate. The Romans used it because it took people days to die. Days of suffering and everyone who passed by that person was reminded that if they stepped out of line, they would be the next person nailed to that cross.'

'Okay. Say he was crucified. So what?'

'A crucifixion is a statement. It's a punishment meant to warn other people of what will happen if they step out of line. And it's being used today by only one other group of people.'

'Christians?'

'No! Not Christians, by Muslims in their so called Islamic State. Haven't you heard this?'

'I've never seen it on the news. Where have you heard this?'

From Cynthia, from Tony... Even from Mary. Danny didn't answer Natalie, just turned back to the victim.

'He was a Muslim.'

'Just because of his skin colour? Now that's racial profiling...'

Danny frowned at Natalie. He turned to the M.P. 'You can check his religion, right?' The officer nodded. 'He will have been a Muslim. That's why he was killed like this, because he fought against them. They saw him as a traitor and wanted to send out a message that any other Muslim who fights against them will suffer in the same way.'

'Boss, I have to say, we've got no evidence whatsoever that this attack was carried out by a Muslim terrorist group.'

Danny pointed at the victim. 'That is our evidence.'

~~~

It had been a difficult morning, trying to hold back a flood of questions and things she wanted to say to Calvin. Sensing that he was an immediate flight risk if pushed too fast, Emma had bit her tongue and nursed coffee after coffee. She had switched to decaf after two knowing that if she was wired it would be harder to stay quiet.

If he knew that he was torturing her with his silence, he didn't show it. She had offered him lunch and apart from saying he would like the soup of the day he had barely said a word since they had entered the cafe. He'd had a few questions but had then clammed up, alternating between looking out the window and studying her.

When her mobile rang it was a relief to be able to talk to someone.

'Emma,' she heard Joan's voice. 'I'm sorry to call you when you're not at work.'

'It's okay, what's up?'

'Do you remember Michael Irving?'

How could I forget him? 'Of course.'

'He's... He has gone missing.'

Emma sat up straighter. 'Michael? How could he?'

'I had security check the CCTV. He walked out the front door. I don't know if the lock failed or something had jammed the door but he just walked out.'

'Has anyone checked his home address?'

'We informed the police and they sent someone round but he's not there. I just wondered if you had any ideas. I know you recommended his evaluation.'

Emma started to say she didn't really know him but then stopped. 'Maybe. I'll call you back, okay?'

Joan thanked her and hung up.

Emma looked across at Calvin who had unashamedly listened to her side of the conversation. 'Do you want to go for a walk?' She asked him.

~~~

'I think I've seen him,' Calvin said.

Emma stopped. 'Where?' She looked around but couldn't see Michael anywhere.

'No, "have" seen him.' Calvin stopped and turned to her. 'Little guy, going bald, looks like a strong wind would blow him away. You have a lot of time to study people when you're begging. I think he might even have given me some money.'

Emma caught up with him and they continued on up Fishergate into York. Ahead and to their right a corner of the Roman wall rose out of a grass slope, trees obscuring the length of the wall that led up to the Barbican.

'It tells you a lot about people,' Calvin said. 'How they treat beggars. How about you, Emma? Are you the type to drop money in a cup?'

She felt herself flush. 'No. I...'

'Yet twice now you've bought a beggar something to drink. If you count the number of drinks and meals you've bought me today separately, well... You better be careful or you might end up dropping money in every cup you pass.'

Emma glanced at him. It was the most Calvin had said since she met him that morning and yet she didn't know how to respond.

Calvin stopped at the pedestrian crossing and they waited for the lights to change.

'We should split up,' he said.

'No!' The word shot out of her mouth before she had time to think.

'I mean, we'll have more chance of finding...' His voice faded as he gave her a quizzical look.

'I know what you meant,' she said hurriedly. 'I just... I don't want to. Is that okay?'

'Of course.'

The lights changed and they crossed, Emma thankful for the distraction. They walked in silence up to the start of Piccadilly, Emma mulling over

Calvin's suggestion. How much time had she spent looking for Calvin without finding him, worrying that as she was walking down one street he might be walking in a parallel street in the opposite direction. She didn't even know Michael would be walking the streets except this was where she'd first bumped into him. If she'd had someone else to help her look for Calvin... She pulled out her mobile, looked up Mary and dialled.

The phone rang several times before Mary picked up.

'Hello?'

'Mary, this is Emma, do you remember the patient I told you about, the one who said I was a ghost?' Next to her she noticed Calvin looking at her. 'He's gone missing from hospital. I think he might be in the centre of York. We're going to look for him, I wondered—would you be able to help us?'

Mary didn't respond straight away.

'If you're busy...' Emma began.

'No. This is important to you, this patient?'

'Yes. He is.'

'Where should I meet you?'

Emma thought. 'How about in front of the Minster?'

'I'll be there in half an hour.'

Emma thanked her and hung up. She looked up at Calvin who was studying her. 'What?'

He bumped into her, pushing her to the side. 'You're not a ghost.'

'I know that.' She bumped him back, ignoring his smile. 'Mary's become a friend. She, we... It's hard to explain.'

'You don't have to,' Calvin said.

'No, I want to, it's just all happened so fast. Have you been filled with the Holy Spirit?'

Calvin stopped dead, his bag falling to the ground. She stopped and turned to him, his face questioning.

'I think I assumed,' Emma said, feeling like she needed to explain. 'Because you said you prayed for me. There seemed to be a connection.'

Calvin had lifted up his hands and was looking at them. 'It's so long ago.' His expression looked pained. 'My father... He prayed for me when I was a boy and for a time I thought I had received the Holy Spirit. Then, things happened... And I wondered if it had all been a lie. Until I found you. Even then, even after you found me and I knew you'd been healed.' He shook his head. 'There have been times when I've heard God speak to me. But I'm not sure what it means any more.'

'You healed me,' Emma told him.

'God healed you.'

She smiled. 'Yes, he did. That's pretty cool.'

He laughed. 'Okay, yes, that is cool.' And then he stepped forward and wrapped her in his arms. Was holding tightly onto her and she held him back. His voice was muffled as she heard him say: 'I'm glad you were healed, Emma.'

She blinked hard. 'Me too.'

After a minute he eased away. 'There's a friend of yours we need to be looking for.'

~~~

There was no sign of Michael on Davygate or Stonegate. Emma saw Mary walking down from Bootham Bar as they reached High Petergate and called out to her.

'Thank you so much for coming!' Emma said when they reached each other. She saw Mary and Calvin both looking curiously at each other. 'This is my mystery man, the one who prayed for me.'

'Man of mystery,' Calvin said. 'I like that. You can call me Calvin though.'

Mary studied Calvin. 'You prayed for Emma? After her fall?'

'Before I got chased away.' He turned to Emma. 'It seems God had other plans for you that night.'

Mary stuck out her hand. 'Then it is wonderful to meet you. I'm Mary.' She shook Calvin's hand and then turned to Emma. 'How will we know what this person looks like? Do you have a picture of him?'

Emma mentally kicked herself. 'No.'

'Well, that will make it difficult.' Mary looked at Calvin. 'Do you know the man?'

'I'm not sure. I think I might have seen him around.'

'Good. Can you at least describe him? What is it they say on those detective shows? Any distinguishing features?'

'I think he will be carrying a sandwich board, you know, one of those...'

'I know what a sandwich board is. You don't see that very often. Very good. What else?'

Emma described Michael to her and gave his name.

'Right,' Mary said. 'How shall we do this?'

'I don't really know,' Emma said. 'I thought we should just look round the streets.'

'Very well, we should split up, I could head round to Goodramgate and then back... What's wrong?'

Emma suddenly felt short of breath. She reached out to Calvin and grabbed his arm.

'Emma, are you okay?' Mary asked.

'I'm sorry, I just... You know, you're right. It will be difficult to find him. Maybe you and Calvin could go together?'

'He should be easy enough to spot if he is carrying those boards,' Calvin said. 'And York might be a small city but it packs in a large number of streets and alleyways. It would make more sense for us to split up.'

Emma looked pleadingly at Mary who was looking intently from Emma to Calvin and back.

'No...' Mary drew out the word. 'Emma might be right. She knows this Michael whereas we are unsure. We can help each other. Very well, that's settled. Emma, why don't you head down to Coney Street and we'll meet at St Sampson's Square in what, fifteen, twenty minutes?'

Emma eased her grip on Calvin's arm, avoiding looking at him. 'Okay, I'll see you both there.'

'Just a minute,' Mary said.

'What?'

'We should pray. Father, help us to find Michael. Amen.'

Emma looked at Calvin who was smiling and to Mary who was looking expectantly at them both.

Calvin laughed. 'So say we all!'

Mary raised her eyebrows. 'Well, that will have to do.' She took Calvin's arm and steered him away with one last look at Emma. 'See you soon, my dear.'

Emma watched them walk off between the Minster and St Michael le Belfrey. She forced herself to turn and headed down High Petergate thinking she would cut through Stonegate. Families with children were walking up the street with ice-creams, passing couples holding hands. A tourist was stopped in the middle of the street taking a photo of one of the many Tudor style buildings that could be found in York.

It was like trying to find Calvin, walking round the streets wondering if she was chasing him in a circle, if he was behind her or parallel.

God help us, she murmured clenching and unclenching her fists.

~~~

In the distance there was a muffled thump. Calvin looked round trying to place what it had been but was distracted by Mary who was encouraging him to hurry up.

'Did you hear that?' He asked.

'No. Pick up those feet, we've a lot of ground to cover in quarter of an hour.'

'Yes, Ma'am,' he said with emphasis. He wasn't used to hurrying for anyone. The only time he'd run in months was... Well, he admitted to himself, there had been a couple of times in the last month he'd been forced to hurry. It was starting to become a habit.

He hoped Emma was okay. She'd acted strangely before they separated...

'What are your intentions towards Emma?'

The question took him by surprise. 'What?'

'She cares for you, do you know that?'

She wasn't looking at him, instead was standing on tip toes every few steps trying to see further ahead over the mass of tourists.

'I don't have any... Intentions towards Emma.'

'Hmm...' She gave him a look that clearly signalled she didn't believe him.

'I was just released by the police. I'm homeless. I've no job, no income and no desire to change. I didn't ask for Emma to try and find me.'

'So why are you with her?'

He had no answer. Would it have been kinder to chase her off than to have let her lead him into that cafe? What was she going to do when it got dark and he needed to find a dark alley to bed down in? He needed to end it, except... How could he do that?

'She came back.'

'What do you mean?'

'She found me. Twice. How could I push her away?' Calvin shook his head at the thought of it.

'You can't. It will break her heart.' Mary sighed. 'I hope you're worth the trust she's placing in you.'

Calvin had no reply to that. Before he could muster his thoughts, Mary had grabbed his arm.

'Did you see that? Is that him?'

'Where?'

'I saw a flash of white, hurry!'

Calvin had to break into a jog to keep up with Mary.

'I think he went into Swinegate,' she called back. As she turned into the street she shouted: 'Michael!'

Calvin reached Swinegate and saw a small figure walking slowly away with what looked like a heavy, white board strapped to his back. Mary caught up with him and he heard her ask him if he was Michael Irving. The man stopped.

Calvin read the words on the board facing him as he reached them:

Repent
The End
Is
Near

He walked round as Mary asked: 'Are you Michael?'

Calvin thought maybe this was the man he'd once seen but he hadn't spoken to him then.

The man shook his head. 'I don't know you,' he said.

'Oh, I'm Mary, this is Calvin.'

The man seemed distant. Calvin looked down and read the front board:

Repent
And Seek
The
Lord

Mary continued: 'Emma sent us, we've all been looking for you.'

At this the man frowned.

'We were going to meet up at St Sampson's Square. Would you come with us?'

~~~

Mary helped Michael turn and led him back down Swinegate and then right towards St Sampson's Square. To her relief she saw Emma across the square as they reached it. She waved and caught Emma's attention who hurried over.

'Michael!' Emma said as she reached them. 'We were so worried.'

'Why?'

'We didn't know where you'd gone.'

'I had to warn them.'

'Warn them about what?' Calvin asked.

Michael looked at Mary. 'You know.'

She felt a shiver chill her whole body. 'I know what?' She asked, regretting the question as soon as it was out of her mouth.

Michael tilted his head. 'You've seen them. You know what's going to happen.'

'What does he mean?' Emma asked.

Mary looked around at the people who were passing. Tourists, business men and women, families with their children—all citizens of York going about their usual business. None of them were safe.

'I told you about my dreams,' she said to Emma. 'Every night, for weeks the same nightmare. York under attack by evil men.' She turned to Michael. 'It's really going to happen?'

'Yes.'

Emma looked at her. 'You both believe York is going to be attacked?'

'I didn't want to,' Mary said.

'Not exactly,' said Michael.

'What do you mean, not exactly?' Emma demanded.

'We're going to be judged. I need to warn people.'

Mary felt Emma's stare. 'I thought it was just bad dreams. Then they stopped. I did try telling a police officer…' She felt herself run out of steam.

'But they didn't believe you,' Emma stated. She looked away. 'Just like we didn't believe Michael, like no-one believed me… We're all as bad as each other.'

Calvin dropped his bag. 'I heard a noise earlier, did you hear it? Like a distant… explosion? I dismissed it, but now…'

'What can we do?' Asked Emma.

'The only thing we can do,' Mary said. 'Pray.'

There was the distant sound of rapid explosions, like a strip of fireworks had been set off a few streets away. Then an answering set of explosions from a different direction.

'We maybe should try running first,' Calvin said urgently.

'But where to,' Mary asked, trying to stop herself from panicking.

'The Minster,' Calvin said. 'Come on, Michael leave those things behind.' He helped Michael climb out and then together they ran.

~~~

Zafar thanked Allah that they had been prepared for the timing to change. Everything they had planned had been based on the assumption they might be unable to launch the attack when they wanted. A day early, a day late and if they were locked into a schedule, the whole plan could have fallen apart.

As it was, he understood almost thirty men were still en route. Their objectives would have to be re-tasked to others but that was to be expected. Plans had to change in the heat of battle and if or when men were injured or killed he would have to adapt the plan.

Around York ten cars, five vans and two coaches—including the one he was on—were converging on the agreed locations. The men were assigned to four and five man platoons, each with specific objectives to achieve: Blockade the roads, control the inner walls, take control of communication and surveillance hubs, subdue local police and the population.

Tariq was co-ordinating the Guerrilla attacks that would distract and provide an outer layer of defence. A second wave of attacks were also planned once their victory in York was achieved. Smaller in scale, they were intended to waken their brothers throughout the country and provide focal points for more public recruitment.

He could feel adrenaline surge through him as the coach he was on pulled into Clarence Street coach park. Was this as it had been for the early followers of Mohammed? He turned to Kadar and offered his hand. 'May Allah watch over us.'

'We are in Allah's hands now,' Kadar replied.

The driver exited to open up the luggage compartments.

Zafar stood up at the front of the coach. 'Balaclavas on. Remember, you are not hiding your faces for your own sakes but for your families and friends—to prevent the Government using them against you.'

Zafar pulled his balaclava down over his face and looked round as his men followed his lead.

'Team one out!' He waited while the men filed past and then called the second and third teams. Outside he could see the first team jogging away, heavy bags in hand containing guns and ammunition and supplies.

Zafar's team was second last and they followed the others out and were handed their bags without any wait. Zafar opened his and removed his rifle, an AK-47. He checked the safety was on and there was ammo in the magazine. Then he looked around. There were a few tourists getting off a different coach. Some had not seen them but a couple of people had and were looking with opened mouths.

Zafar checked his team all had their guns ready, had their bags and then called them to start walking. He clasped the driver on his shoulder and blessed him, then caught up with his team. The driver was to take his coach and use it to block Wigginton Road just North of the Hospital then his team were to work their way across to Haxby and Heworth blocking traffic as they went.

On the pavement, Zafar noticed drivers slowing down as they passed. Other people on the pavement moved aside, uncertainty evident on their faces. Zafar ignored them. His objective was to seize control of the CCTV monitoring building to allow him to direct operations. In the distance he heard gunfire. The battle had begun.

CHAPTER FIFTY-SEVEN
The Stand

'Bit early for Halloween,' Karl said to Thomas who had put an arm out as if to shield him. On the opposite side of the road a masked group of men were jogging past, heavy canvas bags in one hand, the other cradling rifles that until now, Karl had only seen in movies.

Thomas leaned back and looked down Clarence Street. 'There's another two groups heading towards the centre. Kitted out the same.'

'We should get back to our coach,' Karl said. 'And call the others and warn them.'

'Johnson said he was staying on the coach. I'm not sure if anyone else was. I'll call Andy.'

Karl pulled out his mobile, found Keith's name and dialled. They started walking back towards the coach park. Keith wasn't answering. He left a message on his voice mail and then sent him a text. Then copied that text and forwarded it to the rest of the group.

'Guess we picked the wrong day to stop in York,' he said to Thomas when he finished his call.

'Or maybe the right one...' Thomas responded.

Karl watched as yet another group of men jogged past. In the distance there was the unmistakable sound of gunfire.

~~~

To the South of the city centre another bus pulled up outside the Barbican, ignoring the double yellow lines. Cars behind the bus began beeping their horns as the men walked out, grabbed their bags and began crossing the road. The car immediately behind the bus tried to overtake but one of the men raised his rifle and fired a quick burst at the driver. Those first shots reverberated off the ancient walls and modern buildings and could be heard across York.

~~~

The A1237 terminates at the South West corner of York where it crosses the A64 dual carriageway and circles round to join it. Mohammed's team drove onto the overpass and braked to a stop right over the middle of the dual carriageway.

A driver behind them waited patiently until she saw four men get out, balaclavas over their heads and rifles in their hands. She put her car into reverse but took her foot off the clutch too quickly. The car stalled and she could only watch in terror as one of the men raised his rifle.

~~~

The sound of fireworks outside made Najwa look up from her book. She saw others in the library also look around, stop what they were doing.

She put her book down and fished in her rucksack for her earphones. She had come here for space away from her brothers and didn't want to be disturbed by some neds who thought it would be fun to set off fireworks in the middle of the day.

She checked her watch. Okay, not the middle of the day. She'd been here longer than she thought. She sighed, she would need to head home soon.

But not just yet.

Najwa turned up her music and picked up her book. It was getting to an exciting part...

~~~

Having shot at and disabled several cars approaching them on the overpass, there was no way for other cars to approach. Mohammed's team set themselves up at either side and began firing at cars approaching on the dual carriageway. A couple of cars made it through but then Mohammed shot one driver whose car careered over to the left and took out another car. The two vehicles skidded over the road and came to a halt underneath the underpass completely blocking the Westbound carriageway.

One of his team then shot up a lorry approaching on the Eastbound carriageway and found himself having to duck as the cab slammed into a supporting pillar and the rear end pivoted up. A series of cars on both carriageways braked to a halt behind the cars and the truck and the team fired at those until their magazines were empty.

'That should do it,' Mohammed said. He looked round and then North towards his next objective. 'You know, if I had the opportunity to do this again, I would do it differently.'

'Why?'

'Should have parked the car off the overpass and walked here. Then we could have driven to the next bridge.'

'Oh yeah.'

'Never mind, maybe we can use one of these cars up here.' He pointed his gun at the cars they'd shot up. 'Okay, just need to set the explosives and we'll be done.'

~~~

Emma struggled to keep up with Calvin and Michael, regretting her choice of dress. Why hadn't she worn jeans? Calvin was shouting at people to get inside as he ran. Most people were just ignoring his warnings, staring at them. She saw a few laughing.

Looking back to Mary, Emma saw she was keeping up. She waved at Emma to keep going but Emma didn't want to leave her behind. They were just passing St Michael's when Emma saw a group of masked men running towards them from Bootham Bar. They seemed to be carrying guns. She looked back again, 'Mary! Hurry!' She shouted.

Emma saw Calvin and Michael reach the Minster. She wasn't far behind but slowed to help Mary, was suddenly aware of knots of people turning to look at them...

'I'm okay,' Mary shouted at her. 'Keep going!'

The men were too close, there wasn't time, Emma reached the entrance herself turning to call out but then felt herself pulled and she was inside, Calvin pushing past her and reaching for Mary and then he was forcing the heavy wooden doors closed... Shutting everyone else outside...

She became aware of shouts of protest as officials came over.

'You can't do that!'

'Get away from there!'

And then Mary was standing between the officials and Calvin. 'Leave him alone! There are men with guns outside who intend to kill everyone in this church!'

As if to punctuate her point, Emma heard a crash against the door and saw Calvin pushed backwards as the door moved.

'Help him!' Mary demanded of the officials. 'Do you want to meet your maker?'

Emma rushed forward and was joined by one official and together the three of them pushed the door back against repeated attempts to push it open.

'How do we lock it?' Calvin asked.

'Here...' A massive key was inserted in the lock and then a wooden bar placed across the doors.

Emma stood back only to cringe as what sounded like gunfire erupted outside the door causing it to judder.

'Everyone, away from the doors!'

Emma tried to move but her feet didn't respond. Mary, who seemed to have taken charge took her by the hands and led her to one side.

'Emma, I need you to be brave now,' Mary said.

'Yes, of course.'

'There are other entrances to the Minster. We need to seal all of them.'

'But there are still people outside…'

'I know, but this building is strategically important. Those men desperately need to capture it and we must stop them!'

'How do you know this?'

'I've no time to explain, please, will you help me get all the entrances shut?'

Emma forced herself to take a deep breath. 'What can I do?'

'Follow me.' Mary turned to the group that had gathered around the entrance. 'Gunmen are outside trying to get in. I saw at least a dozen men with guns before we got inside. They will not hesitate to kill us if they get in. We must stop them. We must close and seal every entrance to the Minster now before they reach them. Who here can help me do this?'

An official stepped forwards. 'There are six entrances to the building…'

'Then we better hurry!'

The official gestured at her colleagues. 'Quickly, Colin, take Anne and lock all entrances off the North Transept. I'll take the South Transept. You,' she said to Mary. 'Come with me.'

Mary looked at Calvin. 'Go with them. Emma, you come with me. Michael… gather everyone else in the centre of the Nave.'

Emma followed Mary and the official who had set off at a run.

The official pulled out a radio. 'All members of staff, the Minster and all occupants are under attack. Lock all entrances and exits to the building. Report in now to confirm you have received this message.'

A static voice could be heard responding: 'Is this some kind of a joke?'

The official spoke again, her voice filled with anger: 'This is Yvette Stevenson, shots have been fired outside the Nave entrance! Gunmen are trying to break in. Repeat: Lock all entrances and exits to the building. Confirm you've received this message!'

They had almost reached the main entrance to the cathedral and Emma saw that officials there had begun to close the large doors. The doors were nearly shut when Emma saw one of the masked men trying to push his way through, his rifle sticking out of the gap. She dived out of the way as the gun fired, the noise echoing, amplified by the acoustics of the space.

The official—she'd called herself Yvette—fell. Emma crawled over to her, still looking up towards the doors, saw that someone had grabbed the gun out of the masked man's hands and the doors were being pushed shut, trapping an arm. There was a scream from outside, the arm was withdrawn and the doors finally closed.

Emma checked Yvette's pulse but couldn't find a beat. She examined her back and found three exit wounds, one large, but none of which were bleeding heavily. Rolling her onto her back Emma saw an entrance wound over the heart. She felt herself take a great, shuddering breath, fought back the emotion and looked up to see if anyone else had been hit. It seemed only Yvette had been shot.

Emma stood as Mary approached her.

'We should cover her body,' Emma said.

'Let the dead bury their own…' Mary muttered. 'There's no time. We must finish sealing the building… And then we must pray.'

'But we'll be trapped in here.'

'We have to defend the Minster, defend it at all costs.'

'Why is it so important?'

'The towers, they're the highest structures for miles around. If those men get snipers up there, they can control the city.'

Emma struggled to fit what she knew of Mary with the words she was saying. 'How do you know this?'

'I think God warned me, but I didn't listen. I couldn't believe it and yet it's happening.' Mary turned to the officials who had been manning the entrance. 'Who is in charge?'

One of them pointed at Yvette's body. 'Ms Stevenson.'

'This lady gave her life to defend the people inside this building,' Mary said with authority. 'Her last orders were to seal every entrance, make sure this is done immediately.'

~ ~ ~

'There's no attempt to hide their faces,' Natalie said.

'No,' Danny agreed. 'They must have known there would be CCTV on site.'

They had just finished viewing the footage of the initial attack on the sentry. Four men obviously working to a pre-arranged plan had skillfully taken down two soldiers. An M.P. officer was skipping through footage from other cameras searching for the next sighting of the men.

'They had control of the whole base, why wouldn't they try and erase or destroy the hard drives? Did they run out of time?'

Danny shook his head. 'They had time to torture the soldier. No, they didn't care if we saw them, maybe they even wanted us to see.'

His mobile rang and he saw Rudd was calling him. Danny stepped away. 'Sir?'

'Danny, you need to get back to York immediately. We've reports of masked men with machine guns on the streets, multiple reports of shots being fired. I'm implementing Lockdown.'

The knot that had formed in Danny's stomach when he'd first seen the tortured soldier grew tighter. Lockdown was an Argus protocol for dealing with a large scale terrorist assault. Harbrook had quickly talked him through it as part of his overall briefing along with several other protocols that Danny had hoped he would never have to implement.

'Sir, Harbrook is in London today...'

'I know. I need you to co-ordinate...' There was a booming sound from the speaker, interrupting Rudd.

'Sir?' He asked urgently.

'Danny, are you there?' Rudd asked. Danny could hear a shaking in his voice.

'Yes, what happened?'

'I think headquarters has just been attacked. There's been an explosion, I... Danny, I need you to take charge...' There was a louder noise from the mobile's speaker forcing Danny to move it away from his ear. A noise of static and then a dead tone that faded as his hand dropped.

Natalie was looking at him. He turned to the M.P.

'York is under terrorist attack. Under section 63 of the Terrorism Act 2006 I'm assuming command of this base and of your men. You will order a platoon to remain and defend this base, the rest are to arm themselves and accompany me into York.'

'Sir, I'll need to clear this...'

'Soldier!' Danny shouted. 'I've given you an order. Now carry it out!'

~~~

William heard a muted explosion, like a large firework had been set off outside the building. The bed he was sitting on shook and he saw flakes of paint fall from the ceiling.

He stood, listening intently. A few seconds later there was a second explosion, closer and he felt a distinct tremor through his feet.

There were sounds of shouts from other cells and then banging on the doors, people calling for the guard.

He recalled the detective telling him they'd found plastic explosives. Could they have been used against the police? The detective had warned him what would happen if the explosives or guns were used. He hadn't thought it was possible, that he could be involved in any way.

Slowly, William sank to his knees. He'd mocked Calvin for his prayers, ridiculed him for his faith. Knowing he was a hypocrite, William began to pray.

~~~

Cost cutting measures, Zafar thought to himself as his team reached St Leonard's Place, why were the British so short sighted? Having spent hundred's of thousands on their "state of the art" CCTV control room in 2013, they had then moved it to St Leonard's Place to save money.

It was plastered all over the Internet. Articles on the York Council website, the BBC and even York Press, giving him the location and even photos from inside the control room. If he'd had more time for preparation, there was even the possibility he could have had one of his team apply for a job there when the move had occurred the previous year.

As it was, the building was far less daunting to seize than the previous premises.

As they ran up towards the entrance a guard stepped out, perhaps looking to find the source of the sporadic gunfire that had been occurring for a couple of minutes. Beside him, Kadar fired and the guard fell.

Zafar dropped his bag before taking the stairs. Haajib was to take up the rear, securing their equipment and preventing access to the building. Kadar pulled open the door and Zafar plunged through spotting a guard to his right holding a... Zafar shot a quick burst and the guard was punched backwards.

'Get their passes,' Zafar ordered as he went through a metal detector to the sound of an irritating alarm.

Kadar tossed him a pass and Zafar waited for him to join him before opening the security door.

For all the resources on the Internet, Zafar had been unable to find a floor plan that would have indicated where in the building the control room was.

He and Kadar took it in turns to open doors, the other storming the room and executing anyone found there. They cleared the three rooms on the ground floor and then took the stairs. On the first floor Zafar burst into a room to find a woman on her knees, her hands clasped towards him. He shot her as she begged to be spared. They had no resources to take unnecessary prisoners and he had long ago decided they could show no mercy during the initial stages.

There was a helpful sign on the second floor: CCTV Control Centre.

The security pass unlocked the door but it wouldn't open. Zafar and Kadar tied kicking at the door, but it wouldn't budge.

'They've barricaded themselves in,' Kadar said.

'Okay, back to the stairwell.' Zafar took a grenade and jammed it behind the door handle. Pulling the pin, he retreated to join Kadar. The explosion was no louder than a firework. Zafar returned to the door which now had a hole where the handle had been. Lifting his rifle, he peered through the hole. There was no-one in sight. He pushed at the door and it gave slowly, resisting as if someone was pushing from the other side.

Eventually it was open enough he could fit through the gap and Zafar entered the room to find it empty. The bank of wall monitors were black, three chairs were scattered about the centre of the room, the desk monitors also dark. A fourth chair and desk sat towards the rear of the room.

'Where is everyone?' Kadar asked.

Zafar spotted an emergency exit sign at the rear of the room. He kicked one of the chairs in anger causing it to flip over. 'They had an escape route, I should have thought...'

Kadar ran for the exit and disappeared through it.

Zafar lifted his radio. 'Rani, this is Zafar, over.'

He waited for long seconds as he berated himself for not preventing the staff from escaping. His assumption he would be able to force them to show how the equipment worked...

'Zafar, this is Rani, over.'

'Rani, the CCTV is dead, how do I restart it? Over.'

Another wait.

'Zafar, start with any desktop computers you can find. Get them switched on. Monitors too... Over.'

Zafar found the desktop units and turned them on. Immediately the monitors came to life as the computers booted.

Kadar returned. 'No sign of them.'

'Forget it, we need to get these monitors working again.' Zafar gestured at the wall screens. His plan was dependent on being able to oversee action around the city. If that was impossible he'd have to come up with a different strategy fast.

~~~

They met back in the centre of the Minster, the huge overarching ceiling giving an illusion of space that Emma couldn't reconcile with the feeling of being trapped.

'All the entrances to the building are shut,' said a Minster official.

'Thank you,' Mary replied, then looking around at the assembled staff and tourists, she raised her voice. 'Outside are some evil men who have come to steal, kill and destroy. We must fight against them and protect this building and this city.' She hesitated. 'If you follow Jesus then you know he said to believe he would answer us when we call on him, that we should believe for amazing and wonderful things, that our battle is not against flesh or blood but against principalities and powers. Join us now in standing against the evil outside. Pray with us.'

Mary offered her hand to Emma. She took it, unsure what Mary expected them to do. Mary then took Michael's hand. Emma felt her other hand gripped gently and she turned to see Calvin standing beside her. Calvin took Michael's hand as other people standing behind started placing their hands on Michael and Mary's shoulders, then Emma felt hands on her shoulders as well.

'Michael, I feel you need to start,' Mary said.

He nodded, looking straight at Emma, his eyes filled with pain. A wail escaped from his mouth, eased and then he spoke, his voice no more than a whisper: 'Father, open their eyes. Let them see...'

And Emma felt the same sensation she had felt back at her flat when she and Mary had prayed, a heat that spread downwards through her body.

'Show us, Father,' Michael continued, his voice gaining volume. 'Show us what to pray for. Open our hearts and minds to you. The men outside, cause their guns to jam, confuse them, may the bombs they are carrying blow up in their hands...'

And it was as if someone had turned on a projector, Emma could see a group of men in a car, rectangular packages of some grey substance in their laps, wires running out of them. 'Father, stop them,' she whispered.

Calvin's hand shook in her's...

~~~

Raj's team were almost in place to launch their first attack on a key road in and out of York. Raj looked out the window of the car he was traveling in at the fields of golden wheat. It was a prosperous land they were claiming. Perhaps his children could become farmers one day. He was under no illusion that the fight they were about to start would take many years to conclude, but it was their destiny to subdue the world, for all men to one day submit to Allah.

His driver, Eifad, pulled onto the off ramp and slowed as they reached a roundabout.

'Park under the dual-carriageway,' Raj told him.

Eifad stopped the car as instructed to the obvious annoyance of the driver behind who sounded their horn.

'Turn on the hazard lights,' suggested Jadiid from the back.

Raj took six bricks of C4 out of his bag and handed them to Eifad who looked as if he would rather not be handling them. 'They're perfectly safe,' he said. Eifad gave him a distrustful look which he ignored.

Jadiid and Dizhwar in the back seemed impatient, looking back at other drivers who were giving them curious looks.

His plan was to attach the C4 to the underside of the A64 carriageway where it crossed the A19, preferably in the middle where it could also take out the giant concrete struts that held up the road. He needed to tape the bricks into position, insert the detonators and then light the fuses which would give him two minutes to get a safe distance away before the C4 exploded.

The underside of the carriageway was only fifteen feet above the road but Raj glanced nervously up at it. He was afraid of heights. He knew it was foolish, that it was no higher than his first floor flat, but his flat had four walls and a window that he never opened. It at least gave the illusion of being on the ground. The strut was an over sized V. He would have to climb into the V and then straddle the sides as he attached the explosives.

If he attached the detonators now then that would mean he wasn't having to balance and steady himself at the same time while up on the V.

Next to him Eifad drummed his fingers on the window.

'Please don't do that,' Raj told him.

'How long is this going to take?' Dizhwar asked.

'I need to concentrate, okay. I'll be faster if you just let me get on.'

Eifad turned round to the others. 'I'd be happier sitting here if we weren't wearing these stupid balaclavas. Someone's going to call the police.'

'So what if they do,' Jadiid replied. 'They won't be expecting us to shoot them.'

Raj tried to ignore them as they talked. He carefully took the detonators out of the separate bag, the neat coils of fuse dangling from one end of each detonator. He'd considered using mobile phones and electric fuses but as there were so many locations they were targeting, he'd decided they would be safer to go old school in case the phone masts were turned off before everyone was set to detonate.

He needed two detonators for each brick—a primary and backup in case the first detonator failed. Though in truth he knew they only needed one detonator and the others were backups. Once the first brick exploded it would trigger the others.

He slowly inserted the detonators into the grey putty like material.

'Will you need help setting those?'

Raj looked up and, distracted, knocked one of the detonators. He felt the contact and looked down to see the fuse had come loose.

'Not now! Don't you know what will happen if something goes wrong?' Raj shouted at Dizhwar.

Raj once again focused on the explosives. He'd trained seven others, each of them practising again and again crimping the pyrotechnic fuses and had drummed it into them to be cautious. A fuse coming out was not a problem—he had spares. The risk though was when crimping a fuse you had to make sure it was crimped high and away from the pyrotechnic ignition mix and primary explosive which could be triggered by the crimping process.

Raj pulled the now useless detonator from the block and placed it carefully in a separate compartment in his bag. Then he took out one of the spare detonators. He found his crimping tool, inserted the fuse into the detonator and adjusted the crimp tool until he was sure it was in the right place.

'Police car!' The driver warned them, just as Raj was about to crimp the fuse in place. The detonator slipped and exploded as the crimp compressed the primary explosive.

Raj was blinded by the explosion, his hands and face burnt, his clothes set on fire as were the fuses to the other detonators.

Jadiid had been looking at the police car, getting his gun ready to fire. He fumbled and tried to pat out the burning fuses but only succeeded in burning his hands.

Eifad managed to open his door and dived out the car while Dizhwar also fumbled his gun and couldn't open his door.

Eifad managed to get three metres away before the first lit fuse ignited the pyrotechnic ignition mix which in turn set off the primary explosive and output explosive. The first block of plastic explosive did indeed set off a chain reaction, the blocks next to it exploding a millisecond after the first. Then further blocks which had been planned to take out additional bridges on the way into York were also triggered.

The three team members in the car were vapourised, their component parts becoming indistinguishable from the car which was blasted apart. Eifad was crushed against the wall of the underpass and was dead from the trauma before being burnt in the explosion.

While much of the explosion was directed North and South as there was only resistance from the air, the force was enough to crack the bridge in two, pushing the now split road up a full two metres and tossing a West bound lorry and two cars into the air before crashing down. The V struts had also been crushed and the road dropped from both sides forming a new V.

The lorry driver lost control but his velocity carried him past the bridge and he survived. The two car drivers and one passenger also lived, managing to regain control of the cars and braking to a halt just past the now smoking scene.

One driver died as they were unable to stop their car as it plunged into the newly formed chasm, the impact from the crash throwing them through the windscreen onto the concrete rubble.

The police officers who had been responding to calls for all officers to return to York were both killed when their van was thrown backwards by the explosion which shattered their windscreen and crushed them before they could react.

Raj's first attack was a partial success, the A19 now effectively blocked.

~~~

He had never experienced a vision and the sight before Calvin shocked him. It was as if a portion of reality had been ripped away and he was looking beyond to something happening far away. A group of men on what looked like a motorway, rifles held out, firing at cars below them. He didn't question that what he was seeing was actually happening, felt a fear grip him that caused his whole body to shake.

'Father,' he called out. 'Deliver us from these men, deliver us from the evil they are doing, send your angels to protect us, strengthen the police, the army to defend us. Show us how to pray, help us, Father, help us!'

~~~

Natalie drove at speed up Appleton Road, followed by two Military Police Land Rovers. Danny focused on his mobile. He'd sent a group text message shortly after his aborted call with Rudd: "This is not a drill, Implement Lockdown Protocol immediately, Confirmation code: HU5386DF." The message had gone to three dozen contacts throughout York. The hope was that each would forward it on to everyone they were responsible for in a cascade that would ensure the maximum number of people were informed.

He had called FSU to activate all their officers and inform them he was taking command of the situation; called Irene Carr at the Home Office and asked for all available support; tried unsuccessfully to raise Control at Police Headquarters and had moved on to follow up with his key contacts.

'Mr Stark, this is D.I. Martin, did you get my text?'

'I did, I… Is this really happening?'

'Have you begun implementing the protocol?' Danny gripped his mobile as he waited for a response.

'I'm on my way to the studio now.'

'Good, I can't emphasise enough—we need you to warn the citizens of York. By getting this message out you could save countless lives. I'll update you when I can.' He hung up before Jim could answer and dialled his next number.

'Ms Avery, this is D.I. Martin, did you get my...' Danny broke off as Natalie abruptly braked. He was thrown forward, his seatbelt the only thing stopping him from hitting the windscreen. In his ear he could hear Claire Avery speaking.

Ahead of them it looked like the scene of a traffic accident except there were three people running towards them, one of them waving their arms.

'I'll call you back,' he said into his mobile and killed the connection. Natalie was already out of the car. He did likewise, and was greeted by shouts to get back. Danny looked back and saw the M.P.s were exiting their vehicles.

'What happened?' He asked the first person to reach them while holding up his badge.

'Guns,' she said, panting. 'They just started shooting at us... I didn't think I'd get away.'

'How many were there?' Natalie asked.

'Two, three, I couldn't tell.'

'Okay, continue onto Bishopthorpe, try and wave down anyone that tries to drive this way and warn them.'

The M.P.s clustered around, each holding a rifle they'd taken from the armoury.

'We've two or more men shooting at cars from the overpass,' Danny told them. 'Can you deal with them?'

The senior officer nodded. 'We'll take it from here.' He held out a sidearm to Danny.

Danny stared at the weapon. He'd never seen a need to hold a gun.

'Sir, if you intend to defeat these men, you'll need more than a badge.'

Danny reluctantly took the gun.

'The safety is on,' the officer said. 'Switch at the side. Stay back until we give the all clear.'

Another officer handed a gun to Natalie who seemed to be far more comfortable with it than Danny felt.

He watched the M.P.s carefully make their way up the road, wondering if he should follow them, but recalled Harbrook's warning: "If the worst should happen your job is not to try and stop it yourself. Your two main roles are to warn and co-ordinate. You get injured or killed and you'll be no use to anyone."

He pulled out his mobile and called back Claire Avery.

CHAPTER FIFTY-EIGHT
In the Spirit

The attack had been as successful as their previous one. Mohammed was about to call a halt when he heard gunfire from different weapons. He whirled round from his position hearing cries from his platoon. Bursts of gunfire were coming from several locations from the South and he instinctively returned fire, aware he wasn't aiming.

He crouched to present a smaller target but was hit in the chest and thrown backwards. He saw two members of his platoon on the ground, tried to shout out: "Retreat" but was struggling to breathe with the impact.

He had not lost his weapon though. He dragged it round, lifting himself up so he could aim. Where had this counter-attack come from, he thought as he squeezed the trigger. And then there was an overriding pain...

~~~

She was reliving her nightmares, the pictures in front of her scenes that had woken her in a sweat time and again. Emma and Michael's grip on her hands the only thing anchoring her to the reality this was actually happening.

'Lord, forgive me,' Mary cried. 'Forgive us all, have mercy on us, do not leave us to suffer but send your help. We call out in Jesus name, have mercy on us. I know I am a sinner, I confess I am fallen. You said to Abraham you would not destroy Sodom if ten were found there to be righteous. I know I am not righteous except through faith in you, I can't believe there are not many more than ten who follow you in this city, please spare this city on our account and if not for us then because of your great mercy!'

~~~

Jim Stark ignored the ON AIR sign and opened the door to the studio causing Josie and her producer Iain to look round. Josie was in the middle of a weather bulletin and didn't miss a beat at the interruption. He made a "cut it" signal and forced himself to wait while Josie truncated the bulletin.

'…And I have to cut that short. I'll leave you with this song by local musician Scott Mitchell and will be back with you in a few minutes.' She pressed a key on her keyboard and then turned back to Jim.

'What's going on, Jim?' Iain asked.

'There's a high likelihood a terrorist attack is taking place in York right now,' Jim said, trying to keep his voice steady. 'We need to implement the emergency broadcast protocol.' He handed over a folder to Josie.

She took it and started flicking through the few short pages it contained. 'This is one of the pre-recorded government broadcasts, right?' She asked.

'Yes,' Jim replied.

She shook her head. 'I don't think we should do that…'

'We have to!' Jim insisted.

'Wait, I can read this out live. If we switch over with no warning, people will be terrified.'

'Josie's right,' said Iain. 'We can ask people to call in with questions, ask them for information.'

'Okay, okay, just get on with it, I need to call the rest of the team and warn them.'

~ ~ ~

'I don't know if we should be running round the streets with our guns,' Andy said, hefting his Walther Q5 Match. 'Last thing we need is getting mixed up with some terrorist nut jobs and getting shot by the police.'

Karl checked his rifle was loaded, giving Thomas' 308 a glance. In theory his .22 would do sufficient damage at a distance, but for what they were about to do he'd rather have a bit more stopping power. He looked at Andy. 'The police see us and the worst that will happen is a Tazer shot or a face full of pepper spray.'

'Some of us have dodgy tickers,' said Keith. 'A Tazer is probably more deadly than your .22.'

'Maybe, but I'm not running into a terrorist and having him shoot me while I pull my rifle out of a gun bag. Okay, is everyone ready?'

Everyone nodded.

Karl looked at the collection of single shot match rifles and pistols they were all carrying and hoped it would be enough against the machine guns they'd seen the terrorists carrying.

'We split into two groups, hunt the scum down. Watch each other's backs and hope the police are able to tell friend from foe.'

He led his group out of the coach park and in the direction he had seen the terrorists running. Single shot and semi-auto gunfire could be heard in the distance and more disturbingly, there had been muffled explosions as well. The pavements were now clear. Karl hoped most people had seen the danger and headed for safety or at least shelter. As he passed some windows he could see scared faces at the back of shops and cafes.

The competition they had been heading for down in London could wait. Karl doubted there would ever be a more important test of his skill than the one he now faced.

They reached a junction and Karl slowed. He readied his rifle knowing that he was not as accurate a shot from a standing position. He moved out stepping into the road to get a better angle. Shots could be heard to his left, coming from beyond the ancient Bar. He took note of the stairs heading up onto the wall.

'I think we should split up,' he said to the others.

'Isn't it safer to stay together?' Andy asked.

'Maybe, but I would rather have some of us up on that wall. It goes round most of the city, right?'

'There are gaps,' Keith said. 'But if it gives us height I'm all for it.'

'That's settled. Keith, you take Pete and Alex with you. That gives you two rifles and a pistol and leaves us with the same. The rest of us will head down here.' He pointed through the Bar.

The street after the Bar was clear and Karl moved quickly forward. He started to hear shouts and then the street opened up and he could see the bulk of a cathedral with a smaller church ahead.

Two of the masked men were visible outside one of the cathedral doors, they seemed to be trying to shoot the locks out.

Karl motioned for Andy and Frank to get down and he knelt and then lay down himself, taking aim on the terrorists. 'I'll take the one on the left,' he said.

'I've got the right,' Frank confirmed.

'Reckon we're 40 metres away,' Karl said adjusting his sights.

'Maybe a bit less…'

Karl squinted over his sights, aiming at the masked man's head, steadying his breathing. His heart hammering away he could do nothing about, but he breathed in, held it then half out and…

His rifle fired.

The man dropped.

Next to him Frank fired.

The second man turned, his rifle now pointing in their direction.

'How could you miss that,' Karl said, fumbling in his pocket for a bullet.

The terrorist fired a burst at them which Karl thought he could feel whizzing over his head.

'I didn't miss,' Frank shouted. 'Hit him in the chest.'

Karl ejected the spent round and pushed a bullet in the chamber, slammed the bolt down, aimed and...

The terrorist's head flew back, an obvious spray of blood fountaining out behind him as he fell.

Karl turned to Andy who was already reloading his pistol. 'That was you?' He asked in surprise.

'Wasn't going to wait for you two has-beens to get us all killed.'

'Good shot,' he said. 'Do you think you could use an AK-47?'

There was a glimmer of something in Andy's eyes.

'Probably better not to leave guns lying about,' Andy said and pushed himself up.

Karl covered him as Andy ran towards the fallen terrorists. As he scanned the streets that led further into York he tried to decide the best route for them to take next.

~~~

He had lived with the visions his whole life. He'd asked for God to open the others' eyes but had no idea if they could see what was passing in front of him now.

God could see. God could always see, was always watching, a fact that filled him with fear mostly, especially when his thoughts strayed. Now though he was being given a gift, a gift he would rather not receive, but that wasn't up to him. He looked on as evil men set about bringing terror and destruction.

'Father, stop them, halt them in their tracks, these evil men, strike fear into their hearts. Cause the people of this city to rise up against them and strengthen us with your courage. We cannot stand without you, we will fall unless you lift us up, save us, Father, save us!'

~~~

The traffic round the A1237 had been unbelievably slow and Darius was concerned he was well behind schedule. His plan had been to blockade the roundabout where it linked to the A64 then double back and seal off the Monks Cross roundabout. Now he was wondering if he should just have started with Monks Cross...

'Take us onto the main roundabout,' he said to Syed who was driving. 'Stop where the A64 North joins and we'll get out and stop the traffic.'

'If we ever reach the roundabout...' Syed muttered.

'Patience, brother. Not long now.'

They inched forward, eventually reaching the first smaller roundabout and crossing to the short stretch of road that led to the main Hopgrove roundabout.

Syed braked to a stop as there were vehicles passing.

Without warning the car was shunted forwards. Syed cried out, Darius looked round to see the grill of a lorry or truck immediately behind them.

'What's he doing?'

'Look out!'

There was no time to brace as a lorry ran into them from the side.

Darius felt himself flung sideways and then back, his head smacking off his window.

The blow dazed him.

He became aware of unfamiliar voices, people shouting.

'Get the doors open!'

'It's jammed!'

'Get them out through the windows then.'

He felt his body being moved, tried to protest and then was laid down. Tried to open his eyes but everything looked wrong, all blurred together.

'There's guns in here, who are these people?'

No! Darius tried to sit up, stop them, but the world tilted at an odd angle and then everything went black.

~~~

Hands gripped her shoulders, voices rose and fell around her as some people cried out and others wept. A man's voice called out in anger, seeking God to act; a woman begged for her father to hear, to see, to intervene; a child said they were scared and many murmured their agreement.

Mary felt drained by the emotion that had poured out of her, exhausted from the effort. She lifted her face upwards. 'Father, I am so weak, strengthen these tired legs, these feeble arms. Pour out your strength on us, increase our faith, give us hope, do not let us grow weary but renew our strength.'

And as she prayed she felt a renewal of her hope, felt her faith rise. Empowered, she again called out to God.

~~~

'And we have James on the line from the A64, James, what can you tell us?' Josie pressed a button and the external line went live.

'We've caught some of them, these terrorists.'

Josie looked wide eyed at Iain, mouthed: What do I say?

Iain shrugged.

'You should be very careful,' Josie said, shaking her head at Iain. 'We advise all our listeners to avoid placing themselves in any danger.'

'We're in no danger, these guys are all out for the count. Freak accident, it was. Guy's brakes failed on his truck, pushed their car into the path of a lorry. Just not sure what to do with them, or their guns...'

Josie flipped through the protocols she'd been given. There wasn't a single passage that detailed what to do with a captured prisoner.

'I would keep them away from their guns and if you have any rope you might want to tie them up, thank you James from the A64.' She cut his line before he could say anything else she couldn't answer.

She was about to fill in with some more sage advice from the protocol document when Jim burst into the room again. She managed to kill the live feed before he shouted: 'They're downstairs!'

Through the open door came the sound of gunfire.

'Iain, switch to the emergency broadcast, now,' Jim said.

'Wait!' Josie turned back on the live feed. 'Listeners, our station has been attacked, we may have to stop our live broadcast. You are in our prayers.' She nodded at Iain who switched to the emergency broadcast with a click of his mouse. In her monitor Josie saw the broadcast status change, the only visible sign she was no longer broadcasting live.

Jim still had the studio door open and Josie felt panic rise as shouts grew louder and then a masked man appeared in the doorway, an ugly rifle muzzle pointing in her direction. She forced herself to look up to the man's eyes.

Another man appeared behind as the first said: 'You will stop broadcasting now.'

Josie raised her hands.

'This radio station now belongs to Islamic State.'

'I thought Islamic State was in the Middle...' The words came out before Josie could stop them.

'The whole world will submit to Islam,' the man said. 'Step away from the desks.'

Josie stood and walked towards Jim. She prayed none of the men knew how to use the station software...

~~~

Danny had finally raised Control, his fears for headquarters confirmed. They had been attacked, presumably with rocket launchers stolen from the armoury. The sprinkler system had activated shorting out equipment throughout headquarters.

It had taken a while for Control to get a backup system online and as soon as it was active reports of multiple attacks throughout the city had started pouring in. Several officers could not be reached and Danny feared for their lives.

They had abandoned their vehicles, confiscated cars on the North side of the A64 and had headed up Tadcaster Road towards the centre of York. Once away from the dual-carriageway there was little sign of the havoc they had left behind. Passing the racecourse it was almost surreal to be speeding up the road, a bulky gun in his hands. Danny realised he didn't even know what kind of ammunition it took.

Protocol dictated he head back to headquarters but there was still a small battle going on there. Instead, on hearing that York Radio had been attacked he had decided to head there. The station had switched to an automated emergency broadcast and if it was still operational it could be very useful to be able to communicate with a wider audience.

~~~

It was taking too long to work out how to use the system. Zafar paced as Kadar and Laskhar brought up different views of the city. They had found two platoons but each had moved out of the camera's range before they could work out which camera to switch to to allow them to follow their progress.

Zafar pulled out his radio. 'Platoon One, what is your status? Over.'

He waited for the reply, but none came back. Perhaps they were busy. He moved on. 'Platoon Two, what is your status? Over.'

Again, no response.

Kadar glanced round, concern in his expression.

'Platoon Three, what is your status? Over.'

This time a reply came immediately: 'Under attack! Two men down, need assistance.'

'What's your position, Platoon Three? Over.'

No reply. Zafar felt a clenching inside.

'Platoon Three, we need your position so we can send assistance, over.'

Nothing. There were many reasons two platoons might have been unable to report in, and he had 45 spread out through the city, but still…

'All Platoons, report your position in sequence,' he instructed.

He grabbed a notepad that had been left behind and started noting down the responses. But there were more gaps than responses, with several of the Platoons requesting assistance.

'What is happening out there!' Zafar shouted as the last Platoon failed to report in. More than half his men were unaccounted for. He plotted the locations of those who had responded on a map and then began directing Platoons to assist those under attack, trying not to worry about how the police had managed to respond so quickly and effectively.

The Platoon at York Radio had no-one nearby to assist, except for his own…

'Laskhar, try and get this under control. Kadar, with me! We'll rescue the Platoon at York Radio.'

Zafar grabbed his rifle and checked he had spare magazines then led the way down.

~~~

People were looking at her. Whispering. A few minutes before a group of people had run into the library shouting. Najwa had turned up her music even louder. It was inconsiderate of them. She'd tried to continue reading but a large group had gathered now and it was getting impossible to ignore them.

She put her book down with a sigh. She might as well go home. It was certainly no more disruptive than the library this afternoon.

As she walked out a woman made to stop her. She looked uncertain as she did, as if she was afraid of something. Najwa side stepped but pulled out her earphones. 'What?' She asked.

'You can't go out there,' the woman said.

'Why not?'

'People have been shot. We think it's a…' That look again. 'A terrorist attack.'

Najwa felt anger rise up inside. 'I'll be right at home then,' she stated as haughtily as she could. She turned and before anyone could stop her, ran out of the building.

~~~

The M.P.s had stormed York Radio with Danny and Natalie following. Two of the terrorists were killed on the Ground Floor, the soldiers sweeping each room to ensure no-one was hiding. Danny noted the civilians that had been executed, their bodies left lying where they fell.

The lead M.P. was cautious taking the stairs, rifle held high. At a signal, another soldier threw what looked—to Danny's horror—like grenades. An explosion and the M.P.s rushed upwards. Danny followed, terrified there might have been civilians still alive upstairs. Two, three, four gunshots ahead of him and he heard M.P.s calling: 'Clear!'

Danny pushed his way through, saw two masked men lying on the floor. No other bodies…

'What were you thinking!' He shouted at the M.P. who had thrown the grenades. 'If they'd had hostages…'

The M.P. looked bemused.

'Why'd you throw grenades?' Danny insisted.

'You mean the Flash Bangs? What did you think I was doing?' The man laughed. 'Did their job.'

Still confused, Danny didn't have time to fully process what he'd heard as someone else shouted: 'We've got hostages!'

Natalie pushed past him and he followed her into a back office where an M.P. was untying a woman, two other men lying tied and gagged on the floor beside her.

Danny's mobile rang. He stepped out of the room to answer it.

'D.I., this is Control. We've been unable to raise the CCTV Control Centre. It's not far from your location.'

'I'll check it out.' He killed the connection. 'Natalie, I'm going to leave you here. CCTV Control are not responding.' He turned to the senior M.P. 'How many men do you need to secure the building?'

'Two should be enough.'

'I need the rest of you with me. The CCTV Control Centre might also have been attacked.'

~~~

The street outside the library was deserted apart from cars parked at odd angles. Najwa heard a noise that still sounded like fireworks to her, but now she imagined guns firing. She had to get home. She started running. Turned the corner into St Leonard's Place.

No one was around.

No one.

She'd never seen York empty. Ahead the fountains outside the Art Gallery were still operating. It was surreal.

And then she saw uniformed men with guns running towards her. She skidded to a stop and turned only to see two masked men also running at her, their guns lifted. She screamed.

~~~

Danny saw a young girl running towards them, then saw two of the masked men behind her. He shouted at her to get down but she turned away from him.

'Hold your fire,' he shouted at the M.P.s.

There was no cover...

~~~

Zafar held up a hand to stop Kadar. The sight of the soldiers running towards them making him aware how exposed they were. He hadn't even noticed the girl in front of them until she turned to face them, her scream chilling him to his core.

It was Najwa! What was she doing here?

~~~

'Stop!' Najwa cried out, feeling herself shake. 'You can't do this! Put your guns down. Please…' She raised her hands…

~~~

Zafar let his rifle lower but saw Kadar still had his rifle up. He couldn't let him shoot. He grabbed at Kadar's gun. Kadar fought back. The rifle fired.

Zafar let go and turned to see his sister fall to the ground.

He let out a cry of horror and without thought raised his rifle and turned it on Kadar.

There was a feeling like someone had punched him in the arm. Then another blow and another and the street around him tilted.

Faces appeared above him, his rifle was grabbed from his hands and then something dark sped towards him and everything went black.

~~~

Danny knelt by the girl trusting that the M.P.s had dealt with the armed men. She was taking rapid but short breaths, looking up at him with wide eyes.

'I need to turn you over,' he said.

Her hand grabbed his, squeezed.

He knew he should check her back for an exit wound but he didn't want to let go of her hand.

Her breaths slowed until with a sudden finality she exhaled a long slow breath. Her hand in his relaxed and he found himself squeezing her hand tighter.

'Sir?'

He looked up, not recognising the face of the M.P. before him.

'We should go, sir.'

'Of course.'

Danny closed her staring eyes, blinked away tears and stood.

~~~

Danny was prepared for the use of Flash Bangs when they stormed the building containing the CCTV Control Centre. They found and killed one terrorist in the security lobby and another in the control room. Danny let the M.P.s check the rest of the building was clear while he called Control.

'We've taken back the CCTV. No sign of most of the staff. I need people to man the room.'

'Hold on, I've a call coming in for you.'

Danny glanced down as he waited for the call to be put through and saw a map of York, red circles around dozens of locations. Next to the map a notepad with a list of numbers and locations. York Radio caught his eye on the list. He looked from one to the other…

'Detective Inspector Martin?'

'Speaking.'

'This is David Carstairs, Junior Minister responsible for Counter Terrorism.'

'Sir…'

'I'm inbound on a chopper, where do you recommend we put down?'

'I wouldn't advise flying into York at the moment, Sir.'

'I was given to understand the incident was almost under control.'

'We're a long way from that, Sir. I suspect there are still…' He quickly scanned the list. 'A couple of dozen groups active in the city.'

'We've already passed the outer ring road, sounds like you need our help. I'm accompanied by two Apache helicopters and we have a Company of soldiers on two Chinooks meeting us from Catterick.'

'Very well.' Danny examined the map. 'Can you set down at the front of the Art Gallery? St Leonard's Place…'

There was a pause and then: 'We'll be there in a couple of minutes.'

'There will only be room for one of you to touch down at a time.'

'Understood.'

'I'll meet you there.'

Danny grabbed the map and list and headed for the exit.

~~~

Mary let go of her hand and let out a cry. Emma looked round, saw Mary had her hands up to her mouth. A low moan escaped from her.

'What is it?' Emma asked, but Mary just shook her head.

'I have to go,' she said. 'You have to open the doors.' Mary was now looking around. She shook off the hands from her shoulders and grabbed at an official. 'You have to let me out, please!'

'Calvin…' Emma looked at him. 'What's happened?'

He shook his head.

Mary was now pushing her way out of the crowd of people that had gathered round them.

'We should go with her,' Emma said.

'Okay. Michael?' Calvin asked.

Michael shook his head. 'I need to stay here.'

Calvin clasped Michael's shoulder and then led Emma out following Mary.

'Is it over?' An official was asking Mary.

'No,' she said.

The official stopped. 'We shouldn't open the doors then. You said…'

'I know. Close them after I've gone. Please, I have to go.'

The official looked as if he might refuse, but then relented. He strode over to the South entrance. 'Why do you need to go?' He asked.

Mary just shook her head.

'You're going too?' The official asked Emma and Calvin.

'Yes,' Emma said.

The official took a deep breath. 'God go with you,' he said and then unlocked the door.

Mary pushed through as soon as it had opened enough, Emma following into sunlight. She heard the door close behind and felt Calvin's presence beside her.

A voice in her head questioned why she was running out when she knew men with guns were ready to kill, but she forced the doubt away and focused on keeping up with Mary who was hurrying towards Bootham Bar.

~~~

Ignoring the armed soldiers stationed at points up and down the street, Mary ran across St Leonard's Place focused on the small body lying on the opposite pavement. She had recognised the girl immediately she had seen her in the vision, her eyes closed as if asleep if not for the ragged hole in her chest.

She became aware of a man walking over to Najwa's body, kneeling, lifting her and carrying her away.

Mary caught up with him. To her surprise, recognised Danny, saw tears in his eyes, realised she was finding it hard to see.

'What happened?' She sobbed.

'I couldn't stop it,' he said. 'Please, you need to move out of the way.' He took a heaving breath. 'There are helicopters landing here in a minute.'

She followed him round to the other side of the fountain, the noise of the water masking distant gunfire. Danny carefully laid Najwa's body down.

Emma and Calvin joined them. Emma pulled Mary into a hug.

She let herself be held until a whopping sound started to grow quickly louder.

She pulled away from Emma and looked up. A helicopter appeared overhead, the downdraft like a gale of wind. Two other helicopters appeared at either side, higher up, starting to circle. They were menacing: rockets and guns clearly visible.

And Mary had a sense she had seen this all before, had stood in this very spot as giant men strode out of the helicopter towards her, death in their hands...

END OF SEASON ONE

A WORD FROM THE AUTHOR

Thank you for reading Fallen Warriors!

Season Two of Fallen Warriors is being planned. If you would like to sign up to my mailing list and receive news about the book's progress, the chance to get previews of short stories and get occasional notifications about blog posts then please sign up at:
http://www.dragonlake.co.uk

Everyone who signs up to my mailing list will get my short story—Dragon Lake—for free.

Please rate and consider writing a short review for Fallen Warriors on Amazon or Goodreads:
http://www.goodreads.com/book/show/34232497-fallen-warriors.

Your feedback is very valuable to me.

In fact, I would love to hear from you - you can contact me through:
Email: mark@dragonlake.co.uk
Twitter: @my100goals
Facebook: http://www.facebook.com/my100goals/

If you enjoyed Fallen Warriors, why not check out my first novel: The Great Scottish Land Grab, also available in paperback.

The story of how Scotland became independent...

Robert Castle is fighting to save the UK Union when an incident while walking in the Scottish Highlands turns his life upside down.

A search for justice leads Robert to look deep into Scotland's history and what he finds will change not just his life, but the direction of a nation.

Sensing that the theft of Scotland's land over many centuries has robbed the people of their opportunity to be independent, Castle fights for a modern day land grab - to reverse the clearances that stole Scotland's land from the people.

Challenging an out of touch parliament, Robert turns government on its head by introducing Cafe Politics - a way for communities to debate and agree their own policies.

But how far will Robert go in his determination to overturn the injustice of the Highland Clearances and will he lead Scotland to a better future or into civil war?

Find out now in The Great Scottish Land Grab.

ACKNOWLEDGEMENTS

Fallen Warriors has been many years in the making and there have been many who have contributed in different ways to make this novel possible.

To Jesus Christ who gave me life and set me free, all hope and joy in this book is only there because of you.

To my wife and children, thank you for putting up with my habit of disappearing into another world.

To Carol, who encouraged me to write, thank you for seeing potential in me long before I was ready.

To John R. who told me to stop trying to make the beginning perfect and get on and finish the book - you were right! Sorry it took so long...

Thank you Grace for keeping up with me week in and week out and always having an encouraging word to say!

Thank you Alan for your constant encouragement!

Thanks to David for advising me on the correct way to sink a fishing boat and also keeping me on the right track when suspending staff.

Thanks to Sally for sharing your knowledge of injuries and paramedic procedures.

Any errors and omissions are mine and mine alone. While Fallen Warriors has been edited and proofread, it is possible something has slipped through. If you do find any mistakes, please let me know by emailing mark@dragonlake.co.uk which will allow me to correct for future editions.

Thanks to D. Gunn for allowing me to use your name! Sergeant Gunn is in your debt!

Thanks to Paul, Jeanette, Liz, Irene, Jane, Jennifer, Marie and Phyllis for your regular support while I was editing Fallen Warriors

Thank you to Margaret and Tom and Mary and Myrtle and Louise and Norma and Petre and Robert and Don and Alan and Moira and Trudy and Graham and Peter and Lindsay for your kind reviews of the draft and your support!

Thanks to Mark at Covervault.com for amazing cover shot templates and instruction guides.

Finally, thank you for reading this story! For living for a time in my world. I hope you'll join me here again soon...

BIOGRAPHY – MARK ANDERSON SMITH

Mark Anderson Smith is a Scottish author who lived in York—the setting for his latest novel—for ten years.

Mark confesses he had the initial idea for Fallen Warriors while daydreaming through a church service. He longs to see the Church return to the passion and power the early apostles displayed.

Mark has been writing since he was eight and worked on and off to complete his current novel for ten years. He is the author of The Great Scottish Land Grab, a political tale of one man's fight to reverse the Highland Clearances and transform Scotland, first published in 2014.

Married with three children, he works as an IT Consultant in Scotland, developing applications for businesses, databases and reports. Mark is passionate about goals and a few years ago accepted a challenge to write down 100 goals. To date he still hasn't stood on a new planet or learned to fly, but insists there is still time…

GLOSSARY

There are a few terms in Fallen Warriors that may be new to some readers. Hopefully the explanations below will help.

Allah – An Arabic word for God. Used by Christians in Arabic countries and by Muslims around the world.

Caliphate – Islamic region governed by a successor to Mohammed.

Infidel – An insulting term for a person who does not accept ones faith or religion.

Injil – The Arabic word for the Christian Bible, specifically the four Gospels or New Testament.

Jizya – Under Islamic law this is a tax levied on non-Muslims who refuse to convert to Islam to allow them to live in a Muslim country.

Shaitan – Arabic name for Satan or the Devil.

Snicket – A narrow lane that cuts between rows of houses. Used in Yorkshire.

The Ouse – A major river that runs through the centre of York.

Ummah – Arabic word for community of Muslims. Used to describe all Muslims today and also the anticipated future where Muslims hope all people will eventually submit to Islam.

SCRIPTURES QUOTED

Bible verses from several different translations have been used throughout Fallen Warriors. Where these have been quoted, read or paraphrased by a character they are included in the list below. Some additional verses and passages are alluded to, but are not listed below.

NIV: Isaiah 45 v 7

'I form the light and create darkness, I bring prosperity and create disaster; I, the Lord, do all these things.'

Chapter 8 - Expelled
NIV: Luke 5 v 31

Jesus answered them, "It is not the healthy who need a doctor, but the sick."

Chapter 9 - Challenged
NIV: 1 Corinthians 5 v 11

But now I am writing to you that you must not associate with anyone who claims to be a brother or sister but is sexually immoral or greedy, an idolater or slanderer, a drunkard or swindler. Do not even eat with such people.

NIV: 1 Corinthians 5 v 13

God will judge those outside. "Expel the wicked person from among you."

NIV: Matthew 18 v 17

If they still refuse to listen, tell it to the church; and if they refuse to listen even to the church, treat them as you would a pagan or a tax collector.

Chapter 11 - Discarded Sandwich
NIV: Matthew 5 v 39 Paraphrased

But I tell you, do not resist an evil person. If anyone slaps you on the right cheek, turn to them the other cheek also.

Chapter 12 - Tick Tock
NIV: Isaiah 58 v 5

Is this the kind of fast I have chosen, only a day for people to humble themselves? Is it only for bowing one's head like a reed and for lying in sackcloth and ashes? Is that what you call a fast, a day acceptable to the Lord?

NIV: Joel 2 v 28

And afterward, I will pour out my Spirit on all people. Your sons and daughters will prophesy, your old men will dream dreams, your young men will see visions.

Chapter 13 - Argus
NIV: Isaiah 58 v 6-9 Paraphrased

Is not this the kind of fasting I have chosen: to loose the chains of injustice and untie the cords of the yoke, to set the oppressed free and break every yoke? Is it not to share your food with the hungry and to provide the poor wanderer with shelter—when you see the naked, to clothe them, and not to turn away from your own flesh and blood? Then your light will break forth like the dawn, and your healing will quickly appear; then your righteousness will go before you, and the glory of the Lord will be your rear guard. Then you will call, and the Lord will answer; you will cry for help, and he will say: Here am I.

NIV: Romans 7 v 15

I do not understand what I do. For what I want to do I do not do, but what I hate I do.

Chapter 27 - The King's Judgement
NKJV: Luke 19 v 12 Paraphrased

Therefore He said: "A certain nobleman went into a far country to receive for himself a kingdom and to return."

NKJV: Luke 19 v 22 - 23

You knew that I was an austere man, collecting what I did not deposit and reaping what I did not sow. Why then did you not put my money in the bank, that at my coming I might have collected it with interest?

NKJV: Luke 19 v 27 But bring here those enemies of mine, who did not want me to reign over them, and slay them before me.

NKJV: Luke 19 v 11

Now as they heard these things, He spoke another parable, because He was near Jerusalem and because they thought the kingdom of God would appear immediately.

Chapter 32 - Unwelcome
NIV: Job 40 v 2
Will the one who contends with the Almighty correct him? Let him who accuses God answer him!

NIV: Job 41 v 11
Who has a claim against me that I must pay? Everything under heaven belongs to me.

Chapter 35 - Watchman on the Wall
NIV: Ezekiel 33 v 5 - 7 Paraphrased
Since they heard the sound of the trumpet but did not heed the warning, their blood will be on their own head. If they had heeded the warning, they would have saved themselves. But if the watchman sees the sword coming and does not blow the trumpet to warn the people and the sword comes and takes someone's life, that person's life will be taken because of their sin, but I will hold the watchman accountable for their blood.

Chapter 40 - Witness
NIV: Matthew 19 v 26
Jesus looked at them and said, "With man this is impossible, but with God all things are possible."

NIV: John 11 v 5 - 6
Now Jesus loved Martha and her sister and Lazarus. So when he heard that Lazarus was sick, he stayed where he was two more days

NIV: John 11 v 23
Jesus said to her, "Your brother will rise again."

NIV: John 11 v 25 - 26
Jesus said to her, "I am the resurrection and the life. The one who believes in me will live, even though they die; and whoever lives by believing in me will never die. Do you believe this?"

NIV: John 11 v 35
Jesus wept.

NIV: 1 John 1 v 8

If we claim to be without sin, we deceive ourselves and the truth is not in us.

Chapter 41 - Paying Your Debts
NIV: Luke 1 v 79

to shine on those living in darkness and in the shadow of death, to guide our feet into the path of peace.

NIV: Luke 7 V 12

As he approached the town gate, a dead person was being carried out

Chapter 42 - Crossroad
NIV: 1 Corinthians 11 v 5 - 6

But every woman who prays or prophesies with her head uncovered dishonors her head—it is the same as having her head shaved. For if a woman does not cover her head, she might as well have her hair cut off

NIV: 1 Corinthians 11 v 21

For when you are eating, some of you go ahead with your own private suppers. As a result, one person remains hungry and another gets drunk.

NIV: 1 Corinthians 11 v 29

For those who eat and drink without discerning the body of Christ eat and drink judgment on themselves.

NIV: 2 Corinthians 11 v 2

I am jealous for you with a godly jealousy. I promised you to one husband, to Christ, so that I might present you as a pure virgin to him.

NIV: 2 Corinthians 11 v 24 - 27

Five times I received from the Jews the forty lashes minus one. 25 Three times I was beaten with rods, once I was pelted with stones, three times I was shipwrecked, I spent a night and a day in the open sea, 26 I have been constantly on the move. I have been in danger from rivers, in danger from bandits, in danger from my fellow Jews, in danger from Gentiles; in danger in the city, in danger in the country, in danger at sea; and in danger from false believers. 27 I have labored and toiled and have often gone without sleep; I have known hunger and thirst and have often gone without food; I have been cold and naked.

Chapter 44 - Listen
NIV: Luke 24 v 49

I am going to send you what my Father has promised; but stay in the city until you have been clothed with power from on high.

Chapter 44 - Boarding the Rollercoaster
NIV: John 15 v 26

When the Advocate comes, whom I will send to you from the Father—the Spirit of truth who goes out from the Father—he will testify about me.

NIV: John 14 v 26

But the Advocate, the Holy Spirit, whom the Father will send in my name, will teach you all things and will remind you of everything I have said to you.

NIV: Luke 11 v 13

If you then, though you are evil, know how to give good gifts to your children, how much more will your Father in heaven give the Holy Spirit to those who ask him!

NIV: Luke 11 v 9 - 13

"So I say to you: Ask and it will be given to you; seek and you will find; knock and the door will be opened to you. For everyone who asks receives; the one who seeks finds; and to the one who knocks, the door will be opened. Which of you fathers, if your son asks for a fish, will give him a snake instead? Or if he asks for an egg, will give him a scorpion? If you then, though you are evil, know how to give good gifts to your children, how much more will your Father in heaven give the Holy Spirit to those who ask him!"

NIV: James 1 v 6

But when you ask, you must believe and not doubt, because the one who doubts is like a wave of the sea, blown and tossed by the wind.

Chapter 47 - Greater
NKJV: Romans 3 v 23 Paraphrased

For all have sinned and fall short of the glory of God

NKJV: Isaiah 53 v 6

All we like sheep have gone astray; We have turned, every one, to his own way; And the Lord has laid on Him the iniquity of us all.

NKJV: 1 John 1 v 8

If we say that we have no sin, we deceive ourselves, and the truth is not in us.

Chapter 51 - Burnt
NIV: Romans 8 v 28 Paraphrased

And we know that in all things God works for the good of those who love him, who have been called according to his purpose.